Natalie's Wars

Natalie's
Wars

By
Paul Castellani

Polly, I hope
you enjoy the story,

Paul Castellani

The names, characters, and incidents in this novel are the work of the author's imagination. Any resemblance to actual persons, living or dead is entirely coincidental.

The headings of each chapter are headlines from newspapers on or close to the date of the events of the chapter.

Text Copyright @ 2019 by Paul Castellani

ISBN: 978-1-792880-84-1

Donwood Books
Delmar, New York

For Donna

Natalie's Wars is also dedicated to the memory of Joseph Castellani and Timothy Cannan who served in the U.S. Army during World War II; Ruth Cannan who built bombsights at Bausch & Lomb in Rochester and Irene Castellani who served as a volunteer nurse's-aide in Syracuse.

1

March, 1942

New Draft Rules Speed Induction: Men to Go Into Service at Once on Passing Army Physical.

"Marry me, Natalie."

Pretending she hadn't heard him, Natalie slid across the front seat and put her arms around Bill. She kissed him and buried her face in his neck.

When she was a girl, Natalie imagined several romantic places where a man on his knee, holding a ring in his hand, would ask her to marry him. None were in a car parked on the side of a dirt road at Tomhannock Reservoir.

As soon as he picked her up in his father's new Buick instead of his own thirty-six Chevy with the busted heater she'd guessed what was going to happen. But she hadn't figured out what to do. At the dance, they'd met two couples who just got engaged and another who were married last week. With so many of the guys like Bill getting drafted and shipping out, it was as though all the young couples were performing a patriotic duty like buying war bonds.

"I want you to be my wife," Bill said.

She liked Bill – a lot. He was good looking, and they had fun together. His father's garage was a going business that paid Bill a good wage. They'd been going steady for almost a year. But after every date, Natalie asked herself if she was foolishly waiting for a movie version of love with dazzling stars, violins playing and splashes of Technicolor.

1

Give it time, she'd thought. But now, it was as though she was being pulled along in a riptide.

"I love you, Natalie."

A splatter of sleet ran down the windshield. She was suffocating under her winter coat, but she didn't want to unbutton it.

Bill twisted away and dug into his pocket. Leaning back, he pulled out a small velvet-covered box.

"Bill, do you think…?" Natalie wasn't sure what she wanted to say, but before she said anything, he'd opened the box. Their breath had fogged the windows, and in the dim interior of the car, Natalie stared at the small diamond ring groping for the right words. When she finally lifted her head, Bill's eager face was beaming at her. Tears brimmed in the corners of his eyes.

"Will you marry me, Natalie?"

She didn't want to hurt him. She couldn't force herself to say, 'I'm not sure.' She nodded.

**

"Dearly beloved. We are gathered here today in the sight of God…"

Natalie stared at the covered chalice in the middle of the altar as Father Eagan droned on. A hint of incense from yesterday's funeral hung in the air. Standing behind Natalie was her best friend Joyce who'd made the trip from Syracuse with the gas coupons Bill sent her. 'Don't ask', he'd said. She was glad Joyce found a lovely dress. She hated hers. The owner of Capital Bridal explained that she hadn't been able to keep up with the crush of weddings. With the fellows going off to the service and specialty fabrics getting scarcer every day, Natalie should be thankful she had anything in the store that fit her. When Bill's orders to report came earlier than expected, the wedding turned into a slap-dash

2

affair: no bridesmaids in robin's egg blue chiffon, no flower girl or ring bearer, no time to have the kind of wedding she'd dreamed about.

Behind Bill, his brother Mike pulled at the collar of his starched shirt. The florist had to help him knot the tie, and whoever he'd borrowed the suit from was a size larger.

"Do you, Natalie, take William to be…?"

The most important event in her life, and she felt as though she didn't choose. Bill loved her. She hoped she would come to love him.

"I, Natalie, take you, William…."

***

It was a hot fuggy afternoon when Natalie boarded the train in Philadelphia. In the first car, the aisle was jammed with GIs swigging from beer bottles. She made her way to the next car and pushed through a fog of cigarette smoke and sweat. She spotted a vacant seat, but before she reached it, a GI flopped into it. She was about to try the next car when the middle-aged woman next to the window poked him. "Where's your manners, soldier?"

The GI let out a resigned sigh and hauled himself up. 'Thank you," she said. She put her suitcase on the rack. The train started with a lurch, and she fell into the seat. The train pulled away from the station. Clouds sagged over the river, and gulls swooped over the mud flats.

Exhausted, Natalie closed her eyes and wondered how she got here. She felt cheated. Only a three day honeymoon in a freezing motel room in Lake George instead of a bridal suite in Niagara Falls.

She didn't think after her girlish honeymoon fantasies that she and Bill would live in Fred Astaire's and Ginger Rogers's penthouse, but finding a decent apartment for a few months was impossible. The tiny room in a boarding house in Troy smelled of boiled cabbage, and they shared a bathroom with a man who must have been brought up in a barn. There were only so many places to go at night before they had to come back to the dingy room to have sex and listen to the radio, taking turns sitting in the one rickety chair while the other sat on the bed. She was ashamed to admit she was glad when Bill left for basic training, and she suspected he wasn't sorry either.

Moving back to her bedroom in her parents' house, it seemed as though she'd never left. She felt guilty enjoying clean sheets, good food, and a living room.

With only a short leave before Bill was scheduled to ship out, they agreed to meet at Fort Dix and not waste their time together if Bill had to take the train back and forth to Albany. He said the room he got at a hotel near the base wasn't much, but they'd be together. Natalie hoped the weekend would be a fresh start erasing the memory of the ragged first months of their marriage.

It was awful. The hotel was crammed with soldiers on leave from Fort Dix with their wives, girlfriends, and too many women who didn't fit in either category. Maybe it was the sounds echoing through the thin walls, but sex with Bill was coarse, too rough. Outside the hotel, there was no place to go except the saloons where Bill drank too much. She struggled to remember the fellow who asked her to marry him with tears in his eyes.

The conductor punched her ticket. Natalie wanted to think of the good things a life with Bill might bring, but everything about the past few months and the past three days overwhelmed her. Her shoulders slumped, and she began to cry.

The woman next to her handed her a tissue.

"I'm sorry. I just left my husband at Fort Dix."

"He's shipping out to Europe?"

Natalie nodded, sorry for not thinking that Bill must be afraid of what lay ahead. Maybe that explained the way he behaved. But Natalie blurted, "I think I made a mistake."

The woman gave her a quizzical look.

"We should have waited. I'm sorry. I shouldn't have said that."

Pulling another tissue from her handbag, the woman said, "Dearie, every woman feels she's made a mistake at some point in a marriage." She patted Natalie's hand. "I hope you can make the best of it."

Her pity washed over Natalie, and she shrank in her seat.

***

I can't sleep, Bill thought. Something's wrong with me. My fingers and toes are tingling, and my heart's pumping so fast I'm afraid I'm going to blow a gasket. The Drill Sargent would kill me if I went on sick call for anything less than a compound fracture. The snoring, farting, and sleep-talking of the fifty guys in my platoon is getting louder every night. I'm never alone – even for a few minutes. I can't turn around without bumping into someone. Everyone is pressing into me. Sometimes I can't catch my breath. I feel like I'm going to faint.

Every night I finally fall asleep a half hour before reveille and then go through the morning drills like my eyelids have weights on them. Can't wait to see what stupid drill we practice tomorrow. A damn fool nearly killed us all yesterday, gawking at a grenade with the pin pulled like he couldn't figure how it ended up in his hand, everyone screaming '*throw it,*' before a Corporal grabbed it and flung it. Get killed here or overseas: what's the difference? Nothing I can do.

Natalie won't care after what I did. I'm disgusted with myself. She must hate me. It was more like a whorehouse than a hotel, but there was no other place to go. I saved myself for her and wouldn't go along with the ones who screwed whoever they picked up in the bars on the weekend passes. Giving her a case of the clap would have been about the only thing worse than me acting like an animal. If only we could have gone someplace nice. I drank too much. But what else was there to do?

I hate to think that's how she'll remember me. I try to write her nice letters. I want to tell her how much I love her and how I'll make it up to her when I get back. But I read back the words, and it's like I'm in third grade.

2

Watervliet Arsenal.　　　　September, 1944

*Doubled Output of Munitions Ordered: War Production
Board Calls for 62,000 More Workers*

It was ten minutes to eight when Natalie slid into the chair at
her tiny desk. She pulled a stack of ship orders in front of
her and savored the few minutes of eerie quiet between shift
changes. Double-checking the inventory for 60 mm mortar
tubes, she prepared an order for twenty and stuffed cotton
in her ears. At eight, a pounding hydraulic press shook the
pencils in the cup on her desk. Two floors above the
assembly lines, the rhythmic thumping vibrating through
her breastbone made her feel as though she was a part of the
machine.

At noon, she finished the last inventory check for the
morning and decided to eat her sandwich at her desk while
she up-dated her TODO list. At the same time she took a
bite, there was a knock on the door. "Come in," she said
through a mouthful of egg salad.

A tall man stood in the doorway. Safety googles hung
around his neck. "I'm looking for Mrs. Costello."

Natalie wondered what he was doing here. She'd
seen him once punching in, and that's all you needed to
remember Jack Mahoney. Well over six feet tall. Trim with a
rugged face. The black patch covering his left eye and the
black band snaking across his forehead made him stand out.
Black Jack. Captain Hook. She'd heard the nicknames thrown
around by the men. But it was the girls at the lunch table

who giggled when they gossiped about this handsome single man. "I'm Mrs. Costello."

"Can't be," he said. "From what my crew chiefs say, I expected to find a tough old battle-ax, not an attractive young woman."

Natalie wasn't used to flattery, and she stammered, "I am Mrs. Costello – Natalie Costello."

"Sorry. I should go back out the door and come back in. Start over. I'm Jack Mahoney."

Why did this high-ranking assembly manager want to see her? she wondered. He did ask for her and not her boss. Still, she said, "Mr. Holt is not here."

Mr. Mahoney leaned over Natalie's desk. "I know. That's why I'm looking for you."

He leaned in so close, Natalie tipped back in her chair. His finger pointed at her chest like the Uncle Sam poster. "Oh, I see," she said. "What can I do for you, Mr. Mahoney?"

"I need sixteen pallets of 37 millimeter breech rings in Area 5 no later than the start of the second shift on Thursday. It's urgent, and I haven't got an approval yet." He pulled a slip of paper from the breast pocket of his work shirt. "And I've got three other orders pending I'm afraid are going to be late too."

"I'll tell Mr. Holt as soon as he returns."

"Mrs. Costello, I came to you because my line supervisors tell me the only way to get something done around here is to have you do it."

There was a commanding tone under his soft-soaping, and she decided to do what he wanted. "Let's see if I can find the order." This wasn't the first time she'd had to retrieve something while her boss was out to lunch, but she always felt as though she was trespassing. Mr. Mahoney followed her into Mr. Holt's office.

The jumble of papers scattered across Mr. Holt's desk seemed to have multiplied since the last time Natalie was in the office. "I think Mr. Holt has a new system, but I'm not sure if the pending are now on the left or right. Or where he's keeping his inventory records."

"System?" Mr. Mahoney waved a dismissive hand over the mess. "Looks like somebody emptied the trash barrel."

Natalie shuffled though the piles of paperwork. "Here are two of the orders you had on the slip of paper."

Mr. Mahoney checked the paper he'd pulled from his pocket. "You remembered the numbers from one glance?"

"I have a good memory. I'll find the others." Natalie continued shifting through the towering stack on the right side of the desk. Mr. Mahoney began sorting through the pile on the left. One stack began to collapse, and they bumped shoulders as they both reached for them. Natalie jumped back as though she'd been pricked with a pin. "Sorry."

"Here's twenty-seven-forty-five," he said and held up the ship order as though he'd found a pearl in a muck pile. "One more to go: sixty-eight- ninety-one."

Natalie saw it on the edge of the desk. "Got it!"

"What's going on?" Mr. Holt called from the open doorway.

Natalie placed the ship order on top of a pile of papers. "I'm trying to find a ship order for Mr. Mahoney." She gestured toward him as though he'd dropped in from a hole in the ceiling.

"I'm sorry," Mr. Mahoney said. "Your assistant wanted to wait for you, but I insisted she open your office."

"I was inadvertently detained. Mrs. Costello is my

secretary, not my assistant."

"The order is urgent," Mr. Mahoney said.

Mr. Holt swept his hands over the pile of papers covering his desk. "They're all urgent. There's a war on in case you hadn't noticed."

Then why do you act as though it's over, Natalie thought?

Mr. Mahoney and Natalie stood silently while Mr. Holt scrabbled through the mound of papers, knocking some to the floor. Finally, he noticed Mr. Mahoney's ship order on the top of the pile where Natalie had placed it. "Right here," he announced. "I would have had it in a second if you two hadn't messed up my system." He pulled a rubber stamp from the jumble in a desk drawer and stamped, 'Approved' on the order. He handed it to Mr. Mahoney as though passing on top secret plans. "Next time, I'll handle it."

"It was my fault," Mr. Mahoney said, but he didn't sound apologetic.

"Well, now you have it. And I'd appreciate it if you'd come to me directly with urgent requests. Mrs. Costello has her own duties to attend to. If she has to deal with every supposedly urgent request and go … well, there it is."

Mr. Mahoney laid the other ship orders side by side on Mr. Holt's desk. "Would you please stamp these as well?" 'Please' was more an order than a request.

Mr. Holt's hands fluttered over the orders before giving each a ceremonious thump of his 'Approved' stamp. Ignoring Natalie and Mr. Mahoney, he turned his attention to rearranging the papers scattered across his desk.

Natalie let Mr. Mahoney exit first, then closed the door behind them. "I'm sorry about the mess in Mr. Holt's office."

"What I heard is that it's ten times better than it was before you came here. How long have you've been Mr. Holt's secretary?"

"Six months. I was in the tool sheds when I was first hired."

"Right. My guys tell me the tool runners stand around waiting for a drill bit or lathe blade, complaining it wasn't like that when you were there. You should have a twin."

"I like organizing things. I mean it was like nothing I'd ever done before. I discovered I could solve problems I didn't know existed. I…" She felt foolish. "Excuse me, I'm rattling on."

"Not really. And now floor managers are coming to you to when Mr. Holt's …"

"Out to lunch?" She was sorry she'd said that, but she was anxious to be liked by him. "I bring a sandwich and eat at my desk," Natalie said as though she needed to explain herself.

Mr. Mahoney held up the sheaf of ship orders and gave her a broad smile. "Thanks a million. I've got to get going."

"It was nice to meet you, Mr. Mahoney."

"My pleasure, and call me Jack." He pointed at the half-eaten sandwich on her desk. "You saved my day. I should buy you a proper lunch."

Twenty minutes later in the ladies room, Natalie was embarrassed by what she saw in the mirror. Hunks of cotton were sticking out of her ears as though smoke was billowing from a fire in her head. 'Attractive young woman.' It was true what he'd said about the managers coming to her when Mr. Holt was out, but he was still giving her a line. With most of the fellows at the Arsenal older and married, she'd forgotten how to deal with sweet-talkers.

Mr. Holt may be driving her buggy, but it was still better than the tool shed. And she thought she would really be ready for a straightjacket if she spent one more month at the first job she got after Bill shipped out. At State Street Insurance she was assigned to work with three other women reviewing and checking the accuracy of the billing. It was supposed to take all day, but after the first week, Natalie finished her accounts by two o'clock in the afternoon while the other women worked right up to the end of the day. When she finally asked her boss if there was something else she could do to fill the two hours she spent staring at the pile of accounts she'd checked and rechecked, he seemed annoyed.

Thank goodness the Arsenal was taking on another wave of hires. The first day Natalie walked through the main gate and flashed her security badge, she felt as though Saint Peter had let her in. They started her in the tool shed on the main assembly line.

After a several weeks, Natalie realized many of the tools closest to the front were obsolete. Some went back to World War I. The tool runners had to wait while she searched for their orders. Her boss let her move the rarely requisitioned tools to the back and move the most often requested to the front shelves. Most of the runners seemed happy with the shorter waits – although she knew a couple grumbled that she'd cut into the time they could stand around chewing the fat.

When her boss called Natalie into a meeting and she saw the troubled look on his face, she said, "I hope I haven't made a mistake."

"No. You're doing a splendid job," he said. "Too good I guess. You're being transferred."

Great, she thought. When she learned what the women who'd replaced the machinists and assemblers who'd gone into the service were doing, she wanted to join them on the assembly line.

"You're going to be Mr. Holt's secretary in Inventory Control."

Secretary? She'd avoided the secretarial classes in high school and couldn't do more than hunt and peck on a typewriter. And she'd heard about Mr. Holt and Inventory Control. None of it was good. She was going to be a secretary – no different than working as a clerk in an insurance company.

Now, Natalie didn't know what she was supposed to be. At least she didn't have to worry about being bored. With her *secretary's* job, along with dealing with Mr. Holt's mistakes and incompetent dithering she barely had time to finish a sandwich. Buy her a proper lunch, whatever that is. She wasn't holding her breath. Still she cringed at the memory of cotton sticking out of her ears.

In the days after Natalie helped Jack find the ship orders, Mr. Holt became even more confused. He began snapping at her for supposedly misplaced paperwork, but quickly apologized and asked her to help him organize his records. Within days, the mess in his office reappeared. She often found him staring bewildered at the piles of paper on his desk as though mischievous fairies had snuck in at night to scatter them into random heaps. He stopped taking too long lunches and seemed especially nervous whenever the phone rang or a supervisor came to see him.

***

At ten o'clock on Monday morning, the office door opened and Mr. Vincent entered, trailed by Mr. Fox. Natalie jumped out of her chair and stood next to her desk. Good grief, she thought. Why were the Director of Operations and his assistant here? She was sure it had to do with the incident with Jack and the late ship orders. Mr. Holt must have complained about her insubordination. Or maybe Mr. Holt was going to blame the chaos in his office on her. Mr. Vincent knocked on Mr. Holt's door and the two men entered without waiting.

Natalie could barely work as she tried to make sense of the rumble of voices from behind the closed door. At ten-thirty, the door opened, and a haggard Mr. Holt asked Natalie to come into the office. She smoothed down her dress and ran her fingers through her hair. When she entered, Mr. Vincent asked her to sit. Her legs felt wobbly. She expected the ax to fall.

Mr. Vincent set his pipe on Mr. Holt's desk. "Mrs. Costello," he said. "As you know, Mr. Holt has a great deal of responsibility for the smooth flow of materiel from the warehouses and storage to the shop floors."

She'd never exchanged more than a nod with Mr. Vincent as they passed in the corridor, and the fact that he was actually speaking to her had her trembling. "Yes," she finally whispered.

"In fact, we feel that he has been asked to take on more responsibility than any one man should carry. Therefore, we are asking him to assume a different role, one that would allow him to maximize his ability to see the whole picture, as it were."

All Natalie could do was meekly nod. The deflated sag of Mr. Holt's body didn't match Mr. Vincent's words.

"Beginning tomorrow, Mr. Holt will be in charge of reviewing ship orders that come from the floor managers and matching them against the inventory of materials in the warehouses."

Isn't that what he's supposed to do now, Natalie thought? No, he approves them.

"We would like you, Mrs. Costello, to assume the responsibility for day to day approval of orders from inventory. At the end of each week, Mr. Holt will review your approvals to ensure that you have made the appropriate judgements about the priorities of moving materiel to the shop floors."

She was going to do Mr. Holt's job? That didn't make sense. I'm a woman, a secretary, she thought. How will that work? How will I manage the flow of paperwork? How can I decide what is urgent and what is routine? Already thinking about how she would do the job, she almost forgot that Mr. Vincent was still speaking.

"Congratulations, Tim. We have the utmost confidence in your ability to handle this." Natalie was sure Mr. Vincent cast a grim eye across the mess on the desk as he turned toward her. "Thank you, Mrs. Costello. That will be all."

Natalie left and sat at her desk struggling to make sense of what she'd just heard.

A few minutes later, Mr. Vincent came out of the office, tipped his head in Natalie's direction and left a savory trail of pipe smoke in his wake. His assistant, Mr. Fox, stood in front of her desk, and she wished she had a place to hide. Mr. Vincent was admired for exercising calm, under-stated authority. Mr. Fox was feared, and even though Natalie's mother told her to always see the best in people, she thought he was one of the ugliest men she'd seen. She imagined him starting out at six-one before stumbling into one of the hydraulic presses and getting hammered down to five-six. With a flat, acne -pitted face and fleshy lips, he looked like an angry frog. Like everyone else on the floor, Natalie managed to avoid him as he followed behind Mr. Vincent, eyes darting left and right as though searching for a juicy bug. But now he was fixing her with cold gray eyes, and she was afraid his tongue would snake out and snatch her.

"I don't believe I need to elaborate on the charge to you – and to Mr. Holt."

Natalie felt color rising in her cheeks. "No. I understand." She'd been noticed for taking care of Mr. Holt's mistakes and delays. Now, any mistakes and delays were going to be hers.

Mr. Fox surveyed her cramped work space. "Of course, Mr. Holt will remain in his office. I'll order supply to deliver a desk that will give you more – latitude." He gave her a counterfeit smile. "And you'll be pleased to see an additional ten cents an hour in your pay envelope each week."

A raise? It hadn't occurred to her. Ten cents. She'd still make a fraction of Mr. Holt's salary.

"And one more thing," Mr. Fox said. He handed Natalie what he must have taken from Mr. Holt's desk: his rubber stamp—"Approved." His smile vanished. "We'll see how well you use it."

3

OPA Acts to Stop Shoe Buying Rush: "Not a Chance" for
Cancellation of Ration Stamps

Mario Pisano carried the scrap out to the trash barrel behind the shop. He lifted the lid and saw a half sheet of eighty pound poster stock wedged against the side. He guessed it must have got stuck when they emptied the barrel last night. He reached in and pulled it away from the edge and started to fold it so it would go out next time. Underneath the poster stock were several balls of crumpled paper. Red and blue smudged on a white background – misprints. He reached for them, but pulled his hand back as quickly as if he'd seen a rattlesnake in there.

He knew. He didn't want to know. They hadn't done a job with ink in those hard-to-come-by colors for months. He stuffed the scrap in the barrel making sure it covered the crumpled balls at the bottom. Mario slammed the cover back on and rubbed his hands on the thighs of his work pants. He wondered if he should wipe the cover clean with his handkerchief – as if his fingerprints on the scrap barrel were the only evidence the FBI would need.

What now? Mario wondered. It had been two months since Stan started doing this. Damn fool. He must think I fell off a potato wagon. Where was he getting the ink? For sure it's in the old storage cabinet that sprouted a new Yale padlock. The two of them working elbow to elbow in the small shop for three years now and all of a sudden something has to get locked up. The paper must be in there too. He probably brings it in after we close up.

'Too damn much paperwork,' Stan complained when he started staying late. Okay, he's the owner, but he'd been staying late three and four nights a week instead of walking across the street to Ralph's Tavern after locking up for his usual shot and a beer. And giving Mario the razz for heading straight home. Paperwork, my eye. Stan was careful to clean up on those paperwork nights – too careful. But the smell of recently inked presses lingered when they opened up in the morning.

He owed Stan. His first steady paycheck since thirty-one. Nothing but pick-up jobs here and there. Even a couple of months on the WPA. The shame he felt when he had to tell the paperboy they were cancelling the *Times Union*. Tess stretching one scrawny chicken for days. Him having to urge her to put some of it on her plate. The fight they had to keep Natalie from dropping out of school to get a job to help out. What kind of job could she get? How much worse could he feel if his daughter quit school to help feed his family?

Family is what got him the job. It was down to him and Jerry Hanley. He didn't know if he'd have to beg, but Tess reminded him that Stan's mother was related to her aunt on her father's side. Mario was embarrassed when he threw out this supposed family connection that wasn't too far removed from Adam and Eve. But Stan did remember this aunt. And although Hanley had actually worked in a print shop some years ago, he was known as a drinker. And maybe Mario said something that reminded Stan of it.

The first day on the job was as clear as though it was yesterday – him standing outside the shop thirty minutes before Stan arrived to open. It was like it might be some terrible joke, and he really didn't get the job. Stan had to tell him to stop thanking him as he showed him the ropes. And if he lived to be a hundred, he'll never forget that first

Friday, taking that pay envelope home and counting it out on the kitchen table. Him and Tessie and Natalie and Nicky staring at the bills and change as though he'd found a million bucks on the street. It was weeks –maybe months – before he got over the fact that he had a regular job with a regular paycheck.

What was he going to do? He felt helpless. He couldn't think of any other possible explanation than forged ration coupons. Gas stamps? Food stamps? Ration books? B and C windshield stickers? What difference would it make? He'd read the stories in the paper about forgery rings. The government was making it up as it went along with rationing and food and gas coupons. When they first got theirs, Stan and Mario laughed at the crappy job. 'We could do a better job on our worst day,' Stan said.

All Mario saw was blue and red smudged scraps. He wasn't going to pull them out of the barrel and confirm his suspicions. What would happen if he confronted Stan? He could deny it. He could fire Mario. Then what: go to the police? Two printers working side by side every day, and he didn't know or didn't suspect? He dreaded what might happen, but what was he going to do?

4

Scarcity Affects Standard Lines of Goods. Cotton Dress Situation Declared Critical

On Friday morning, two guys from supply squeezed a gray steel desk through the door of Inventory Control. It was twice the size of Natalie's old secretary's desk, and it certainly would give her the 'latitude' Mr. Fox promised. However, the dents, scrapes and grime covering it made her wonder if it had been in the supply room since World War I. And it would take a bucket of *Spic n Span* to clean the swivel chair that came with it.

She was wondering where to have it placed when one of the fellows began to turn her old desk on end. "Hold on," she said. She hadn't formed a clear idea of what she wanted, but she walked to the doorway and faced the room as though she was entering. "I'd like to keep it."

The man who held the paperwork said, "We're supposed to return the old furniture to storage."

He had to be at least sixty, Natalie guessed, and she'd noticed the other fellow, who was still taking ragged breaths, had dragged a leg behind him when they arrived. Neither of them was probably fit enough to be working on the assembly lines. "I'll take responsibility," she said. "Besides, you won't have to carry that old desk and chair down two flights and all the way over to the back of Building 4."

The man with the gimpy leg shot an approving glance at the fellow with the paperwork, and before he had a chance to think about it, Natalie grabbed the paperwork from his hand and quickly scrawled her signature across the bottom. She put her hand on his arm and as she was nudging him toward the door, she said, "Thanks, guys. I'll tell Mr. Fox what a great job you did."

Now what? Natalie thought as she surveyed the jumble of office furniture. The vague notion that had shot into her head a few minutes ago began to form into the makings of a plan. Sorry she got rid of the fellows from supply so quickly, she barely managed to shove the new gray desk back toward the door to Mr. Holt's office.

Mr. Holt apparently heard the scraping of the desk legs on the linoleum. He poked his head out of his door.

"Mr. Fox," Natalie said. "Latitude."

As though watching for an ambush, Mr. Holt's eyes darted left and right before pulling the door closed.

Mr. Fox, Natalie thought. She wondered if those might be magic words to use again on Mr. Holt.

After fifteen minutes of shoving and grunting and sweating, Natalie's plan began to take shape. Her old secretary's desk and chair were now set just inside the office door. The Inventory Reports In-Box sat on the left, the Out-Box on the right. Natalie's old-new desk was three feet behind it and a foot closer to the wall. On the desk was the up-right file metal file holder she'd ordered. In the right top drawer was her "Approved" stamp and ink pad.

After a preliminary swipe of her handkerchief on the dusty swivel chair, Natalie sat and took in the new arrangement. Somewhere in the Personnel Office she was listed as Secretary Grade 2 – Temp, but if she was going to perform the most important duties of Mr. Holt's position, she should have her own office. *"My office,"* she whispered.

Late in the afternoon, Natalie knocked on Mr. Holt's door and entered. Mr. Holt, fingers folded, sat behind a completely clean-topped desk. Natalie held a sheaf of carbon copies. "These are the orders I approved this week, Mr. Holt." She laid the pile neatly on the left side of the desk. Mr. Holt nodded toward the stack of paper. "And here are the inventory records matched to the orders." She laid them next to the first sheaf. Natalie didn't know what was supposed to happen next, and she shifted from one foot to the other as she waited.

"Is that all?" Mr. Holt asked.

Was there supposed to be something else? "Yes," she answered, unsure of herself.

"Thank you." Mr. Holt inclined his head toward the two stacks. "That will be all."

Back behind her desk, Natalie wondered whether she should wait for him to tell her the results of his review.

Minutes before quitting time, she was startled by a knock on the office door. Jack Mahoney stepped in. He spread his arms to take in the new office arrangement. "Things must have changed for the better since I was last here."

"Just a small adjustment," Natalie said.

Jack detoured around Natalie's old secretary's desk. "Now I have to run an obstacle course to get to you."

"I'm sure you can manage."

Jack hesitated for a moment. "In any case, I'm glad I caught you."

"Here I am, Mr. Mahoney."

He gave her a jokey frown.

"Jack, I mean."

"I'm sorry I haven't been back sooner. Two major breakdowns on the line this week."

"I heard." She'd re-routed supplies to deal with them. Thank goodness she didn't have to wait for Mr. Holt to approve the orders any longer.

"And I heard how well you handled the mess."

"I'm doing my best."

"I'm not here just to deliver thanks. I want to make good on my offer of lunch."

"Oh, that's not necessary."

"When I say something, I mean it. Is Monday okay? Nothing special. Mel's Diner on Broadway. I'll swing by a few minutes before noon."

Natalie said, "I, ah. I guess – I suppose that will be okay. I'm not…"

"Have you taken your full lunch hour since you got this job?"

Aside from the few times she'd managed a short lunch with the girls in the cafeteria, she spent most lunch hours at her desk, pencil in one hand, sandwich in the other. "Not really."

"Then you're entitled to one. And it will do you good to get out from time to time. See you a few minutes before noon on Monday."

Natalie's brain started to swirl the moment he left her office. What should she wear? Should she ask Mr. Holt for permission? What should she order? Should she offer to pay for her lunch?

***

Monday morning Natalie stood in front of her closet in her slip pawing through the dresses she wore to work: three from one Butterick pattern and the other two from another pattern her mother made up from whatever decent fabric she could find on sale at Whitney's. More than a few times, she'd run into other women at the Arsenal and around town wearing the same dress in the same material. If she had a job on the line, she would change into overalls in the ladies'

23

locker room that had been slapped together in the far corner of Building 4. Not too fancy, not too plain. It was a 'thank you' for expediting his orders. Nothing more. That's it. I'm not going to the prom, she thought. But she couldn't stop running a comb through her hair, wishing her appointment at Cathy's Cut &Curl was this week instead of next.

When Natalie got to the office, she couldn't concentrate as she tried to imagine what Jack and she would talk about at lunch. She wished for an emergency that would postpone their lunch. By the time Jack rapped on her office door two minutes to twelve she was in a frazzle.

As Jack and Natalie headed to the exit of Building C, she was afraid she was walking too close to him. Then she hung a couple of steps back until he glanced over his shoulder as though wondering if she was going to bolt. By the time they slid into a booth at Mel's, she was convinced this was a big mistake. They were surrounded by men in booths and tables: some of the brass from the Administration Building, two women in dresses that weren't homemade who Natalie was sure didn't work at the Arsenal, but no couples, none of the women from the cafeteria lunch table. She felt as though she'd stumbled into the wrong room.

"You don't get out to lunch much do you?" Jack asked.

"Is my nervousness that obvious?"

"Maybe a little," he said. "But I felt I needed to do something more than 'thanks' for the terrific job you've been doing. I can't tell you how many of the managers have been singing your praises."

"That's nice. I'm not sure my husband would be happy to know several men are talking about me."

Jack nodded his chin toward Natalie's left hand.

"Your husband's in the service."

"Fourth Infantry Division. He's in France, at least as far as I can tell from his censored v-mails."

"The Fourth. Utah Beach. I'm glad he made it."

"Yes, we didn't hear until weeks after the landing."

"You should be proud." Jack pointed to the patch over his eye. "I'm afraid my war is going to stay right here at the Arsenal."

"How did it happen?"

"Stupidity." He fingered the collar of his shirt where his safety glasses would hang. "I was in a hurry. If I'd gone back to the bench for them, they would have blocked the sliver of tungsten flying off the lathe."

The waitress arrived at their booth. Natalie couldn't remember the last time she was in a restaurant, even a diner. Going out to eat, even at a diner, was a rare luxury. She felt flustered, and Jack said, "With rationing, Mel's is one of the few places that actually has beef in their burgers."

"Okay," Natalie said. "I'd like a hamburger and a Coke, please."

"The same," Jack said and handed the menus to the waitress.

Natalie didn't know what to do with her hands. Ordering a hamburger and a Coke made her feel as though she'd barely passed a difficult test. Even the clatter of plates being delivered to the tables around them startled her.

When a Major marched by their booth and snapped a look at Natalie and Jack, she felt a sting of disapproval.

Jack's eyes followed him, and he said, "I hope you don't feel uncomfortable with just the two of us." He laughed. "I could have brought along at least three other floor managers who wanted to buy you lunch. If you knew how many times I've heard how you've gotten them out of a jam, your ears would burn."

Natalie didn't try to hide her blush. "And you'd be surprised how often a ..." She bit back 'young and handsome' ... "single man gets mentioned at the girls' table in the lunch room." Jack lifted his palms and gave her a playful shrug as though he heard her unspoken words. And vain too, she thought.

The waitress set two glasses of Coke on the table. Jack picked up his and raised it toward Natalie. "Here's to burning ears."

She clinked her glass on his. He joked about the room he'd rented from an elderly widow in Green Island who pampered him so much he was afraid she'd come into his room and tuck him in at night. Natalie relaxed a little. She told tell him that she was back living at her parents' house and how her mom had a hard time not treating her like she was sixteen again. They traded stories about their teenage years.

Jack smiled easily. His hands chopped and fingers pointed as he talked. And when Natalie spoke, he leaned toward her. His one eye looked at her as though her every word was important. Now she understood why there were naughty giggles from the girls in the lunch room when his name came up – and confessed she was being carried along by his charm.

They dug into their hamburgers, and they both laughed when catsup dripped on their fingers. It hit Natalie that this was the first time since Bill left that she'd had a meal with a man who wasn't a relative. It was only lunch with someone from work, a thank you for doing a favor, she thought. Still, he made her feel like an adult rather than an over-grown teenager living at home and someone who'd been given an important job to do.

They finished their lunch and walked back to the Arsenal, making small talk, joking about things she couldn't recall later – except how he made her feel more comfortable.

Inside the Building C entrance, Jack held out his hand. "It was a pleasure."

"Thank you. I enjoyed it."

"It was nice that we didn't talk shop," he said. "And I'm glad you're doing so well in the new job."

"Thanks, but I'm still pushing paper and too often guessing what's a priority."

Jack said, "I bet you could do it even better if you could actually see how the materiel moves from storage to the shop floors. Let me see if I can arrange a tour."

"I'm not sure."

"It will be good. Get you out of the office and down on the shop floors."

"Perhaps," Natalie said. She felt unsure about his offer. Lunch was nice, but Jack was a flirt, and maybe she enjoyed talking to him too much. She was glad Bill came up at lunch. It was good to be reminded that he was somewhere in danger in France. It had been two years since she married Bill. Sometimes it seemed like it was a lifetime ago.

***

First thing Wednesday morning, angry voices hit Natalie as soon as she opened her office door. Mr. Fox and a man she didn't recognize were standing inches apart.

Mr. Fox's squished-down face was flushed, and the hairy fingers of the other man's hands were gripping the edge of her desk.

"You're finally here," Mr. Fox snapped as though she'd spent the entire morning dallying around Watervliet.

The clock over his head confirmed that Natalie was ten minutes early, but she didn't think it would be a good idea to point that out.

"Let's get to the bottom of this," Mr. Fox said.

The other man, with *Brillo Pad* hair and black eyebrows snaking across his square face, waved a piece of paper at Natalie as though it was a warrant for her arrest. He said, "I'm supposed to get seven gun carriages for 240 millimeter howitzers, and I get four 240s and three for the 105. I get written up for falling behind schedule while my guys sit on their – hands waiting for the three missing carriages to get delivered to the line."

Natalie was sweating under her coat, but was so alarmed by the man's accusations she kept it on. "May I?" she asked, and he passed her the paper he'd been waving. Her hands shook as she placed what she recognized was a ship order on the top of the desk. "Mister..?"

"Tartanian," he said as though it was none of her business.

As calmly as she could manage, Natalie said, "This is your request for the seven 240 gun carriages." She pulled the inventory report for that date and laid it next to the ship order. "These show there were thirty in Building SH on that date. I matched the request with inventory and approved the delivery."

"Paper pushing," Mr. Tartanian snarled.

Mr. Fox muscled in behind Natalie to look at the two pieces of paper side-by-side on her desk. "I see what happened. We got a bigger-than-expected shipment, and SH was re-shuffled to make room two days after this order was sent."

"I told you it wasn't my fault," Mr. Tartanian said.

Mr. Fox said, "Let's go." He turned to Natalie. "You should be extra careful."

Mr. Tartanian glared at her as though it was her fault

and followed Mr. Fox out the door. Tartanian's hair crept down his neck and into the collar of his shirt, and Natalie cringed as she imagined a carpet of tight black curls on his back.

Natalie wanted to give the closed door a kick. "Damn it." She was extra careful. She doubled and triple-checked every order before she stamped 'Approved.' No one told her the supplies were re-shuffled. It was their fault, not hers.

Natalie tried to get back to work, but she was so angry she kept breaking off pencil points as she wrote up ship orders. She'd been at the Arsenal almost two years, and she didn't know what a gun carriage looked like. She needed to see how supplies were actually moved from inventory to assembly. Jack said he'd arrange a tour, but she hadn't heard from him in more than a week. Another come-on line, she supposed. But she typed a note and put it in the interoffice mail out-box. Every few minutes she stared at it, and moments before the mailman arrived, she almost grabbed it back.

**

The next morning, Natalie was still angry. She'd bet Mr. Tartanian still thought it was her fault, and Mr. Fox looked as though he agreed. Mr. Holt was terrified she'd mess up his cushy life. When she gave him approvals at the end of the week, he cringed as if she'd handed him hand grenades with the pins pulled out. She was a paper-pushing drone who counted for nothing except when they were looking for someone to blame.

Natalie slammed the 'Approved' stamp on an order so hard, pencils jumped off the desk. There was a rap on the door. "Come in," she snapped.

Jack said, "I got your note."

"I shouldn't have sent it."

"I'm sorry I didn't answer sooner, but it's been crazy. Three more rush orders for mortars last week. We're gearing up for a big push into Germany for sure."

"It's been difficult. I mean. I'm not sure what I mean."

"Wow. You look like you've climbed out of the furnace pit."

Natalie shoved inventory reports and ship orders to one side of her desk. "It's like there's no connection. I can't see what's going on down there."

"I heard about Tartanian's beef. We all get the wrong parts delivered."

"It happens a lot?"

"Too often, but most of us handle it ourselves." Jack dropped her note on the desk. "I agree. You should see how the supplies move from inventory to the lines. It's overdue, and I've cleared Tuesday morning."

She heard the steel in his voice. She understood why he was known as a take-charge guy. "Tuesday would be good." He was standing so close she smelled machine oil on his hands.

"You look very nice, pretty dress and all."

Natalie felt a flush on her cheeks. "Thank you," she said in a hoarse whisper and vowed to get better at dealing with his flirting.

"But you'd better wear a pair of overalls. Some sturdy shoes and a kerchief. I'll bring a pair of safety goggles."

Natalie felt like a jerk thinking he was complimenting her. "Of course."

"I'll meet you here. Eight-fifteen."

***

On Tuesday morning Natalie found her way to the Women's Locker Room. Informally, it was off-limits to those who didn't have jobs on the assembly lines, and a couple of the women eyed her suspiciously. Still in her dress, Natalie tried not to stare as they stripped to their underwear and pulled on overalls. Thank goodness, her old high school friend, Flo Rudenko, said she had an extra pair she could use.

"Hey, Natalie," Flo called as she entered the room. "Welcome to the broom closet." She waved to the other women. "Relax. She's not going to steal a locker."

"Hi, Flo. I appreciate this."

"I swear they made this so small, we'd be forced to change out in the hallway." Flo opened her locker and took a pair of gray overalls off a hook, handed them to Natalie, then reached in for another pair.

"I'll wash them tonight and bring them back tomorrow morning," Natalie said. She was disconcerted when Flo unbuttoned her dress, quickly stripped it off, and pulled her slip over her head. Even in what passed for gym in high school, the girls rarely took off their clothes, but Flo didn't seem embarrassed to be standing there in her bra and panties. Natalie was the one who was embarrassed when she realized even though Flo was only an inch taller than her, she had the hour-glass figure of a pin-up while Natalie was much smaller on top and hips.

Natalie quickly undressed and stepped into Flo's overalls. As soon as she pulled them up, she realized they were too big.

Flo said, "Sorry. I hope you don't fall out of them when you're on your tour with Mahoney."

"Black Jack?" the woman next to them asked. When Natalie nodded, she said, "I wouldn't mind falling out of my overalls touring around with him."

"Can it Gertrude," Flo joked. "My friend is *not* a girl like you."

A busty red head at the end of the room gave Natalie

a nasty look. "Jack – Mahoney," she said, biting off each word before slamming her locker shut and stalking out of the room.

Blood rushed to Natalie's face as smirks and snickers slid around the room.

Natalie quickly put on the shoes she'd been using in the garden and tied one of Dad's paisley handkerchiefs over her hair. She stepped toward the mirror at the end of the row of lockers. Good grief, she thought. I look like Charlie Chaplin.

When Jack entered the office at eight-ten, he threw open his arms in mock surprise and said, "From secretary to Rosie-the-Riveter."

The girls at the lunch table were sick to death of Rosie-the-Riveter comments but she didn't tell Jack because she was afraid he'd think she was a scold.

"You'll need these to complete the outfit." Jack handed her a pair of safety glasses. "

Natalie slipped them over her head, and they flopped down her nose.

"Here," he said and stepped behind her to adjust the elastic band so the glasses fit snugly. The feel of his callused hands on her cheeks sent a tingle in places it shouldn't. His fingers adjusted the goggles, and she saw tiny black hairs on his knuckles and breathed in the aroma of *Boraxo* soap. "Are you ready to go?"

"I'm ready," she said and followed Jack down the stairs.

"Let's start at the beginning." Jack led Natalie around several assembly lines. He carried himself with energy and intensity, and she struggled to keep up. After what seemed to be a mile from where they began, he said, "Here we are,

Storage Building H. Siberia."

"Like Russia?"

"Like not heated. None of the storage sheds are, but this one is the coldest place in Albany County for sure."

There were endless rows of parts on pallets. Natalie tried to guess the size of the building and thought of the football field behind the high school. The roof of this building must cover four or five football fields. And she knew from Inventory Control that this was only one of four storage buildings. "I never imagined it was so large."

"It's too small," Jack said. "We've got materiel jammed in here and the other storage buildings and supplies stacked outside next to the tracks." A fork-lift came down the aisle, and Jack put his hand on Natalie's arm and nudged her toward the pallets as it passed.

The gentle power of his hand surprised her. "I'm glad you agreed to show me. I go through the front gate to my office and never see the buildings back here."

"Right now, the Arsenal is manufacturing twenty-eight different kinds of ordnance. And most big guns have 40 to 70 parts." His hand swept across the rows of parts. "In six weeks they'll be in howitzers aiming at the Jerries."

"All those parts. It's a wonder we haven't had more mistakes like Mr. Tartanian's." They walked down the rows of pallets. At the front were neatly lettered signs: 'Breech rings – 105', 'Breech rings – 240.' Further along, dozens of pallets were labeled, 'Firing mechanism – 37mm' and 'Firing mechanism – 75mm.'

"What are breech rings?" Natalie asked.

"It's part of the sliding block mechanism at the base of the gun tube."

"I see," she answered but hadn't a clue what he meant.

Jack seemed to hear the hesitation in Natalie's answer. "I think I'd better stick with how the parts get stored and moved for now."

Jack gestured toward the far wall. "The tracks are out there. We're getting nearly one hundred carloads of supplies a month. That's almost double what we did a year ago. And we've got too much in open storage." As they neared the end of the storage building, the neatly lettered signs give way to crudely chalked labels on cardboard. By the time they reached the end, dozens of pallets were un-labeled.

"I never realized how complicated this is," Natalie said.

"Imagine being on the assembly line, and your crew is standing idle while someone is sent back here to find the *one* part out of seventy that keeps them from finishing a howitzer?"

She couldn't. And then she heard chirps. Sparrows were perched on the metal beams thirty feet above them. Natalie had a vision of being up there with the birds gazing down on this ocean of parts that made her a little dizzy.

"You okay? You look a little woozy."

"I'm fine," she said. "I was imagining a bird's eye view of this building."

A quizzical look skittered across Jack's face. "Seen enough storage?"

Natalie nodded, but something kept her staring at the rafters and then back to the rows of parts.

Jack walked her by the shrink and furnace pits, and she heard a wolf whistle as they walked along a wall at the end.

A guy shouted, "Hey, Black Jack. Nice chick."

Natalie pretended she didn't hear him, but she was embarrassed by the idea they were together.

Jack shot the guy a nasty look. "Let's move on to the Field Artillery building."

Over the next two hours, Jack took Natalie through the shops where the materiel in Building SH was turned into howitzers. At first, she was startled by the clanging of enormous machines and the scrum of men moving back and forth. But then she realized it was a strange dance as teams of men grabbed parts from hoists and walked them into place as other teams welded and bolted.

Jack pointed to a line of lathes and shouted a description of what the workers were doing. Natalie couldn't hear him, and he grasped her shoulder and pulled her closer to shout into her ear. She flinched at his touch, and he stepped back. "Sorry," he said.

"No, it's all right." The black band snaking across Jack's forehead made Natalie wonder how many men did go deaf. She thought she'd grown accustomed to the noise, but when they entered the last building before the gun shop, the banging made her head throb. She couldn't help herself from covering her ears.

"It's a ten thousand pound cold-working press," Jack shouted.

"What?" she shouted back.

Jack leaned so close to Natalie, she felt his breath on her cheek. "Cold-working press," he yelled into her ear. "Ten thousand," he repeated. "You should stick more cotton in your ears."

Natalie was going to but remembered how foolish she looked the first time she met Jack. Now she was sorry because the noise was deafening. "I couldn't find anymore," she lied.

"Here." Jack dug in the pocket of his pants and pulled out a wad of cotton. He broke off a couple of pieces and handed them to Natalie.

Natalie was sure the pieces she pushed in each ear were sticking out. "I must look like a rag doll."

Jack pointed to the black patch under his goggles. "Can't have the blind and the deaf working here."

They walked through the ends of two assembly lines and stood at the end of a vast open space. An overhead crane with a long tube hanging below it slowly moved along the rails until it hovered over a huge machine.

Jack said, "That's a gun tube for a 240 millimeter howitzer." A moment after the memory of the tiff in her office flitted through her head she heard, "Is that our paper-pusher in a real worker's outfit?" She turned to see Mr. Tartanian with his hands on his hips and a sneer on his flat face that looked as though he'd run into a brick wall at forty miles an hour.

"Stuff it, Sam," Jack shot back. "Sorry about the language," he said to her.

Natalie shrugged. The girls who worked in the shops complained about the rude comments they got. But it was rough work, and they'd picked up some of the language themselves.

"You see the crayon mark on the gun tube?" Jack shouted.

Natalie bent her head next to Jack's arm and saw a big yellow 'C' chalked on the tube.

"That tube was found out of line after it was forged and straightened in a hydraulic press in Building 22. It's not far from your office. You probably hear it all the time."

"So that's what's giving me headaches," Natalie shouted.

He pointed at the machine below the gun tube. "Once that's in place and secured, they'll begin reaming and rifling the barrel."

Jack pulled her around the side of the reaming machine to where, ten yards farther along, a gun tube was already clamped into its twin. The high-pitched scream of the machine made her flinch despite the cotton in her ears. Sparks flew everywhere, and curls of steel fell around the feet of the workers like thousands of scattering lightning bugs. The air tasted like metal. Workers shouted at each other over the clanking of another enormous barrel being set into place.

A few feet behind them, a borer sent out a screech like a hundred fingernails dragging on a blackboard. Further along, Natalie felt the grinding blades of a lathe in her teeth as a finished gun tube was being rifled. Borers, reamers, grinders, lathes: it was as though each machine played a different instrument in a hellish symphony.

They reached the far end of the building. Natalie's head was pounding. There was an oily taste in her mouth. She snatched air into her lungs and realized she'd been holding her breath. It was nothing like she'd imagined. It was fantastic.

Natalie remembered that Tina went from being an inspector to a welding job last month. And Mary in the tool shed was being trained to be a crane operator. She did her boring desk job every day, and every evening she ate dinner with her parents, listened to the radio, and went to bed. This is where she wanted to work.

Jack walked Natalie to the end of another assembly line. "I think you've seen enough for one day."

"Okay," she said. But she was confused, not sure of where they were in this vast array of shops and assembly lines. "But I don't know where I am. You'll have to lead the way home."

Thirty yards along the back of one of the assembly lines, Jack stepped around her to stand on her left side as they passed the end of a large open space filled with several huge misshapen hunks of metal.

"Not what you want to see," Jack said.

"What are they?" Natalie said a moment before she identified the hulks. "Oh, tanks."

"I'm afraid so," Jack said. "This is the Tank Repair Shop. We're one of three places in the country with the equipment that can repair or salvage damaged tanks."

Jack insisted on walking Natalie back to her office. Inside, he nodded toward the folders on her desk. "I hope what you saw makes sense of your paperwork."

Waving her hand toward the door, Natalie said. "I think I'm getting a feeling for what goes on down there."

Jack let out a snort of a laugh. "Lady, you ain't seen nothin' yet. Let me know when you up for it, and I'll show you more." He tipped his head and left.

Exhausted and thrilled, Natalie collapsed into her chair. Following Jack from the cavernous cold of Building SH to the searing blasts from the finance pits, she felt as though she would crack like an icicle dropped into a pool of hot water. Even in her quiet office, her head was still ringing from the banging and screeching of hundreds of machines. She gazed around the room and recalled her year at the insurance company and her stint in the toolshed. Compared to what she'd seen today, her life had been one long bore. She needed to see more – and do more.

She swiveled around in her chair and realized the goggles Jack lent her were still dangling around her neck. She started toward the door to call him back and then stopped. She took off the goggles and laid them carefully in the bottom drawer of her desk.

***

Bolting upright, Natalie was sweating. Her breath was coming in gulps. She stared at the Big Ben alarm clock on the bed stand: 2:00 a.m. She tried to shake away the nightmare but she couldn't. She was in the Tank Repair Shop. Mr. Tartanian had her by the arm, squeezing so hard it hurt. He was dragging Natalie from one twisted hulk of metal to the next. She was crying and begging him to stop, but he still pulled her up onto the turret of a tank and yanked open the hatch. 'Not here,' he shouted and pulled her to the next one. She put her hands over her ears. He pried open the burning metal of the hatch and pushed her to see what was inside. Bodies. Mr. Holt. Jack. Bill.

5

Sending Women to Germany Urged to Curb Fraternization

I had too much to drink. What else was there to do? Finally, a two day break back from the line. A shower, clean underwear and socks. Who cared where the hell we were. Five of us from the squad crowded in what used to be a restaurant. It's a wonder the guy behind the makeshift bar didn't pull out an old hunting rifle and shoot us. GIs with everything they didn't have – money, cigarettes, sugar – and their women – at least the handful that filtered out of the wreck of the town acting like every ugly dofus was Cary Grant, even though we could barely understand each other.

I don't remember how I ended up with her. When me and my buddies staggered out, we each had a girl. What was I supposed to do, walk back to camp by myself? That would have been the right thing to do. She had my arm in a tight grip, and when I asked where we were going in the few words of French I picked up, she said her place. I wasn't that drunk. Damn, I'd been faithful to Natalie. My buddies had gone off with their girls. I should have left right then.

It was awful, and the moment I shot my wad, I felt miserable. And then she wants a handful of script and two packs of Camels. What a damn fool I was to think she liked me. Betraying my vows to Natalie. Knowing I did it with a whore instead of taking up with a real girlfriend didn't help much. I couldn't keep from scratching myself all the way back to the camp, convinced I'd already caught the crabs.

I'm so ashamed and angry at myself, and I can't stop thinking about our last weekend outside Fort Dix.

6

Women Mastering Jobs in War Plants: Hundreds Work at
Machines in Propeller Factory

Fiddling the plug with her toe, Natalie let out more water
and turned on the hot tap. A bath usually relaxed her, but
she was still keyed up from her tour of the Arsenal with
Jack. She replayed the infernal noises of the machines as men
wrestled so many parts into cannons, howitzers and
mortars, surprised at how they excited her after her initial
shock. She picked up the sponge floating next to her knee
and squeezed it, embarrassed by what she felt when
memories of Jack leaning into her and touching her crept
into her head as she washed herself down there. Confused
memories of screeching lathes, Jack, and pallets of breech
rings rattled around in her head. But there was one vague
memory that haunted her. She lay her head back and stared
at the peeling paint in the corner of the ceiling trying to
bring the blurry picture into focus. That's it, she thought as
she imagined herself as a sparrow in the rafters peering
down on the hundreds of pallets of equipment and supplies
in Storage Building SH. She saw it now.

***

At every knock on the door, Natalie ran her hand through
her hair and straightened the front of her dress. It had been
three days, and she hadn't heard a word. Finally, there was
Jack. She didn't hear him knock. "Oh, it's you."

"Disappointed?" Jack said.

"No. I'm surprised."

"I got your note," Jack said. "I feel like we're a couple

of kids at the back of homeroom."

Natalie ducked her head to hide her blush. "I've got an idea for re-organizing some of the materiel in Building SH."

Jack seemed surprised. "It was just a tour. I didn't think you were paying that close attention to how the materiel was laid out."

Natalie was annoyed that he wasn't taking her seriously. "I'm always paying attention," she said sharply. "Otherwise, I'd still be handing out wrenches in the tool shed."

Spreading his hands in surrender, Jack said, "Sorry. Let's hear it."

"It's probably a pipe dream, but I'd like you to take a look."

Natalie pulled out a paper from the top drawer and spread it across the top of the desk. "Storage Building SH," she said as she waved her hand over the drawing. "Or as best as I can remember it."

"Pretty good considering you were only there once," he said. "You're not a Nazi spy, are you?"

"I have a good memory." Natalie pointed to the dozens of squares she'd drawn in rows. Each had tiny writing inside: breech rings, firing mechanisms, shell channels. "These represent only the front quarter of the building, but I hope it gives you an idea of the overall picture."

Jack ran his finger over the rows. "An excellent memory."

"I was thinking about the wrong parts being delivered to the assembly line."

Jack said, "It happens at least a couple of times a week."

"I think the problem is that similar parts are stored together: breech rings for all the guns here." She pointed to several boxes. "All the firing mechanisms here. My guess is that the part-timers assigned to the warehouse don't easily see the difference between a breech ring for a 37 millimeter and a 75."

"You're right. Many of them are working for us after a full day at another job. They're tired and inexperienced."

Natalie pulled another sheet from the top drawer, and Jack leaned forward. His goggles dangled over the drawing, and she smelled a tang of sweat and grease. Jack swung the goggles around so they hung down the back of his neck. The ones he'd lent her were still stashed in her bottom drawer.

Pointing to rows of re-arranged boxes, Natalie said, "Instead of all the similar parts in the same place, why not put all the materiel for each gun in a row? See," she ran her finger along a row.

Jack's fingers traced the rows as a low hum came from the back of his throat. "Okay."

Natalie worried he sounded unsure and was afraid he thought she was wasting his time. She needed him to see what she saw. She rushed on. "Breech rings, firing mechanisms, shell channels, carriages all for the 37 in this row. Breech rings etcetera for the 75 in this row. Even the part-timers can find the right part by staying in the proper row." She slumped back positive Jack would come up with a dozen reasons why her idea wouldn't work.

Jack put the two sheets side by side on the desk top. Natalie glanced at his face. His razor had missed a small patch of stubble. She wondered if it was because he'd lost an eye. She caught a hint of witch hazel and savored his smell. She felt sorry he lived alone with no one to take care of him.

"I think you've got something here. How did you

come up with this idea?"

Natalie felt a rush of relief. "The sparrows," she said. "I imagined Building SH as though I was perched up in the rafters. I could see it like this." She pointed to the sheet with the re-arranged rows of pallets.

"If this works, they'll requisition a crane and build you a nest in the rafters."

"Do you really think it will work?"

"It might. You should take these drawings up the line."

"Mr. Holt?"

Jack cast a dismissive glance toward Mr. Holt's office. "From what you've said, he's out of the loop. I guess Mr. Fox."

People detoured around Mr. Fox. Natalie thought her idea was something she could give to Jack and let him refine it. It would give him a feather in his cap if it worked. But now she pictured Mr. Fox looking at these rough sheets, scoffing, and getting her in trouble. "I did it just for the 37's and 75's. I'm not suggesting it will work for the other guns."

"It's a very good idea. You have to take the chance." Jack tipped his head toward Mr. Holt's office again. "They won't send you back to the tool sheds."

"I just want to do my part."

Jack took her hand. It fell between a handshake and … she didn't know what. "If it works, someone owes you dinner."

***

Natalie spent much of the next day trying to make the rough drawings of the pallets in Building SH look less like hen scratching. Late in the afternoon, she screwed up her courage and walked off the linoleum and onto the carpets in the executive suite with the drawings in a large envelope and the note to Mr. Fox she'd re-written five times.

She lurked in a corner near Mr. Fox's office until his secretary picked up a handful of papers and headed toward the other end of the suite. Natalie hurried to her desk and dropped the envelope in the in-basket. She was about to dash away when she heard, *"Yes?"*

Mr. Fox was glaring at her as though she'd flitched a pencil from his secretary's desk.

Her dry tongue stuck to the roof of her mouth. She pointed to the envelope in the in-basket. "Mr. Tartanian's problem. I took a tour of Building SH," she babbled as Mr. Fox's face screwed into a scowl. "The parts. All together." She made another feeble gesture toward the envelope. "In there," she croaked and remained rooted to the carpet.

Mr. Fox's mean stare sent a shiver through her. Finally, he made a quick nod toward the entrance, and Natalie forced herself to walk rather than run back to her office.

***

It had been two weeks since Natalie put her suggestions for reorganizing the parts storage in Mr. Fox's in-basket, and every day she tried to come up with reasons why they wouldn't work. The more she thought about it, she was sure they would work, and she had other ideas about reorganizing storage that would be even better. But she hadn't heard a word. She slapped a work order into a folder, convinced the bosses would stick with the same stupid ways they'd been doing it since the last war.

On Friday afternoon, Natalie stepped out of Mr. Holt's office after handing him her weekly approvals. Jack stood at her desk. A large roll of paper was upright on the edge. "Good afternoon," she said as evenly as she could manage.

"I'm glad I caught you before quitting time," he said. "Sorry I haven't been back sooner." Jack unrolled the paper. "Do you mind?" he asked but spread it across the desk and anchored it with Natalie's stapler before she'd answered.

Natalie saw why he was known as a take-charge guy but felt a flicker of annoyance at him taking over her desk.

"Look at what got handed to the managers from the corner offices," Jack said. He slid the other corner of the roll under Natalie's in-box. "It's your drawings dolled up."

Natalie moved to the other side of the desk. Draftsmen had precisely drawn to scale the rough drawings she'd put in Mr. Fox's in-basket. She was taken aback. "I can't believe they're actually using my suggestion."

"It's early days, but so far the assembly managers like it."

She thought she heard a hesitation in Jack's voice. "But?"

Jack said, "I'd steer clear of the guys in storage. They've been moaning and groaning about moving the parts around."

"Now I've started something."

"I hope you've got some other great ideas in that – head of yours." Jack shrugged. "I mean don't be shy. Fly up to that perch in the rafters and tell us what you see that helps us keep the snafus to a minimum. Take them it up the line. If they work out as well as this one, Mr. Vincent will take you to dinner."

Natalie was too embarrassed to tell him how these ideas came to her while sitting naked in the bathtub, staring at the ceiling and imagining herself up in the rafters with the sparrows. "He barely knows I exist."

"Until he catches on, will you settle for popcorn?"

"Huh?"

"Do you like high school basketball?"

"I guess." Natalie didn't tell Jack she was a cheerleader for the Watervliet Cannoneers and spent every game jumping up and down facing the bleachers while the game was being played behind her.

"I'm going to the game tonight. If I see you there, I'll spring for popcorn." He checked his watch. "I'm late for a meeting."

Natalie stared at the door he'd closed behind him. She hadn't been to a basketball game since she graduated. But what else was she going to do on Friday night, wash out her underwear and listen to Fibber Magee and Molly with Mom and Dad? He'd said 'if I see you there,' so it's not a date. She tried to picture herself arriving at the game, where she'd sit and what she'd do.

Later Natalie stared at the tuna and noodle casserole her mother prepared every Friday. She could predict what she would do every single minute from now until she went to bed. She'd been thinking of Jack all day, unsettled by his offer of popcorn at the game. It's only a basketball game, she thought. She walked around the house, but she couldn't settle. She'd already washed out her underwear.

"You going to the game?" Natalie asked her brother.

"Nah," Nick said. "They'll get thumped as usual. I'm going to the town park and volunteer as an aircraft spotter for the Ground Observer Corps."

"When did you catch this burst of patriotism?" she asked and wondered whether that blonde with the big bust she saw him with last week might also be volunteering.

Nick pulled a sheet out of his pocket with silhouette drawings of airplanes. "Look at this. Maybe I'll spot a Heinkel 111 swooping in to bomb Ralph's Tavern." He put the sheet back in his pocket. "Hey," he said. "Did you know why the moron took a ladder to church?"

"What?" Natalie asked, still distracted by deciding what she was going to do about the game.

"He heard it was going to be high mass," Nick said. "And why did the moron...?"

"*Stop it.*" Mom barked. "That's not funny, and I don't want to hear those cruel words in our house."

Natalie was startled by her mother's angry words and the anguished look on her face. It was more than her usual scolding of Nick's foolishness.

"Jeepers, Mom. I'm sorry," Nick said. He gave Dad and Natalie an apologetic shrug.

Mom swept her hand across her face as if brushing away cobwebs. She pushed her chair back and left the room.

Twenty minutes later Mom returned to the kitchen and helped Natalie finish washing the dishes. She acted as though she'd forgotten Nick's jokes.

Natalie dried the last of the dishes and stacked the plates in the cupboard. "I think I'll head over to the high school and catch the game."

"Game?" Mom said.

"Basketball. The Cannoneers are playing tonight," Natalie said as though high school basketball was an in-grained Friday night habit.

"At the high school?" Mom said as if she'd forgotten where Natalie spent four years and where Nick was a senior.

"I need to get out," Natalie said. She hoped she didn't sound as though she was complaining, but coming back to live with her parents had been a lot like reverting to her teenage self. When she'd gone out in the evening, her parents' 'where are you going?' and 'who with' lurked just beneath the surface. "It's been a rough week at the Arsenal," she added. "I've been stuck in my cramped office every day.

A change of scene for one night might clear my head." She gave Mom a kiss on her cheek as she took a glass from her hand. "Not that I don't love being here with you and Dad."

Mom shook her head as though she knew she was being jollied along.

"I'll probably meet a couple of the girls from the Arsenal. We were talking about seeing how our old team is doing these days."

Forty minutes later Natalie came down the stairs after changing her blouse twice. She gave Mom and Dad kisses on their cheeks and took her coat from the closet next to the front door. "Couldn't find my pom-poms," she laughed as she went out the door and heard the unspoken, "Be home early," and "Be careful," stuck in their throats.

Savoring the aroma of burnt leaves lingering in the October night air, Natalie walked up 16th Street. But the closer she got to the school, the more she felt like she'd slipped back to being a teenager with a crush. Was she supposed to take a seat in the bleachers and pretend to watch the game until Jack noticed her or a girlfriend sidled up to whisper that Jack liked her? This was foolish. She should turn around and go home and tell Mom and Dad a headache suddenly came on.

Ten minutes later, Natalie walked along the corridor by the boys' locker room. A sweaty smell hung in the air. At the doorway to the gym, she realized she'd entered on the visitors' side – the hated Cohoes Tigers. She stepped onto the polished floor boards to cross to the home side. At half-court she felt as though she standing in the cone of a spotlight. With her head down, she hurried to the bleachers and stumbled up the first two rows, plunking down as far from the nearest people as possible. She was gulping air, and her face felt flush. What a stupid, stupid idea.

Natalie finally got her breath under control and focused on the scrum of boys huddled around the coach. They looked so young. She picked out one or two of the older ones and thought that next year they would trade their green and gold shorts and tee-shirts for khaki uniforms. And Nick too.

The buzzer startled her. The game got underway, and she watched the boys running up and down the court as though one of them was her son. The cheerleaders bounced on the balls of their feet, and she remembered waving her pom-poms as the crowd looked over her head at the game, with no idea if we were winning or losing.

"Not going well for the Cannoneers."

Natalie let out a startled yip and pivoted around to gape at Jack who seemed to have dropped silently into the space next to her. She looked at the jumble of boys scrabbling for a loose ball. She had no idea what was happening. "It's you," she finally managed.

"None other," he said. "I'm glad you could make the game."

Natalie struggled to regain her composure. "It's good to get out of the house once in a while."

"When I first stayed in on the weekend, Mrs. Larson offered to teach me to play two-handed canasta. I quickly became a big fan of the Cannoneers."

"I haven't been in the gym since I graduated."

One of the Cohoes players tripped and crashed to the floor. The ref called a time-out as his teammates and coaches gathered around him.

"I'll be right back," Jack said. He clambered over the spectators in the first few rows and headed out the door on the home side.

Natalie chanced a look around and spotted Rosemary

Davis several rows behind her. They weren't close in school so Natalie didn't imagine she'd climb down to join her. They exchanged waves but not too enthusiastically. The war had up-ended everyone's life, making memories from just a few years ago seem as though decades had passed. She gazed around the gym and spotted the cheerleaders at the end of the bench. A little over three years ago, she was there probably giggling about some cute guy on the visitor's team, knowing that even thinking about dating a fellow from Cohoes was treason. She and her girlfriends were already talking about getting serious with their steadies, going to the weddings of their older sisters and cousins as though they were dry runs for theirs, even seeing babies in their mothers' arms at the store and wondering how long it would be before they had their own children. Trying to make sense of what was then and what was now made her head swirl.

With two bags of popcorn in his hands, Jack stepped over the people in front and sat next to her. "You save the Arsenal thousands of dollars in wasted time, and you get popcorn," he said, and handed her one of the bags.

The game resumed, and Jack and Natalie munched their popcorn and watched the game wordlessly except for cheers when Watervliet scored a basket. Natalie remembered their easy conversation at Mel's Diner, but now she pretended an avid interest in the game because she didn't know what to say. At the buzzer signaling half-time, Natalie licked her salty fingers. "I need to wash my hands."

"Me too."

She waited until Jack started in the direction of the Boys' before she climbed down the bleachers and headed for the Girls. She kept her head down as she walked.

"Natalie. I thought it was you."

Jane Taylor stood in front of Natalie with her hands

on her hips. Miss Head Cheerleader. Miss First Class Stuck Up. Every slight she'd delivered flooded back.

"You're still in town," Jane said as though Natalie was trapped in Nowhereville.

"Still here," Natalie said brightly, trying to make it sound like something other than a defeat.

"It's so nice to see my old friends," Jane trilled. She nodded to the man in uniform standing next to her. "George is on leave, and I wanted to visit Mother and Father." She put her hand on Natalie's forearm. "Father isn't in the best of condition," she said in a conspiratorial whisper. "I thought I'd show George some of our old haunts."

Good thing he's with a witch, Natalie thought. The daughter of the president of Watervliet Savings Bank, Jane was the richest girl in school. Off to Syracuse University after graduation. George, she presumed, stepped forward and shook Natalie's hand. With all the brass at the Arsenal, Natalie recognized his First Lieutenant insignia.

"George is in a special intelligence program at Syracuse," Jane said. "It's all hush-hush isn't it dear?" Jane put her hand on George's.

There was a rock of an engagement ring on Jane's finger. Did she waggle it or was it Natalie's imagination? Natalie curled her left hand. The tiny diamond and thin gold band Bill bought at Meyer's were barely visible.

"I heard you and Bill Costello tied the knot." Jane turned to George. "Bill was such a cut-up. Always good for a laugh," she said. "And where is Bill?"

"He's in the Fourth Infantry Division," Natalie said meanly to George. "In France – fighting." Not in some posh university program she hoped to convey, but the indulgent looks on their faces didn't seem to register her lame accusation. But Natalie had to admit she was here pretending she had just happened to run into another man – who had her fluttering like a teenager at the sock hop while her husband was fighting the war in Europe.

"And I heard you're a Rosie-the-Riveter at the Arsenal," Jane said as though it was the most amusing thing she'd ever imagined.

Natalie pictured five foot two Angie Demarco hefting her two-handed power drill and boring a hole in Jane's forehead. She couldn't figure out how to explain she was really acting as deputy director of Inventory Control but realized there was no way she'd win this game. She was about to deliver a flip end to the conversation when Jane looked over Natalie's shoulder.

Jack stood very close behind Natalie. Should she pretend she didn't know him? "This is my friend Jack Mahoney," Natalie announced. The surprise Natalie saw on Jane's face was matched by the confusion she felt. Why did 'friend' pop out of her mouth? Was it simply easier than trying to explain how she came to be here with 'a man I work with at the Arsenal?'

Jack was at least two inches taller than George. And with the black eye patch and a take-charge posture that commanded any space he was in, he seemed more important, more manly, than this junior officer. "How do you do, Lieutenant," Jack said. Jack dealt with the top brass at the Arsenal and Natalie heard the hint of dismissal in Jack's emphasis on the junior officer's rank.

"And this is my friend, Jane," Natalie said hoping Jack heard the drop of her voice on 'friend.' The four of them stood mute for a few moments while Jane eyed Jack with a mixture of confusion and shock. The buzzer sounded, and Natalie said, "So nice to see you Jane – and you too – George. We'd better get back to our seats." Natalie turned to cross the gym floor. Jack walked beside her, and five hundred pairs of eyes followed them to their seats. I must be crazy, Natalie thought.

The game was a welcome distraction from having to talk, and Natalie and Jack watched with the concentration of die-hard fans. Natalie thought of several clever and cutting remarks she should have made to Jane. She glanced at the scoreboard. There were two minutes left in the game, and the Cannoneers were being trounced. Natalie wanted the game to go on for a long time because she didn't know what to do when it ended. But it did.

Everyone stood and began to leave. Jack followed close behind as they joined the crowd shuffling toward the exits. Outside, Natalie said, "Thanks for the popcorn."

"Thanks for the company."

Since Jack lived in Green Island, Natalie knew he had to walk back along 16th to Broadway before turning north. She also had to walk back along 16th before turning south. They stood wordlessly for a few moments. Natalie was sure they both realized the necessity of traveling the same route with dozens of others heading home. They started walking. Natalie didn't look ahead or behind her, or across the street, because she was positive that several people must know who she was – and some surely knew Jack from the Arsenal.

At the end of 16th, Jack said, "I hope you've rekindled a warm feeling for your Cannoneers."

"Perhaps. And thank you," Natalie said. She reached out to shake Jack's hand. She hoped someone – everyone – saw the formality of her gesture. Briskly she turned toward home. A chance meeting of two co-workers, they'd guess – she hoped. Two blocks along Broadway, Natalie held her head erect. Her step was purposeful and business-like, but unwanted tears welled in her eyes.

Natalie turned into her street and almost ran smack into Mr. Podoski, standing in the middle of the sidewalk. His Air Raid Warden white helmet was strapped tightly under his chin, and he wore an armband clearly visible against his black jacket with the collar turned up. She expected he'd begin blacking his face with burnt cork soon. He inspected Natalie head to toe as though she was about to whip out a large flashlight and guide a German bomber Nick missed to the center of the Arsenal. He was a neighborhood nuisance, patrolling the streets for hours each night, shouting warnings at anyone letting as much of a glimmer of light to seep out an opening door or curtain. He was a self-important pest most people ignored, but tonight Natalie felt guilty and ducked around him as she scurried to her house. As she mounted the steps she couldn't avoid seeing the Blue Star flag in the window. This had been a foolish thing to do.

***

Natalie tried to go through Saturday as though it is simply another day, but she felt it looming over her head. At times during the day, she wanted to face either her mother or father and beat them to it. I met a man from work at the game.

Dinner on Saturday evenings was at the dining room table. Without looking up from her plate, Mom said, "How long has it been since we heard from Bill?"

"Last week," Natalie needlessly reminded her. "Remember, we got two V-mails at the same time." Bill was never very articulate, and she was sure writing letters was difficult for him. Each was a repeat of the previous one: very short sentences reporting rain, bad food, and censored lines which Natalie guessed tried to tell of the war in France. She shouldn't complain because her letters contained mostly details of her boring life.

"How was the game?" Natalie's father asked.

"We lost."

Natalie's parents concentrated on the green beans Mom had canned from her Victory Garden. Her mother glanced at her father.

"Did you run into any of your old friends?" her father finally asked.

His attempt to sound casual fell flat. Natalie guessed they decided that Dad would take the lead.

"I saw Rosemary Davis."

Out of the corner of her eye, Natalie caught the jokey look on Nick's face.

"And Jane Taylor is in town," Natalie continued. "Says her father isn't doing well." She took a bite of green beans and thought about how she'd deal with the questions that hung in the air. "I ran into a man from the Arsenal I've been working with. Jack Mahoney," she said unsure about putting his name out there. "He helped get me the new job in Inventory." She decided to see if they'd leave it at that.

Natalie's father and mother nodded and returned to their food.

"I imagine it's difficult for single men," her mother said. "Living alone in a strange town."

Natalie had to stifle a bitter laugh. Mom was not a shouter. Natalie never met anyone who dealt out disapproval so economically: sighs, movements that became sharper, doors that closed just shy of a slam, dishes put in the cupboard with almost a thump – an entire toolbox of subtle censure.

"Yes," Natalie said brightly. "Mr. Mahoney sat with me. He rents a room in Green Island. He bought me popcorn," she added. "A reward for an idea I gave him for reorganizing the parts storage. We talked about it at the game and while we walked back along 16th." She wondered if there were other bald facts she should lay out to confirm what friends and neighbors had reported.

Her parents looked at each other, apparently deciding to leave it at that. They finished dinner wordlessly.

Mom scraped the little fat from the beef tongue into the can at the back of the stove, and started doing the dishes. Natalie waited. This was when Mom would caution her about hanging around with the wrong crowd, wearing too much lipstick, and other youthful misdemeanors.

"We realize it's difficult for you. Bill being overseas. A hard job," she said as she spent too much time washing a serving bowl.

"Mom, he's just a man I work with at the Arsenal. I appreciate your and Dad's concern," Natalie said. "But I can't spend every weekend night at home. And I work with married and unmarried men all day. The war has turned the world upside down, and we – I – have to learn to live in it. Don't worry,"

"I know," Mom said. "It's just that people talk. They don't know any better."

"I can't live my life worrying about what ignorant people are talking about."

They finished putting away the dishes. Later her parents listened to Major Bowles Amateur Hour while across the living room, Natalie made a show of writing a letter to Bill.

7

Roosevelt Says Call to Older Men Is Needed for Victory --
Group Not in Combat Age

For days after the basketball game, thoughts of her and Jack
sitting in the bleachers, sharing popcorn, and walking home
along 16th Street kept creeping back. She tried to recall what,
if anything, she meant when she told Jane Taylor that Jack
was her 'friend' – then decided she should just drop it.
Besides, more than a week had gone by without a word from
Jack. And if a memory of what she'd felt walking home from
the game ambushed her, the sharp words of that redhead in
the locker room let her on that Jack wasn't spending every
evening playing two-handed Canasta.

Natalie had almost erased Jack from her mind when
she walked into her office from picking up an order of office
supplies and found him perched on the end of her desk as
though it was a regular stop on his afternoon rounds.
Natalie almost dropped the typing paper and envelopes.
"What are you doing here?" Her voice sounded like a scold.

"Sorry." Jack made a show of looking back at the
office door. "Do I need to make an appointment?"

Natalie put the supplies on the vacant secretary's
desk and gave Jack a cold look as she tried to sort out what
she wanted to say. Should she have expected him to come to
see her shortly after the game and stop by for a friendly chat
to see where they were going? Had she read too much into
what he felt for her after the tour of the Arsenal and the
basketball game? "No," she said carefully.

Jack slid off Natalie's desk and stood so close to her

that she leaned back to half-sit on the secretary's desk. "Here's the deal. You helped get SH re-arranged, and we need to see if Wonder Woman has some other great ideas for reorganizing what we do."

Natalie was annoyed Jack had barged into her office and jumped right in on her helping reorganize something as though he was a Major giving orders to a Private. But him standing inches from her with a commanding look brought back those disturbing feelings she'd felt on the tour and then at the basketball game. "I don't understand."

"Sorry," Jack said. "Let me back track. Here's the problem. We're getting rush orders for mortars and smaller bore weapons because the Army is expecting to move more rapidly across Belgium and into Germany with lighter equipment. But too many of our assembly lines are set up to manufacture the bigger guns."

"I remember those huge hydraulic presses and borers when you took me on the tour."

Jack said, "We spent two months replacing the steel-tipped borers with the new tungsten carbide-tips for rifling the large gun tubes. With these new orders, we've got to move them back." Jack nodded in the direction of the executive suite. "I just returned from a meeting with the carpet-walkers. I've been assigned to a team to figure out a solution."

"Good for you. I hope you get a promotion." She imagined Jack in a uniform with lots of gold braid and battle ribbons. Most of the top brass assigned to the Arsenal were veterans of the last war. The gossip was that they ordered the civilian managers around as though they were all Privates, and no idea was a good one unless it came from a Colonel or higher.

"I got something better. You."

"Me?" Natalie was stunned. "I don't understand."

"I pulled Mr. Fox aside and reminded him about your suggestion for reorganizing SH." A sly smile stole across Jack's face. "I hinted that I might make it more widely known that it was your idea that he took to the managers' meeting."

"I had one good idea, but that was for rearranging parts. I don't have any idea about how to move machinery that large in a hurry."

"Neither does anyone else, so I suggested that he let me have a couple of hours of your time over the next week or so. Tag along with me. Give me a fresh pair of eyes." He leaned toward her. "Whisper more of those brilliant ideas in my ear."

Jack asked for her? Now she was suddenly flustered remembering the tour and how he grasped her arm, leaned into her to point out something. Dozens of thoughts tumbled through her head. "When? "How? I only saw the large gun borers for a few moments."

"We'll figure it out as we go along."

Natalie couldn't imagine having anything useful to say about this problem, but the fact that he wanted her was surprisingly exciting. "Alright, if you think it might help."

"Great. We'll start on Tuesday. Mr. Fox has cleared it with Mr. Holt." Jack gave Natalie a salute as he headed for the door.

Wonder Woman, indeed. Once she found the comic pages turned to the Wonder Woman strip on the sink just after Nick had left the bathroom. When she handed him the paper and told him he'd left it, his blush was as deep as the one she felt now as she pictured herself in Wonder Woman's star-studded strapless outfit alongside Jack.

***

On Tuesday morning, Natalie waited for Jack in her office wearing her new coveralls. She'd tried to get her infatuation with Jack under control by telling herself this project might be a step that would get her a real job on the lines instead of assuming Mr. Holt's duties for ten cents more an hour and the threat of messing up.

"Well," Jack said when he came in. "You look like you're ready to roll."

In her hand were the goggles she got from supply. The ones Jack gave her when they did the tour were on the desk. "These are yours," she said and held them out to him.

Jack looked in her eyes for several seconds. "I want you to have these." He took his goggles from her hand, walked around behind her and put them over her head.

"Thank you," Natalie said as though they'd completed a small ceremony.

For the next three days Natalie followed Jack through the Liner Shop, the Heavy Field Artillery building, and the shrink and furnace pits. Then they went through the Seacoast Cannon Shop and back to the storage buildings and rail sidings. She never realized how many buildings there were at the Arsenal. She didn't see how she could imagine an improvement when the vast array of lathes, borers, presses, reamers, and forges was a confusing mass in her head.

Although she carried a steno pad and took as many notes as possible, she was lost. On the third day, she was about to tell Jack he'd made a big mistake. She had one, maybe two, ideas that were lucky guesses. That was it. No more. Her head was empty. An overhead crane slid into position over a reamer, lifted a mortar tube off and moved it to toward the end of the building. She watched the crane operator slowly lower a rack of mortar tubes onto a pallet of other finished tubes. "How much does each mortar tube weigh?" she shouted into Jack's ear.

"Thirty-seven pounds," he yelled back. "Why?"

Natalie made a note in her pad. She looked at the scrawl of notes she'd taken. They didn't make sense. She stepped back to the wall and stared at the crane. She thought Elsie Higgins was the operator. She wished she could do that instead of sitting at a desk. Even if she managed to come up with a decent suggestion, she'd probably be back pushing paper.

Waving to the unseen Elsie, Natalie turned the page to a blank one and began to draw a rough sketch. She wasn't sure what she was drawing. Maybe this small box was the reamer. And this rectangle was the crane. And these circles could be the mortar tubes.

"What are you drawing?" Jack asked. She felt his breath on the back of her neck as he leaned over her shoulder. For once she wasn't distracted by his closeness. She scribbled more lines at the edge of the page and then some arrows pointing in different directions. "I don't know," she finally answered.

"Are you up in the rafters again?"

"No. It's nothing." Natalie closed the notebook quickly. She didn't want Jack to see what she'd drawn because she wasn't sure what it was. She needed quiet. It was probably nothing. All the noise was pushing the unclear picture she formed out of her head. "We've got to go."

Twenty minutes later, Jack was seated across from Natalie in the cafeteria. People glanced at them as they passed their table. They'd been side-by-side for three days, and it was getting harder for her to keep pretending it was just work.

"Come up with anything, yet?" Jack asked. "I've got a

couple of ideas, but they're small potatoes. Nothing that's going to solve the big problems."

The closed notebook was next to Natalie's elbow. "Right now my head is empty." She needed quiet. She needed a bath.

"You were making a sketch back there."

"That's the way I see things. Pictures."

"Did you study art in school?"

"Goodness, no," Natalie said. "At my school, art stopped at finger painting in kindergarten. Later, in history classes, I'd see the battle of Gettysburg like a movie in my head." She shrugged. "In English classes, no picture, no movie." Natalie recalled the guidance counselor looking stumped at her aptitude tests and grades spread across his desk. 'Peaks and valleys,' he'd said. 'Top marks in math and history, but not so hot in others.' "I was good in math," she said. "Sometimes I didn't need to do the calculations. I'd look at the problem and see the answer like a drawing in my head."

Jack said, "Sounds like a hidden talent. With your math skills, you should have gone to college, maybe RPI."

RPI, she thought. What a joke. For kids like her, RPI on the hill lording it over Troy was like Oz. "College wasn't in the cards," she said. "My family had it rough in the Depression. Before my father got a job in a print shop, he was barely making any money." Natalie remembered Dad and Mom trying to stretch the few dollars Dad managed to make from odd jobs, pretending to her and Nick that everything was okay. "After I graduated, it was this and that including a stint at an insurance company in Albany before I took the job at the Arsenal."

"Best hire the Arsenal ever made."

Natalie listened more carefully to Jack's tone and

thought about the way he looked at her. It was more than just the kind of flirting he did when they were first together. This was the first time she really heard it in the tone of his voice and the way he'd cocked his head. His sly grin was unmistakably sexual. Natalie reached for her cup and hit the handle, sloshing coffee into the saucer. She gulped the coffee, and drips from the bottom of the cup splattered on her overalls. "I better get back upstairs."

***

Natalie closed the bathroom door and sat on the toilet. She stripped off her dress, kicked off her shoes and ran her hands over her legs between the tops of her cotton socks and where the hem of her dress fell. The faintly darker skin on her calves reminded her of tan lines after a summer day at Burden Lake. The girls at the lunch table complained about the dust-filled air and the infinitesimal particles of metal filings that settled on everything at the Arsenal. Now back on the shop floors with Jack, she savored the feel of it on her at the end of the day. She didn't resemble the raccoon-eyed machinists who worked in casting, but it was a reminder that she wasn't just a paper-pusher any more.

The sound of a car driving by startled Natalie awake. She settled back on the pillow and stared at the ceiling. What was she seeing there? Illustrations from her history book. The Crusades. She loved those stories. Richard the Lionhearted. Evil King John. But underneath the arrows in the diagram, knights and caravans of crusaders marched from Venice and across the Balkans to wrest the Holy Land from the Saracens. In the pre-dawn light she stared at the ceiling where she'd projected the picture and wracked her brain. What was the phrase that was just out of her reach? Saracens. Muslims. Yes. That was it. Sometimes the mountain comes to Mohammed.

Big Ben read 5:00 a.m. She wished it was six. Should she write this down? If she fell back to sleep, she might forget. She pulled back the covers. Shivering in her thin nightgown, she scrabbled around in her dresser drawer for a pencil and paper. Nothing. She went down the hall to the bathroom and pulled some toilet paper off the roll and scrawled 'Mohammed' on it with her lipstick. She lay awake with her mind racing until she fell asleep five minutes before the alarm clanged.

Sitting behind her desk at 7:30, Natalie couldn't make sense of the diagrams she'd been drawing. I'm a mess, she thought. My hair looks like a fright wig. I'm sure my lipstick is smeared. When she arrived early at the Arsenal, she went first to Jack's work station hoping he'd be there. She left a message with 'URGENT' on the envelope.

Natalie couldn't work while she waited to hear from Jack. She tried to clear out her in-basket but she was distracted and kept making mistakes.

Finally, the office door opened and Jack stepped in. She wanted to blurt out her idea but forced herself to calm down. Like she did with the Building SH, she'd made some rough sketches, but they looked like children's drawings. She wished she could draw better.

"Okay," Natalie said. "Here's the gist of it. Reorganize the supply chain instead of moving the equipment. We've been stuck thinking heavy artillery. I think we should move the lighter materiel closer to the machinery already in place. Instead of moving the mountain to Mohammed, move him to the mountain. It's easier." Over the next several minutes, she showed Jack her drawings and explained how the materiel could be moved.

Jack seemed to be listening, but he didn't seem excited, and Natalie was disappointed. When she finished explaining her plan, Jack simply nodded again, and said, "You might be on to something. I'll bring it to the meeting."

Natalie waited. It isn't until mid-afternoon that Jack appeared. He stepped into the office, and she forced herself to remain seated. She scanned his face for a sign of what happened. "So?"

A broad smile spread across his face. "Sew buttons. I think it's going to work."

She was excited. "Will you get a promotion?"

He seemed surprised. "No. Before the meeting, I laid out the outline of your proposal to Mr. Fox and showed him your drawings. At the meeting, he pushed your mountain and Mohammed idea. At first, the other managers and execs were opposed, but the more they argued it wouldn't work, the more the holes in that line of thought didn't hold up and they had to keep coming back to moving the materiel to the machinery already in place. Finally, the head of Heavy Artillery got behind it."

Natalie wanted Jack to get the credit. It was her gift to him, not to Mr. Fox.

"I've got to get back to the floor," Jack said. He reached for her hand.

His gentle squeeze was more than a handshake and set off a swarm of bees in Natalie's stomach.

8

France   September, 1944

*Germans Sweep West Through Luxembourg: Panzers
Smash 15 Miles Past Bastogne.*

Piece of cake, my ass. Bastards from the 1st think they won
the war already, like Utah was a walk in the park compared
to Omaha. Next time we run into some of them, we'll kick
the shit out of them. I pull my poncho tighter, but my back is
soaked under the rip. I try to keep my M-1 dry, but I'm
afraid it got soaked when we dug in. I just hope I don't have
to use it. I shot off a couple of clips into the trees, but I
haven't actually aimed at a kraut. Haven't even seen one
except for the prisoners we took after we landed. And I
don't care if I never see one with a rifle aimed at me.

For now I'm dug in outside Caen waiting for the
Shermans from 70th Tank Battalion to take out the krauts
along that ridge. The first time I saw one back in England, I
wondered if Natalie built the gun tube. Or at least knows
someone who did because she writes that she's doing
inventory or something like that. The CO says we'll mop up
after the Shermans finish off most of the Jerries. Our Second
Louie says we just follow behind the Shermans and we'll be
okay. Sarge doesn't sound so sure it'll be that easy. Don't get
too close to the tanks, he said. In case one gets hit. Great. I
want to hide right behind those big bastards.

I hear them. They're coming. I grip my M-1 tighter.
Damn, they're so close I hope they don't run over us. My
head is splitting from the noise. There's one, two, now three

bucking across the field. *Jesus,* the cannon blast makes my head ring. Fire you bastards. Take them out. *Fire.*

I see four, no five, Shermans swerving toward us. One cuts in front of us and starts toward the ridge. *"Get moving,"* Sarge yells. I can't. My legs won't work. *"Move out,"* Sarge screams at us. He pokes me in the back with his Thompson. I crawl over the top of the foxhole. Riley crawls up next to me.

"Move in behind the tank," Sarge yells. *"Not too close."* I hear loud pings. Shit, rifle fire hitting the tanks. The tank belches a cloud of black smoke and starts up a rise. We're taking fire from the ridge line. I hunker in closer behind the tank, but it's pulling away from us.

I'm on my back. I hurt all over. What happened? My helmet's blown off. The Sherman in front of me is a ball of fire. A deafening roar to my left. A second Sherman explodes into flames.

The hatch on the one twenty yards in front of me flies open. A tanker scrambles off the turret. Christ, he's on fire. Screaming he falls off the turret and runs in circles. A human torch until he falls to the ground. A second tanker jumps free. He makes it ten yards before he pitches forward.

"Eighty-eights! Fucking eighty-eights," Sarge is yelling. *"Pull back to the trees."* Riley gets up. Blood splatters on me. He's still standing, staring toward the ridge with a surprised look on his face. Blood is spurting from a hole in his neck. He staggers a few steps and falls next to me.

I'm running for the trees. Sarge is yelling for us to re-group. A shell hits to my right, and chunks of dirt hit me. I fall, then crawl toward the trees. Another shell takes off the top of two or three trees in front of me. I swerve to the left.

Forty minutes later, what's left of our platoon is flopped on the ground behind a shattered house. A Captain approaches. He stands over me. "Get up you cowardly bastard."

I can't make my legs work. I'm not the only one still on the ground. I get to my knees, then struggle to stand. My legs are trembling. My knee is jerking. And then as though the strings of a puppet have been cut, I tumble to the ground. The Captain kicks me in the side. "Fucking, coward."

Where the fuck was he when the 88's opened fire? I didn't see him anywhere near the line.

"The 88's took out most of the Shermans," our Second Louie says.

The Captain punches the Lieutenant.

"Nobody knew they had 88's up there," our Louie whines. "The Shermans didn't stand a chance."

"Yellow-bellied chickens," the Captain mutters and stalks away.

It's been an hour, and my heart won't stop pounding. I can't breathe. I'm suffocating. I can't stop thinking about Riley still standing with a hole as big as a golf ball in his throat before he keeled over. A guy I think was Amato lying in two pieces back in the woods. The top of him was staring up at the trees. Everything from his waist down was five feet away. Not a drop of blood. Neatly cut in two like he went through a band saw at the butchers.

I hear voices. I reach for my M-1. Never fired a shot. Never saw a kraut, just the Shermans exploding like Fourth of July fireworks. Jesus, that tanker. I'd take a round in the head instead of running around on fire.

Two of our guys approach from the dirt road. Four krauts with their hands over their heads are in front of them. "What are we supposed to with them?" one of them asks our Louie.

I didn't see him before, but a tanker gets up from

where he was sitting. One side of his face is a mass of blisters, and the other is covered with gauze. His jump suit is burned black. He grabs Sarge's Thompson.

He starts toward our guys and the krauts. The GIs dive toward the side of road. The krauts just stare at the tanker, their hands still over their heads. *"Nien, "*one of them cries, but the tanker unloads the Thompson into the four krauts. They stagger in an awful dance and fall to the ground. The tanker walks back to Sarge. He takes a clip from Sarge's belt, ejects the spent clip and re-loads. He goes back to the riddled bodies of the krauts and empties another clip into them.

I puke all over myself. I want to go home. I'm crying. So what? I don't want to die. I want to go home.

9

Soldiers in Italy Gain Morale: Advances Help Losing Feeling They Fight on Forgotten Front

Natalie sat at her desk with her head in her hands. She'd hoped that acting like a foolish moon-struck teenager at the basketball game was behind her. When Jack asked for her to work with him on this project, she should have said she was too busy. Now, after three days close to him, she couldn't get him out of her head. She was ping-ponging between trying to sort out her feelings for Jack and concentrating on her job and making a hash of both.

Natalie glanced at the clock and decided to meet Flo for lunch. At the door of the cafeteria, Natalie scanned the women's tables for Flo. Only one or two women dared to sit with the men, and she'd heard snide remarks about them. The tables where the women sat were also segregated: line workers in the first two, office workers in the back. She didn't see Flo and wondered if her tours of the shop floors with Jack entitled her to sit with the line workers. Still debating about where she should sit, Flo arrived and apologized for being late.

The two women slid into empty seats near the end of the workers' table. Natalie flipped open her lunch pail. The smelled of egg salad sandwiches seeped through the waxed paper. So help me, she thought, when this war ends, she was never going to eat another egg – sliced, deviled, fried, scrambled or poached.

Flo set a lunch pail on the table. "I'm afraid to open it." She pulled an envelope from her pocket and took out four sheets of V-mail. "Nothing for a week and I get four v-mails in yesterday's delivery."

"Bob is quite the writer."

Flo grinned. "One every day, although they're been longer gaps between batches lately. I have to lay them out on the kitchen table to make sure I'm reading them in the right order."

From her seat, Natalie saw there weren't too many spaces where the censors had erased anything military. More than half of Bill's rare v-mails were blanked out, leaving nothing but his usual complaints about the bitter cold, the lousy food, and aches and pains. Natalie supposed the blank spaces referred to where his unit was in France. "You're lucky."

"I hope we can visit Italy after the war," Flo said. "Bob writes about the beautiful old churches and monasteries around Naples he's visited when his unit gets a day or two back from the lines. Now he's on a short leave in Rome. The Coliseum, St. Peter's. Gosh, I hope he doesn't want to stay."

"I'm sure Bob wants to get back to you ASAP."

Flo turned a page, read for a several seconds and grinned. "He's learning Italian from the kids who hang around the GIs."

Natalie remembered Bob Cady from when he was in her social studies class senior year. A nice guy, but nothing that hinted at a future desire to visit ancient churches and learn Italian.

After turning another page of Bob's v-mail, two crimson spots painted Flo's cheeks. "Oh, my. I wonder how that got by the censors." She quickly folded the v-mail and stuffed it in her pocket. "I'll save this one for when I'm alone at home," she giggled.

The last time Natalie saw Bob Cady, he was working with his father on a plumbing job next door, unclogging a sewer drain. He was wearing gray stained overalls and wiping his grimy hands on a rag. She couldn't imagine him as a bi-lingual art lover and author of steamy letters to his fiancée. "I hope you don't do something you'll have to confess."

Flo colored again. "Natalie Costello, you are a sinner, putting evil thoughts in my mind." She opened her lunch pail and made a face. "After Bob and I are married, I'm not going to eat an egg for two, no make that three, years."

"You're sure?"

"Absolutely. No eggs," Flo said and made a sour face at the sandwich in her hand.

"About Bob?"

"Of course." She stared off in the distance. "I can really picture the house, Natalie. A Cape. Out of the city. Maybe Greenbush. A house full of children, the more the merrier. And a car. And a washing machine."

"Keep putting in for those overtime shifts," Natalie said.

Flo leaned toward Natalie. In a quieter voice she said, "I can tell you because you know I'm only half crazy, but I lie awake at night and think about the colors we'll paint the rooms. I've even chosen the patterns for the curtains."

"You've been sucking in too many fumes in the casting pits." Natalie took a bite of her sandwich and tried to put the picture of her future out of her mind. It was easy because there wasn't any picture, certainly not like the one in Flo's head. It was the same one she'd heard from many of the other girls at the lunch table. Bob's experiences seem to have changed him. Maybe Bill will be a different person when he returns. She would be.

"I'm off overtime for a week. Want to catch a movie Friday night?" Flo asked.

"What's playing?"

Flo said, "Depends."

"On what?"

"Whether we want to be naughty or nice," Flo said.

"Nice would be *Song of Bernadette* at the Paramount."

Flo said, "Why don't we go to church instead?"

"And I suppose naughty would be *The Outlaw* at the Strand." Natalie nodded toward a nearby table where the men hooted in that way when one of them had told an off-color joke. "And we'd sit smack in the middle of those guys drooling over Jane Russell."

Flo said, "The Legion of Decency flyer said it's morally objectionable in part. You can tell me when that part is on the screen, and I'll close my eyes."

"*Meet Me in St. Louis* is at the Palace, and *Mrs. Parkington* is at the Ritz," Natalie said.

"Let's check the *TU* for the times and decide whether we'll be good girls, bad girls, or just a couple of tired girls trying to stay awake after the cartoons." Natalie felt a hand on her shoulder, and before she could turn to see whose it was, she heard a voice that sent a shiver through her.

"Hey, Nats. I thought it was you."

Oh God, what's she doing here? Natalie turned slowly and confirmed that it really was Genny LaFleur. *Nats,* the hateful nickname Genny and her friends pinned on her in sixth grade. Genny was in overalls. Her hair, now brassy blonde, curled out from under her kerchief. She was cracking chewing gum, and a wicked smile spread across her face. "Hi, Genny," Natalie said with little enthusiasm. "I'd ask what you're doing here, but I don't suppose you're on a USO tour."

"You got that right, Nats. I was hired on last week. I'm over in Warehouse B learning how to operate a fork-lift."

Natalie tried to fix her with as mean a stare as possible. "Genny, It's *Natalie*."

"Jeez. Don't go high hat on me, Nat-til-ee." Genny turned to Flo. "You'd think we weren't just a couple girls who go back a long way."

"Where did you work before you were hired on here?" Natalie asked.

Genny shrugged. "I was a secretary to an accountant over on North Pearl. Then I hooked up with a lawyer in Lansingburgh." She paused. "A couple of others. Everyone's short-handed. Somebody gives you the guff, and you can take a powder."

"You get around," Natalie said.

"A girl's got to do the best she can," Genny said. "Got to run." She sash-shayed by a table of guys who made no bones about locking their peepers on her buns as she walked by.

"Too bad peroxide isn't rationed," Flo said. "I wonder if she'll last long here."

"I hope not. That girl's a commotion."

***

Friday afternoon Natalie was punching out when she saw Jack walking toward her. It had been three days since the Mountain-Mohammed meeting, and she'd been unsettled and unable to concentrate. She tried to convince herself it was natural to like him. Even a little crush was understandable, but that's it.

"Are you on overtime this weekend?" Jack asked.

His smile was disarming. Natalie tried to keep her voice even, as though they were simply a couple of people who worked together, but she was not hitting the right casual tone. "No. I'll have a couple of days to take it easy."

"Are you just going to put your feet up and relax?"

Natalie sensed there was something lurking in his question. "Flo and I are going to catch a movie tonight."

"What are you seeing?"

"Probably *Meet Me in St. Louis*," Natalie felt as though she was standing in front of a class groping for the right answer to the teacher's question.

"It's great. That Judy Garland's a real grown up gal. I think I'll catch *Mrs. Parkington*."

"Tonight?"

"I have to get out or my landlady will invent another reason to take up my entire evening," Jack said. "I've changed the washers in every faucet, learned two-handed canasta, and listened to her long stories about her dearly-departed Henry. I've got to get out."

They stood silently for several awkward seconds. It seemed that neither of them knew what they wanted to say. The silence stretched. Finally, Natalie said, "Well, I better get going."

"Sure. Well, maybe I'll see you around."

Natalie rolled 'I'll see you around' in her head trying to discover whether there was more to it than a simple good-bye.

After supper, Natalie helped her mother clean up the dishes and announced, "I'm going to the movies with Flo."

"I would have thought you'd want to relax after a hard week at the Arsenal," Mom said. Natalie's parents hadn't gotten used to her going out as often as she could. The whole town was out and not just on weekends, but her parents' heads were still in the Depression. Save every penny because you never know when the bottom will drop out. Stay home. Stay safe. The world is full of danger.

In her bedroom, Natalie paid more attention to what she was going to wear than if it was just a night out with Flo. She stared in the mirror and decided that she should stop fooling herself. Was it because Jack was the only man who'd paid the slightest attention to her since Bill left? She enjoyed having lunch with him, and she was excited to work with him on her suggestions for improvement. She should, but she couldn't, get him out of her mind.

Twenty minutes later, Natalie met Flo at the bus stop. Natalie was chilly. There was a hint of winter coming in the fall evening air, but she wore the lighter jacket she thought looked smarter than her heavier coat.

Flo said, "I heard that *Meet Me in St. Louis* is pretty good."

"I heard it's not. What do you say we see *Mrs. Parkington* instead?" Natalie couldn't believe she said that without thinking. It wasn't planned, but the thought must surely been pushing to get out. She needed to get herself under control.

"*Mrs. Parkington*? I can't stand Greer Garson." Flo said. "Let's stick with *Meet Me in St. Louis.*"

Flo was right. What's the matter with her? She should stop playing with fire.

The bus pulled up to their stop, and the sound of Flo's sigh and the whoosh of the brakes melded. Natalie stepped up first. They paid, and Natalie started down the aisle. Jack gave her a slight nod. She passed by the two empty seats behind him and continued further back. She wasn't sure what she saw in his face. Was it a smile or just acknowledging he saw her? She felt as though they were two spies who'd passed a secret message.

Flo slid in beside Natalie. "Well, I wonder who's on his way to see *Mrs. Parkington?*" she said in a huff and fiddled with her purse.

Wordlessly, Flo and Natalie rode into Albany. The bus approached the stop at Clinton and Broadway. Jack stood and walked to the front of the bus. Natalie and Flo got out at the rear entrance. Flo and Natalie walked briskly up Clinton toward the Palace. At the light, Natalie turned. Jack was twenty yards behind them. *Mrs. Parkington* was playing at the Ritz on South Pearl. What was he doing here?

Inside the theater Natalie and Flo walked down the center aisle, and Natalie didn't look for Jack.

The theater lights dimmed, and the newsreel featured General MacArthur wading ashore in the Philippines. Natalie tried to push away thoughts of Bill in France and Flo's Bob in Italy. It was a bit sick to follow with cartoons, but Natalie chuckled through a new Donald and Daisy Duck. Out of the corner of her eye she saw Flo grimly staring at the screen. The coming attractions didn't have much appeal. And she couldn't concentrate on *Meet Me in St. Louis* as she struggled with what it meant that Jack had followed them – her – to a movie he'd already seen.

The movie ended. Natalie slid quickly out of her seat and hurried up the aisle as the lights came on. She stood in the middle of the doors to the lobby scanning the faces in the crowd. She didn't see Jack.

Flo joined her. Natalie was about to apologize to Flo when she felt a tap on her shoulder. It was Jack.

"How did you like the movie?" he asked.

"I loved it," Natalie said. She felt Flo's eyes on her.

Jack said, "What do you say we get a cup of coffee."

His question hung in the air for seconds. It's just a cup of coffee, and I'm with Flo, Natalie thought. "Sure. Why not?" Out of the corner of her eye, she caught a question on Flo's face.

Flo's eyes flicked from Natalie to Jack and back again. "Why not," she said flatly.

They pushed through the crowd. Jack pointed toward North Pearl Street. "How about the Victory Café?"

Flo tugged the arm of Natalie's jacket. "You know, I'm feeling very tired. Too much overtime. Why don't you two go ahead? I'm going to catch the bus back home."

"Are you sure?" Natalie searched Flo's face for answers to the jumble of questions that were ricocheting around inside her head.

Flo said, "Really. I'm likely to fall asleep at the table. I guess the movie was too exciting for me. Nice to see you, Jack. Maybe another time." She waved and turned toward the bus stop on Broadway, and Natalie swore she heard her whistling the tune to *Don't Sit Under the Apple Tree With Anyone Else But Me.*

Ten minutes later, Jack and Natalie were hunched over a marble-topped table at the café. They'd exchanged a couple of sentences about the weather on the walk there. The café was jammed. The waitress poured two cups of coffee.

Jack pulled a small paper sack from his jacket pocket. "Sugar?"

"That's some pick-up line."

"I like mine black, and Mrs. Larson seems to have a source we don't talk about."

Natalie let Jack pour her a teaspoon full. She spent too much time stirring.

Jack said, "Did you like the movie?"

Natalie wondered how long they could keep up this charade and whether she wanted to. "Why did you follow us to the movie you saw last weekend?"

A sly grin spread across Jack's face. "Why do you think I did?"

Natalie gave him a sharp look. "I asked you," she snapped.

Jack seemed taken aback for a moment. "Because I wanted to see you." He reached across the table and laid his hand over hers.

All she could do was stare at his hand. There was nothing else to add to what had been made crystal clear.

They finished their coffees. There were people standing inside the doorway waiting for a table. "I think we should give up our table," Natalie said.

"I'll walk you to the bus stop."

They stood wordlessly looking up Broadway for the Number 22. When it arrived, they both got on and sat together. At her stop, Jack rose from his seat. Natalie started to say something, but he was walking toward the back door. He held it open, and they stepped out onto the sidewalk.

"It will be twenty minutes before another one," Natalie said.

"I didn't want to just leave," he said. "I wanted to say good night – properly."

Natalie rolled 'properly' around in her head. They stood searching each other's face for several seconds. The chill evening air seeped through her thin jacket and she shivered.

Jack pulled her into him, and she felt the warmth of his arms around her. She knew what he was doing. She knew if she let him, she had crossed that line she'd been toeing too closely – dancing back and forth over it as though it was a meaningless child's game.

Jack kissed her. She didn't pull away. He scanned her face and kissed her again.

Natalie tried to say something, but didn't know what. She turned toward home still feeling the scratch of his beard on her cheek and the coffee taste on his lips.

Mr. Podoski, wearing his white helmet, eyed her from across the street. He took a small notebook from his pocket and scribbled something in it.

***

On Monday morning Natalie banged her thigh on the sharp corner of her desk. Good, she thought. She should suffer pain for what she did – what she let happen. All weekend she fell into fitful sleep and then jolted awake at the memory of Jack kissing her – her letting him kiss her. She should take it back somehow and tell him it was a mistake. She was tired and not thinking straight. The Arsenal and Mr. Holt. Home with Mom and Dad. Her life had been back and forth on such a narrow track, she forgot how to behave when someone like Jack knocked her out of her groove.

Five minutes after the noon whistle blew, Natalie slid into the seat next to Flo in the lunch room. Flo opened her lunch pail and sighed so long Natalie expected her to deflate.

Natalie couldn't stand Flo's silence any longer. "Okay. How many Hail Marys and Our Fathers?"

"It's not funny, Natalie."

"I know. And I should go to Confession, but it's more important to me that you forgive me than Father Eagan."

"Now *I* have to go to Confession."

"You didn't do anything," Natalie said. She poured coffee into the top of her Thermos. She could see the bottom because her mother brewed it with too much chicory and too little coffee. She got a cup of water from the cooler and took a sip. It tasted stale.

"It was what the nuns called a sin of omission," Flo said. "I should have insisted we go home or, at the least, gone along with you two."

"Come on, Flo. To them everything outside Holy Orders was a sin or an occasion of sin. Besides, what could we do in a crowded coffee shop in downtown Albany?"

"Hanky, but not panky?"

Natalie wasn't going to tell Flo what happened at the bus stop. "He's a nice guy. I enjoy being with him."

Flo's face took on a serious cast, and she spent too much time pouring coffee from her Thermos. Finally, she asked, "So you and Jack Mahoney will simply go on making goo-goo eyes at each other around the Arsenal and just happen to run into each other at basketball games and the movies?"

Natalie didn't like the sharp way Flo said Jack's name. "Why not? He adds a little sparkle to my dull life." From pinch on Flo's face, Natalie felt like the teacher knew she'd been handed a forged excuse. "I deserve a little fun."

Flo took a bite of her sandwich and chewed as though savoring a pre-war sirloin steak. After several seconds she asked, "And you believe you can simply go along with this…high school going steady thing with Jack Mahoney?"

"Why not?" Natalie snapped. She hated the way Flo kept repeating his name, as if she was a Mr. Podoski shining a flashlight on every dark thought she'd had since she met Jack.

Flo concentrated on carefully folding the wax paper that wrapped her sandwich. "You're a good friend, Natalie.' She paused. "I don't want to see you hurt." She stood and patted Natalie's shoulder before walking away.

10

OPA Delays Ration Cut for Canned Fruits: Grocers Are Confused and Housewives Perplexed by Ration Mix-Up

I re-ink the small press. Concentrating on a job used to help. But now, the burn in my gut won't go away. It used to come and go, but now it comes and stays. I thought only big-shots got ulcers.

Last night I almost told her. Tess and me alone. But what could I say? She doesn't need one more worry. Last week, I caught her crying at the kitchen sink because Salvetti had run out of pork just minutes before she got in the door – after waiting an hour in the rain. No matter how many times I tell her it's not her fault, she takes it too much to heart when she's putting meals on the table with scraps of god knows what end of the cow. Me and Natalie and Nicky telling her how great the sawdust frankfurters taste and pretending the cake made with saccharine doesn't taste bitter.

Tess is smart in her way, but watching her spread out the coupon books on the kitchen table, counting and recounting the stamps, trying to figure out how many red points and blue points she has against the prices and how many days left in the month is painful to see. And I know she feels like she's let the family down when it all comes undone when she gets to the store and has to refigure everything when this or that is out of stock or the prices have gone up or that bastard Salvetti won't let her buy two cans of peas unless she agrees to taking a pound of his mealy sausage. Thank god Natalie helps her out. The girl has a knack for laying out the coupons and ads and the calendar and seeing a plan – even though the plan comes unglued when Tess goes to the market.

What would I say? I think about the straw and the camel, but this is more like bricks on our heads – each one heavier than the last. Tess is going crazy with running the house. Nicky's fooling around with that girl, and I hope he's got enough brains to buy some protection from one of the GIs at the USO. If she knew, Tess would say it's a mortal sin. Accounting for that is a long way off, we hope, but that's better than a bun in the oven now. Telling Tess I think I got an ulcer would be a relief compared to the ten-ton block I could drop on her head. What would I say? 'Tess, Stan is forging ration stamps, and if we get caught I'll go to jail.'

Stan's in the back room. I got to clear my throat to let him know I'm coming so he won't jump out of his shoes. And I think he's lost fifteen pounds in a month. Okay, he's got big bills for his wife at the TB place in Saranac and a son missing a few marbles, but the FBI isn't going to give a damn when they catch us. And it is us. Ever since I discovered the misprints in the trash, the walls of this place have been closing in on me. There's no way I'd get off if – no when – we get caught. Stories in the papers about the feds breaking up forgery rings jump out at me. I see our names – mine and Stan's – on the page instead of the latest ones that got nabbed. Last week I was at the front desk when a black sedan pulled up. Two men in suits and hats got out: FBI for sure. Before they walked by the shop, I had to squeeze my cheeks to keep from shitting myself.

I don't know how long I can do this. The other day I almost laid it out to Stan that I know what he's doing. But then I'd be in on it. The moment I saw what was in the trash I knew I should quit. There's a lot of shops begging for workers. But I'm fifty. I'd start at the bottom, and then out the door as soon as the war's over. If, and it's a big if, we don't get caught, the print shop could be long-term. If. If.

11

Army Asks Labor to Speed Output: Pay Demands Urged Not Interfere with Ammunition Needs.

At 3:50 on Monday afternoon, Natalie waited outside Mr. Vincent's office as if she was a misbehaving student about to be punished by the principal.

'Please meet with Mr. Vincent at 4:00 PM.' The note summoning her to the office of the Director of Operations was so upsetting that she'd crunched it into a sweat-soaked clump. Precisely at 4:00, Mr. Vincent's secretary ushered her in. Mr. Vincent pointed to the chair in front of his desk.

Natalie sat with her hands tightly clasped and waited for the axe to fall. Mr. Vincent's long thin, slightly hooked nose reminded her of a hawk.

Mr. Vincent said, "Well, well. I meet the estimable Mrs. Costello – again." For a thin man, his soft voice had surprising weight. It cast importance.

Estimable. Was that good or bad? Natalie whispered, "Yes."

Mr. Vincent made a steeple under his chin and seemed to be carefully considering his words. "When Mr. Fox brought me a plan for reorganizing the parts in Building SH, I thought he was demonstrating a previously hidden talent for organizational innovation." Mr. Vincent paused. "Mr. Fox has many talents, but that isn't one of them. And when he promoted the idea of moving the materiel instead of the heavy machinery – moving the mountain to Mohammed as he put it – I wondered anew what refreshing spring of innovation he'd been tapping." Mr. Vincent pursed his lips as though he'd discovered the answer. "At the risk of bringing in another metaphor, it seems that your talent has been hidden under a basket. Those were your ideas weren't they?"

"Yes," she said in a barely audible voice.

"Indeed, when I queried Mr. Fox, the chain of innovation stretched back to you through Mr. Mahoney. You have a champion in Mr. Mahoney."

She pictured Jack sitting on a white horse with a medieval lance in his hand. "Thank you," she said.

"Mrs. Costello, I have already expended too much time discovering the source of these excellent suggestions. You seem to have an uncanny ability to see and solve certain types of problems. I've carefully reviewed the suggestions you've made. I've even gone back to the source documents – your original drawings. A grasp of logistics and organization is your gift."

All Natalie's teachers said she was organized. She thought it was like being a runner-up like Miss Congeniality. She bowed her head. "I'm trying to do my part."

"As you know, we have critical tasks here at the Arsenal," Mr. Vincent said. "In my role I'm charged with seeing the big picture, and if good suggestions for doing our jobs better and faster come from the trash men, the security guards – or from a secretary, indeed a woman, then I need to employ them." He leaned toward Natalie as though expecting a comment.

"I understand."

"I hope so."

Mr. Vincent handed Natalie a stack of thick file folders. "What you have in your hand are backlog reports on which assembly lines have experienced delays. I've had some of our staff analyze them, and some good suggestions for improvements have been made. Not enough, I'm afraid." He gestured toward the door. "As you saw with the issue of rush orders for mortars and smaller field artillery, the assembly lines cannot turn on a dime. Mr. Mahoney reluctantly revealed that you *see* solutions. Mrs. Costello, I don't care if you use an Ouija Board or conduct séances. I want you to study these reports. I don't care if you see, smell, taste or feel an answer, but I want you to take a crack at these."

"I'll do my best. I can't promise I will come up with something, but I'll try."

"I want this to be very discreet, Mrs. Costello. If and when you have something for me, call my secretary and we will meet."

"I may have to go back to the shop floors." Natalie was already thinking about Jack and her side-by-side as they walked through the shops, meeting to discuss their findings, and... nothing.

"I will arrange whatever you need," Mr. Vincent said. "And I am assigning Miss Agnes Martin to your office to assist in inventory and shipping duties."

She was getting her own secretary? "Thank you."

**

That evening Nick stared at the French toast on his plate as if he couldn't recognize what it was. One word and I'll hit him with the skillet, Natalie thought. Nick poured a too large dollop of Aunt Jemima syrup on it, and cut a piece of the burnt toast. Dad had finished his and was rinsing his plate at the sink.

"Thank you, Natalie. Delicious," Dad lied. "I'm going to check on your mother." He left the kitchen.

"You don't have to eat it if you don't want to," Natalie said to Nick.

He put a piece in his mouth. "It's okay."

Natalie was lousy with French toast and wondered if she wanted to chance a couple of slices for herself or just fry the eggs. "I'm sorry I forgot and didn't have anything else to make."

"I forgot too," Nick said. "November tenth. *Every* November tenth she goes to early Mass and spends the rest of the day in her room in bed I guess. Do you know why?"

"No, and I'm tired of asking." Natalie cracked two eggs and dropped them in the pan. "I was eight or nine when I first caught on to her once a year thing. I asked her and got a weird answer about a special saint's day. I even looked up the saint for November 10 – Saint Euphemia Martyred Virgin of Chalcedon. She died in 307, tortured and eaten by a wild lion because she refused to attend a pagan ceremony."

Nick said, "Not up there with Saint Lucy or the other ones the old ladies pray to."

"It didn't make sense to me. I asked Dad. He muttered something about her not feeling well." Natalie shrugged "I can't remember her ever being sick, but every year on the same day?"

Nick said, "It's been happening all your life?"

"As long as I remember and before I'll bet."

"And tomorrow, back to normal," Nick said.

"I suppose we're lucky that our mother is only weird one day out of three hundred and sixty-five."

Nick said, "Three-sixty-six this year. Leap year. Does that throw her off, like it's like so many days into the year?

"Two hundred and fifty-nine this year."

"Cripes, Natalie. How do you do that?"

"Special talent like being double-jointed. Funny and useless."

"You should be a math teacher or something," Nick said.

"I can count coupons, and I can guess the weight of the sugar you've been nipping from the sack in the cupboard."

"Sorry. I'll go light from now on. Thanks for pitching in on dinner."

"You're welcome." Natalie slid the eggs onto a plate and sat across from Nick. She pushed the plate toward him. "Want some of my eggs?"

Nick took a small forkful. "Only one bite. You Rosie-the-Riveters need your energy."

"You say that one more time, and I'll stick this fork in your eye."

"Sorry, Sis."

Natalie realized that she and Nick were rarely alone together, with her at work or out and him out with his buddies – or the blonde with the big breasts. He was graduating in June, and she couldn't imagine her kid brother in uniform, in the war. "What are you going to do in June?"

"Go in, not that I have a choice."

"I suppose you can choose which branch."

"Yeah. I can sign up before graduation and pick my service." Nick looked troubled.

"What's wrong?"

He shrugged. "I don't want to get killed."

"Who does?"

Nick said, "Some of the guys talk big. Let's join the Marines and take on the Japs in the Pacific. A couple want to get into the Army Air Corps, fly B-17s or Mustangs."

"And you know the odds for those?"

"Yeah."

"Sign up for the Army," Natalie said. "I see the orders

for different types of artillery. We're gearing up for a final push. Maybe by the time you finish basic training, the war in Europe will be over, or mostly over."

"Not as exciting as the Air Corps or Marines, or even the Navy."

"You don't need excitement."

"You're right. Thanks, Sis."

Natalie wondered whether to bring it up, but when would they be alone like this. "And you don't need more to worry about than staying safe in the Army." She let her words hang in the air for a few seconds. "So stay *safe* when you're with your girlfriend."

Nick's face went crimson. "*Jeez*, Natalie.

"Be careful," Natalie said and finished her eggs. She felt ridiculous for giving Nicky prudent advice when her life was spinning out of control

12

On Tuesday morning, Natalie shuffled through the dozens of backlog reports again and again, but she was still confused. It had taken three days to make sense of the list of parts and processes that were only in shorthand. One entry read, 'Recast (M3) – (M4) - 76mm cannon- 22hrs.' She finally figured out that the 76mm cannon had to be recast from its former use on the M3 General Grant Tank to the M4 Sherman Tank, and it was 22 hours behind schedule.

Natalie scanned the monthly and weekly schedule charts for each department which showed the operational times and where each part was supposed to be and the explanations as to why production was behind schedule. Except that the explanations – late delivery of components, incorrect or damaged parts, told her what happened but not why it happened. And she didn't' see a pattern in the delays and backlogs.

Sorting the reports by type of backlog didn't work. She re-sorted them by department. When she thought she had a glimmer of an answer, the next ten reports pointed in an opposite direction. She was lost in too much paper. She knew it was not only on her head. Mr. Vincent had weekly meetings, and some of the problems had been solved. She was his wild card. Still, if she helped solve this problem, maybe he'd let her work in the shops. She needed to do something besides shuffle paper.

She fought back angry tears. Damn. She glanced at

Agnes who seemed to be trying to ignore this crazy lady muttering at stacks of paper. The five o'clock whistle blew, and Agnes grabbed her coat off the hook. "Good night," she said and scurried out the door.

Glad to be out of here is what she meant.

Mr. Holt came out of his office and stuttered to a stop as he cast a perplexed look at the stack of folders. "Good night, Mrs. Costello." It seemed as though he couldn't get out fast enough.

She should go home. Take a bath. Stare at the ceiling. For days, she'd been shivering in cold water every night searching for answers in the cracked paint in the corner. *"Damn."* Now she let the angry tears flow. In moments she was sobbing. "Damn. Damn. Damn." She swept the folders off the desk. A flurry of paper swirled and settled in clumps around the office. It would take her forever to put the reports back in order. She should shove them in the wastepaper basket and burn them. Bless me father, I cursed and destroyed government property.

Hiccupping back the end of her tantrum she wished she could make sense of the scatter of reports. She leaned to pick up one nearest her and stopped. She should go back to where she started: up in the rafters in Storage Building SH, she thought. But she couldn't. She got down on her hands and knees and tried to put the reports in batches. First, she put the backlogs caused by broken machinery in one pile. She put the delays caused by missing parts in another and backlogs caused by injuries and other personnel problems in still another. It wasn't working. She couldn't see behind the top sheet of each pile. She'd been on the tour with Jack before she made the recommendation on reorganizing SH. And they'd spent three days on the shop floors before she came up with the Mountain and Mohamed idea. Maybe being with Jack was the key to solving these problems.

Natalie reached for the nearest stack and spread the reports along the wall. Reports from the next stack were lined up in front of the first. Pushing back her chair she made room for a line of reports from the third folder. Shoving her desk back, she cleared a space for the rest of the reports. She backed up to Agnes' desk. The office floor was papered with reports.

Kicking off her shoes to tip-toe through the paper, she took a black pencil and a red pencil from the jar on her desk. The five-thirty whistle blew. Her parents would wonder where she was, but she couldn't stop now.

For several minutes she stared at the reports. The bird's nest in the rafters wasn't going to work. Injuries and machinery breakdowns couldn't be predicted. She pulled all the backlog reports that had those explanations and set them behind Agnes' desk. She reshuffled the delays due to incorrect or delayed parts into a line from the coatrack to the office door. She stared at them for minutes, but nothing came to her. Natalie took the black pencil and circled delays caused by incorrect parts delivered. She used the red pencil to circle backlogs due to delays in delivery of parts. She still couldn't see anything.

Carefully, Natalie stepped onto her chair and then gingerly up to the top of the desk. Better. The office floor looked like the start of a giant game of Solitaire.

The office door opened.

"Stop," she shouted as the reports closest to the door scattered.

A security guard gawped at her. "Mrs. Costello! You all right?"

"Yes." She waved at the papers. "I'm working on a project. I need to see them from here."

Following the arc of her hand, the guard shook his head. "You didn't punch out, and I didn't see your name on the overtime roster."

"I'm sorry. I got carried away on this project. For Mr. Vincent," she added hoping the guard would think her a little less crazy.

"You going to stand on that desk for long?" From his worried look, it seemed as though he'd spotted a noose dangling from the light fixture. "I wouldn't want you to get hurt or something."

She held out her hand. "Watch the papers please." He stepped around the ranks of reports as though negotiating a mine field. Natalie took his hand and stepped down from the desk and the chair. "I'll be alright."

The guard didn't leave. She would love to stay and finish, but thought she'd better go. She took one last long look at the reports trying to burn them in her memory.

It was getting dark as she walked home. November's fading light depressed her. When Natalie explained that she had to finish work on an important project, her mother gave her the look Natalie used to get when she offered a lame excuse for coming home late. Ever since the basketball game, 'my friend' lurked unspoken on her parents' lips every time she went out in the evening. With an exasperated sigh, Mom said she'd reheat the baked ziti after Natalie's bath.

Slipping into the tub, Natalie hoped a hot bath would bring her another *Eureka*. But twenty minutes later, she finally climbed out of the cool bath water. She couldn't see an answer from the tub or the corner of the ceiling. It only started to form when she imagined herself surveying the reports from the top of her desk. The security guard probably alerted the medical staff, and they'll be waiting for her with a straitjacket when she tried to punch in tomorrow.

After two hours of tossing and pummeling her pillow, Natalie couldn't fall asleep. Her brain was clogged with reports. She swung her legs out of the bed and switched on the bedside lamp. She retrieved a sweater from the dresser, reset Big Ben, and draped the sweater over the clock to muffle the alarm.

Finally, at 5:00 A.M., Dad, in his pajamas and robe, caught Natalie tiptoeing across the kitchen floor, shoes in hand. He looked at her as though recalling a bedroom farce movie.

"Emergency at the Arsenal. Forgot to mention it last night. Overtime. Backlogs. Big meeting." Natalie waved and darted out the back door. She forgot to put on her shoes, and last night's rain seeped through her stockings.

In cold, wet feet, Natalie hurried up Broadway. Streetlights struggled to cast light through the pre-dawn fog. Inside the gate, workers in overalls stared at her, seeming to wonder what she was doing at this hour.

Up in Natalie's office, the reports were where she'd left them. Among the dozens of worries that kept her awake last night, she was afraid security would confiscate the papers as evidence of an employee gone nuts.

Over the next two hours, Natalie circled more delays and backlogs in black and red. She climbed up and down the chair to the top of her desk to survey what she'd done. It wasn't making sense. Or maybe there was a hint of it over there in the corner near the coatrack.

Natalie clambered back down and crawled among the papers. She held the red and black pen together in one hand and began to draw double arrows and lines from circle to circle. She put rips in some of the reports and wished she had crayons instead of sharp pencils. More arrows, more lines. Again and again, she clambered up on the desk, looked over what she'd done before climbing down to draw more lines and arrows.

At 7:30, she was standing on the desk top thinking she finally grasped the outlines of an answer. Maybe it was there as she scanned the papers and red and black arrows. Or perhaps it's the work of a mad woman? She glanced at the wall clock. She took a piece of paper, wrote 'Please knock' in large letters, tacked it to the outside of the office door and locked it. This better work or she was off to the rubber room.

At precisely eight o'clock, Natalie heard an impatient rapping. She unlocked the door and opened it a crack. Of course it was Agnes, never a minute late and never a minute early. "Agnes, I'm working on a special project for Mr. Vincent. Would you please step in very carefully?" Natalie relocked the door and guided the obviously perplexed woman around the few inches of floor not covered with paper until they reached her desk. "Would you please stay here? It's very important that the papers not be disturbed." Agnes looked at Natalie as though she was disturbed. "I'll bring your work to you." It was only then that Natalie wondered what she was going to do next.

When Natalie heard a tentative rap on the door, she knew it was Mr. Holt, always at least ten minutes late. Natalie shot a warning look at Agnes: *Don't move.* She flinched as if Natalie had pulled a knife on her.

Natalie eased the door open and explained that she'd been assigned a special project by Mr. Vincent. Mr. Holt peered over her shoulder as if he'd find his boss behind Natalie. She let him enter, guiding him around the paper to the door of his office. He glanced at Agnes as if wondering if she had anything to do with the strange arrangement of paper covering most of the office floor. As Natalie closed Mr. Holt's door, she said, "Mr. Vincent. Hush-hush," hoping he'd cower in this office fretting about how his secretary was going to get him assigned to a real job.

Now what? She'd like to climb back up on the desk for another look, but she was sure that would really send Agnes into a swoon. Natalie took a deep breath. She had to do it. It couldn't wait. "I'll be back in a few minutes," she said to Agnes. "Please don't touch the papers."

Natalie straightened the front of her rumpled dress and walked down the hall to the executive offices where the faces of the secretaries were pinched in permanent disapproval. In front of Mr. Vincent's secretary, she said, "I need to see Mr. Vincent as soon as possible."

The secretary stared at Natalie as though she was collecting for the Red Cross. "He has a meeting in five minutes and can't be disturbed."

"It's very important. He gave me an assignment, and I need to tell him that I've solved... well perhaps have an idea... and need his advice." Natalie's voice trailed off. What exactly was it she was going to tell Mr. Vincent?

"I'll inform Mr. Vincent that you requested a meeting."

From the way she glanced at the calendar on her desk, Natalie guessed she was thinking sometime next month.

"Please tell him ..."

"Mrs. Costello?" Mr. Vincent said from the open door of his office.

"Mr. Vincent. I'm so glad. The backlogs and delays. I think I've found a solution. I mean I have an idea of how to see the problem." Natalie heard her mother's *I can't believe what I'm hearing* sigh from the secretary and guessed she was making an appointment for Natalie sometime late next year. Oh my God, Natalie realized she was shoeless.

Mr. Vincent followed her gaze to her feet. She wanted to run from the office. "You have a solution?" he said.

"An approach to it." Natalie pointed toward the hall. "In my office. Laid out. You have to see it there."

"Mr. Vincent. You have a meeting with the maintenance foremen…" the secretary made a point of staring at the wall clock… "in three minutes."

Mr. Vincent gave Natalie a long appraising look. "Please reschedule them. I'll be in Mrs. Costello's office for…?"

"I just need a few minutes," she lied. She didn't think she could explain what she'd done that quickly but it couldn't wait any longer. She would forget. She'd lose her nerve. She was running on two or three fitful hours of sleep. Her mouth was ahead of her brain, and she was afraid her spring would suddenly wind down and she'd slump to the floor. Natalie resisted grabbing Mr. Vincent's hand, willing him to follow.

After Natalie had carefully opened her office door and led Mr. Vincent just inside, Agnes jumped to attention. Natalie knew she was out of line but said, "Agnes, we think it would be better if you took an early break. No need to charge it. I'll come for you when we're done."

Agnes picked her way along the wall and out the door.

When Natalie turned back, Mr. Vincent was surveying the reports. She wondered if she was in trouble for marking them up with red and black pencils. She was either going to explain how her scheme made sense or pack her stuff and punch out – forever.

"Mr. Vincent. I know this sounds strange, but, well,

maybe I'm a little strange." Natalie hoped his smile meant to continue and not to confirm that she was indeed very strange. "I could try to explain what I've done, but the thing is you have to see it – from up there." She pointed to the desk top.

"From the desk top?"

Natalie gingerly stepped onto the chair and then up on the top of the desk. She let out a chuckle she hoped said, "See, it's easy."

"Shall I take off my shoes?"

"It's not necessary. I didn't want to dirty the desk."

"Well then, neither of us should damage government property." Mr. Vincent untied his black brogans and slid them off.

Natalie almost held out her hand to help him up, but he surprised her with his agility as he stepped quickly from the chair to the desk.

"Over the top. Just like Passchendale."

Natalie told herself to slow down. Make herself sound rational even though she hadn't thought out exactly what to say. "Okay," she started. "Over there." Natalie pointed to the stack of folders next to the coatrack. "Equipment breakdowns and injuries. Unpredictable – for now." She swept her hand to take in the reports that covered most of the floor. "Backlogs due to delays in delivery or incorrect parts delivered." She dared to glance at Mr. Vincent. He seemed to be taking in the mess on the floor. She wished it didn't look like a busted up paper drive.

"The arrows and lines," Natalie continued. "The red arrows are delayed deliveries. The black lines are where incorrect parts were delivered to the shops." It was there she was stuck. "Do you see how the lines and arrows converge at certain points?" She hoped she didn't sound like a kindergarten teacher.

Mr. Vincent put his hand under his chin and stared at the papers for what seemed like an hour.

Mr. Holt's door opened. He gaped at the two of them standing on Natalie's desk as if they were about to jump off a dock into a lake.

"Carry on, Lieutenant," Mr. Vincent said. "Everything is under control."

Natalie remembered Mr. Holt also served in the first World War. He ducked back into his office as though diving for cover from an artillery barrage.

Natalie and Mr. Vincent turned back to the mass of paper, lines and arrows. Mr. Vincent let out a long, "Hmmm" and then said, "Mrs. Costello. The dates on the reports. I'm afraid I can't see them from here. Could I trouble you to climb back down into the trench and read them to me?"

Natalie made her way off the desk, relieved that Mr. Vincent hadn't ordered her to sweep up the papers and report back to the tool shed.

Mr. Vincent pointed to a set of papers where several black lines converged. "Over there, please – where your lines come together."

Natalie tiptoed to where he'd pointed and kneeled. "August fifteen."

"And the time if you would."

"Five-fifteen. Afternoon."

"And over there, that group of red lines."

"September fourteen. Eight thirty. Morning," she reported.

"And there, please."

Over the next several minutes, on her hands and knees Natalie crawled from one batch of reports to another, reading out the dates and times where the lines and arrows converged.

"Thank you, Mrs. Costello."

Natalie tried to hear whether he'd thanked her, or she was being dismissed. She was relieved when he asked her to join him on the desk and delighted when he held out his hand to steady her as she stepped from the chair to the desk top.

"Well, Mrs. Costello. What do you think we have here and there and there?" he said pointing the places where the lines and arrows met.

She was exhausted – and exhilarated – She couldn't think straight.

"Patterns, Mrs. Costello," he said before she could answer. "Your arrows and lines have shown us patterns of where delays and backlogs have been occurring. A very important part of the answer to this puzzle."

"But not the answer."

"Mrs. Costello, in my experience too often people only see a part of the answer to a riddle and go off thinking they have solved it. You have illustrated *where* the problems of delay and backlogs are occurring. Very important indeed. Congratulations."

Natalie was so happy she wanted to hug him.

Mr. Vincent pointed to one group of papers. "You allowed me to build on your insights by adding *when* the problems occur: at the beginning of the work weeks and on shift changes."

"You knew the days when all I read off were the dates?"

"A modest talent," he said with a dismissive wave of his hand. "Now with our talents in tandem, we may be on our way to a solution."

It took her a moment. "Ah, I see. We have the what and the when, but we need to discover the why." Natalie felt an overwhelming swell of accomplishment and satisfaction.

"Exactly. I have some notions about that, but I think we've done enough for one day." He stepped off the desk onto the chair and then to the floor. He held out his hand, and Natalie felt as though she was stepping out of Cinderella's coach holding the hand of an elegantly attired footman.

"Have you had much sleep, Mrs. Costello?"

She was sure she looked like she'd slept in her clothes. "Not much."

"I strongly suggest you take off the rest of the day. Get some well-deserved sleep – on the Arsenal's clock."

The papers were still spread across the floor. Natalie was afraid the cleaning staff would throw them out or Agnes or Mr. Holt would make a mess of them.

Mr. Vincent must have sensed her concern. He rapped on Mr. Holt's door. Mr. Holt peeked out. 'All clear?' was written across his brow. "Lieutenant, I want you to guard Mrs. Costello's papers. They should remain just as they are."

Natalie was sure Mr. Holt's hand almost rose to a salute. "Yes, sir, Mr. Vincent," he said uncertainly.

Mr. Vincent put his hand in the small of Natalie's back and guided her toward the door. He leaned toward her and whispered, "Holt's a good soldier. Your secret papers are safe." Natalie was shocked when he winked.

13

Fuel for Home Front Will Be Short Again: Output Has Risen, But So Have War Demands

On Monday afternoon, Natalie took her place in a chair next to the wall while the managers gathered around the conference table. The talk was loud and animated. A fog of cigarette and pipe smoke stung her eyes. Mr. Vincent stood at the head of the table, and the room went silent. He said, "Mrs. Costello will take notes for me." His voice was soft but strong, and the men leaned forward to catch his words. Natalie wondered if she was the only one who heard 'for me?' And when Mr. Vincent smiled at her, she got curious looks from the men. A swell of satisfaction made her sit up straighter.

The discussion of the delays and backlogs got underway. Mr. Vincent reviewed the problems and the suggestions for improvements from the last meeting. He turned to Mr. Tartanian. "Sam has some interesting ideas on what's happening. Sam, why don't you sketch out what you and I talked about this morning?"

Tartanian? Why was Mr. Vincent asking that jerk to explain what she'd done? She should have told Jack and let him take part of the credit.

"Well, you see, it's got to do with weekends," Tartanian said. "What I mean is, well, you know it's not always really on Mondays. Oh, and you got to pay attention to the shifts – when they change, that is."

What? In less than a minute of hearing him stumble along, Natalie wanted to leap out of her chair and whack him on the head with her steno pad. She turned toward Jack, but he was staring at Mr. Tartanian as though he was listening to the Sermon on the Mount. Mr. Vincent was nodding along at Tartanian's tortured explanation. You bastard, Natalie almost said aloud and wondered which bastard.

Tartanian sputtered on, occasionally casting pained looks at Mr. Vincent, until he came to a break point.

"That's a useful overview, Sam." Mr. Vincent said.

Tartanian let out a long breath as if relieved to have finished reading the Declaration of Independence at a school assembly. Natalie wondered what Mr. Vincent was doing, giving her idea to Tartanian instead of Jack or one of the other managers who wouldn't have made hash out of it. She glared at Tartanian and hoped colonies of biting insects were nesting in his thick hair.

And the idiot got half of it wrong. Natalie tried to calm down. She thought she got a hint of a smile from Mr. Vincent, or maybe it was a warning to keep her mouth shut. She still wanted to drop Tartanian in a shrink pit.

Mr. Vincent took a roll of paper from next to his chair. "I've taken Sam's ideas, along with the several other excellent suggestions you all made, and had this diagram drawn by our draftsmen." He gestured to Tartanian and another manager who unrolled the paper and held up the ends so that it could be seen by the others.

It was a picture of Natalie's office floor all dressed up. There were a couple of minor changes, but it was hers. She choked back angry tears. The smoke made her cough, and she buried her face in her hands to hide her anger.

Over the next hour, Mr. Vincent and the managers discussed the diagram and considered ways special attention could be paid to delays and backlogs that occurred at the start of work-weeks and shift changes. Natalie struggled to pay attention while she imagined ways she could torture both Mr. Vincent and Tartanian.

When the discussion came to a close, Mr. Vincent said, "Gentlemen, I think we've had a very productive meeting." The men began to gather their papers. "I'd like to add an important footnote before we adjourn." The men settled back. "I would be remiss if I didn't mention that Mrs. Costello made an important contribution to solving the problem. It was she who reminded me that with speed-ups and shifts in assembly lines, Monday to Friday work-weeks and shift changes at pre-war schedules are no longer the norm."

I never said that.

"Fresh thinking," Mr. Vincent continued. "We have twenty-nine hundred women in our workforce. They're doing remarkably well in every job." One of the men cleared his throat, and Mr. Vincent glared at him. After a cold-staring pause, he continued, "We need to use every resource at our disposal. If we fail, it won't be because we've sold fewer Fords or washing machines. If we fail, men die." Mr. Vincent gestured toward Natalie and waited until all eyes were on her. "I've asked Mrs. Costello to take on added responsibilities. From time to time, you may see her on the shop floors. When I see an opportunity for her to assist you, I will temporarily assign her to work with you on a problem. I expect you to regard her as *my* aide-de-camp. Thank you, gentlemen."

The men glared at Natalie as they left. Mr. Fox stood next to the door. His fleshy lips were pulled back in a greasy imitation of a smile, and Natalie had to duck around him to leave.

Twenty minutes later Natalie sat in Mr. Vincent's

office, her mind reeling. Mr. Vincent had just repeated what he said in the meeting without adding much if anything to what she'd do as his aide. He took a pull on his pipe and set it in a large round glass ashtray with a cork knob in the middle. He looked like a college professor – or at least Natalie's image of one.

"Mr. Vincent, I don't know if I can do what you want."

"Neither do I. You may have exhausted every good idea in your head," he said. Then he surprised Natalie with a little chuckle. "But I'm betting you haven't."

She finally screwed up her courage. "Mr. Vincent, I want a real job. I want to work on the lines. I'll do anything, weld, drive a fork-lift, learn to operate a lathe. I don't want to spend the entire war as a paper-pusher." Oh, God, now she'd' called a top executive a 'paper-pusher.' She'll be mopping floors in the locker rooms tomorrow.

"Alas, some of us have talents we'd rather kept hidden." A hint of a smile creased Mr. Vincent's lips. "Mrs. Costello, indulge me for a moment or two. In nineteen-sixteen, I was a boy on my father's farm in Iowa. All I could see was corn to the horizon. And I knew that all I'd see for the rest of my life was corn. I'd never been to Des Moines. I enlisted, and by nineteen-eighteen I had seen Paris and London and Brussels." He stared at the top of his desk for several seconds as though something important was there. "And I saw death and destruction beyond imagination." There was a slight shake of his head as he leaned toward Natalie. In a hoarse whisper as if revealing something shameful he said, "I was afraid. More frightened than I thought one could be. I saw comrades and friends die, and I was sad beyond belief. I killed other men, and even though they were enemies, I will never forgive myself." He leaned back. "It was the most exciting time of my life. Nothing since has come close to the exhilarating highs and fathomless lows I felt." He drew in a breath as though he needed to confess, he said, "Mrs. Costello, I loved the war."

Natalie couldn't believe Mr. Vincent actually *said* what she thought was her shameful secret.

Mr. Vincent continued, "I desperately wanted to serve in this war. But a dubious talent for administration acquired at a washing machine plant – and my age – has me here, pushing paper."

"I didn't mean…"

He gave Natalie a dismissive wave. "I could assign you to any of those jobs in a minute."

She already heard, 'But.'

"Mrs. Costello, you are my secret weapon. You have a talent. We need what you have much more than one more person operating a lathe."

Natalie slumped back in the chair, resigned.

"You will be out on the lines, I assure you. Perhaps not every day, but when I see a need for your special talent I'll have you there. I'm confident Miss Martin can handle the routine aspects of your responsibilities – of course with your supervision."

"I'm sorry I was angry when you let Mr. Tartanian explain what I – we – had done in my office."

"Let me give you a piece of advice, Mrs. Costello. I wouldn't call Mr. Tartanian your enemy. Indeed you will surely discover many more managers and workers who dismiss us as mere paper pushers. But as my Drill Sergeant pointed out in bayonet practice. 'Get as close as you can to your enemy." He paused. "Or as my first boss at the washing machine plant said, 'Be extra kind to your enemies. It confuses the… daylights out of them."

"I will."

Mr. Vincent seemed to be considering what to say next. "In this new role, you will be working closely with many of the managers." He paused. "Discretion, Mrs. Costello." He gave her a searching look. "I trust you understand the need for discretion."

"Of course," she whispered.

"Good. I'm confident we understand the need for discretion."

Natalie kept hearing Mr. Vincent's saying, "I loved the war." Over and over in her head. "I loved the war."

When Natalie stepped out of Mr. Vincent's office, Jack was standing in the hallway. His eyes played over her, and she positive everyone in the executive suite had stopped working and was staring at them. Natalie felt a bubbling in her chest as if someone had uncorked a bottle of seltzer between her breasts. "I thought you'd left."

Jack put his hand on Natalie's arm. "I have to see you again – soon." His voice was an urgent whisper. "Not a supposedly chance meeting at a basketball game or a movie. In the real world, like real people."

For a moment Natalie was confused, and then she realized what he'd proposed. Yes," she said, thrilled and frightened by what her answer meant. "But not in Watervliet. "

"Let's go bowling. The Bowl-Mar Lanes in Albany, Friday. We'll meet at the bus stop on Broadway and 6th at seven o'clock."

Natalie liked the way he took charge, steamrolling over her doubts. "Yes. I'd like that." Finally she said, "I should get back to my office."

14

*General Assails Home Front Laxity as a Danger to
Soldier's Fighting Spirit*

Friday after dinner, Natalie was helping her mother with the dishes. She put away a glass, and faced Mom. She couldn't pretend any longer. "I'm going bowling – with a friend." The two women stared at each other for several seconds.

Finally, Mom let out a strangled, "I hope you know what you're doing."

To Natalie, her reflection in the window over the sink was that of a shameless adulterer. Her mother's face was screwed into a mask of worry and anger, but she seemed unable to speak.

Why doesn't she let me have it, Natalie thought? She should scream at me, call me a harlot. It's always been like this with her. Natalie got the usual motherly rebukes for teenage misdemeanors. But for more seriously bad behavior her mother hesitated and then slipped into pauses and silences with dense unreadable textures. It was as though something held her back.

"I do." Natalie headed upstairs to change. No need to put a fine point on it. Mom and Dad can think what they want.

In her bedroom, Natalie said, "I'm going on a date." There, she'd said it if only to herself for now. "I'm not sneaking around at the Arsenal. I'm going out with Jack." On her dresser was the photo of Bill in his uniform taken when he finished basic training. She restrained herself from saying, 'Sorry,' to Bill because she wasn't. She needed the photo to remind her what he looked like. The memories of him just after they were married and at Fort Dix were all she could conjure. She couldn't remember him before they were married, and she hardly had a life with Bill after. She didn't know what was ahead with Jack, but she was going to find out. She was finally making a choice.

Forty-five minutes later, Natalie waited at the bus stop on Broadway. She'd slid off her wedding ring and put it in her purse. The number 22 rolled to a stop. Jack stood in the well at the front door, and she hopped on. They found two seats and rode wordlessly along Broadway until they got off at Madison. Two blocks up Madison, people were streaming in and out of the Bowl-Mor. Natalie and Jack squeezed in the door and found the line to rent bowling shoes.

Jack said, "Bowling alleys, movie theaters, night clubs, bars, restaurants, jammed every night." He pointed toward the cash register. "These people are going to be sorry when the war's over."

"It's crazy," Natalie said. "Guys like you shoe-horned in tiny rooms, some doubled –up or worse. Women back home with their parents. Overtime pay in their pockets. They can't wait to get out."

Jack made a mock hurt face. "Is that why you agreed to come out tonight?"

Natalie faced Jack and put her hand on his arm. "No. I want to be out with you."

A broad smile covered Jack's face, and he squeezed her hand. "I'm glad."

They got their shoes, and Jack went for a couple of beers while Natalie sat at a table behind the lanes to wait for one to open. Groups of gals and groups of guys and mixed groups were roaring and hugging like it was New Year's

Eve.

Jack returned with two Hedricks just as the manager called their number. They started toward Lane 7, and a fellow behind them called out. "How about we double up? It'll be an hour before we can get a lane."

Jack and Natalie looked at each other and shrugged. Natalie felt giddy recalling their declaration of wanting to be with each other. It would show they were a couple. "Sure. Why not?" Natalie said.

Ted and Sarah joined Jack and Natalie on Lane 7, and they decided to challenge each other. Natalie loved it. Jack and her on the same team. They were all rusty and admitted they didn't give a hoot about bowling, but it was a great night out.

The guys weren't bad, and Sarah and Natalie kidded about bowling and archery in high school.

When Jack missed a split on his last frame, he came back to the table shaking his head. "I ought to get another chance. I closed my good eye."

Ted said, "How'd it happen?"

"Sliver of tungsten off a lathe, and my safety goggles sitting on the bench."

"Keeps you out of the war," Ted said.

Jack's said, "What about you?"

"I hit every check on the 4-F list: bad heart from rheumatic fever as a kid, bad eyes, flat feet. You name it." He shrugged. "Don't get me wrong, but I wish I had something like a patch over my eye instead of looking like I'm dodging the war."

"Okay," Sarah said. "You won the first game, and we won the second. Now it's the rubber match."

"Hey, you jerks going to fart around all night?" a thick-set Private in a rumpled uniform shouted at them. He was pushing his way through the people waiting for a lane. He had a girl on his arm, and the two of them were leaning into each other. From his loud, nasty tone and slurred speech, it was obvious he was drunk. Following him was another Private with a shriveled ear. He had what Natalie's mother would call a 'hussy' in tow. She had buck teeth, and her nose looked as though a lump of cookie dough had been slapped on her red-pitted face. A USO girl. Not that they were all ugly, but the USO was a magnet for girls who knew it was a sure bet for a date with guys desperate for female company. Or maybe she was one of those girls from Green Street. They were all drunk.

"One more game," Ted replied.

The loud-mouth dragged his girl to the bench. The other soldier and his girl followed. "We're shipping out and got no time for one more game," he slurred. "We got to win the war while you conchies and 4-Fs sit on your asses playing one more game." He grabbed Ted's jacket off the bench and threw it at Jack. "Take your crap and beat it."

Jack stepped in front of the Private. "We said one-more-game."

"And I said, beat it – or I'll punch out your other eye."

With a laugh like a hyena, the Private's girl doubled over as though it was the funniest thing she'd ever heard.

"Calm, down, *Private*," Jack said.

For a second, it seemed like the Private heard the voice of his Drill Sergeant. He straightened, and then glared at Jack. "Fuck you," he spat and took a wild swing at Jack.

Jack grabbed the soldier's forearm before it made contact and twisted his arm around. The Private's buddy lurched toward the two men, and Jack shoved the Private at him. Both men fell sprawling back onto the bench.

Natalie was shoved from behind, and when she

turned, the Private's girlfriend clawed at her face. Natalie tried to push her away, but her hands grasped Natalie's blouse, tearing off a button. Sarah grabbed the girlfriend by the shoulders and pulled her off Natalie. The other girl collapsed on the bench and was still laughing when she put her head between her legs and threw up.

Jack lifted the girl who'd attacked Natalie by her upper arms and plunked her down on the bench. The two Privates and their girlfriends glared at Jack.

One of the Privates snarled, "Fucking 4Fers and their pussies."

Jack took a menacing step toward him. "Get out."

The manager pushed his way through the crowd that had gathered. "Enough. It's over. You two, clear out," he said to the soldiers.

They staggered to their feet. One pulled back his fist as though he might punch Jack, but keeled back and put his hand on the scoring table to steady himself. He sneered at Jack and cocked his head toward his date. "Who wants to hang around with these losers?"

The two soldiers and their dates stumbled out. At the step, the girl who clawed Natalie shouted to the crowd. "And I'll bet their boyfriends are in the service."

Natalie was breathless. She put her hand on her stinging cheek.

Sarah said, "You're bleeding." She took a handkerchief from her purse and dabbed at Natalie's cheek. There was blood streaked on it. Natalie tried to hand it back. "Keep it," she said.

Jack put his arm around Natalie and drew her into him. "Are you alright?"

The crowd was staring at them. The reek of vomit made Natalie gag. She pushed herself further into Jack.

"Yes."

A kid with a bucket and a mop arrived. The manager said, "You want to continue after he cleans this up?"

Natalie shook her head. She didn't care what the others wanted to do. She wanted to get out of there.

They took their coats off the bench and headed through the crowd.

Sarah started to cry, "I'm sorry."

"There's nothing to be sorry about," Jack said.

Sobbing, Sarah said, "My fiancée is in the Navy. I shouldn't be here." She took a few steps toward the door.

Ted said, "I'll take you home." He turned to Jack and Natalie. "We're just friends. We work in the same office. It's not like that."

Jack and Natalie watched them leave. Jack said, "Would you like a cup of coffee, a drink?"

"It's not right," Natalie said.

"I'm sorry. Maybe this wasn't a good idea."

Jack placed his hand on Natalie's shoulder. She wanted to turn and kiss it. "No. That's not what I mean. It's not…" She didn't know what she meant. She grasped his hand. "Let's go."

Outside the building, people were still crowding to get in.

"Hey, Natalie."

Sweet Mother of God. Was she being punished for all her sins now, right here on earth? It was Genny. She and another girl bounded up to Natalie and Jack.

"Great night." She cracked her gum and gave Jack a flirty smile. "Hey, I know you. Jack Mooney. I see you around the shops." She turned to Natalie with a sly grin, "All the girls know Jack."

Natalie sighed. "It's Mahoney. Jack, this is Genny

LaFleur. We go back to the dark ages."

"Pleased to meet you," Jack said.

"Got to scoot," Genny said. "Only got a couple of hours before my shift starts."

Natalie said, "You're working a weekend night shift?"

"Yep. I'm stashing away my overtime for when this is over: nylons, steak, maybe a Chevy convertible. Toodles," she trilled and headed into the bowling alley.

Jack said, "The other day, I grabbed a guy a second before he fell into the working end of a reamer. Asleep on his feet. Party all night and show up to operate equipment that can kill you."

"It's not right."

Jack seemed uncertain. "Coffee? Something to eat?"

"I don't want to be near people." When Jack flinched, she said, "Other people."

"What do you want to do?"

Natalie took Jack's hand. "It's a beautiful evening. Let's walk home."

It was a little over two miles from downtown to Watevliet, but Natalie wished it were ten as they strolled hand and hand along Broadway. Neither of them said a word. She just wanted to walk and walk and walk holding his hand.

At the corner of 6th, they stopped. The air was crisp, and stars were visible in the clear sky. They stood silently, smiling at each other. It was as if neither wanted to speak.

Natalie pulled Jack into her, and they kissed. And again. And again.

Gently, Jack ran his calloused fingers over Natalie's cheek and she savored everything about his touch, even the sting from the scratch on her cheek. This was not good. She shouldn't want this. But she loved him.

***

With no word from Jack for two days, Natalie felt abandoned. She was desperate to see him, and she jumped every time the office door opened. The first inter-office mail was delivered, and there was a sealed envelope with nothing but her name written on it. She tore it open. 'Seacoast Cannon. 1:00 PM. Far end near the loading dock.' There was no signature.

Natalie left a message for Flo that she wouldn't meet her for lunch and ate her sandwich at her desk. With her new assignment from Mr. Vincent, it was easy for her to leave the office at odd times. It was 12:30, and she knew it would take her twenty minutes to get to the far end of the Seacoast Cannon Building.

At 12:35, Natalie picked up her clipboard. "Mr. Vincent's project. I'm not sure when I'll be back," she said to Agnes. Agnes shrugged, apparently not seeing the flush on Natalie's cheeks or hearing the lie in her voice.

Natalie walked with a studied purposefulness through the Liner Shop, making sure her clipboard and calculating appraisals of the machinery showed she was on an assignment. When she arrived in Seacoast Cannon, she lifted her chin, paused occasionally, and pretended to be examining a lathe. Looking as though satisfied with her inspection, she walked on shaky legs to the far end of the building. She was at the loading dock, but Jack wasn't there.

"Over here."

Jack stood at the doorway of a room and she stepped toward him. She was no more than a foot from him, searching his face.

Jack grasped Natalie's wrist and pulled her into a small storage room with floor to ceiling racks of broken parts

118

smelling of grease and dust. She maneuvered herself into the tight space where Jack stood grinning.

"Jack…" Before she could finish the unformed sentence, he pulled Natalie into him, took her face in his hands and kissed her.

They kissed urgently, grasping each other's shoulders and arms as though saving themselves from drowning.

"I…" Natalie started a sentence but didn't know what she wanted to say. Jack squeezed her to him before they finally pulled apart.

"I want you. I need you," Jack said. He gave her another kiss and said, "I'll get in touch" and dashed out.

"I, I," Natalie stammered as she watched him walk briskly along the end of the building toward his shop.

Natalie waited until her heart returned to a normal beat. She straightened her clothes, lifted her clipboard and left the room. Struggling not to rush, she walked along the reamers and presses, smiling and pretending to make important notes on her clipboard.

Natalie stopped in the Ladies' Room before returning to the office. There was a smudge of grease along her jaw. She wondered how many saw it as she made her way back. She scrubbed the smear from her face, double-checked her clothes for other tell-tale signs of what she'd done, and entered the office as though returning from an assignment.

Every morning, Natalie pounced on the first inter-office mail like a cat leaping at a mouse. Dropping everything on Agnes' desk except that one envelope with Jack's handwriting, she was positive her hands trembled as she tried not to tear it open as though it contained the Virgin's third secret of Fatima.

Tuesday. ' Supply room behind the time-card racks.'

Wednesday. 'Building SH. 10:30. At the end of the 75mm. breech ring pallets.'

Thursday. 'Field Artillery. 2:00. Vacant supervisor's office next to stairs.'

They were reckless.

Drawing surprising energy from her meetings with Jack, she threw herself into Mr. Vincent's assignments.

Now, Natalie and Gene Farley were crammed in the doorway of his small office in the Mortar Assembly Shop.

"Thanks," Gene said. He started to reach out toward Natalie, then hesitated.

It was always awkward when she was on a special assignment. Natalie grabbed Gene's hand, and they shook. "You're welcome, Gene."

"I got to tell you, I wasn't happy when Mr. Vincent told me you were coming over to help me out."

"An unwelcome visit from the trouble-maker."

"I never said that." Gene laughed. "Maybe once."

"If my ears turned red every time someone called me that, I'd look like one of Santa's elves."

"We like to think we know what we're doing."

"You do. I'm just a fresh set of eyes. You guys haven't got time to step back and review the way you're working."

Gene said, "We're under such pressure to produce more mortars, we just try to do it faster. No time to figure out if we can do it better."

"All you needed was a little tweak."

"Well, at least I'm off Mr. Vincent's...."

"Shit list?"

Gene shook his head. "You gals. I don't know how we're going to handle you when this is over."

"You're not," Natalie said. "Got to run." She stepped out of the office and glanced back at the mortar assembly line. A little tweak? More like radical surgery. Not one of these assembly crews had time to re-reassess how they were working. When she was on her way to one assignment for Mr. Vincent and walking through another shop, she had to tell herself to keep her eyes straight ahead. But she couldn't. Too many of these assembly lines were laid out in World War I.

Natalie would put a bug in Mr. Vincent's ear, and she was off to another trouble-shooting assignment. She could see work for her if this war lasted for ten more years. But it wouldn't. Already, Natalie had heard workers talking about what's going to happen to them when it was over. She knew she'd never get a real job on the lines, but at least now she was down here in the shops most of the time.

Natalie was at the north end of Building B. The shortest route back to her office to write up her report was through the shrink pits to her left. Jack's area was on the other side of the Liner Shop. They'd been stealing meetings around the Arsenal as often as possible, but she still longed to see his face every day. She re-tied her bandanna and started walking to the end of the Liner Shop.

Inside Shop 35, Natalie leaned against a wall trying to make herself invisible. She watched a crew lock a 175 mm gun tube into a rifling machine. If she stayed long enough, she was sure she would see something that could be improved.

A foreman spotted her. "Hey, girl. Something I can do for you?"

His voice was a challenge not a question. "No thank

you," Natalie said and felt guilty as she took a step toward the Liner Shop.

He drilled her with a black glare. "You're Vincent's girl."

It was a nasty snarl, and Natalie flinched before turning around. "Yes?"

"You girls better enjoy lording it over us while you can. When this is over, you'll be back in the kitchen where you belong, listening to your husbands tell you what's what."

She was dumbstruck by the venom in his voice. The foreman's words chased her along the wall leading to the Liner Shop.

When she reached the end of Jack's area, she was torn about what to do. It was as though a miniature Mr. Vincent was sitting on her shoulder whispering *'discretion'* in her ear. Natalie decided to take the stairs and go directly to her office.

"Hey, Natalie." Jack was striding toward her. When he reached the bottom of the stairs, he said, "You're all the way over in Shop 35, and you don't stop in to say hello?"

"I thought you might be too busy." She was on the fourth step, a few feet above Jack. She'd never seen him from this angle. Now she was overwhelmed with the desire to see him from every angle. She wanted to stand right there for as long as she could.

Jack said, "If I took two minutes to say hello, would you report me to Mr. Vincent?"

"Is my reputation that bad?"

"Terrible. The avenging angel. The black widow." Jack took a step up and reached for here. She flinched. Jack's fingers grasped the goggles dangling around her neck. "I'm glad you decided to keep these."

"Do you want them back?" she teased.

"No. I want you to wear them as a reminder of me wherever you are. Especially when you're working with all the other men on your special assignments." He looked over his shoulder. "I want to see more of you." He took another step up, and kissed her.

"I do too," Natalie said as Jack backed down the steps and strode toward his assembly line. She remained rooted to the stair. Natalie snatched air into her lungs when realized she'd been holding her breath.

Friday at 5:00, Natalie sat at her desk waiting for Agnes and Mr. Holt to leave. She tried to make sense of what had happened. They hadn't exchanged more than a handful of words: first Jack, then her finally saying it aloud. "I love you." What happens now?

Natalie wasn't surprised when the door opened without a knock. Jack entered and closed the door behind him. Natalie stood and they embraced and kissed. They jumped apart as the door opened. Mr. Holt stood in the doorway. He seemed embarrassed.

"Forgot my sweater," he stammered. He walked around Jack and Natalie as though they might explode.

Mr. Holt came out of his office holding his sweater out as though he needed to explain his interruption. "Cold snap this weekend," she said as he rushed out.

As soon as the door closed, Jack took Natalie in his arms. He laid his hand gently on Natalie's cheek. "I wanted to see you this weekend, but my group just pulled overtime. I'm here all day Saturday and Sunday."

"Oh." Every secret meeting with Jack was a thrill she didn't want to end.

"I hoped we could get together and find somewhere private."

She'd gone way over the line meeting him in secret places around the Arsenal. Dangerous as their meetings had been, she knew that finding somewhere private meant crossing a line she could never step back over.

15

Latest War Casualties From New York, New Jersey and
Connecticut as Reported by Army

Emotionally exhausted from her secret meetings with Jack, Natalie trudged home along Broadway. Today, even the aromas wafting out of Schuyler Bakery didn't give her their usual boost for the last four blocks. She started to cross the street but stepped back as a dark olive-green sedan with government plates passed in front of her. Two men in uniform, staring straight ahead, sat in the front seat. The car slowly turned up 7th Street. Natalie stared at it for a second before she realized what was happening. "Oh, no," she said aloud, and a woman coming out of the bakery turned toward her with a surprised look on her face.

Natalie crossed and began walking faster up 7th. Jeff Wilcox? The auto hesitated at the corner and then made a left on 5th. Her mind raced but she couldn't come up with any names on 5th. But when the sedan turned toward Manor Place, she froze for a moment, then began to trot in the wake of the car. She tripped off the curb into the street and clutched her dress front as the car slowed. "Oh, no," Natalie cried as the car slowed to a crawl. The soldier in the rider's seat gestured with his right hand, and they drove by her house before coming to a stop three doors down the street.

Natalie stood rooted in the middle of the street. The car remained at the curb for several moments before the doors opened. The two men stepped out and smoothed down the fronts of their uniforms before slowly walking side by side up the sidewalk.

Before they were halfway up the sidewalk, the front door of number 27 flew open, and a scream ripped through the air. Mrs. Morelli stumbled down the steps. "You go back," she howled at the two men. "No. Not here. Go away," she cried and fell to her knees on the sidewalk, raking her hands through her hair as though wanting to yank off her scalp. Mr. Morelli stood at the open door staring at the two men who had stopped in front of his wife now crumbled into a sobbing ball, her right hand pounding the ground.

Mr. Morelli's hand covered his mouth. He staggered down the three steps to where his wife had fallen. He leaned down and said something to her. She shook her head and shouted something Natalie couldn't make out. Mr. Morelli put his hand under his wife's arm and raised her to her feet. Angela and Tony Morelli clung to each other, their bodies heaving. One of the men stepped forward and said something to them. After a few moments, the Morellis, still wrapped in each other's arms, slowly made their way toward the house. The two men, ramrod straight, followed them.

Oh, Sweet Mary and Jesus. Chuck. He's dead. Joyce. She's in Syracuse. Natalie pictured two men in uniform arriving at Joyce's apartment. She glanced at her watch. She'll be home from school. The Morelli's door closed, and Natalie tried to picture this scene in Syracuse. What will Joyce do? Natalie felt a gentle tap on her shoulder. She turned, and their next door neighbor, Mr. Evans, softly said, "Natalie, it's terrible, but you should get out of the street." His car was behind him. "Yes. Thank you. I'm sorry." He took Natalie's hand and led her to the sidewalk.

Natalie turned toward her house. Her mother and father were standing on the top step staring toward the Morelli's house. Other neighbors stood on their front steps.

Women weeping. Children clinging to their mother's skirts. Men with their hands on their wives' shoulders. She didn't know what to do. Her high school best friend's husband. Joyce teaching third grade in East Syracuse. Natalie stared at her house and the blue flag in the front window for Bill, and her soul sagged.

***

Natalie wished it was a dream, but it wasn't. Memories of her and Jack at the basketball game, walking home after the movies, bowling, and their frantic secret meetings around the Arsenal had been playing in her head like a speeded-up film. She got out of bed, walked to the front window and stared across the street at the Morelli's house. It was two o'clock in the morning but lights were still on. Chuck's brother had driven to Syracuse to bring Joyce home, and Natalie only had a few moments to hold Joyce in her arms and cry as Chuck's and Joyce's parents and other relatives sobbed and hugged each other in the Morelli's crowded living room.

She couldn't shake away the idea that what she'd done was somehow connected to Chuck's death. It didn't make sense, but what did?

Natalie turned from the window. Even in the dark room, she felt Bill's eyes on her. She'd turned over his picture before going out with Jack. Upright again, Bill gazed at her, not angry, puzzled, maybe wondering why Natalie had betrayed him. Joyce's life was ruined. She was ruining her life, and Bill was in mortal danger.

***

Sunday, Mrs. Morelli refused to go to Mass after telling Joyce and her husband that she hated God for what He let happen to her son.

On Monday evening at Parker Brothers Funeral

127

Home, Natalie sat four rows behind Joyce, Mr. and Mrs. Morelli and Chuck's brother and sister. Banks of flower arrangements covered the end and sides of the room. Instead of a casket, a framed photograph of Chuck in his uniform sat on a lectern.

It was ten o'clock and there was still a line snaking in from the adjoining parlor. Father Eagan whispered to Mrs. Morelli. The priest stepped forward and announced that he would lead the Rosary.

"The first Sorrowful Mystery. Our Father who art..."

Natalie scrabbled in the bottom of her purse for her rosary. Every chair was filled. Men and women were standing four deep at the back of the parlor. Others lined the walls. She heard people in the adjoining room intoning the prayer.

Out of the corner of her eye, Natalie picked out two other families who had sons in the service. Chuck was the third serviceman from Watervliet to be killed in action this month. She didn't know the others well, but she stopped in for a few minutes at their wakes. It was the right thing to do, but she couldn't help feeling that somehow there was a quota on how many men from their town would die in the war. It was a shameful thought but she'd already heard of many families' special prayers, charms, and strange behaviors. Mr. Grady refused to move his son Tom's Plymouth from the exact spot where it was the day he left for the Navy and washed it every single day, even in the rain and snow. Their lives were fragile.

No one thought that Chuck Morelli would need a special charm. He and Joyce were charmed already.

"Hail Mary, full of grace..."

Joyce Brewster, the prettiest and smartest girl in town, and Chuck Morelli, star athlete and King of the Prom:

steadies since their junior year. Everyone in town agreed those two would set the world on fire.

Chuck won a football scholarship to Syracuse, and Joyce enrolled in Albany Normal School. Natalie remembered how excited Joyce was when they got engaged after each finished their first year. Natalie recalled ohhing and ahhing over Joyce's diamond ring. They were married when Joyce finished the two year course and moved into the university's student housing. Joyce got a job teaching third grade in East Syracuse.

"The second Sorrowful Mystery. The Scourging at the Pillar. Hail Mary..."

Chuck graduated in May, 1942 and was immediately drafted.

"The third Sorrowful Mystery. The Crowning with Thorns. Hail Mary full of grace..."

And killed in action on Luzon in the Philippines last week.

Why was this young man who'd led a charmed life – who had a charmed life ahead of him – dead? No one would think that Bill Costello was charmed. Chuck was dead. She was here. Bill will come home.

***

Joyce walked through the funeral like a zombie. Mrs. Morelli fainted after wailing that she needed to see her son one last time. The chaplain sent by the Army assured the Morellis that Chuck would be given a funeral with full military honors and buried in one of the cemeteries being set up by the Army. Yet, it seemed unfinished: no following the hearse to the cemetery after the funeral, no casket over an open grave, none of the final rites that marked the finality of death.

In the days after the funeral, Joyce would cross the

street to Natalie's house, and sit on the sofa with Natalie. Mom would bring in coffee, and the two women would sit and talk quietly.

"I'm ashamed of myself," Joyce said. "I can't help wondering what my life will be like now."

Natalie said, "Don't be. That's natural," she said although she had no idea what was natural.

"Chuck hasn't been dead a week, and I'm worried about me." Joyce put her hand on Natalie's arm. "I prayed for Bill – and you."

"Thank you." She needed prayers, Natalie thought. But God decided that no matter how many prayers were said for Chuck, God let him die and she hoped Bill was still okay. Would praying for Bill make any difference?

"I was remembering the times we double-dated." Joyce said. "We were in Verdile's after a movie, and you accused Bill of having a huge crush on Barbara Stanwyck. And he claimed you were probably imagining Cary Grant in your arms every time he kissed you." She laughed. "And right in the middle of the restaurant he pulled you out of your chair and gave you a huge hug and a dozen kisses. Some of the folks at the next tables applauded."

Natalie smiled but felt a stab in her heart as the memory of Jack, not Bill, kissing her shot in her head. "We had some great times together." They were great together – before they got married. She couldn't remember an argument more serious than whether they'd go to a dance at the Henrich Hudson Hotel ballroom in Troy or meet friends at the South End Tavern for an evening of cheap beer and laughter. Bill was a nice guy. She needed to put this foolishness with Jack behind her. She'd allowed the ragged start to her marriage cloud her thinking. She was going to look forward to re-starting a good life with Bill when he returns.

On Thursday, Joyce came to the house, and told Natalie her principal had called and wanted to know her plans. Joyce told Natalie she was going back to East Syracuse. Chuck's brother and sister were here for his parents, and she couldn't bear the thought of simply sitting in his parents' house with nothing to do but mourn Chuck. She urged Natalie to go to work, and while Natalie made a small protest, she was relieved. Her head had turned to mush with too much time to think, not that she'd come up with a clear plan for her life ahead.

***

Stinging sheets of icy wet snow strafed up and down Broadway as Natalie slogged toward the Arsenal. She turned her face into the wind hoping to wash away the cloying stench of gladiolas and incense that seemed to cling to her even after a week.

Inside the office, Natalie saw that Agnes had taken care of the backlog. She was a fussbudget, but efficient and that's what Natalie needed now that she was spending more time on the shop floors on Mr. Vincent's special assignments.

At precisely twelve, Agnes gathered her purse and left for lunch. Mr. Holt came out of his office, asked once again if she was alright, and went to lunch. Natalie didn't see Jack at Chuck's wake or at the funeral, and she was glad. Maybe he was in the crowd at Parker Brothers or at the back of the church, but she didn't want to see him there. And now she was still unsure if she wanted to see him at all.

A few minutes after twelve, Jack entered the office and pulled Agnes' chair up to Natalie's desk. After several seconds of tense silence, Jack said, "Are you alright?"

A bolt of anger shot through Natalie. She wanted to

shout, *I'm not alright.* Chuck Morelli isn't alright. Joyce isn't alright. Mr. and Mrs. Morelli – none of them will ever be alright. She was exhausted. Her brain was frazzled. For the past week she wanted to see Jack – and not see Jack. Now he was here, and she didn't know what she wanted.

"It's a terrible thing," Jack said.

"Yes."

"Do you still want to see me – outside?"

Even though she'd chewed over them for the past several days, she still didn't know what her choices were. She should bury herself in Mr. Vincent's assignments and pray for Bill – and at least try to imagine a life ahead with him. "I don't know."

Jack seemed hesitant. "Do you need some time to yourself?"

She didn't want to be by herself, but she said, "Yes, I need to think."

Jack stood and Natalie didn't know whether or not she wanted him to kiss her. "Good bye."

Jack scanned Natalie's face. "Take as much time as you need. Let me know when – if – you want to see me."

***

For the rest of the week Natalie threw herself into Mr. Vincent's assignments, and she didn't get in touch with Jack. On the following Monday, she was walking through Jack's shop with another manager on their way to check on a parts shortage and bumped into him. She thought his face was searching hers for an answer before she hurried away, still befuddled by a roil of guilt and helplessness.

The first week without meeting Jack stretched into the second. Was she testing herself to see if this self-enforced pulling away would tell her something important about her and Jack?

In her bedroom Natalie stared at the photograph of Bill in his uniform trying to remember the good times they had – before they married. It had been two and a half years since he'd gone overseas. When she imagined Bill coming home, she recalled reading about arranged marriages in traditional societies where the bride meets the groom for the first time on her wedding day. She hoped they could put those awful first months behind them and start fresh.

Back at the Arsenal, when Natalie was an assignment, she ran Jack ran again. He acted as though she was a girl from a blind date he hadn't called back. She didn't know what message her face sent as they exchanged curt hellos and good-byes. But Natalie still woke every morning with her head full of him.

***

On Tuesday of the third week of her self-imposed exile from Jack, Flo sat next to Natalie at the lunch table. They chatted about what was going on at the Arsenal, and she shared a few tidbits from Bob's v-mails. Flo seemed to be deciding whether to say something. Finally she said, "I saw Jack coming out of the Palace Monday night."

From the tone of Flo's voice, Natalie suspected where this was going and couldn't decide whether she wanted to hear it. But she nodded for Flo to continue.

"With another woman."

"*Another woman?*" Natalie said. Was she angry because Jack was seeing another woman instead of waiting to see if she would come back to him? What did she expect? She sighed, but as she shrugged as if to tell Flo she could deal with it, there was something else in Flo's eyes. "Oh, no. It can't be."

"I'm afraid so. Genny LaFleur."

"Oh, for goodness sake." They held their gazes for a

few seconds, then surprised themselves as they burst into laughter. The women at the other end of the table turned to see what caused the uproar.

Flo said, "None other."

Natalie didn't know if she wanted to strangle Genny or Jack or both of them. "How many hundreds of single women are working here?"

Flo said, "Does she hate you that much?"

"Who knows?" Natalie said. She didn't ask, 'Does he?'

"Well, it's probably for the better," Flo said.

Natalie tried to give Flo a mean glare but she couldn't hold it. "Thank you Mother Superior. I really needed that." Still, her heart felt crushed.

16

*Secret Service is Set Up by OPA in Fight on
Counterfeiting Coupons*

Mario heard pounding on the bathroom door.

"Mario. Mario. Open up."

How the heck did he end up on the floor?

"*Mario*. Can you hear me?"

Mario tried to answer, but his voice was weak. "Tess.
I'm alright," he barely croaked.

"Please, Mario," Tess cried.

"Okay. Just a second." Mario grabbed the back of the
toilet and hoisted himself up. What a mess. He had shit on
his leg. He reached for the toilet paper. "A second, Tess." He
wiped away as much as he could before flopping back on
the seat. He didn't want her to see him like this, but he felt
light-headed. He leaned forward and unlocked the door.

"Oh my God. What happened?"

"I don't know. I think I might have passed out for a
second. I'm alright." He tried to lift himself from the seat.
Even after twenty-five years together, he was embarrassed
to have her see him like this, but he felt as weak as a baby.

Tess put her hand on Mario's forehead. "You're not
alright."

He tried to stand. He reached for more toilet paper
and wiped, doing his best to hide the paper from her. But it
felt wet. Blood. His head felt like it was floating away. Tess
grabbed Mario's wrist.

"You're bleeding."

He stuffed the toilet paper between his legs. He was

afraid to look down.

Tess put her hands under Mario's armpits and lifted him a little off the seat. "Mario, you got blood coming out."

He flopped back. "Give me a minute. I'll be alright."

"You stay right there. Don't try to get up." She turned. "Leave the door open."

"Where are you going?"

"I'm calling Dr. Townsend."

"Tess, I just need a few minutes."

"Don't move."

As soon as Tess left, Mario wiped and saw more blood-red shit. He flushed. He didn't know how much Tess saw before, but she'd have a bird if she saw this. At least Natalie and Nick were out of the house.

Five minutes later, Tess returned. "Dr. Townsend can fit you in at ten."

"I got to go to work."

"You're not going anywhere except to Dr. Townsend's after you lay down."

Mario couldn't pretend he was going to be okay. "Call Stan. Tell him – I don't know – tell him you had a spell or something and I'll be in after lunch."

"I'll call Stan and let him know you won't be in. We'll see what Dr. Townsend says."

Twenty minutes later, Tess had helped Mario clean up. He felt a little better. "Did you call Stan?"

"No answer."

"You dialed the right number?"

Tess snapped, "I know how to use the telephone. I called back two times. No answer."

By nine-thirty, Mario felt better, still weak, but better. He and Tess took the crowded bus to Dr. Townsend's office even though it was only ten blocks away. Tess had a hold of

Mario like he was an old man. Mario tried to act like he wasn't, but he felt eighty. And he couldn't understand why Stan wasn't answering the phone. He had Tess call twice more and still no answer.

Dr. Townsend checked Mario out. Tess insisted on coming into the examining room with him. Mario said he had a little blood in my – what do they call it? – stool.

Tess chimed in. "A lot. And he passed out," she added.

When the doctor asked Mario about other symptoms, Mario told him he had a little heartburn from time to time. He thought about making a crack about Tess's cooking, but she didn't look in the mood for jokes. And he didn't want to worry her if he told Doc Townsend he had a corkscrew twisting in his gut most days. The doctor asked Mario if he was under any stress. "What, like there's not a war on?"

Finally Doc Townsend was done poking and prodding, which hurt more than Mario let on and told Mario to cut down on red meat, especially liver and other blood rich cuts. At that Tess and Mario couldn't help laughing. Doc Townsend didn't seem to think that was funny, and Mario wondered if the doc got hold of some of Stan's counterfeit ration stamps.

Tess insisted they take the bus home, and she wanted Mario to take off the rest of the day. He was too tired to argue. Back at the house, Mario called the shop, then Stan's house. No answer. He tried a couple more times before he finally agreed to take a nap. He conked out until he heard the phone ring. He looked at the alarm clock. Holy Toledo: 4:30.

Tess came into the bedroom. Her face was a crease of worries. Something wrong with Nicky or Natalie? Mario didn't like telephone calls. Most were bad news.

"Stan's son Jimmie is on the telephone. He's not making much sense. I think you have to talk to him."

Maybe something's happened to Stan, Mario thought. He made his way downstairs. Tess walked next to him like he was going to topple over. "I'm okay, Tess. A nap was just what I needed." She didn't look convinced.

Downstairs in the front hall, Mario picked up the phone. He listened to Jimmie blurt out that his father called him and told him to call Mario. "What did he want you to say to me?" Like always, Jimmie was confused. He mumbled for a bit, then said his father wanted Mario to come and get him. "Where is he?" In the second before Jimmie answered, Mario wanted him to say, 'the hospital,' or 'at a garage because his car broke down,' or anywhere besides what Mario feared he was going to say.

A bleeding ulcer saved my bacon, Mario thought. Maybe. When he finally sorted out what Jimmie was supposed to tell him, he and Tess and Jimmie made their way to the federal court house in downtown Albany. Stan wasn't answering the phone because two FBI agents arrested him when he opened the shop.

On the bus, Jimmie tried to give Mario the wad of fifties he brought with him. He was telling Mario, and half the others on the bus, about the stash behind the coal bin Stan told him about, but Mario pretended he didn't hear him. Jimmie will get off because he's simple. Mario couldn't come up with a reason why he'd get off.

Mario stood outside the courthouse like it was the entrance to the Albany Home for the Incurables – no exit. Was the FBI after him too? He wondered if he should grab some of the cash Jimmie was holding and give it to Tess to bail him out. But he didn't want to touch it. He didn't even want to touch Jimmie. Crazy, he knew.

It was awful, but they finally bailed out Stan and got him home. Mario had seen better looking corpses at Parker Brothers. Mario wanted to grill Stan about everything that had happened, but it was already seven o'clock and they were all dead on their feet.

Mario didn't sleep that night, and he didn't think Tess did either. They gave Natalie a quick recap, and Mario knew she understood how serious this was. There was no use sugar-coating it, because there it was in the *TU* the next morning. Stan's only piece of good luck was the front page story about the bombing raid on Hamburg pushed, 'Local Printer Arrested for Forging Ration Coupons.' to page 4. Mario was positive he read his name in 12 point bold in the article. Maybe he wanted to see it, but it wasn't there – only Stan's.

***

The following morning Mario didn't know what to do. He tried calling Stan's house, but the line was constantly busy. Off the hook, or angry citizens threatening to lynch him? Mario had the key, but he didn't think it was a good idea to go to the shop. Finally, Mario and Tess took the bus to Stan's house. At this point Mario had to argue with Tess to be allowed to take a pee by himself.

Mario felt every eye in the neighborhood burning into his back as they made their way up the sidewalk to Stan's house. Stan peeked out the closed curtain, then let them in.

Mario had to pretend he was sorry and concerned for Stan, but 'What about me?' was in every question Mario asked and behind every explanation that tumbled out of Stan. The pressure of paying his wife's bills at the sanitarium, who was going to take care of Jimmie, the cousin who had a fool-proof scheme for a one-time print run of gas coupons, and then hardball pressure to keep doing it or someone tips off the feds. Mario followed along faking sympathy but listened to Stan's jumble of excuses and worried for what they meant for him.

Finally, Stan convinced Mario that the FBI agents only wanted him. They asked who else was involved, but Stan claimed he told them Mario wasn't in on it. Stan said Mario was too dense, not skilled enough. He'd kept Mario out of it because he was afraid he'd screw it up or inadvertently spill the beans. Mario guessed he should be grateful, but he wondered how much of what Stan said to believe.

Mario still didn't believe he was out of the woods. Was he going to be arrested despite Stan's claim that he didn't know what Stan was doing? Stan said his lawyer figured the feds had bigger fish to fry than Mario. He guessed he should be happy he was a little fish, but now he didn't have a job. Stan's lawyer said he was would likely get eighteen months in jail and a fine that would wipe out his savings and then some. Mario was on his own until the FBI needed some little fish to fry.

***

Four days later, Mario sat at the kitchen table scanning the want ads, still waiting for the knock on the door or the phone to ring. Lucky that with so little they could buy, they had enough put away to pay the bills for a while. But Mario didn't know how long before he could get another job, and he couldn't stop thinking about the years he didn't have steady work. He was hoping to splurge a little on Christmas presents, but now he didn't know what he could afford.

Natalie came home from the Arsenal. She leaned over Mario's shoulder, gave him a kiss on his cheek and sat across from him. "How are you doing?"

"Okay." Mario pointed toward the paper. "Lots of openings."

"Did you see anything you'd like?"

"Maybe a few possibilities."

Natalie said, "Nothing for printers?"

"I can do other jobs."

"Your shop was doing well, wasn't it?" Natalie said.

"Stan's shop. Pretty good. We were turning away some jobs, and Stan was hoping to hire a printer's helper. But the job market's so tight, we couldn't get anybody at what he could pay."

"Who's going to take up the slack?"

"What do you mean?"

Natalie said, "If you and Stan were doing pretty good, who's doing the jobs you did?"

Mario hadn't given it a lot of thought. "Maybe McGraw down on Pearl. Crandell over in South Troy."

"You think your customers are going to them?"

"They can do the jobs, but the problem is delivery. Most of our accounts were here in Watervliet, some up in Cohoes and over in west Albany: grocery stores, small shops, hardware, restaurants. None of them can waste gas ration stamps picking up flyers, posters, and menus. We walked most of the jobs to the customers or took the bus to a few."

"And those other printers aren't going to drive around to your customers either."

"I guess they'll have to do without, until they figure out something else."

"Dad, I was thinking."

Mario laughed. "You're always thinking. Should have sent you to college, maybe normal school like Joyce."

"Yeah, like Joyce," she said. "Like I said, I was thinking about what you could do now." She paused. "What about taking over the shop?"

Mario wasn't sure he heard her right. "Stan's shop? The Feds closed it down. It's *kaput*. They're not going to let me reopen it, and no one's going to do business with a forger."

"Not all those shops who take forged coupons like they don't know they're fake?"

"They can pretend to be holier than us, but Stan's going to jail."

"Right," Natalie said. "And you're not." She paused for several seconds. "What would you think about opening your own shop?"

"I take back what I said about you being so smart. I can't do that. Where would I get the presses, all the other equipment? None of that's available, and how would I pay for it if it magically appeared?" But as Mario finished he understood what Natalie was driving at. She was smart, and he was slow on the uptake. Still, he didn't have the money.

"I've been running this over and over in my head," Natalie said. "Yesterday, they were digging up a broken water main on Broadway, and I had to detour up First and back around. Remember Zemke's Hardware?"

"Sure, they were one of our customers until they closed up. He had a stroke. His son's in the Navy. Three, maybe four years ago."

"Right. The shop is empty. It has a For Sale sign on it, but I bet you could rent it for beans."

"Natalie, that's crazy. You're figuring I buy what's in Stan's shop?"

"All of it. Lock, stock, and barrel," she said. "The whole package, just like when they began putting all the gun parts together."

"Okay, Miss Arsenal, put the money together." As soon as the words are out of Mario's mouth, he wished he could grab them back. "No. Absolutely, not. No way. That's yours and Bill's."

"Why not?" Natalie leaned across the table at Mario. "I was putting some figures together." She pulled a pencil and notepad from her purse and moved her chair around so she was sitting next to Mario. "Here's a rough plan," she said and pushed the pad toward him. "This is what I have in the bank," she said pointing to a figure at the top of the page. "That's the total I can contribute to a down payment." She sat back. "You want to tell me what you can put down?"

They kid me – the silent *patrone* – keeping the family finances secret, he thought. Maybe he was old fashioned, but he did it to not scare Tess and the kids, especially the years when he was mostly out of work. Mario would give Tess what he could for groceries, maybe a nickel to Natalie and Nicky when he could, not letting them know there wasn't another nickel left. There were other figures under Natalie's total. He knew what he had – him and Tess – and even added to Natalie's total, it wasn't enough to buy the equipment and supplies in Stan's shop. "I got some, but the two of us, we don't have enough – even if I agreed to go along with this – which I'm not."

"Play along with me for a minute." Natalie pointed to the numbers under the first total. "This is my weekly salary. And this is my monthly wife's allotment from the Army."

"That's part of Bill's pay."

"It's mine," she said quickly. "That's what I can bring in every month."

"We don't have to eat or pay the electric?"

"We're not spending what we make. There's nothing to buy."

"Not now," Mario said thinking about Natalie's savings and Bill's allotment. "The war isn't going to go on forever. When it's over, you're going to want to buy a house, maybe a car."

"Now is now," Natalie said sharply. But as soon as she said it, a thought about the future crept in. The war will end, and what will she do? Maybe the print shop will figure in her future.

"I'm not agreeing to this one bit. I know what I'm making – was making – at the shop. I might have barely enough brains to guess what I could make on my own. And I'd have to have at least a printer's helper, and if it's my shop I got to pay the electric, the supplies."

"Dad, I'm not sure it will work either, but why don't we at least lay out what we have to put down and what we have coming in each month?"

Mario knew she was smart and eager, so he hated to pop her balloon. "We sit here and put these numbers together, there's still something big missing." From the crinkle on Natalie's forehead, he was glad he had her stumped, at least for a minute.

"What?" she finally asked.

"Stan."

Natalie made circles on the pad with her pencil. "Stan doesn't have much choice, does he?"

Mario was surprised by her cold, hard tone. "He's got a world of trouble."

"Stan is going to jail," she said. "He's got bills for his wife at the TB place. He doesn't have any idea what's going to happen to Jimmie. Stan doesn't have a lot of bargaining power." Natalie waved toward the papers on the table. "Dad, Stan takes what we offer, or he gets nothing."

Did he raise this hard case? Is she learning this at the Arsenal? Is this what happens when these girls go to work? "Stan was good to me. You don't remember, but we were in

144

bad shape when he gave me the job."

"I do remember," Natalie said. "And you went to work every day and did a good job – I'll bet a better job than what your pay was." She paused. "And Stan forged ration coupons and put you out of that job." There was a catch in her voice. "And dragged us in the mud along with him."

He'd seen it in the neighbors' eyes. Tess didn't say much, but from the way she acted when she returned from the market, she heard it there too. He was sure Natalie heard about it at the Arsenal. Mario didn't know what Nicky heard. "Stan had a lot on his mind. I don't know what made him do it."

"Right now, I don't care what made Stan do it. I care about you and Mom and Nicky – our family. *Damn it,* we have to take care of ourselves."

Mario didn't think it's a good time to remind her to watch her language. God, how he wished this war was over and Natalie was out of the Arsenal. Two years now, and he hardly recognized the girl who went out the door and into that job. She was as hard as a gun barrel. She was right. "Let's see what we've got. I'm not saying I'm agreeing, but we can see how it would play out."

After supper, Mario told Tess that he and Natalie had to go over some money stuff. He didn't need Tess in on this. She wouldn't understand, and she'd flutter and fuss and think of a dozen things that wouldn't help them.

Natalie and Mario were at the kitchen table with a couple of larger pads of paper, pencils, and their bank books. They went back over the figures Natalie laid out earlier. She had them right on the money. Mario didn't know how she did it. He could tell she was leading him along, making it like some of the ideas were his, not ones she'd planted in his head as they talked. They finally came to the end. "What do

145

we do?" Mario asked.

Pointing to a figure on the big pad, Natalie said, "This is the total we have for a down payment." After Mario glanced at the figures, she said, "And this is what we offer."

Mario said, "It's less than what we have. That's all?"

"We need to have a reserve. You don't know what all the costs might be to re-fit Zemke's for a print shop."

"Okay," Mario said as if he had a choice.

Tapping her pencil point on another total, Natalie said, "And this is what we offer to pay Stan, or his wife's doctors, every month." She must have seen the question in Mario's. "I don't want us eating day-old bread and thin soup for the rest of the war. We need to take care of our family."

Mario didn't like the way she said, 'We need' which made it clear that she was in charge. Mario was worn down. "Okay," was all he could manage.

"Stan may not like it, but I doubt if he's getting offers from anyone else," She paused. "Dad, I'm sorry I didn't bring this up earlier. If Stan has any reservations about the deal or what we're proposing, what would you think about keeping on Jimmie as a printer's helper? And Nick can quit the part-time jobs he's doing after school and come in when he can."

"Jimmie? He has a hard time tying his shoes," Mario said. "He cleans up and carries stuff in and out." Then Mario thought that maybe, just maybe, he could teach the kid enough to give him a hand. Mario wouldn't have enough at the start to hire a full-time guy even if he could find one. Besides, it would make Mario feel better about sticking this deal to Stan, even if he was a criminal that cost Mario his job. "Maybe that could work."

Natalie leaned back in the chair. "It will work, Dad. We'll make it work."

17

New Plants Approved to Provide Mortars for Infantry: Consumer Goods Delayed.

It was snowing Tuesday morning. A sudden gust of cold air swept down Broadway, and Natalie pulled the collar of her coat tighter around her neck. She was exhausted from working through all that had to be done to rent Zemke's, arrange the purchase of Stan's equipment, and set up the new shop. With Dad still slowed by his bleeding ulcer, Natalie was pleasantly surprised by how Nick dove in to help her. They'd all tried to make Christmas less dreary. Mom proudly roasted two plump chickens she'd been hoarding in the freezer, and they exchanged simple gifts. New Year's Eve was just another day except for the glasses of Dad's last year's wine they sipped early in the evening. On New Year's Day, Natalie went to Mass and joined in the prayer for those in the service, and Natalie wondered if God would forgive the sins she'd committed. The newscasts reported a German counter-offensive in Belgium and northern France they were calling the Battle of the Bulge, and she hoped Bill was safe. She hadn't received a v-mail from him in weeks.

Natalie was a block away from the Arsenal when she stopped and stared toward the gate to the Heavy Artillery building. Something wasn't right. What was it? Then it hit her. Everyone was walking in the gate. Where were the night shift workers who ought to be streaming out by now?

Inside Building G, Natalie punched in and waved at one of the foremen she'd worked with. He looked harried, and his face was grease-stained. "Emil, what's going on in Heavy Artillery?"

"Two one fifty-five rifling machines broke down in Shop 35. The first one froze up around three this morning. The second one crashed an hour later."

"Holy Smokes" Natalie's mind ran through her shipping orders. "That's two out of four."

"Don't stand in front of any fans, doll, 'cause it's hittin' big time." Emil pulled his goggles up over his raccoon eyes. "I got to run." He sloped off toward Heavy with a cocksure bow-legged gait.

When Natalie got to her office, there was a piece of paper in the middle of her desk with one message scrawled in large letters: 'Mr. Vincent's office. ASAP!'

She walked into the executive reception area and was nearly run over by General Gillespie, trailed by a Major and a Second Lieutenant, marching out of Mr. Vincent's office. The Arsenal Commander stabbed her with a sharp 'who the hell are you?' glare and she almost brought her hand up in a salute. Mr. Vincent's secretary was standing at attention behind her desk. She cocked her head toward the office door. "He wants you in the meeting," she said in a tone that implied Mr. Vincent had suffered another bout of temporary insanity.

Outside Mr. Vincent's office Jack was among the men milling around, tense with purpose. Jack and Natalie caught each other's eyes. Did he smile? She couldn't read his face. Mr. Vincent's secretary announced that the meeting would commence in five minutes. Jack and Natalie glanced at each other again. After a few seconds, he approached her.

"This one takes the cake," Jack said.

"I guess." Natalie shifted from one foot to the other and glanced toward Mr. Vincent's office. She didn't know if she wanted the meeting to start right now – or not.

"How have you been?" Jack asked.

"Good, mostly. How about you?" Natalie wanted to keep the conversation casual, but her stomach was in a roil.

"Okay."

A second before she asked 'Just okay?' Mr. Vincent's door opened.

"Gentlemen. And Mrs. Costello. Let's get underway."

Natalie edged into the office and stood as far as she could behind the men crowding around the conference table. The room vibrated with anxiety. She recognized assembly managers, foremen, and the head of the Arsenal repair team gathered around the conference table. Several charts and diagrams were spread on the surface.

"Mrs. Costello, please join us," Mr. Vincent said. He pointed to a spot between one of the foremen and the head of the repair team.

Natalie cautiously stepped toward the table, waiting for the two men to make room. Only at the last second, as Mr. Vincent's eyes shot a warning, did they shift to leave her a place so narrow that her hips were snug against both men.

Jack stood at the far end of the table. He glanced at Natalie and quickly turned his attention to a diagram spread out on the table. Natalie was confused by a sudden rush of longing fighting with anger at how quickly he went with other women – and Genny LaFleur. She tried to calm herself and piece together snatches of what the men were saying. It wasn't good.

The head of arsenal repairs said, "The last time we shut down one of the rifling machines for maintenance, it took us three days to get it back on line."

Mr. Vincent rapped his knuckles on the table. "Gentlemen, unless anyone has something new to add, I believe we have a keen grasp of the dimensions of the challenge. The repair teams are already working on Machine 1.They will move to Machine 3 by noon. "Sweeping his hand over the papers in front of him, Mr. Vincent said, "These are outlines of what needs to be accomplished to get Machines 1 and 3 back on line without risking breakdowns of 2 and 4. We will break into two teams to lay out the details and plans for implementing them. He pushed two large charts to the edges of the table.

"Jenkins, Hartunian, and Martin," Mr. Vincent said. He handed one of the charts to Mr. Jenkins.

"Mahoney, Snyder, and Bellini." Mr. Vincent said and handed the other chart to Jack. "Mrs. Costello," he said. "You will remain as a resource."

Jack said, "Mr. Vincent, we'd like Mrs. Costello on our team." He paused. "She has a talent for seeing things those of us close to the work have missed."

Mr. Vincent gave Natalie a long look. Finally he said, "It's at your discretion, Mrs. Costello."

Natalie felt Jack's eyes on her. She didn't have to do this. But she chose him, and Genny LaFleur can't have him. "Yes, I would like to be on Mr. Mahoney's team."

Mr. Vincent turned to the others around the table. "These tasks are of the utmost importance, and they must be completed as quickly as possible. We will meet at noon to review your plans. Thank you."

The men regrouped into their teams and staked out places along the conference table. Jack tried to spread their chart, but there wasn't enough room. The voices of the men got louder. Jack said, "We need a quiet space to work on this."

Natalie knew that Jack's cramped floor office in Heavy Artillery was barely large enough for two people.

Men at Snyder's and Bellini's rank only had stand-up desks right next to the assembly lines. "We can use my office," Natalie said. "It's down the hall."

Natalie waited for Jack to make the first move, but he gave her a 'ladies-first' sweep of his arm, and she led the three men to her office. She felt as though he'd recognized what her decision to join the team meant.

Inside the office, Jack asked, "May we?" and before Natalie could answer, he nodded to Mr. Snyder, and the two men turned Natalie's desk around and pushed her chair against the wall. Jack eyed Agnes's desk, but she grasped its edges as though she was afraid the men were about to pick it and her up.

Jack spread the diagram across the top of Natalie's desk and started to lay out an action plan. She tried to concentrate, but she couldn't help glancing at Jack as he turned to speak to the other men. Natalie remembered every word they exchanged outside Mr. Vincent's office, but she struggled to find the meaning in the tone of his voice, the way he stood, how he looked at her as he spoke and what she sounded like to him.

"Ain't going to work like that on this fix," Tito Bellini said. He jabbed a thick finger at the arrows on the diagram drawn from the rifling machines to a box labeled, 'Field Artillery.' He cocked his head in the direction of the door. "Them carpet-walkers see artillery and artillery and draw a straight line."

Natalie liked Tito. He was one of the managers she worked with on her first trouble-shooting assignment. At first, he came across as unfriendly, and she worried that he wouldn't work with a woman, especially one that was supposed to help solve a problem in his shop. But Natalie learned that his gruff manner and blunt way of talking was because he had no time for niceties or fools. She glanced toward Agnes who was stapling shipping orders as though their conversation was interfering with winning the war. If it wasn't for Mr. Vincent, Natalie would be over there – forever.

"He's right," Mr. Snyder said.

Unlike Bellini who told Natalie to call him 'Tito' right away, she didn't know Snyder and wondered if he'd ask her to call him 'Martin' – or maybe it was 'Marty.'

Jack asked, "What's the problem?"

Tito said, "We got machinists, assemblers, and runners." He pointed at Snyder. "You got machinists, assemblers, and runners. But we do it different, right?"

"I worked in Field before I transferred to Heavy," Snyder said. "Took me forever to figure out what they were doing."

"No way in Hell it's a straight line," Tito said, "Sorry, Mrs. Costello."

"Tito, when we worked on the parts delivery issue, I was Natalie. Remember? If you guys are going to stammer and stutter every time you want to say, damn, hell, and worse, we'll never finish this."

Snyder held out his hand. "Call me Marty." At first, Natalie couldn't place it, and then she realized he smelled like mustard. She glanced at his hand expecting to see him clutching a hot dog.

Tito and Marty explained what might work or not if they transferred idled Heavy staff to Field. Natalie began to feel more confident as the two men traded ideas. Tito's blunt, decisive manner seemed to mesh instead of clash with the air of constant energy that surrounded Marty like a pulsing halo.

"The 'nots' are winning," Jack said.

"Hold on a minute," Tito said. Marty started to say something, but Tito held up his hand. "I got it. I got it." He turned to the others, all with expectant and impatient looks on their faces. A big smile creased his face.

"So?" Marty finally asked.

"Tinkers to Evers to Chance," Tito said like he'd answered the jackpot question on *Information Please.*

Jack said, "Who?"

Thank goodness, Nicky was a baseball fan. "The famous Chicago Cubs double-play combination," Natalie said. "Johnny Evers, the second baseman, was from Albany. Local hero."

"She's got it," Tito said. "We go around the horn." He grabbed a pencil from the jar on Natalie's desk and drew another box on the chart – 'Seacoast.' Then he drew a line from Heavy to Seacoast to Field. "Tinkers to Evers to Chance," he said as though the answer should be obvious to a child.

"The Seacoast Cannon Shop?" Marty asked.

Tito said, "I put in five years at Seacoast before I went to Field. They set up almost the same as we do, and orders are dropping off for their big guns. They won't admit it, but they got slack. They'll raise holy hell, but it'll work."

Jack said, "If I see where you're going with this, it will be one heck of a lift."

"You got two choices," Tito said. "One we can butt heads trying to get the crews from Heavy matched with the crews from Field. Or we put together better-matched crews from Seacoast and send them to Field. They'll pick it up right off the bat. I trained half of them."

"We're putting a lot on our heads," Marty said. "We try to turn the double-play and drop the ball, we're done for."

Jack said, "Tito, you realize that if we go with your plan, it's going to be a lot more work for us."

"You in?" Tito asked the others, and after a few seconds, they all nodded.

Tito said, "I'll head to Seacoast to see if they're on board with this."

"I'll go to Field," Marty said.

Jack said. "I'll get some big sheets of paper, and draw up Plan B to take to the meeting."

Natalie said, "I need to take care of something."

A few minutes before noon the team reassembled in Natalie's office. Tito and Marty reported that they got the managers of Seacoast Cannon and Field Artillery to agree to their plan.

"It just might work," Tito said. "But it might be an all-nighter."

Jack, then Tito and Marty looked at Natalie. It was as though all three had the same idea at the same time. Jack said, "I haven't thought that this might have you staying over."

There was a knock on the door. It opened, and a man in coveralls stepped in. "Mrs. Natalie Costello?"

"Yes. I'm Natalie Costello."

He stepped back out the door and returned with a folding canvass cot under one arm, and a C5 infantry sleeping bag under the other. "Where can I put these?"

Natalie pointed, and he stood the cot and the rolled sleeping bag in the corner. "It occurred to me. Just in case."

The crisis made her feel more alive than she'd felt in weeks. And she finally admitted that being on the team with Jack and pulling her share of the load was exhilarating. The others might not be one hundred percent okay with that, but she was not going to let them push her aside.

Tito and Marty reviewed what the managers of Seacoast Cannon and Field Artillery agreed to. Satisfied their plan would work they headed to the executive wing to give Mr. Vincent a briefing before the meeting.

Now, they stood together in a wordless huddle outside Mr. Vincent's office, shifting back and forth as though they were the offense on the sidelines ready to get sent into the game. Electricity hummed among them. When the meeting got underway, the men grumbled about working around the clock, but there was excitement in the air as well. It was a break in routine and a challenge to overcome.

Mr. Vincent rapped his knuckles on the conference table and looked at each of them as though assessing their readiness. "I assume you all have completed your specific work plans and are ready to go."

Jenkins explained how his team was rotating workers between the two still-functioning rifling machines and their plan to phase in the workers once the broken machines were brought back on line.

"Mr. Mahoney," Mr. Vincent said. "I assume your team has given a great deal of thought to your plan to how you are going to rotate workers from Seacoast Cannon to Field Artillery."

Natalie heard skepticism in Mr. Vincent's voice even though he agreed to their plan earlier.

Jack said, "We're confident it will work." He paused. "But we need one additional resource."

"But?" Mr. Vincent asked. "This is late for *buts.*"

Tito leaned into the table. His huge hands splayed in front of him. "We're sure it will work, but if we add commandos to the teams they will be additional insurance."

Mr. Vincent gave Tito, Jack, Marty, and Natalie a skeptical look.

Tito said, "Natalie, explain. It was her idea."

Natalie didn't want to explain. Mr. Vincent's chin lifted, and he was looking down his thin, sharp nose at her. She felt the stares of all the other men of the room on her. Why couldn't Tito explain? Finally, she said, "The commandos, sir." Natalie didn't know why and when men who had full-time jobs outside the Arsenal and worked here part-time were named 'commandos,' but they're going to be important to making their double-play plan work.

"Explain, Mrs. Costello," Mr. Vincent said.

"We watched the machinists and assemblers in Seacoast and Field this morning, and we realized that some of their tasks could be done by commandos."

"What?" one of the foremen from Seacoast Cannon growled. "We're talking about highly skilled and experienced men, not monkeys on a Ford assembly line turning one bolt and handing it off to the next guy. No part-timer is going to do my guys' jobs."

Now, with everyone in the room except the men on Natalie's team glaring at her, she wanted to drop into a hole in the floor.

"Gentlemen," Mr. Vincent said. "Let Mrs. Costello finish. She has shown an uncanny knack for seeing things others have missed."

Natalie said, "With two rifling machines down, we have commandos who mostly did running for supplies standing around. If we get the surplus commandos organized into a couple of teams, they can do simple things the machinists and assemblers do themselves. Just handing them tools they had to get for themselves will save minutes that will add up."

Mr. Vincent said, "Our own Frederick Taylor."

"Who?" Natalie asked.

"Never mind," Mr. Vincent said. "Proceed."

Natalie explained their plan, and Mr. Vincent agreed to assign four commandos to their team.

Two hours later, Jack and Natalie gathered the crew from Seacoast and the four commandos they'd recruited and headed for the Field Artillery building.

The Seacoast crew and the commandos gathered at the end of the assembly line. The Field Artillery men stood behind their manager. It was like two football teams ready to square off. They waited, and Natalie thought it was going to all come apart.

In a loud voice, the Field Artillery manager said, "This ain't the stag line at a USO dance. You Seacoast guys pair up with our men, and let's get this show on the road." The men began moving together. "Jack," the manager said, "I'm leaving it to you to figure out how to use the commandos so they help instead of getting in the way."

The assembly crews began work, and Jack and Natalie stood off to the side, each with two commandos at their side. The moment before Natalie said she wanted one commando to start handing tools, Jack said, "We should get one commando to start handing tools."

The commandos were getting into the rhythm of the work. When one of the machinists began to wipe down a lath, at the same moment, Jack and Natalie pointed to a commando and said, "You take those rags and wipe down his lathe." It was a duet, and it went like that all afternoon.

Natalie started to make a suggestion, but before she spoke, Jack said exactly what she was going to say. They finished each other's sentences. She'd never felt closer to anyone in her life.

By late afternoon, Natalie was exhausted but thrilled that their plan was working.

"We need a break," Jack said.

A few minutes later they sat across from each other in the cafeteria. Natalie hadn't eaten since her that morning, and she didn't realize how hungry she was. She tried to not wolf down her sandwich.

Natalie said, "It's as though we're reading each other's thoughts."

"We make a good team," Jack said.

Natalie let that hang between them for several seconds before she said, "Yes. We would make a very good team."

By ten o'clock Natalie, Jack, Tito, and Marty were leaning against a wall. Tito's head tilted back and his eyes closed. Natalie was exhausted. They had shoveled down more sandwiches and bowls of soup around seven, but they'd run out of gas.

"I can't see straight," Marty said.

Tito said, "Should we go back over to Seacoast and see if the night shift is doing okay?"

"If we go there one more time, someone's going to drop a pipe wrench on our heads," Jack said.

"You're right," Tito said. "We should get some rest and wait until the first shift shows up."

Marty said, "You going home, Tito?"

Tito said. "I'll lose more than an hour of sleep walking home and back. And Emily's going to make me get out of these dirty clothes and take a bath before she'll let me get in bed. I'm going to drag myself over to where the cots are set up and flop just the way I am."

"Sounds like a good idea," Jack said. "I'll be more tired dragging to Green Island and back."

The three men turned toward Natalie. Tito said, "Natalie, we got the drill down. You don't have to stay. Go home and get some sleep. Meet us when the first shift starts."

Natalie managed a tired smile. She didn't want to go home. She was asleep on her feet but she was staying. She was on the team, not a cheerleader jumping up and down waving pom-poms. "I'm afraid you guys will mess it up. Remember, I've got a cot in my little hide-away."

Twenty minutes later in the dimmed lights, Natalie tip-toed to the executive area. She went into the Ladies Room and washed as much of the grease and grime off her face and hands as she could.

Back in Natalie's office, the cot was against the wall. A sleeping bag and a green GI blanket were rolled at one end and a thin pillow at the other. She turned on a desk lamp in Mr. Holt's office and left his door ajar leaving her office in semi-darkness. She would feel better if she could take off her coveralls and sleep in her underwear, but the notion of taking off her clothes in the office stopped her. She took off her shoes, and fell back on the cot. She slid into the sleeping bag and pulled the blanket up to her chin. It felt great to be off her feet.

She was exhausted. She wanted to fall fast asleep, but she couldn't. She stared at the ceiling. *We would make a great team.* It just came out like that. Finishing each other's sentences and finishing each other's thoughts. Why can't it be like that?

Natalie turned on her side to move away from the wood frame of the cot digging into her back. She recalled when Jack and she had the same idea about how many commandos they'd need. They'd both blurted out the exact same words together, and Tito gaped at them as though they were a vaudeville act. And when they were figuring out the work schedule, she'd finish a sentence, and Jack picked up the thought and continued as though they were reading from a script. She and Jack were a team – more than a team. What?

She must have finally fallen asleep, but her eyes shot open when she heard the office door slowly open. Her heart fluttered, but she wasn't afraid. She knew who it was.

Jack's shadow fell across her.

Their eyes searched each other's for several seconds.

Jack eased himself down to perch on the edge of the cot. Natalie sidled over to keep his weight from tipping it.

Jack's hand caressed Natalie's forehead, and it mobbed her brain. Wordlessly, the fingers of his left hand traced around her face, over her lips, across her nose. The fingers slid into her hair, gently massaging her scalp, then lightly touching her ears.

With her skin humming, Natalie opened her lips but didn't know what she wanted to say. She tried to slow her breath when his right hand slid into the sleeping bag and undid the top button of her overalls. Natalie stared into his eyes as his fingers slowly undid the other buttons. His fingers lightly slid across her bra, and she lifted and slid her left hand around under and undid the clasp. Jack slipped his fingers under the loosened cup and gently rubbed her breasts.

A tear coursed down Natalie's cheek. The fingers of Jack's left hand continued to trace through her hair and across her face as his right hand moved down from her breasts until they stopped at the waistband of her panties.

Jack's chin lifted a fraction, and Natalie nodded the answer. His fingers slipped in and gently rubbed as her legs parted. After a few moments, Jack's fingers slipped back out. He pulled the gap of her overalls together. He leaned forward, kissed her forehead, her eyes, and then her lips. She tasted the sweat on his lips. He stood, stared down at her for several seconds, then tip-toed out of the room.

Natalie heard a rap on the office door and bolted upright. Where was she? Oh, God. She grabbed the lapels of her unbuttoned overalls and pulled them together. "Yes?"

"Natalie, it's Tito. You all right?"

She glanced at her watch: seven –fifty. "Yes, I'm okay." She swung her legs over the side of the cot and had to lean back when it almost tipped over. "Sorry. I over-slept."

"Okay," Tito shouted from behind the closed door. "I'm heading over to Field. We'll meet you there when you're ready." There was a pause. "Agnes is out here. Should I tell her to wait?"

"Yes. Thank you. I'll be a second." Natalie stood. She was late. She'd let her team down. The office door opened. Agnes gawped at Natalie, and Natalie turned away scrambling to fasten the rest of the buttons on her overalls. "I stayed overnight. The rifling machines. Emergency." She felt as though Agnes had discovered her and Jack naked. "I've got to clean up and get over to Field Artillery." Natalie dashed by Agnes to the Ladies Room.

In the Ladies Room Natalie splashed cold water on her face and ran a comb through her tangled hair. She had to pee, and when she unbuttoned her overalls and pushed her underpants down a flush covered her body.

Ten minutes later, Natalie found her team huddled with the Field Artillery manager. No one looked at her as she sidled up behind Tito. Three commandos were standing against the wall. Jack was reviewing the overnight work with the manager.

Jack turned toward Natalie, and she felt as though everyone had stopped to gape at her – at them. "You okay?" Jack asked.

"Sorry. I over-slept." She avoided Jack's eyes. "Everything okay with the first shift?" Natalie felt as though her attempt at a business as usual tone sounded like a lie.

Jack said, "We're going to swing by Heavy and see how the repairs to the rifling machines are going. We're meeting with Mr. Vincent at nine."

Natalie followed Jack, Tito, and Marty and felt like she'd lost her place on the team.

At Field Artillery, Tito and Marty made room for Natalie in the circle as they got an update on the repairs. Natalie hadn't been able to look Jack in the eye. He sounded like he did yesterday, but she couldn't help listening to every word for a hint of something different in his voice. She tried to say as little as possible, but her voice sounded strained as she thought too much about every word she spoke.

The meeting with Mr. Vincent and the repair teams ended. The repairs on the rifling machines were almost complete, and the reassignment of workers had kept production on schedule. Mr. Vincent congratulated everyone on a job well done. It was decided that there was no need for any more special over-night crews, and he urged those who slept over to go home and pick up their normal work schedules beginning with first shift tomorrow.

Natalie's team gathered outside Mr. Vincent's office, and Tito said, "I don't care what Emily says. I'm going to start shedding these clothes as soon as I walk in the door and flop into bed. She can throw me and the sheets in the tub together." He put his hands on the small of his back.

"God, those cots are murder. I must have a huge black and blue mark on my... well, you know."

"Slept like a baby," Jack said.

Natalie and Tito laughed, but Natalie noticed a stone cold look on Marty's face.

"Just like Sleeping Beauty here," Tito said.

Natalie hoped Tito's joke forgave her for over-sleeping. "Sorry, guys."

"Even Natalie can't be perfect all the time," Marty said sharply.

Tito said he needed to clear up something with Jack and pulled him a few feet away. Now, Natalie felt Marty's eyes burrowing into her.

"Sleeping Beauty," Marty spat. "You got a husband." It wasn't a question. And before Natalie could even nod, he continued, "A pretty young woman like you ought to think twice about getting carried away with being the belle of the ball. All them fairy tales don't turn out so good in real life." He wheeled around and headed for the lockers.

Natalie was stunned. 'Sleeping Beauty.' She shot a look at Jack who was still head to head with Tito. Did he...? Was it obvious what had happened? She looked at the other managers who still gathered in twos and threes apparently reviewing what they'd done to solve the crisis. Or were they talking about her – and Jack. She knew many of them resented her being Mr. Vincent's new aide – tattle-tale she guessed they thought – and a woman to boot. Now a rash crawled up her back, and she wanted to get away. She started toward her office.

"Natalie," Jack called. He caught up with her outside her office. "Natalie, I still want to see you – outside. Can we meet tomorrow?"

"I need to think, Natalie said. "Friday."

"Good," Jack said "Let's meet at the bus stop at seven-thirty."

***

Each morning since she'd left Jack, Natalie woke with her head full of him. She couldn't deny what she felt anymore. She couldn't control how much she loved him.

At six o'clock on Friday evening, Natalie put the last dish in the cupboard. All day, she'd pretended to work, taking care of the most mindless tasks while letting Agnes handle anything important. Natalie pushed routine inventory reports from the In to the Out basket and argued with herself about what to do.

No, Jack, it's not right. And then what? She didn't need a crystal ball to see herself marking time as Mr. Vincent's Fix-it girl until the war ended and Bill came home. Was she going to fool around with Jack until he got tired of her and went off with a Genny who would give him what he wants?

And if she did, what then? She didn't know, but it had to be better than the dead end that lay ahead.

"I'm going out," Natalie said to her mother.

Mom put a glass in the cupboard too carefully. "Aren't you exhausted after what you've been through this past week?"

Natalie faced her mother. No more shillyshallying or making up cover stories about going to the movies with Flo. She'd become reckless. "I'm meeting a friend." She paused. "Jack. We work together. I'm fond of him." There she'd said it. She didn't have to say 'I love him.'

Mom scrubbed her hands on her apron. "It's not right. You're a married woman."

"Mom, I backed into marrying Bill. The world's turned upside down. The war has changed everything. I'll have to deal with Bill when he returns."

"Don't be so sure everything's changed," Mom said.

"I'm not, but I have to follow what I think is best for me."

Natalie waited for her to yell at her. She deserved it. She was committing adultery. It's a mortal sin. Mom put her hands on the edge of the sink and stared out to the backyard. "I don't know how I failed to teach you right from wrong."

There it was again, Mom's fault. "It's my sin, but I'm not going to give him up."

Natalie put her arms over her mother's shoulders and hugged her. She might as well be hugging a marble statue. She kissed the back of her mother's head and went upstairs to change.

Forty-five minutes later, Natalie stood at the bus stop on Broadway. The number 22 pulled up, and Jack stepped out. The bus pulled away, and Natalie put her arms around him. They kissed.

Jack said, "Where shall we go?"

"With me." Natalie took his hand and turned back toward the direction he'd come from. An uncertain look crossed Jack's face. Natalie led him back toward the Arsenal. A block before the main entrance, Natalie tugged Jack's hand and they turned up Seventh into 1st Avenue. They stopped in front of 437 1st Avenue. A freshly painted sign on the building read, 'Pisano Printing.' From the bottom of her purse, Natalie pulled a key to the front door she'd made.

She unlocked the door, and they entered.

Natalie motioned Jack to stay, and she felt her way to the door to the back room where Dad had his small office. She turned on the lamp on top of the roll-top desk and signaled Jack to follow her. When he was in the office,

Natalie closed the door.

Jack started to say something, but Natalie put her fingers over his lips.

Fifteen minutes later they lay naked on the bed they'd made on the floor from their coats. Natalie shivered, and Jack pulled her tighter. He wrapped his coat over her.

Thirty minutes later, Jack eased off Natalie, stripped the second condom off and stood.

Natalie was freezing, but she wanted to lie there and gaze at him in the soft light cast by the lamp.

Jack knelt, put his coat over her and stroked her forehead. After a few minutes, Natalie stood and they began to get dressed. It had been over an hour since they'd spoken, but tonight Natalie didn't want to talk.

At the front door, Natalie was putting the key back in her purse when a patrol car pulled up. An officer got out of the car and shined a flashlight at Natalie and Jack.

He approached. "What's going on here?"

"I'm Natalie Costello. Mario Pisano is my father." She pointed to the sign. "I was showing my friend my dad's new shop."

The officer followed her gesture, then took a step closer. "Natalie. I'm Victor Rudenko, Flo's uncle." He shot a suspicious look at Jack.

"Flo and I work at the Arsenal. We see a lot of each other." Natalie wanted to divert his interest away from Jack, but she knew how small this town was and wondered how soon it would be before Flo heard about this and before her father found out. She followed Officer Rudenko's gaze and realized that Jack has taken her hand in his.

Officer Rudenko's head swiveled from Jack and Natalie to the sign, then back. She heard the tumblers falling into place. "I'm glad your dad took over Zemke's place.

Shame to let it stay vacant."

"Thank you for checking on it. *I'll* tell my father. He'll appreciate it."

Officer Rudenko gave Jack a long searching look. "Be careful going home," he said and got back in the patrol car.

Natalie felt Jack's grip loosen, but she squeezed his hand into hers. They walked hand in hand along 1st Avenue.

The patrol car behind them hadn't moved.

18

Red Cross Warns Some Wives Hurt Soldiers' Morale:
Letters Asking Divorces Upset Men Abroad

Flo plopped down next to Natalie at the lunch table and slammed her pail down with a bang.

"What's got into you?" Natalie asked.

"They're closing down one of the 240 howitzer lines."

"I know." Natalie had approved the shift in inventory to meet the higher demand for smaller guns. "Why the long puss?"

Flo grabbed a sandwich from her lunch pail. "A bunch of assemblers from the 240 line showed up in our shop like they know everything – certainly more than us girls who've been doing the job for two years."

"You've handled that before."

"I know, but it's getting worse," Flo said. "A couple of them got extra porky, and Doris Kennedy told them to go to Hell in a handbasket. They got all huffy, but we backed Doris and told the foreman that we'd lay down our tools and let those jerks figure out what they don't know."

Natalie had heard a few other stories like Flo's. "Did that take care of the problem?"

"We can handle guys who can't stand to see a woman do their job, but now they're cutting our overtime."

Natalie said, "That should be good news. The Army must figure it's got enough big guns in the pipeline to the end of the war."

"I was counting on the extra money."

"The Cape Cod with the picket fence in Greenbush."

"You bet," she said.

What Flo didn't know was that everything Natalie had saved, including all of Bill's monthly allotment, went into Dad's print shop. She hoped she could make it up before Bill came home, but she didn't want to picture how the future would unfold. "I'm sorry that the idea that the war could end soon is causing problems."

"We're still getting the Cape," Flo said. "Maybe the picket fence will have to wait awhile." She took a vicious bite of her egg sandwich.

Flo and Natalie sat wordlessly for a couple of minutes, and Natalie sensed there was something on Flo's mind. She could guess. Mom, now Flo. Flo might as well let her have it. "Okay," Natalie said. "You might as well get it off your chest."

"Genny LaFleur," Flo said bitterly. "She's putting it about that Jack rebounded back to you because you're doing things with him she wouldn't."

"We're not."

"Not what?"

"Whatever those things are." But Natalie supposed that having sex on the floor of her father's print shop might fit Genny's idea of those things.

Flo looked Natalie in the eye for several seconds. "Natalie, you're a good friend. I don't want to see you hurt."

Every day, she was on the shop floor using her so-called uncanny ability to see ahead to recommend improvements and fixes. But Natalie couldn't see what was ahead in her life. "I'll be alright," she lied.

***

The next day Jack and Natalie were finishing lunch in a vacant office near Jack's line. Jack carefully folded his waxed paper and put it in his lunch pail. Often they ate wordlessly, but she felt they were telling each other important, life-changing things that went beyond mere words. They didn't have to talk. They knew. And then it became clear that they had to say something about what lay ahead for them. But what could they say beyond vague notions of wanting to be together? Natalie set aside her ability to see the big picture because she was afraid of what she'd see.

Natalie had never lived anywhere but Watervliet: growing up, going to school, and except for her stint at the insurance company in Albany, working at the Arsenal. Her entire life had been lived inside two square miles. Even Flo's dream of a house in Greenbush seemed exotic. Where would they go? What would they do? And even if she could conjure a vision of Jack and her in an apartment, working at jobs, living not too far from her parents – if they ever wanted to see her again – there was still the question of what she had to do about Bill.

"Tonight?" Jack asked.

"Yes," Natalie said. Even if she couldn't make sense of their future, she was going to live as much of their life together as she could. Their life. Quick exchanges of whispered endearments as they passed each other on the shop floor. Lunch together. Slipping into the small cocoon of the print shop, a walk to the river and home to the cloud of accusation hanging over her.

That evening after dinner, Natalie walked out of the house with an "A" sewn on her back by her mother's searing glare. At the print shop Jack and Natalie stepped into their separate world. In each other's arms, nothing else – no one else – mattered. Later Natalie and Jack walked from the print shop toward the Hudson River. They each had one of the Army blankets Jack had stashed at his locker and picked up earlier. They were alone, but what they'd done hung over them like a barrage balloon following them everywhere. How long could they go on before one of them finally acknowledged that they had to decide what they would do?

They reached the bank of the river, and Jack unrolled one blanket and spread it along a bench. He wrapped the other around them. Under the blanket their arms entwined. Natalie lay her head on Jack's shoulder. After several minutes of staring at the river, Jack said, "My crew is getting cut back to forty hours."

"Flo told me that they laid off almost all the commandos in her shop."

"It's going to end," Jack said.

"The war," Natalie said and heard a question lurking in her voice. Her mother's scarlet letter was nothing compared to what she was thinking. She didn't want the war to end. She recalled a picture of the damned souls in Hell tormented by demons with pitchforks. She didn't remember how many circles there were in Hell, but loving the war and not wanting it to end would surely condemn her to its lowest depths.

After a few seconds, Jack said, "Yes."

Defying the rarely enforced blackout, lights filled windows across the river in South Troy. Natalie said, "I want to be with you – always."

Several seconds of silence stretched between them. Finally Jack said, "Yes."

Natalie couldn't bear to not hear him say it. "Do you want to be with me?"

"I do."

He'd said it firmly, but Natalie still heard a flicker of hesitancy in his voice. "But?"

Jack shifted on the bench so he was facing Natalie. "You know what I want. You tell me what you want, but I'm sorry that it falls on you. I wish it didn't, but we have to see what you do."

"I will. I will make it so we will be together – always." Natalie pulled his face to hers and kissed him. She put her hands behind his head and held him to her. She didn't want to let him go. She didn't want to think of what she had to do.

***

Two days later, Natalie hung around the time clock after she'd punched out. The Liner Shop crews were coming in from the far end of Building G, always a few minutes behind her. Natalie saw her, and after she punched out, Natalie came up beside her.

"Stephanie? Stephanie Miller?"

She turned and scanned Natalie's face.

"I'm Natalie Costello. Do you have a minute?"

"I've got to catch the twenty-two."

"I'll walk you to the stop," Natalie said.

Outside the entrance, Natalie glanced around to see if anyone she knew was near. She fell in step with Stephanie. They were two blocks from the bus stop. No time for small talk. "Stephanie. I heard you divorced your husband."

She stopped and gave Natalie a suspicious look. "Yeah," she said.

"I don't have time to beat around the bush. How? I mean. We live in New York. It's not easy."

"You can say that again."

When she'd gone to the Watervliet library to research the law, Natalie felt as though she was peeking at dirty books. Desertion, adultery, cruelty were the only grounds. "But you did manage to divorce your husband."

Stephanie glanced toward the bus stop. "Listen, honey. I'll give you the headlines. The asshole came home on leave with the clap and every other variety of VD. After I got cleaned up and refused to do it with him again, he beat the crap out of me. I wanted out, but he says he's sorry and won't go along with the pretend adultery game. It took me almost two years and a lot of dough, and then the judge wanted me to see if *I* could reach reconciliation. The judge said the asshole was serving his country so I should be more understanding of the stress he'd been under. Can you believe it? It cost me – actually my parents – a pile to pay a lawyer to keep pushing to prove the cruelty claim. The black and blue marks had long healed. Fortunately my lawyer discovered he'd beat up a prostitute in Jersey City. There was an MP report, not even an arrest."

Natalie knew the grounds. She knew it wasn't easy. She hoped Stephanie would have some advice – some inside dope. Now she felt worse. Natalie couldn't see how Bill would agree to fake adultery or lie about cruelty. Maybe she and Jack could simply run away. "Thanks."

"Lots of luck," Stephanie said. She started toward the bus stop and stopped. "Or you might get as lucky as Lisa Cantore over in casting. Her total loser of a husband got his at Arnhem so she's rid of him and gets her ten thousand bucks widow's allowance to boot." She dashed toward the stop.

Natalie gawped at Stephanie. She couldn't believe Stephanie said aloud the damning thoughts Natalie pushed out of her head in the middle of the night.

19

Belgium   January, 1945

*Slain U.S. Captives Found in Belgium: 100 Bodies
Discovered Under Snow.*

I follow Sarge and three other guys from the squad to what's
left of a barn. Where the hell are we? Germans everywhere.
Panzers crashing through the woods like the trees are
matchsticks. We're looking toward the woods on the other
side of a field when a mortar round explodes twenty yards
behind us.

Sarge yells that we got to make a run for the woods.
He gets up and waves for us to follow him. The rest of the
squad hunkered behind a shed starts to follow Sarge. I'm
still in a crouch when the world explodes. I'm on my back.
There's a gong going off in my head. I reach for my M1, but I
can't find it. Sarge would ream me out no end, but what's
left of him is splattered against the side of the barn. Another
round hits ten yards to my left, and a leg drops out of the
sky. They got us zeroed in. Get out before another round
finds us.

I can't see and trip over a fallen limb. Face down in
the snow, I listen. I don't hear anything. I'm freezing, but I'm
afraid to get up. I lift my head and look left and right. I don't
see anyone. Cassidy and the rest of the squad went left at the
stream. I was last in line and lost track of them. When I
heard the MG 42 firing in the direction they'd gone, I turned
around and went right. The krauts got better machine guns

174

then we do, and I don't even have my M1. I'm stumbling knee deep in snow with no idea which way our lines are. I hear gunfire but I'm not sure from which direction it's coming. I find a rock wall. It's got to lead to a farmhouse somewhere. I hope that's where I'll find our guys.

I plow through the snow until I come to where the wall ends at the edge of a field. I'm soaking wet and freezing. My head's still ringing. My hands are numb. Hundred yards across the field, there's a farm house, a barn, some sheds. There's people standing near the house. Ours? I can't tell from here. Hundred yards of wide open field. No way I'll make it across if they're krauts. I figure to stay low along the inside edge of the woods until I can get a better look. I crouch down and start to move to my right. I hear voices behind me. Germans. I try to stay low. The blood is thudding so loud in my ears, I'm afraid they'll hear it.

At the same time I hear the shot, a thousand knife points dig into me. *Jesus, I've been shot.* I grab my ass. My pants are shredded, and I dig a sharp piece of rock out of my butt. My hand is bloody. I drop to the ground and crawl as close as I can to the wall. I think I hear voices going away.

Aufstehen. Hande hoch.

Oh Jesus. Two krauts are standing over me, and one's got an MG 42 pointed at me. The other one's holding a rifle.

I roll onto my back and hold my arms up. "Don't shoot. I surrender." Oh God, the one with the machine gun aims it at me. "*Please.* Don't shoot."

The other guy pushes the barrel away, says something to his buddy and motions for me to get up. "*Hande hoch.*"

I scrabble to my feet and hold my hands over my head. "I surrender. Don't shoot." I don't know what that is in German, but I'm praying they get the idea.

The one with the machine gun keeps it trained on me while the one with the rifle goes through my jacket and pockets. He throws what he's pulled out on the ground. He grunts and wipes his bloody hand on my jacket. I feel like I got hit by a thousand pieces of glass.

Rifle steps back and motions in the direction of the farmhouse. I stumble over the wall, my hands as high as I can hold them. My pants are soaked by the melted snow, and hot piss is spreading across my crotch.

I walk leaden-legged across the field. Every ten steps, one of them jabs me in the back with a gun barrel.

Twenty yards from the farm house, I see the yard in front is crawling with Germans. We approach the house, and one of the men behind me shouts something. An officer, I can tell from the uniform I'd seen on ones we'd captured back by the beach, cocks his head toward the barn. I follow the direction of his look and see fifteen, maybe twenty GIs sitting on the ground, hands behind their heads.

Rifle jabs me hard in the back, and I stumble toward the GIs. There's Cassidy and Stevens, but I don't see the rest of the squad. I don't recognize any of the others. The guy behind me shoves me, and I flop to the ground, draw up my legs and sit with my hands behind my head like the others. I'm shivering. I've lost my helmet, but I see out of the corner of my eye that none of the GIs is wearing one. The piss between my legs is stinging.

We sit like this for maybe forty minutes. I see my left pant leg and the left side of my jacket are shredded. Back there, I thought I was shot, but I guess I was hit by shards of rock from the wall. The left side of my ass is killing me, and I remember digging out a chunk of rock after the first shot. My back feels like a hundred pins are sticking in it.

I hear a moan to my left. I'm afraid to turn my head,

but out of the corner of my eye I see one of the guys keel over. One of the krauts who'd been standing in front of us with machine guns trained on us, steps toward the guy. He prods him with the tip of his boot, then gives him a kick. I can't see, but I don't hear anything from the guy, and it doesn't look like he sat back up.

I sense movement to my right, and six or eight more GIs are walking across the field towards us. One is hopping on one leg, leaning on a buddy. Two krauts are behind them. These guys are shoved into sitting positions next to me. Another ten or fifteen minutes go by. I can't tell. I try to think, but my brain has turned to mush. Geneva Convention. Am I supposed to know something, say something, not say something?

I hear loud voices, and I see the krauts near the house shouting at each other. There's at least two officers. After a couple of minutes and more yelling, two peel off and walk toward us. The officer paces along the GIs sitting in front of the barn. He stops about halfway and points to a GI. He turns to the soldiers behind him and barks an order. One with a MG42 gestures for the GIs from where he's stopped to get up. They stagger to their feet.

The two guys with machine guns shove the GIs toward the end of the barn. There's about fifteen of them. They stumble and stagger across the open space between the house and a couple of sheds. I dare to turn my head a fraction and see them walking beyond the sheds toward a stand of trees thirty yards further on. Oh Jesus. My brain won't connect with what I think is happening.

The guy next to me starts to blubber. I stare at a broken window on the house. I can't stop thinking about what happened the day we got clobbered by the 88's back in the hedgerows. I can't shut out the memory of the tanker shredding the four kraut prisoners with Sarge's Thompson. That wasn't the only time prisoners were shot, ours and theirs. Jesus. I don't want to die. And the moment I think it, the sound of machine gun fire comes from the woods where the krauts had taken the guys. I hear more sniffling and crying. Somebody is saying the Our Father aloud.

Five minutes go by, and the krauts who took the GIs away come back. More back and forth with the officer. The ones who took our guys away come over and stand in front of us.

One of them yells, "*Aufstehen.*"

I stagger to my feet with the rest of the GIs. I try to remember the Act of Contrition, but all I think of is all the sins I've committed. The chaplain gave us all a blessing before we climbed into the landing craft. I don't want to die. One of the krauts shouts and motions in the direction the first group of GIs went. I hear more crying and praying. We start to walk towards the woods. For a second I wonder whether I can make a break for it. I'll be cut down before I get ten steps. Maybe that's better. Since we landed, I've been afraid of being killed in action, but being lined up and shot – executed – is worse.

We get to the sheds, and the woods are twenty yards ahead. The guy next to me falls to his knees. The kraut yells for us to keep moving. The guy stays on his knees, and I hear him praying. The kraut with the rifle drops back, and I when I hear a shot, chunks of skull and gobs of brain splatter on me. I feel like my guts twist into a knot, and I shit my pants. Oh, Jesus. Shit is running down my legs like water.

The kraut yells. We stumble forward. When we're almost to the woods, I hear a truck. The krauts turn and stop. A shout comes from back by the farm house. We stand in the mud. My crotch and legs are covered in stinking, runny shit. A kraut approaches from the direction of the house. He says something to the ones taking us to the woods. They shrug and motion for us to walk back toward the house.

When we get to the house, there's two German brass. I think one's maybe a Colonel. They're giving orders to the first officer when another truck pulls up.

We stand in the mud by the sheds for maybe twenty minutes before the guys with the machine guns order us to get into the truck. My pants are a mess of shit. I smell awful, but I'd eat my shit right now. I'm alive.

20

German Attack Halted: Salient in Belgium Caves In

On Friday morning, Natalie was in the Repair Shop because Mr. Vincent asked her to review how the re-assignment of workers from Seacoast Cannon was going. Not well. A big guy from Repair had a handful of the front of a Seacoast assembler's coveralls. The fist he'd cocked was held back by a foreman.

The foreman pulled Repair away from Seacoast and shoved him toward the two other Seacoast assemblers who looked like they'd like nothing better than a brawl. "All of you," the foreman shouted. "Calm down or I'm going to dock you."

Repair pointed to the Seacoast guy he'd almost punched. "I got seniority. At least two years on you."

"You couldn't do my job if you had five years to learn it," Repair shouted back.

"Can it," the foreman yelled.

"And what about them?" one of the other Seacoast guys said and pointed at three women who seemed as though they wanted to melt into the wall.

The foreman's eyes followed Seacoast's finger to where the women were standing. He shrugged.

He didn't have to say a word. Surplus. Scrap. Natalie felt as though she'd been included in the foreman's shrug.

Later that afternoon, Natalie sat in Mr. Vincent's office. He'd closed the folder of her reports on reassignments in Seacoast, Repair, and the Shrink and Furnace Pits. He stared at the closed folder as though he'd memorized what he'd read. Then, he said "I'm afraid I've put you in some very awkward situations."

Natalie wasn't sure whether to answer, but said, "I can handle them. I've developed a thick skin on these assignments."

"Yes you have, and you've made exceptional contributions to our work."

Natalie felt the same unease she felt when the Seacoast guy pointed at the women. "The slowdown is creating problems in reorganizations and reassignments all over the Arsenal." She bowed her head when she realized she was telling Mr. Vincent what he knew better than anyone. "I'm sorry. It's just that there's a lot of work to do. It won't be easy, but I can do it."

Mr. Vincent's hands made a steeple under his chin. "These past four years have been challenging – and exhilarating."

Natalie felt as though Mr. Vincent was sharing their secret about loving the war.

"I greatly appreciate how you helped me solve some of those problems."

Natalie held her breath, afraid she too was about to be dumped on the scrap pile. But when Mr. Vincent started speaking again, she stifled a huge sigh of relief.

"The problems you so admirably dealt with will seem mere skirmishes as we slow down and contract operations. People will be hurt in this process."

Mr. Vincent paused and seemed to be considering what to say next. "I think of the Arsenal as one large family, Mrs. Costello. We take care of each other. We try to protect each other. We all suffer when someone is injured. And beyond physical injury, we all suffer if someone's good name is damaged."

The first time Natalie saw Mr. Vincent his thin face reminded her of a hawk. Like her up in the rafters, he surely had a hawk's eye view of everything that went on in the Arsenal. Now she felt she had a mouse's-eye view and was sure her flaming ears were giving her away. "Of course," she whispered.

Mr. Vincent stared at Natalie for several seconds. "Good." He stood and led her to the door.

She wanted to tell him she was sorry. She was letting him down, but she couldn't stop seeing Jack.

After punching out, Natalie walked down Broadway. At the corner, she glanced in the window of Schuyler Bakery and decided to buy a treat for dessert. Mrs. Bohjalian assured her that there was real butter in the cake – don't ask. She put the cake in a box and tied a pretty bow at the top.

Inside the house, Natalie shouted, "Hello," and took off her coat. She didn't hear her mother's usual return, 'Hello.'

"We're in here," her father called from the dining room.

It wasn't the tone of his voice that sent a shiver through her; it was that he was always home after her on Fridays with his end-of-the-week paperwork and double-checking supplies for the next week's jobs.

In the dining room, Dad and Mom were standing on opposite sides of the table. It was like they were at a wake at Parker Brothers. Nicky was against the wall staring at his shoes. Oh no, was he in trouble with the blonde? She told him to be careful. "What's the matter?" Natalie finally asked.

Mom pointed to the table. "It came an hour ago."

"I got Dad from the shop," Nicky said.

Natalie stared at the envelope on the table.

Dad said, "Do you want me to open it?"

Natalie put the cake box on the table and picked up the envelope. She carefully opened it and unfolded the telegram.

WESTERN UNION

WB30   45 GOVT=WASHINGTON DC 20 1233A

MRS. WILLIAM B. COSTELLO 1945 JAN 11 PM 2 13

THE SECRETARY OF WAR DESIRES ME TO INFORM YOU THAT YOUR HUSBAND CORPORAL WILLIAM B. COSTELLO IS A PRISONER OF WAR OF THE GERMAN GOVERNMENT BASED ON INFORMATION RECEIVED THROUGH PROVOST MARSHALL GENERAL FURTHER INFORMATION RECEIVED WILL BE FURNISHED BY PROVOST MARSHALL GENERAL J A ULIO THE ADJUTANT GENERAL.

THE COMPANY WILL APPRECIATE SUGGESTIONS FROM ITS PATRONS CONCERNING ITS SERVICE

Natalie dropped the telegram on the table. The bones in her legs felt rubbery. Dad picked it up and standing next to Mom read it aloud.

"A prisoner," Nicky said. "That means he's not dead."

Dad glared at Nicky.

Natalie took the telegram from Dad's hand and re-read it. She remembered the day she followed the car up the street to the Morellis. One of the guys at the Arsenal whose cousin was killed in action told her that sometimes they send a car but lately it's mostly telegrams. No car and two solemn soldiers for 'Prisoner of War' she guessed. An image of Bill walking in a file of soldiers with his hands over his head flashed. Bill was a prisoner.

Mom and Dad stared at Natalie. Was she supposed to scream or faint? Her mind was going blank. "I brought dessert."

After Dad offered some empty assurances, dinner was wordless. Every time Natalie looked, Mom's thoughts were written on her face: *This is what you get for your sins.* Was there a ranking of mortal sins? Was committing adultery worse than what she thought when she saw the envelope on the table. She'd left the telegram in the living room, but recalled exactly what she thought as her mind raced ahead of the words, '… desires to inform you that your husband William B. Costello is…" Did she really finish those words in her head?

An hour later, Natalie closed her bedroom door and sat on the edge of the bed. A hot sweat broke out on her forehead, and the sick sweet taste of the cake filled her throat. She put her head between her knees and waited for the wave of nausea to pass. She lay back on the bed and stared at the ceiling. She'd seen photographs in the *Times-Union* of German prisoners: a line of men with haggard faces with hands behind their heads being marched along by GIs holding rifles. Do they march American prisoners all the way back to Germany? Was it as terrible as the 'Death March of Bataan?' She pictured Jack waiting outside the Arsenal main gate, the two blankets under his arms, and she wondered what he was thinking.

***

Monday morning, Jack was waiting for Natalie at the time-clock. She punched in, and they walked to a quiet side of the room. His face is full of questions. Natalie didn't know what her face said.

"Flo told me," he said. "She found me on Broadway."

"I'm sorry I couldn't get word to you."

"I guessed that something important had come up." He glanced at the workers streaming in. "Lunch?"

"Yes"

Jack took Natalie's hand and squeezed it before leaving.

Natalie wondered if it would have been different if the telegram had come on Monday or Tuesday or any day besides Friday. Two days trying to tune out her parents, Bill's parents, everyone who offered her sympathy or assured her that the Red Cross would make sure Bill was taken care of. Two days during which she didn't have her work to absorb her or Jack to assure her that they were going to be alright. Two days in which Natalie had nothing else to do besides think about what this meant. She kept thinking about Limbo where the unbaptized babies go. It wasn't Heaven or Hell, not even Purgatory. How long do they stay there? Bill was in Limbo. She was in Limbo. And now she waits. It was agonizing, the not knowing.

When Natalie got to her office, Mr. Vincent greeted her. Mr. Holt and Agnes hung behind him. He offered something between condolences and confidence that Bill would come home safe. Natalie recalled him telling her we're all family here at the Arsenal, and she hoped she wasn't scarlet with shame for betraying her Arsenal family. Natalie assured Mr. Vincent that the best thing for her was work. When he left, Natalie dove into writing her report on reorganizing the equipment storage in Building C.

A few minutes after noon, Natalie met Jack in the vacant office. He pulled up a chair and sat across from

Natalie. They ate their lunches in silence. What was different from when Bill was still fighting? Were they both hoping he'd be killed and solve their problem of what to do next?

They finished lunch. The ticking of the wall clock was agonizing. The air seemed taut.

Jack said, "When can we meet?"

Natalie hesitated. Maybe this was like falling off a bike. Get right back on. "Tonight." He seemed surprised.

Late that afternoon, Nick burst into the kitchen. "Where's the *TU?*"

Tess pointed to the folded newspaper at the end of the kitchen table. "You're home early. I thought you had something at school this afternoon."

Nick ignored his mother, grabbed the newspaper and began rifling through it. "Here. Here it is." Still standing, Nick said, "*Jesus.*"

"*Nicholas Pisano,*" Tess said.

"Sorry, Mom." Nick jabbed his finger at the newspaper. "Artie killed himself."

"Artie who?"

"Artie Johnson."

Tess said, "One of the Johnson's who live up on 24th?"

"Yeah," Nick said. "Man found dead in Watervliet garage. Police investigating," Nick read. "That's it. I didn't even see it this morning. Two sentences."

"Your father didn't mention it before he left, and you were running late – as usual."

Nick said, "I heard about it as soon as I got to school. Jim Kiely lives on the next block from Artie."

Natalie had been upstairs cleaning up after work. She walked into the kitchen and sensed that something was amiss. "What's going on?"

"Artie Johnson hanged himself," Nick said. "The paper didn't have anything, but I found out it was Artie when I got to school."

"Oh my God," Tess said. "That's awful."

Natalie said, "Artie, the boy who rides his bike all over town?"

"Yeah, he delivers telegrams for Western Union."

Natalie asked her mother, "Did he deliver the telegram informing me that Bill was a POW?"

"Maybe. I don't remember. I was so upset. Telegrams," Tess said. "What could be worse than getting a telegram?"

"Two soldiers parking in front of your house," Natalie said.

Tess flinched, surely recalling the day when the Morelli's were notified of Chuck's death.

"Do you – did you – know Artie from school," Natalie asked.

"No, he quit when he was sixteen. I saw him a few times in the next lane when I set pins at Zack's. "

Tess said, "I'm glad you quit that job. Not only the black and blue shins, but I never liked you hanging around a bowling alley at night."

"Jim knows Artie's younger brother," Nick said. "He went over to their house last night. Jim says the Army and the other services couldn't keep up with sending men out to notify the families like they did with Chuck Morelli."

"Let's pray this war ends, and the telegrams stop," Tess said.

"From what Jim got from his brother, Artie came home crying at the end of every day. The people he delivered the telegrams to fainted, cried, slammed the door in his face. Some even yelled at him like it was his fault."

Natalie shivered at the memory of that terrible afternoon when she'd followed the Army car to the front of the Morelli's house.

Nick plopped down in a chair. "His family kept telling him it wasn't his fault, but he got worse and worse. They never thought he'd kill himself."

Tess said, "Poor boy. It's a shame. I'll pray for the repose of his soul and hope he is at rest in Heaven."

"I thought you couldn't be forgiven and go to Heaven if you killed yourself," Nick said.

Was she beyond forgiveness? Natalie thought. Wasn't there something in the Bible about the Israelites heaping their sins on a goat and driving it into the desert to die? He died for our sins. Maybe whatever was supposed to make her feel ashamed and guilty had been shifted onto Artie.

After she'd finished dinner, Natalie announced, "I'm going out."

Tess let out a shocked cry as though she couldn't believe what Natalie had said. When she realized the implications of what Natalie meant, a breath rose from the depths of her body, and she let out in one long gasp, *"How could you?"*

An hour later on their blanket bed in the print shop, Jack twisted his body as if to relieve the pressure on his arm. Natalie pulled him tighter to her. Their love-making was urgent, and now she was desperate to have him again. He started to say something, but Natalie pressed her lips to his. This was the only place she felt alive. This was where, for an hour, she'd banished shame and guilt.

21

New Ninety-Day Limit for Veteran to Ask For His Former Job Is Made Retroactive

Tuesday morning, Natalie was on her way to meet with the manager of the Number 3 Mortar Assembly line on rescheduling. Closing down assembly lines had been more difficult than when the Arsenal was expanding production. Thirty feet from the line she heard shouting. Backs of men formed a ragged circle. Two women leaned against a wall, crying. "What's going on?" Natalie asked the women.

Before either of them answered, Natalie heard, "I'll kill you, you bastard," and "You son-of-bitch," and worse. The circle opened, men started trading punches, wrestling, while others shouted at the fighters and at the men across the circle.

The manager yelled, "Break it up." He and two other men waded in to separate the fighters.

Most of the men stepped back, but two others, grabbing and punching each other, tumbled out of the circle and fell to the floor. The man on top pinned the other and savagely punched the man on the bottom. Blood spurted from the man's nose, and Natalie lurched back. The foreman grabbed the back of the top man's overalls and yanked him to his feet. Before the foreman pushed him away, the man launched a kick into the fallen man's side. Several men started toward the kicker, but the manager stepped in front of them.

"One more step, and I'll fire the lot of you," the manager shouted.

The two gangs faced each other, snarling and pointing.

Oh my God. Natalie remembered the two men almost coming to blows in the Repair Shop last week. That was nothing compared to this. She knew there might be some friction as workers were reassigned, but she hadn't expected a riot.

The manager pointed to one group. "I want you new guys down at the end of the building until I come for you."

"New guys, my ass," one of them shouted. "I been here since forty. I ain't no new guy."

The man standing next to him said, "My brother's at Ford. The UAW wouldn't stand for shit like this."

"You're in the Army now," a man said in a sing-song.

The foreman yelled, "Shut up."

"Move it," the manager said, and they shuffled off toward the end of the building, muttering and tossing nasty cracks over their shoulders. "The rest of you, get to work."

The remaining men began moving toward the assembly line. Two passed close to Natalie, and she overheard one say, "They fire me, and I'll change the settings on my lathe. They can see how long it takes those bastards to figure out what's what."

Natalie heard sniffling. The two women had picked up their lunch pails and were walking toward her. "Not very pleasant," Natalie said.

The tall redhead gave Natalie a dirty look. "What did you do to keep your job?"

"What?" Natalie said before she realized what she'd meant.

The stocky woman next to the red head said, "I guess we didn't put in enough *overtime*." She let out a sneering bark. "Or maybe it's the under-time."

Natalie said, "They let you go?"

"Jeez, she's a regular hundred watt bulb," the redhead said to her companion.

Ten minutes later, Natalie was crowded in the manager's small office with him and the foreman. The manager said, "You got any bright ideas?" He cocked his head toward the assembly line. "For a second back there, I'm thinking I was going to let them fight it out and work with the ones left standing."

Natalie glanced at the folder in her hand. Her carefully laid out plans for rescheduling were useless.

The manager said. "I appreciate you trying to help out, but I'm a flunky on a sinking ship. Forget the lifeboat drill. It's every man for himself."

"What about the two women?"

"Wasn't my call. They were a couple of my best workers. You're lucky you're Vincent's" – he paused as though searching for the right word – "trouble-shooter."

"I guess," Natalie said. She felt wretched as though the layoffs was her fault.

The manager said, "You'd think we should be dancing for joy with the Jerries on the run and the Japs falling back." He cocked his head toward the door. "They know the returning vets are going to push out the ones that are left. I'm close to retirement, but if I was younger, I'd get out." A screech from a lathe cut the air, and Natalie flinched. "You're too young to remember the Bonus Army after the last one. When this finally ends, I don't know whether we'll all be out of work or making 1946 Chevies."

Natalie pointed to the assembly line. "What are you going to do about the new guys?"

"Let them cool their heels while I wait for word from your boss."

"Mr. Vincent?"

"From what I heard happened in the shrink pits, your boss and a squad from security will show up around 10:30 with a list – mostly by seniority, but not necessarily," the manager said. "Your name's on it, and you're gone. They got some MPs detailed here in case security can't handle it. If I was you, I'd clear out before then."

Natalie realized the folder in her hand was useless.

"Come back later in the week. Maybe you can help me sort out what to do with the survivors." He said. "If you're still here."

Back at her desk, there was a note from Jack. 'Can't meet for lunch. Have to deal with a situation.' Situations were breaking out all over the Arsenal. Earlier Agnes asked Natalie to put in a good word with Mr. Vincent. She needed the job, she said. The sole support of her aging parents. How did Natalie get to be her savior?

At the lunch table, Natalie sat as far away from the others as possible. Flo, along with four hundred women, were laid off last Friday. Flo told Natalie it was awful. They were pulled off the lines and herded to the now empty building where one of General Gillespie's flunkies, a Captain, not even a Major, thanked them for their service. According to Flo, tears, hoots, and catcalls greeted the announcement. One woman near Flo said that if the Captain said 'Rosie the Riveter' – even hinted at the term – there would have been a riot and serious bodily harm.

Natalie punched out. The Arsenal was in complete turmoil, but she didn't want to go home. She couldn't see what lie ahead. She and Jack at the print shop was all she wanted. They'd planned to meet tomorrow, but she couldn't wait. She was desperate to see him. She ran to where Jack would be punching out, hoping to catch him before he hopped the bus to Green Island. When she rushed up to him, she called, "Jack."

He seemed surprised and momentarily unable to recognize her. "Natalie, what are you doing here?"

She searched his face for signs of regret at seeing her. Every time they were together, she listened to his words, sure she was hearing doubt. "I wanted to see you before you left."

Jack took Natalie's arm, and they stood off to the side. "What's the matter?"

"Does something have to be the matter?" She paused. "Can we meet tonight?"

For a second, Jack's eyes skipped away. "Tonight?" After a few seconds he added, "Okay. That would be good."

Natalie sensed something underneath his words. Jack's usually vibrant voice sounded like the starch had been boiled out of it. She was going crazy. "Are you sure?" she said and waited for a fervent declaration of love and a need as desperate as hers.

"Yes, I'm sure," Jack said.

She was so reckless with desire, she heard it.

That night in the back of the print shop Natalie stood naked in front of Jack. She wanted him to see everything she wanted to give him. "I want to do it again."

Jack propped himself up on his elbow. One of the blankets was draped across his body. "You're gorgeous, but you'll catch your death."

"I want you."

"I know."

Natalie couldn't stand it any longer. She knew something was on his mind when they parted this afternoon, and she'd been driving herself crazier every minute since. Finally, she asked, "What is it?"

"Why don't you put some clothes on?"

Something was not right. His voice sounded like a rotor with a bad ball bearing. Now, she was ashamed of her nakedness and dressed hurriedly.

Jack had put his clothes on. He leaned against Dad's work table and gestured to the chair.

Natalie knew what he was going to say. Maybe not the exact words but she felt it in her bones. For a moment, she thought she'd simply say 'Goodbye' and walk out the door, but she slumped into the chair and felt her life splintering.

Jack said, "We can't go on like this."

"Like what?" Did she expect they'd go on forever slinking off two or three nights a week to make love wrapped in army blankets on the cold, hard floor of her father's print shop? But she never imagined how it would end.

"I'm damaging you. The longer we continue, the worse it's going to be."

Natalie wished he would shut up. "I'm already damaged goods." Was there a precision instrument like one of the gauges at the Arsenal that measured damage?

"No, you are a wonderful and beautiful young woman, and you have your whole life ahead of you."

She was shattered by his hollow words and afraid that if she looked at him she'd collapse into a thousand pieces of glass. "Without you," she said not wanting him to finish the sentence.

"I was going to tell you on Friday. I'm taking a job at GE in Schenectady. They're gearing up for post-war production, and it makes sense for me to get ahead of the guys getting laid off at the Arsenal and the returning vets."

Natalie felt as though her mouth was full of mud. "When are you leaving?"

"Next week. My last day is Friday."

For a second Natalie wanted to beg him to stay, to take her with him, but she realized he'd practiced this speech. She felt like a fool. She'd been sloughed off. She tilted her head toward the floor as if listening for a sound, the click of a timer counting off seconds. Finally she said, "I guess that was our last time."

"I will never forget every minute I spent with you, not just here."

Natalie gathered herself. She couldn't bear to listen to him a moment longer. "There's nothing more to say." She wanted to drag knives over her skin so she felt something other than shame.

Jack reached for her and tried to kiss her. But Natalie pulled away angrily. The calloused fingers she'd savored before now felt like sandpaper scouring her skin. "No, it's over. We should go."

Outside, Jack took her arm as Natalie started toward her house. "I'll walk you home."

"No. Let's not make it harder than it is." She turned and started walking, willing herself to not turn around.

22

*Preparing the Way for Soldier's Return: His Place in the
Community and His Right to a Job.*

After a sleepless night, Natalie washed, dressed, and ate
breakfast as though wading through a swamp of molasses.
With that built-in motherly sense that something wasn't
right, her mother eyed her suspiciously as Natalie kissed her
before leaving for work. At the front door, Natalie sniffed
her shoulder before putting on her overcoat. It wasn't the
dress she wore last night, but she thought it smelled like
printer's ink.

Natalie dragged herself up Broadway and wished she
could simply turn around and walk all day between
downtown Albany and Watervliet – away from home and
away from the Arsenal. Her life was in shambles. She
walked to her office feeling the pity and barely concealed
scorn on every face chasing after her.

How long would she have continued lunging forward
with no end, no hope in sight for them? Natalie knew it was
a jerry-built structure bound to collapse. For some unknown
reason, she had the knack of standing on the margins of an
assembly line for less than an hour and seeing the whole
picture. Almost immediately she'd grasp what was working
well, what was not, and what could be improved. She
deserved to have her affair with Jack collapse. She refused to
use that talent to understand what she was doing and realize
it was hopeless. He was selfish. She was selfish, and now she
deserved the wreckage she'd made of her life. The only hope
she had of keeping some shred of sanity, if not decency, was

to work harder and try to ignore the ridicule and scorn she deserved from everyone she'd betrayed.

***

For the next weeks, Natalie begged Mr. Vincent for more assignments. Perhaps sensing how fragile she was, he agreed, and she threw herself at them as though her life depended on them. Every morning, Natalie checked in with Agnes, but she'd completely taken over Natalie's old job. She was glad to be on the shop floors every day instead of out the door along with hundreds of other men and women who'd been let go. She had her own locker where she changed into overalls and exchanged no more than passing greetings with the few women who remained. She'd heard Genny LaFleur skedaddled shortly after Jack left. In the few unguarded moments Natalie allowed them to creep into her head, she pictured Jack abandoning Genny or Genny leaving Jack. That was thin salve for her wounded ego, but she suspected it would eventually heal. Natalie feared the wounds she'd inflicted on herself, her husband, her family, and her friends had disfigured her life and would never heal.

***

The coldest January on record slid into February. Natalie walked home letting the frigid wind scour her face as though it was a small penance for what she'd done.

Natalie's evenings were empty. She had dinner with her parents and Nick who seemed afraid that any remark that even hinted at what everyone knew happened would unhinge her. Then she spent an hour listening to radio programs she couldn't remember and writing letters to Bill that the Red Cross assured her would eventually reach him. From the framed photograph in her bedroom, Bill stared at her with a knowing, disappointed frown.

On the very few times Natalie met Flo for lunch on the weekend, Flo proved to be a friend Natalie didn't deserve. Natalie might tell her about a project she was doing for Mr. Vincent, but Flo had put the Arsenal behind her. Natalie could tell Flo was reluctant to tell her about Bob's letters that looked forward to coming home. Occasionally, Flo cajoled Natalie into a movie, but it seemed that everything Natalie did reminded her of the bad choices she'd made. Her worst penance was when she helped her father at the new print shop. Working with him to organize the book-keeping he'd never done before, suggesting ways to arrange the new equipment, setting up a routine for Jimmie and finding tasks for Nicky helped fill the weekend days when she wasn't at the Arsenal. But when Natalie stepped inside the shop, she expected to see her father pointing at the spot on the floor where she and Jack had sex. She struggled to erase the memory of him, knowing if she let it haunt her, she'd go crazy.

Weeks scraped by, and Natalie was afraid to lift herself up from the grindstone she'd shouldered. She knew what was ahead, but she didn't want to face it.

***

An uncertain March rain fell as Natalie stepped outside the front door. The purple and yellow crocuses pushing through the scrim of wet snow seemed surprised to be tricked into a promise of spring. There was a tremor of anticipation in the air at the news of massive bombing raids on Japan and the tightening noose around Germany. The end might be in sight, but Natalie continued to slog along as though she could soldier on forever. But as hard as she tried, she couldn't turn off her brain. Every time Natalie met with Mr. Vincent, she only relaxed when she left his office with another assignment. But on Tuesday afternoon, Natalie was summoned by Mr. Vincent's secretary, and a pang of dread gripped her.

"Please sit down," Mr. Vincent said.

Natalie sat in the chair in front of Mr. Vincent's desk. She was still wearing her overalls because she'd punched in early and went directly to storage in Building GW to confirm that the materiel had been reshuffled exactly the way she'd laid out in her memo to the foreman. She decided to not change into the dress she'd left hanging in her locker. "Thank you. It's good to sit for a bit. I've had a busy morning."

"All your mornings are busy," Mr. Vincent said.

"There's a lot to do. I'm sorry I didn't change," Natalie said. She cast her eye to the sleeve of her overalls. "I wanted to make sure the reshuffling of materiel in Building GW was done right. And I want to get to the project I mentioned some time ago: reorganizing the shift changes on the second line in Field Artillery." She was talking too fast. "And…"

Mr. Vincent put up his hand. "Mrs. Costello, you are a veritable Whirling Dervish."

"Even with the war in Europe almost over, there's still a lot to do." She couldn't stop. She was on a bicycle flying down a hill, and if she stopped or slowed down, she'd crash. Her days were a frenzy of Mr. Vincent's assignments. And she rushed around the Arsenal prospecting for other problems to solve because she couldn't look back and she couldn't see ahead.

"Mrs. Costello, I'm sure that you could reorganize the entire Arsenal if given enough time."

Natalie had worked with Mr. Vincent long enough to hear the 'but' in his statement. "Thank you."

"I'm afraid you won't need to take on the shift

changes on the second line in Field Artillery." He paused. "It's being shut down."

"Oh."

Mr. Vincent knocked his pipe three times on the cork knob of his ashtray. Natalie was sure he was going to deliver bad news.

She wanted to tell him of the other projects she had in mind, but she knew it was no use. Natalie felt herself shrinking in her chair.

"Events are over-taking us. We must see the big picture. We are on the verge of winning the war in Europe and are on the cusp of winning the war in the Pacific. This is great news. And we have made an important contribution to these victories." He paused. "And you, Mrs. Costello, have played a part I never imagined when I first met you."

Natalie didn't want to hear him. Her throat swelled, and she felt prickles in her eyes. "Thank you," she said in a hoarse whisper.

Mr. Vincent let out a rueful chuckle. "You have an uncanny ability to look farther ahead than most everyone else. So, you realize that we are going to have to end your work here at the Arsenal."

Natalie guessed that was better than what happened to the others who were let go in gang meetings in which a manager announced the layoffs.

"Mrs. Costello, I understand that this is unwelcome news. It's the closing of an important chapter in your life." He paused. "It closes an important chapter in my life. But we all turn the page and go on to the next chapter. Because of the work you did for me, for the Arsenal at my direction, indeed for the work all of the women who worked at the Arsenal has changed my life. I will never see women the same way I did before the war. I hope because of the example you set, I will try to look at every women as having talents and ambition that are not readily apparent."

Oh goodness, Mr. Vincent was brushing a tear from the corner of his eye. "Thank you," was all she could manage again.

Mr. Vincent handed Natalie the envelope that had been sitting in front of him. "I don't propose that you read it now, but in the envelope is a letter signed by General Gillespie and cosigned by me commending you for the work you did at the Arsenal. Of course, it is a well-deserved recognition of your extraordinary performance. But I hope you think of it as," he paused, "a license of sorts. It should say to you, I can do exceptional work in situations yet unknown." Mr. Vincent stood and walked around his desk. He grasped Natalie's hands as she stood. "Mrs. Costello, a new world lies ahead of all of us, for the men and women returning from the war, for those of us who manned the home front and for you."

"I hope so," Natalie said. "I can never thank you enough for the faith you had in me, for giving me the chance to…" She stopped as an image shot into her head. "…to let me fly up to the rafters and see the world differently."

Mr. Vincent ushered Natalie out of his office. A surprised look skittered across his secretary's face, and Natalie realized that they were both sniffling back tears. Mr. Vincent said to his secretary, "Mrs. Costello will hand in her badge today after she has had a chance to pack her belongings. She will remain on the payroll through Friday in compensation for the many, many hours of unpaid overtime she has earned." He took both of Natalie's hands in his. "Thank you, Natalie. I wish you well."

Out of the corner of her eye, Natalie caught the shocked look on Mr. Vincent's secretary's face.

23

August 1945

Troops Returning Home: 25,000 Soldiers Due on 10 Vessels Today

The phone on the table in the hall of Bill's parents' house rang. Conversations stopped as Bill's father picked it up. He frowned and then said a few words into the phone. When he hung up and turned back toward the people crowding the living and dining rooms he looked annoyed. "Everybody," he shouted. "Our soldier boy's a little delayed. Let's go ahead and eat."

Natalie glanced at the clock on the living room wall: 7:15. Bill's train was supposed to arrive at Union Station at 4:30. Bill's brother left the house at four, and the call Bill's father took was the second one. Natalie's and Bill's parents, aunts, uncles, cousins and friends headed to the dining room table where Bill's aunts were setting out casseroles, platters of cold cuts, bowls of macaroni and potato salad, and rolls. Everyone expected Bill to arrive around five, and after a celebration drink, they'd eat around five-thirty or so. Natalie was starved, but her stomach was tied in knots and she was afraid she'd throw up if she had anything to eat. Someone handed her a plate.

The guests were digging into the food balanced on their knees or teetering on the arms of sofas and chairs. Natalie was sure that they were not only hungry, but glad to have something to do besides rehash the conversations that started as loud and happy two hours ago.

"Snafu," was what Bill's cousin said. Bill's ship

docked in New York on Wednesday, and he was supposed to catch a train to Albany on Friday. The cousin who'd mustered out last month assured Natalie and Bill's parents that sometimes the brass simply handed out the three hundred dollars mustering out pay and a train ticket and told the ex-GI's to beat it. He'd heard others were held back because the trains out of New York were overloaded. Natalie had read that there were near riots in Europe as tens of thousands of GIs waited in holding camps for enough ships to ferry them back to the states. Eleanor Roosevelt was booed when she visited one of the camps.

Natalie dropped a piece of baked ziti on her new dress. She carefully picked it up and dabbed at the small red splotch.

"Cold water," Flo said. Flo dipped her napkin in her water glass and carefully dabbed the spot. "There. Now you're perfect again."

Flo wasn't joking, but Natalie knew she was a world away from perfect. All evening, she wondered how many of Bill's and her relatives had heard rumors about her and Jack even though she'd been doing her best impression of Saint Bernadette since Jack left and she got laid off at the Arsenal. These past five months seemed endless as she picked up short-term jobs and helped Dad with the print shop's books.

But the time also let her leap-frog back to the months before she and Bill were married. As though following an obscure religious ritual, each night instead of saying her prayers Natalie scoured her memory for the good times she and Bill had before their marriage. She'd compiled a catalog in her head of the movies they'd seen, their picnics at Burden Lake, and the parties they'd attended. She'd ransacked her closet to see if she'd kept any of the funny presents Bill liked to give her, surprised to discover at the bottom of a box the Kewpie Doll he'd won at a ring-toss at the Altamont Fair. It was a Eureka when she recalled a date roller-skating at Guptil's or a dance at the Wellington in Albany she could add to her storehouse of happier times.

She'd vowed to forsake all others, but she hadn't. As the date of Bill's return approached, Natalie hoped this inventory of better times she shared with Bill would overwhelm the shame that still ambushed her on those sleepless nights. She couldn't fool herself into believing she was waiting for a man she loved deeply. But now she vowed to begin their new life on the foundation of these memories.

"Thanks, Flo," Natalie said and smoothed the dress over her knees. She was wearing new underwear and a pair of silk stockings and felt ridiculous having the butterflies in her stomach she imagined blushing brides were supposed to feel before the wedding.

Sitting across from Natalie on the sofa, Flo and Bob Cady were as close as Siamese twins.

Bob leaned toward Natalie and picked up where he'd left off when Natalie spilled her ziti. "Natalie, you wouldn't believe it," he said. "I'm standing in the middle of the Roman Coliseum, and I can't help thinking about Mr. Neuman and our world history class. Remember him? What a dunce."

Natalie did remember Mr. Neuman stuttering and mumbling his way through the class while most of the students tried to finish their geometry homework. What Natalie couldn't make sense of was the Bob Cady who sat four seats in front of her, and not paying one iota of attention to what Mr. Neuman was saying. And Natalie remembered the Bob Cady in a pair of greasy overalls and grimy gloves following his dad around, snaking out clogged drains. What she couldn't do was match those images with this eager, fresh-faced, crew cut man enthusing about the Roman Coliseum, St. Peter's and jokingly tossing out bits of Italian.

"That must have been exciting," Natalie said. She stopped herself from glancing at her watch again.

"Don't get me wrong," Bob said. "The war was terrible. I lost some good buddies. But it changed me. When I left, I hoped I'd make it through and come back to take over my dad's plumbing business."

Flo gave Bob a playful punch in the arm. "And start a family with me."

Bob faked a flinch and with a wide grin on his face put his arm around Flo. "Well, that goes without saying."

"It's not going to be easy," Bob said. "But Mr. Neuman inspired me."

"I find that hard to believe," Natalie said.

"History," Bob said. "The more I thought about what I'd do if I got out alive, the more I was convinced I wanted to teach history."

Natalie struggled to substitute an image of enthusiastic Bob Cady for lazy Mr. Neuman at the front of a class at Watervliet High. "Teach?"

"The GI Bill, Natalie. The government's going to send me to college – for free."

Natalie had read about the GI Bill, but somehow she didn't connect college with most of the fellows she grew up with – and certainly not Bob. "Where would you go? When?"

"Right here in Albany," Bob said. "Albany State Teachers College. The government pays the tuition and even some living expenses."

Flo said, "And I'll get a job." She blushed. "At least until our first one comes along."

"And living in town, I can work for my dad part-time. In four years, I'll have my degree, and give old Mr. Neuman the boot."

"Maybe not in Watervliet," Flo said. "But some old Mr. Neuman someplace."

Bob leaned even more forward. "When Bill comes home, you better tell him to cash in. Before the war – before I got to see the world and the possibilities ahead of us – I never thought about college. It's a big brass ring, and anyone who doesn't grab it is nuts."

One of Bob's uncles came over and slapped Bob on the back. The Costello's house was jammed with aunts and uncles and cousins waiting to celebrate Bill's return. Natalie took a longer look at Bob Cady as he grasped his uncle's hand. Why not? If the war inspired Bob Cady to start an entirely new life, maybe she and Bill could. At least that's what she'd been hoping these past months.

People had finished eating, even those who've gone back for a second helping. Natalie imagined they'd eat like pigs once rationing ended. Already, there were a lot of people looking the other way, but she didn't expect they'd let Stan out of jail.

It was getting late. The guests were standing around in tight groups murmuring, checking their watches, and eyeing the cake Bill's aunts had placed in the middle of the dining room table.

The phone rang, and Bill's father rushed to pick it up. From the way he was hunched over the phone with his left hand opening and then closing in a tight fist, Natalie was sure it was not good news.

He hung up and stepped into the living room doorway. "Folks," he said with a forced grin. "I'm afraid Bill is going to be delayed."

"He didn't re-enlist?" an uncle said.

Bill's father said, "The Army, I guess. You know, Snafu." He glanced toward his wife who was frowning at the cake. "What the heck. We haven't seen that much sugar in one place for who knows when. Let's eat and leave a piece for Bill."

Bill's mother brought Natalie a piece. Natalie set her plate with her uneaten dinner on the side table and poked at the cake. She didn't want to think about why Bill was late. She wanted the life she'd led during the war to come to an end. She recalled what Mr. Vincent said. Turn the page and start a new chapter.

After a while, folks thanked Bill's parents and shuffled out. Natalie told her parents to go home. The plan was for Natalie to stay here at Bill's house. Her small case with a new nightgown was upstairs in Bill's old bedroom. When everyone had left, Bill's mother suggested Natalie go to bed. "No," Natalie said but agreed to take off her shoes and stretch out on the sofa. Mrs. Costello covered her with an afghan.

Natalie tried to stay awake, but she'd fallen asleep and now she was startled by loud voices. She propped herself up on one elbow. Two men came into the living room. Bill was leaning on his brother. Bill's tie was undone, and his shirt tails dangled out of the waist of his trousers. A lop-sided grin covered his face.

"Natalie, I'm back."

24

Watervliet, New York   **March 1948**

Hoover Sees 'Tough Time'': Nation Needs Quaker Ideals to Combat Frustration, He Says

"Mommy, read me a story."

Snot dripped from Marcia's nose. Natalie pulled a hanky from the pocket of her chenille bathrobe and wiped it. "I just read you a story. Mommy wants to read the paper." Natalie pried Marcia's hands from the grip she had on her legs and took a picture book from the scatter near the fridge and handed it to her.

Marcia looked at the book as though Natalie had handed her dog poop. "I don't like that one. I want a story." She tossed the book aside and gave Natalie a teary pout.

Natalie was sorry Marcia was getting over a cold, but she'd been whining and clinging since she awoke at six. Natalie glanced at the clock over the stove. Nine o'clock and she was already exhausted. She snatched another picture book from the pile. "Look at this one. It's your favorite."

Marcia's chin trembled. "No it's not."

"I don't want to hear it. You sit quietly with this book or you're going back to your room." Where she'll throw a tantrum. Dr. Spock should have a chapter on threats and bribes that really work on a two-year old.

"I'm going to read the Sunday paper, and I don't want to hear a peep out of you." Twenty minutes. Even ten minutes to herself was all she asked. Marcia glared at Natalie and turned the pages so angrily Natalie was afraid she'd rip them.

At the kitchen table, Natalie tried to find the front page she'd left forty minutes ago, but somehow the Society section had ended on top of the pile. The daughter of the President of the Patroon Savings Bank took up half the front page. Natalie's eyes scrolled down through the usual for these front page brides. Vows were exchanged at the Cathedral with Bishop Gibbons presiding. Loudonville and Lake George, Schuyler Meadows Country Club, honeymoon in Bermuda. Blah, blah, blah. No need to mention cleaning ladies and nannies in her future as Natalie surveyed the kitchen. Last night's dishes were still in the sink. A dirty pot sat on the stove. She turned her head and smelled sour dried spit-up on the shoulder of her frayed bathrobe. She was in the wrong society.

Natalie pushed the smiling brides and symphony benefits aside. The next section was the Obituaries. Where was the front page? She scanned the list of names at the top of the page. No last names ending in a vowel. Good. Not that Grams might not imagine a distant connection so she and Gramps can head off to an afternoon wake. Natalie knew it was the only way they met friends these days, but they assumed Natalie had nothing better to do than drive them to a funeral home and stand around while they gossiped. Wait. Who's this? Vincent. Samuel Vincent. Guilderland. Age 49. Oh my goodness. Suddenly. Born in Ames, Iowa, 1899. Nieces, nephews the only survivors. So young. Heart attack?

An image of Mr. Vincent the last time they met flooded back, and the back of her throat tightened. The letter of commendation was in the envelope with Marcia's Baptismal Certificate and her and Bill's Marriage Certificate. Natalie recalled sitting across from him on her last day at the

Arsenal. She knew her days there were numbered, and when he told her she was being let go, she felt as though she'd been hollowed out. Her license to do exceptional work in the new chapters of her life, he'd said. For a moment Natalie believed him. Still, when he took her hand and called her Natalie, she felt as though they shared something special.

Natalie looked around at the dirty dishes and pots and pans littering the kitchen and didn't know whether to laugh or cry. A new chapter in her life. She didn't even want to think about the mess in the living room. She couldn't bear to go into the bedrooms. Natalie didn't know how long she could go on hoping that her life was temporary and she and Bill were still adjusting to life after the war. But everyone else had put the war behind them. More than two and a half years in this crappy apartment, and they hadn't turned the page in chapter one.

Bill walked into the kitchen. Reaching over Natalie's shoulder, he shuffled through the paper and grabbed the Sports. His rank breath made Natalie turn her face away.

"Can't you at least say, please or excuse me? Or possibly, Good Morning?"

"Which one?" He waddled toward the coffee pot on the stove.

"And I wish you wouldn't parade around in your undershirt and shorts."

Bill seemed surprised that he hadn't dressed. "I had a bad night."

Didn't she know it? Another bout of mumbles and nonsense phrases, yanking the covers off both of them and bolting upright before falling back on his pillow with a strangled moan. "You could still put some clothes on."

Bill poured a mug of coffee and plunked down at the other end of the kitchen table.

Natalie shoved the remaining sections of the paper toward him, knocking into his coffee mug and spilling some on the paper.

"You going to make me some breakfast, or do I have to say, please?"

At the counter Natalie cracked two eggs hard on the rim of the bowl, and chunks of shell floated in the white. She started to pick them out, then left them.

Forty-nine. Natalie tried to recall other details in the obituary then yelped as bacon grease splattered on the back of her hand.

"You're acting strange."

Natalie set the plate of bacon and scrambled eggs in front of Bill.

"Where's the toast?"

She burst into tears.

"What the hell is going on?"

Natalie made a feeble gesture toward the paper. "Someone I know died."

"Who?"

"You wouldn't know him. A man I worked with at the Arsenal."

"Three years later, and you're broken up because he died."

Natalie slammed two slices of bread in the toaster, and Marcia started to wail.

25

Job Offers Wait Veterans Graduating From College

Natalie leaned toward the mirror over her dresser to check her makeup then reached for a tissue to wipe the smeared lipstick. Out of practice, she thought and carefully reapplied it. Her one decent dress felt a bit tight as she'd stepped into it. "Bill, zip me up please." When she turned, Bill had sat back on the edge of the bed. "Bill," she said sharply, "my mother will be here in a few minutes."

Bill levered himself up and stood behind Natalie.

"Careful, I don't want to jam the zipper." She drew in her breath and sucked in her tummy. Whew. Barely.

Bill settled back down on the bed. Earlier, Natalie had cajoled him into his slacks, dress shirt and sport jacket.

"Why don't you wear the red tie I gave you for our anniversary?"

"I've got to wear a tie all day at the dealership," Bill said. "I should be able to relax when I come home. Now I got to get dressed up again."

"You've off in the morning, and you take off your tie and jacket the minute you come home. This way I'll get to enjoy looking at my handsome husband all evening."

"I don't know."

Natalie sat on the bed next to Bill. "Come on, we'll have a good time."

"Bob can be a pain in the neck. Who'd want to go to college for four years so you could stand in front of a bunch of snotty kids all day yammering on about the Roman Empire or some other stupid thing?"

Natalie gave Bill a nudge. "Let's finish getting dressed. Mom will be here in a few minutes."

Bill hauled himself up. He stood in front of the mirror and picked up the tie Natalie had set out as though it was a dead snake.

Fifteen minutes later, Marcia was wrapped around Mom's legs. Natalie made one more check of the apartment to make sure everything was ship-shape. The last time Mom babysat, she'd vacuumed, and Natalie was sure she re-washed some pots and pans she must have thought didn't come up to her standards.

Natalie couldn't wait to get out of the apartment. March had been awful. One more day of rain and she was going to be carted off to the looney bin. Even when it let up for a bit, she still had to haul Marcia's trike and the teddy bear she could never be without down the back stairs. How many stories had she read? How many games had she invented? Bill may hate going to the dealership, but at least he's out with adults all day instead of cooped up with a two-year old.

Thirty minutes later, Bill turned off Route 20 into Greenbush Gardens. He made a left on Diane Drive, a right on Jane Court, then right on Mary Louise Lane. Natalie guessed the Morellas who built this new development had a slew of daughters and nieces. They passed ranks of virtually identical ranches with ten-foot high maples staked in the front lawns and newly planted shrubs hard by the naked cement block foundations. Not the Cape Flo dreamed about, but affordable houses filled with vets who've plunked down their savings and GI Bill loans for the down payments. Natalie didn't want to think about that now and just have a pleasant evening out of the apartment.

Inside 52 Mary Louise Lane, Bob hung up their coats

while Natalie followed Flo into the living room. "Oh, Flo, I love the sofa."

"I just had to have it. Whitney's was having a sale. And with my employee's discount, I couldn't resist."

"It goes beautifully with the chairs," Natalie said. Almost every stick of furniture in Natalie and Bill's apartment was a hand-me-down from Bill's or Natalie's parents. She was sure Mom and Dad bought new dining room chairs and table so they could give their perfectly good set to them.

"I'll be right back," Flo said. "Make yourselves comfortable."

Bill settled into a chair next to the sofa. He eyed Bob's tie-less tweed jacket and gave Natalie an annoyed look.

"How about some cocktails?" Bob asked. He walked to a blonde maple sideboard. "I like Manhattans. Flo's into whiskey sours. Hey, Flo," he shouted toward the kitchen. "Do you have some whiskey sour glasses in the freezer?"

Flo shouted back, "I've got four, just in case."

"If Flo's having one, I will too," Natalie said.

Bob said, "How about you, Bill?"

"Yeah, a Manhattan, I guess if that's what you're having."

"You'll have us looped before dinner," Natalie said. She wouldn't mind getting a little tipsy. She needed a fun night out.

At the sideboard Bill fussed with the bottles of whiskey and vermouth, leaning down and squinting at the open *Old Mister Boston Bartender's Guide* as he checked the levels in the glasses as he poured. He added a dash of bitters and spooned a couple of Maraschino cherries into the glasses. He took a sip from his glass and handed the other one to Bill.

Flo returned from the kitchen and set a glass tray on the coffee table. In the center, several flower-cut radishes were surrounded by a fan of cream cheese stuffed celery sticks. "Horsey-dervies."

As Natalie watched them, she thought Bob and Flo were following step by step directions in a how-to-join-the-middle-class owner's manual. They may be trying too hard – but they were trying. The war split people's lives in two. Men like Bob and Bill who went off to war were not the same men who came back. And the women were not the same women they left three years earlier. Bob and Flo had a plan for a different life. Natalie wished she and Bill did.

"Flo's becoming very continental," Bob said. He took a leather tobacco pouch from his pocket, filled his pipe, and lit it with a Zippo.

Natalie waited for Bill to make a crack about the spine-less French. Usually he couldn't let a plate of French fries go by without launching into a tirade about how the French didn't come out of their hidey-holes until the war was over. He reached for a celery stick. Lately, he'd been more touchy. The smallest thing, a phrase you'd think didn't mean a thing, and he was into a rant. Maybe, just maybe, they'd have a pleasant evening. "The pipe makes you look like a professor," Natalie said.

"I'm afraid not. I'll be happy to find a job teaching tenth and eleventh grade history." Bob stared at the pipe bowl and relit it. "But first, I have to finish my collegiate adventure."

Bill rolled his eyes and took his pack of Camels out of his shirt pocket. He shook out a cigarette and lit it with his Zippo. Natalie wondered if the Army issued every GI a Zippo. Bob had pulled a small folding tool from his pocket and began fussing with his pipe. Natalie remembered Bob working for his father before the war, usually in greasy overalls with a plunger in one hand and a pipe wrench in the other. She was sure those memories will fade as this too-dapper college man sails off on his *collegiate adventure.*

Flo said, "I'll get us girls our whiskey sour glasses." She said. "Silly me, the first time I made them, I kept peeking in the freezer to see if they'd frosted. Finally, I said the heck with it and took pulled them out. *Voila.* I guess I'm not yet up to par yet for Mister *Sue-Wave* here." Flo did a little curtsey and pirouette before heading to the kitchen with a swish and crinkle of petticoats under her shirt-waist dress.

Natalie thought Flo looked as if she'd stepped out of this month's issue of *Ladies Home Journal.* If Natalie wasn't overwhelmed with taking care of a terrible two-year old, maybe she wouldn't spend all day in a dress, stockings, and high heels, but at least something other than a bathrobe. Would she feel better if Bob went back to working in his father's plumbing business and Flo went around in the overalls she wore at the Arsenal?

Bob took a sip of his Manhattan. "What do you think of the new Fords?"

Flo was coming out of the kitchen. "Here's our frosted glasses," Natalie said. She did not want a conversation about cars because she was afraid of a rant instead of a conversation.

"Junk," Bill muttered.

Bob took the glasses from Flo and busied himself mixing the whiskey sours. He handed Natalie hers and gave Flo hers. Sitting back on the sofa, he said, "Cheers."

They raised their glasses. Natalie took a sip of her drink and peered over the rim at Bill. He was staring at his Manhattan as though he was trying to figure how it appeared in his hand. He'd let Flo and Bob's little thing about the hors d'oeuvres pass. 'Cheers' might have set off a nasty comment about the English, and who knows where Bob's question about the Fords might have gone. Instead, Bill seemed to be shrinking into one of his long, sullen wordless stretches.

"Do you remember Stosh Zemke?" Bob asked Natalie.

Natalie coughed and wiped a dribble of whisky sour from her chin, struggling to squash the memory of what she and Jack Mahoney did in her father's print shop. "Yes," she said.

"Stosh was – probably still is – dumber than a post. But his son Pete's in my Early American History class, and he's absolutely brilliant. All 'A's' in every other class as well."

Bill grunted and shoved a stalk of celery in his mouth.

Flo popped up. "I think I'd better see how dinner is coming?"

"I'll help." Natalie followed Flo to the kitchen.

Flo stood at the counter, and Natalie heard a sniffle.

Natalie put her hand on Flo's shoulder. "Are you alright, Flo?"

"Just ducky. A little case of the cramps I get just before my period."

Silently they got the roast out of the oven and vegetables off the stove. Natalie followed Flo, carrying a roast beef on a spiked wooden platter to the dining room table where Bob was holding the carving knife and fork from the set she and Bill gave them for a wedding gift. Flo didn't want her period to come. She desperately wanted to be pregnant. Three miscarriages that Natalie knew of and who knew how many late periods followed by gouts of blood.

From her seat at the table, Natalie watched Bob carve

the roast while Flo beamed at the husband Natalie knew she loved so much, the soon-to-be teacher she was so proud of, the man she yearned to be the father of her houseful of children. They were on a path to get everything they hoped for – except children.

Natalie cast a glance at Bill. Thankfully, he was sitting quietly like a large obedient dog.

"Seconds anyone?" Bob said. "I don't want roast beef sandwiches for the entire week."

Bill said, "Sure," and Bob forked a large slice onto Bill's plate.

Without asking, Flo dished out a scoop of peas from the bowl. "I can remember shelling peas," she said. "Mom and me sitting on the back step splitting the husks and dumping the peas into a pan. It seemed like it took forever, and then we got about a mouthful for each of us. Give me Birdseye any day."

"No canned peas for me. I hate canned anything," Bob said. "Right, Bill? We ate enough K-rations to last two lifetimes."

The expression on Bill's face showed he was wondering what Bob had said.

Natalie took a chance to say something that might prod Bill out of his funk. "No Spam for Bill either. Right, honey?" She gave him a playful poke in the arm. "He won't even go down the aisle in the store where they stock it." Thank goodness they got a shrug from Bill and maybe the hint of a smile.

"I hope you all have room for dessert," Flo said.

"You're going to love this," Bob said. "Betty Crocker has landed in East Greenbush."

Flo protested, but Natalie helped clear the dinner dishes. In the kitchen, Natalie stacked the dirty dishes next to the sink. "Great dinner, Wonder Woman."

Flo didn't weigh a pound heavier than when she graduated from high school, and with her carefully coiffed hair, pearl necklace, shirtwaist dress and high heels, she did look as though she'd stepped off the pages of *Ladies Home Journal*. And Natalie bet tonight's dinner was taken from the pages of *Good Housekeeping.*

Flo turned on the oven, opened her new Frigidaire and pulled out a Baked Alaska.

"You *are* Wonder Woman," Natalie said. "I didn't think you could do that at home."

"We're not there yet. This could go terribly wrong."

"I doubt it," Natalie said as Flo slid the meringue covered ice cream into the oven. She twisted the knob of the kitchen timer. "We should pray," she said.

It was a quip, but Natalie knew Flo had taken to special prayers in the hope that God would grant her wish for children. And not once, not even with a hint, had Flo mentioned or alluded to what happened between Natalie and Jack.

Several minutes later, Flo was proudly serving them perfect slices of Baked Alaska. Bill ate two big slices. Natalie worried that he was bursting out of his shirts and suits. Not only couldn't they afford a lot of new clothes, but it wasn't healthy. And he had an extra twenty pounds hanging around his waist.

Natalie and Bill were putting on their coats, and Natalie almost cried with relief when Bill said, "Thanks. Nice dinner." She had been afraid she was going to have to call Flo tomorrow and apologize for Bill's virtually wordless evening and pretend he was suffering from a non-contagious ailment.

"You're welcome," Bob said. "It's always nice to see

you two."

Natalie gave Flo a hug. She'd give her a call anyway to thank her and to catch up on her female troubles.

Outside in the driveway, Natalie stood next to the car waiting to see if Bill remembered to open the door for her. It was one of the small things she'd asked in the hope he'd shed the rough ways of the Army and the months he spent in a POW camp. Bill opened the driver side door, and a second before he got in a flicker of recognition crossed his face. He came around the car and opened the door for Natalie.

Natalie gave Bill a peck on his cheek. "Just like the gallant young man who came a courting," she said and slid in. One more small step in her hope to get Bill back to the sweet guy she married.

They backed out of the driveway, and Natalie wondered if Flo and Bob thought there might be something in the water or dirt out here that would grow kids.

On the ride home, Bill was silent, and Natalie wasn't sure if she was pleased.

26

New Fords Stress Comfort: Company Sees Continued
Prosperity, High Employment, Price Rises

God how Natalie hated these. Still, a Baptism party for her second cousin's son got her out of the apartment for a couple of hours. But Natalie was afraid the future of her social life would be First Communion, Baptism, and Confirmation parties every weekend.

Marcia squirmed and Natalie shifted her from one hip to the other. It was unusually warm for April, and from the kitchen window Natalie saw a handful of men filtering out to the back yard. The lawn must be drying from last night's rain. There were a dozen children banging around in the house, and Natalie hoped they got outside before they drove everyone crazy. She slid Marcia off, but she squeezed into Natalie as two boys ran by. Behind Natalie a baby cried as her cousin Rita bounced her in her arms while waiting for the bottle on the stove to warm. Natalie's cousin Nancy maneuvered her very pregnant body around her. There were two more pregnant women waddling around the house with a couple of toddlers in tow.

In the far end of the living room, Grams and the other old women were clustered around a coffee table vying for the last word about which long-dead relatives were related to whom, on which streets they lived, and the details of ill-advised marriages. On a sofa, Mom was buried in a clot of Natalie's aunts. Thank goodness, Marcia saw her. She let go of Natalie's hand and ran to her grandma. Mom pulled her onto her lap and began showing off her granddaughter.

Natalie sidled along the wall hoping Marcia didn't miss her.

In the dining room, Natalie backed into another bunch of cousins. Snatches of conversations leaked out: who had the longest labor, which kid had the mumps, what new housing development was the best deal. Natalie's cousin Angela rolled her eyes when she heard her mother loudly re-telling the story of six-year-old Angela falling off the playground jungle gym and breaking her arm. And back in the living room, Angela's grandmother was arguing with Grams about whether Angela's husband was related to the Corellis.

Natalie needed to get away from this vision of her future and ducked down the stairs to a knotty-pine rec room. As soon as she stepped off the bottom stair, she felt the glances of the nearest men and realized she'd stumbled into the uncles' club. A pall of cigarette and cigar smoke hung in the room. Clumps of middle-aged men were talking loudly. She didn't have to hear each conversation because she could repeat their stories word-for-word. The biggest walleye ever caught. The winter the garage roof collapsed. The worst or best car I ever owned. Each of them waiting for the other to finish a story they'd heard dozens of times, nodding in the right places, laughing at the same punch-line. They were the same stories she'd heard all her life. She waved to one of her uncles and headed for the stairs leading out to the back yard. The younger men were stealing a march on spring, hauling tables and chairs out of the basement and setting out food and drinks.

The sun pushed through the clouds, and children poured out of the house like a swarm of gerbils. The mothers stuck with their kids inside had decided that washing dirty dresses and short pants was a small price to pay for getting the kids out from under their skirts. Marcia was running in circles with two other girls.

Bill was sitting on a folding chair near the fence – away from the other men his age. He seemed preoccupied with the label of the beer bottle in his hand.

Natalie neared a group of men and heard one of them say, "Lucky Strikes put more guys out of action with the clap than the Jerries," The man next to him said, "For a pack you could get…" He stopped when one of the men gave him a warning nod in Natalie's direction.

All these younger men were veterans, and at parties like this one, she'd heard the good-natured Army versus Navy, Pacific versus Europe ribbing. From the joking and back-slapping, you'd think they'd all been on extended hunting or fishing trips. But from quiet conversations with her cousins and other wives of veterans, Natalie knew there was a darker side to their lives. She'd seen veterans with missing limbs, but no one she knew returned damaged in the way Bill was. Still there were unseen wounds caused by these interrupted lives.

A couple of her cousins complained about missing out on the first years of marriage, not having the chance to build a loving relationship with their husband before the inevitable children arrived. And one or two confided that they too were confounded by a man very different from the one they'd married two, three or four years earlier. When annoyed about something at home, her cousin Rita bitterly referred to her husband as 'Sargent Fred,' ordering her around as though she was a Private in his squad. Natalie once overheard a snatch of a whispered *tete-a-tete* in which a tearful woman asked the other woman if her husband made her do what apparently he'd done with women overseas, unapologetic as though it was a fringe benefit of a three day pass. What could we all expect from vibrant young men ricocheting from boredom to the terror of combat, untethered from family and the conventional lives they'd left behind? Natalie didn't want to know what Bill did overseas. What the young wives did while their husbands were away wasn't off-limits because no one she knew had strayed. She was sure rumors about her and Jack still floated around.

Natalie started toward a couple of mothers who were keeping an eye on the scampering kids when she heard, "Natalie."

Natalie's brother Nick, home on spring break, waved her over to where he was standing next to Tony Spadaro. "Hey, look who's here," Nick said.

Natalie grasped Tony's out-stretched hand. "Good to see you Tony. It's been a long time."

"He's too busy making money to hang around with the peons," Nick said.

"I'm doing alright," Tony said. He shifted from one foot to the other.

Nick said, "Alright? He's opening another store. What's that make, two?"

"Three," Tony said sheepishly.

"He's going to be the appliance king of the Capital District before long," Nick said.

Natalie thought of the stove in their apartment with only three of the four burners working. The oven was so unreliable she couldn't kill herself if she stuck her head in it all day.

Tony said. "I was telling your brother, I'll be a pauper not the king if I don't hire a smart guy like him to bail me out."

"And drop out of Syracuse and the free ride he's on?" Natalie gave Nick a playful punch on the arm. "You're not majoring in business."

Nick said. "Sociology."

Natalie asked Tony, "What could you possibly do with a guy who majors in sociology?"

Tony said, "I can sell appliances. Thank God, I finally figured out something I was good at. But I need a manager." His right hand worried coins in his pocket.

"Don't you have a business manager?" Natalie asked.

"I do, but he's strictly a green eyeshade accountant. It's the other stuff that's going to sink me."

Natalie gave Tony a questioning look.

"The first store, I could handle because everything was right in front of me," Tony said. "I opened the second store and was still able to run back and forth between the two. With the third, I began losing the handle. Too many fridges in Central Ave, not enough in Latham, why the shipment of washers and dryers from Amana go to Cohoes instead of Central Ave, paying guys to truck appliances to the wrong location, losing customers who won't travel across town to see the range they want."

"Are you stretching yourself too thin?" Natalie asked and sensed Tony bristle a bit.

"Latham is growing like crazy. If I didn't open the store out there, Feiden would have the entire area to himself." He opened his arms in a gesture of surrender. "I'm going to charge ahead and hope to God I figure it out – or get someone to keep me from going bankrupt or nuts."

Natalie heard a familiar sound. Marcia sat on the ground, bawling. Two muddy handprints covered the front of her dress. "Good to see you, Tony. Motherhood calls."

She said to Nick. "Sociology?" She cocked her head toward Tony. "Good luck on keeping your head above water."

Five minutes later, Natalie had Marcia's tears dried

and her dress sort of cleaned up. She'd also explained as best she could to a two-year-old, that if you push someone, they are going to push you back. But now, instead of going off with the other toddlers, Marcia was clinging to her. Natalie was leading her toward where food and drinks had been brought outside when she heard, "Hey, trouble-maker."

Natalie wheeled around, and there was a red-headed barrel-chested man grinning at her. It took her a moment or two before she recognized him. "Gene Farley. I'll be darned."

Gene stepped toward Natalie and grasped her hand. "I wasn't sure it was you without the coveralls and safety glasses."

Marcia huddled behind Natalie. "This is Mr. Farley," she said to her, "Mommy and Mr. Farley worked together back in the war."

Gene leaned close to the ear away from Marcia and whispered, "I don't want to corrupt innocent children, but her mommy kicked my behind back in the war."

"You were absolutely not the biggest pain in the you know where." Natalie glanced around the folks scattered in the yard. "What's a Farley doing here?"

"Beats me. "Gene said. "I think my wife's a cousin of your cousin – or something like that." His arm swept around to take in the growing number of people moving out to the back yard. "Quite a bash to include cousins of cousins."

Natalie chuckled. "Your wife will explain it." Inside the house her exhausted cousin Rose was still slumped on a sofa holding the prize in her arms – her newborn son Angelo, Junior. Her two daughters hovered like piglets pushed off their teats, already sensing the supporting roles they were destined to play in their brother's life. "So, what have you been doing since I messed up your life?"

"I stuck it out at the Arsenal until forty-six. Then Ford Radiator started expanding and offered me a better deal. I'm supervising one of the lines."

"Good for you. When you're hiring, you should think about the *girls* who were operating just about every piece of machinery at the Arsenal."

Gene waved his hand toward Marcia. "All you *girls* are popping out kids to beat the band and staying home baking cakes." He paused. "Frankly, I'm making enough that Shirley could quit and stay home with the kids." Gene pointed to Marcia. "Your only?" he said as though Natalie was hiding something.

"Just this one," Natalie said and wondered if I he was accusing her of being un-American.

Marcia tugged on Natalie's arm. "I have to go to the potty," she whispered.

"Got to go," Natalie said. She held out her hand. "Good to see you, Gene."

Ten minutes later, Natalie pushed Marcia toward the other toddlers playing in the backyard. She scanned the yard for Bill, but he wasn't where she last saw him, sulking in a folding chair far from the clots of other men scattered around the yard. She didn't expect him to become a back-slapping hale-fellow-well-met, but he spent too much time brooding, often staring at his hands or something in his lap for minutes on end. Natalie hoped for just a glimmer of the old fun-to-be-with Bill, not a joker, but a man who enjoyed being around people.

Natalie was about to see if Bill had gone down to the rec room, when he spotted him standing with three other men near a table laden with warming pans and tubs of drinks in ice. Good. They seemed to be having a pleasant conversation. Natalie's cousin Ruth sat on a metal lawn chair, fanning herself. She appeared to be about twelve months pregnant, and Natalie wouldn't be surprised if Ruth went directly from here to the hospital. She started toward Ruth and heard a loud, angry voice – Bill's. A red-faced Bill was angrily stabbing a finger at a man who had his hands spread in a conciliatory stance.

"Okay. Okay," the man said. "I didn't think you'd take it the wrong way."

Bill took a step toward the man. He seemed about to punch him. "You watch what you're saying."

"Hey, take it easy," the man next to Bill said and put his hand on Bill's shoulder.

Bill shook off the man's hand, and then stalked across the lawn shaking his head and muttering something Natalie couldn't make out. The three men and now several people close to them followed Bill with *what-was-that-all-about* stares.

Natalie didn't know what to do. Should she follow Bill? Marcia was playing with another girl, so she headed off to find Bill. At the front of the house, Natalie saw Bill sitting in their car. Bill was gripping the steering wheel and talking to himself. Natalie rapped on the window. Nothing. She rapped again more insistently. Bill turned his head but seemed not to recognize her. Natalie made a roll-down-the-window motion. After a few moments, he rolled it down.

"What happened?" Natalie asked.

"Nothing," He stared straight ahead.

Natalie didn't want to argue. "I'll get Marcia, and we'll go home."

"Stay if you want." He rolled up the window.

He went back to staring out the windshield, but his lips were moving. Natalie wondered if he was saying something to her, but then realized he was talking to himself.

Heading back to the house, Natalie skirted around the side to the back yard. She was afraid to ask the men Bill had been talking to what caused his outrage. Just then, Nick sidled up to her.

"Is Bill alright?" he asked.

"Do you know what happened?" Natalie said, cocking her head in the men's direction.

"They're not sure," Nick said. "Apparently one of the guys was telling a story about getting a break from combat in France and something about being in a local bar on a weekend pass." Nick cocked his head toward the men. "Ted said he was kidding about the local girls laughing at their jokes because the GIs were buying all the drinks. That seemed to set Bill off. Surprised them. They couldn't understand what upset Bill."

This wasn't the first time that Bill blew up. Natalie understood how dropping a fork or misbuttoning a shirt would provoke a 'darn' – even a 'damn,' but Bill might yell at the stove if the water wasn't boiling fast enough. Things that might annoy her would set Bill off on a rant. "He's got a lot on his mind," Natalie said. Like not making more than his low base pay the last three months at the dealership.

Natalie thanked Nick for the information and walked across the lawn towards Marcia, feeling the stares from those who heard or were told about Bill's outburst.

"Come on, Marcia." Natalie took her hand and tugged her up from where she was sitting with another girl. She couldn't figure out who among the scads of children this girl belonged to.

"I don't want to go," Marcia said and pulled her hand away from Natalie's.

"We have to go, now," Natalie said in an insistent

whisper.

"We haven't had the cake," Marcia whined.

"*Now*," Natalie repeated. She grabbed Marcia by the wrist and pulled her upright. "I will get you a piece of cake on the way out."

Forty minutes later Natalie sat across the kitchen table from Marcia. She was in her pajamas and finishing the cake Natalie managed to pry from her cousin before the formal cake-cutting. Bill had headed for the bedroom as soon as they arrived – complaining of a headache. Natalie's gentle inquiry about the argument got her nothing more than a grumbled, "Nothing. It was nothing."

Natalie stared at the closed bedroom door and recalled Bill playing with Marcia that morning before they'd headed off to the party. Marcia had sat on Bill's lap while he patiently read her two stories. And then, the two of them went off hand-in-hand for a walk around the block while Natalie cleaned up the kitchen. Their return was announced by Marcia's loud giggling at the nonsense jokes Bill was telling. Natalie would like to take that Bill and freeze him like a block of Birdseye green beans and thaw him out to serve up instead of the sullen, angry and unpredictable Bill they'd seen at the party. Unfortunately, the sunny Bill rarely peeked through the constant clouds, giving Natalie no more than occasional hints – and hopes – of what might be.

Right now, Natalie didn't feel too guilty that Marcia was stuffing herself with cake before dinner because she didn't have much, if anything, in the fridge. She was counting on taking home the paper plates full of leftovers that were doled out by the hosts who always put out twice as much food for the number of guests. Her stinging eyes surprised her. She faked a cough and tried to take her mind away from how close to the bone they lived. Take away from a First Communion party, Dad slipping a ten in her pocket after Sunday dinner – her hands holding enough leftovers for three nights' dinners.

Bill was sulking in the bedroom, and Natalie wondered how she was going to get him off to the dealership tomorrow morning. Millions of Americans with money falling out of their pockets and a pent-up rage for new cars, and he couldn't make sales.

27

Coal Strike Fails to Halt Industry: Another Week of Shutdowns Will Create Serious Condition

Can't catch my breath. I got to sit down.

Jimmie comes in from the back room. "You okay, Mister P?"

"I'm okay, Jimmie. I might have strained a muscle lifting that last barrel of ink." I rub my left shoulder. I can't shake the dull ache in my left arm that's been nagging me all morning.

"You take it easy, Mister P. I got the last of the ink, and I'm going to start on the paper in a minute."

"You're the one that should go easy. Take a break."

"As soon as I get the cartons on the end of the dock inside. Looks like rain."

Jimmie heads to the back of the building. He's a good kid. When I kept him on when Stan went to prison, I figured it was the right thing to do for Stan and Mildred. Both dead within a year. I never thought Stan gave Jimmie his due, just fetch and carry. That he does like a demon, but I taught him more about printing, let him take on more parts of the job. He's never going to handle the whole shebang, but he's come a long way.

"Jimmie," I shout toward the loading dock, "take a break I'm telling you." My breath's coming back. And I think the ache in my arm is easing up.

Jimmie comes back in and plops down on a stack of cartons. "The new shop is going great, Mr. P."

"Only if I can count on you to help me out," I say.

Since I decided – or since I agreed to Natalie's proposal to expand I haven't slept through the night. Run myself ragged trying to keep up with orders with the old shop or run myself ragged trying to generate new business to pay for the equipment in the new shop?

And when I finally fall asleep, that dream keeps coming back. It's been three years. Stan's dead. J. Edgar Hoover is chasing commies, but the two guys in suits and hats coming in the front door of the shop has me bolting awake in a sweat.

Natalie says I need to hire another printer. The numbers she showed me made sense, but I don't want to go out on a limb before I see how much new business we bring in. I can still put in the extra hours. 'Let's wait and see,' I told her. She's not happy. Tess isn't happy. Thank goodness Jimmie's always happy.

28

Sharp Gains Made by Studebaker: Huge Sales Rise Shown

Natalie took her time at the kitchen sink. She never thought washing dishes would be a relief, but she told Bill that he either watches Marcia or does the dishes. Don't give me that look, she'd said. Natalie wondered if men had a secret handbook that listed what they can or cannot do, and washing dishes was definitely on the 'do not' list.

From the living room, Natalie heard a newscaster's voice. Darn, Natalie thought, Bill was listening to the radio instead of reading Marcia a story like she'd asked. "Bill," she called. "Are you reading to Marcia?"

Natalie didn't hear an answer. She wiped her hands on a dish towel and walked to the doorway of the living room. Marcia was still in her pajamas because Bill didn't get home yesterday in time for her to get to the laundromat. Taking the clothes to the laundromat was likely on the 'do not' list. Natalie thought she could dig out an outfit for Marcia from the hamper that wasn't too smelly. Bill had pulled on a pair of pants, but he wasn't dressed for work. "I'll handle Marcia. You better get changed or you're going to be late."

Bill shrugged.

Not again. Natalie told herself to remain calm. "You are going in?" she asked in as casual a tone as she could manage.

She got another shrug.

"What does that mean?"

"It means that Mike can see how well it goes without

me."

Natalie fought the urge to scream. The last time she did scream, but Bill still stayed out two days. This was draining her, but Natalie decided to play the loving, concerned wife. "Does that work?" she said cautiously. She didn't want to set off one of Bill's explosive tantrums. Sometimes she thought Marcia had more self-control.

"Daddy, finish the story," Marcia cried.

Bill got up to turn down the volume and flopped back on the sofa next to Marcia.

Don't ignore me, damn it, Natalie thought. She felt as though she was taking care of two children. "What's the problem this time?" Natalie asked in a soothing tone and sat next to him.

"The big cheese. Dealer of the month. I'll bet Studebaker dropped a few shekels in Mike's pocket, not that I'd get even a tiny piece of the pie."

If they're dealer of the month someone was selling a lot of cars, Natalie thought. But it wasn't Bill. And he wasn't going to sell Studebakers if he was home pouting.

"He's giving the other guys the best leads. All I get are the tire kickers and be-backs."

Natalie was at a loss as she felt Bill slump against her. Day to day, sometimes hour to hour, she didn't know which Bill was here. Right now he could be on the verge of two days of black moods, wordlessly sitting on the edge of the bed staring at the wall. Natalie didn't know whether those were as frightening as the rages set off by the most trivial thing. She patted his shoulder. "Come on, Bill, you've been through a lot worse than having a brother who's a pain in the you-know-what."

"I'm just not cut out to be a car salesman."

Oh, no. You can't quit. Natalie couldn't take more of

the financial roller-coaster they'd been on for the last three years. Okay, you've been through a lot, more than most – combat, wounded, prison camp. Natalie guessed he deserved to lay around the apartment for a couple of months even though that chewed through his mustering out pay and what Natalie had saved.

Natalie wanted to say – but couldn't, You had the brass ring handed to you when Studebaker offered to turn your father's garage into a dealership. He expected you to take over when he retired. But you couldn't see yourself working for your father and being a partner with your brother, Mike. You let them buy you out so you could go off to three other jobs that wouldn't put up with your temper, black moods, absenteeism, and the notion that someone was always out to get you.

It stuck in your craw, but we were broke when your father retired, and Mike asked you come in as a salesman. Millions of Americans with a pent-up rage for new cars, and you can't sell cold beer in a desert. Your monthly base is a gift from your brother, and you'd go crazy if you knew my father slips me a ten or a twenty on the way out the door when we visit. You can't quit.

Instead, Natalie said, "Bill, honey. Give it a go. Don't worry about Mike. Keep your mind on what's good for you, for me and Marcia." Natalie listened to her words and hoped he didn't take them as a complaint about what he was earning – or not. She coaxed Bill off the sofa and into the bedroom. She hoped she wouldn't have to dress him like a child, but he needed to go to work. They needed a normal life. She was dragging her old life behind her like gum stuck on her shoe.

29

Surgeons Warned by Pius; Pope in Address Condemns Sterilization and Birth Control.

Flo was due in ten minutes, and Natalie didn't know whether to wash the dishes or pick up Marcia's stuff scattered about the apartment. She reached under the table for a piece of a puzzle then looked around the place. What a mess. She was a mess. Lately she was spending almost every day in her bathrobe. She should at least get dressed and comb her hair.

Last Wednesday Natalie was so sick of herself that late that afternoon she put on one of her nicer dresses, fixed her hair, and even dabbed on a bit of makeup. Bill came home and stared at her for several seconds. 'What's the matter?' he asked. 'We got to go to a wake or something?' Natalie burst into tears and ran to the bedroom.

To hell with the dishes. She'd check to make sure Marcia was playing quietly, then put on a pot of coffee.

Fifteen minutes later, Flo settled into a chair at the kitchen table.

Marcia came running into the kitchen, and cuddled up next to Flo. Flo pulled Marcia onto her lap and gave her a big kiss. "I love to squeeze my favorite girl." She wrapped her arms around Marcia and pulled her tight to her and kissed her again. "If you play quietly and let me and your mommy talk for a few minutes. Well…." Flo raised her eyebrows. "there just might be a surprise hiding somewhere."

Natalie gave Flo a playful scolding smile. A shopping bag from Whitney's had been left by the door. No matter how many times Natalie told her not to, Flo never visited without bringing small presents for Marcia.

Flo gave Marcia another kiss and gently nudged her toward the living room. "Remember, quietly," she whispered.

"You're spoiling her," Natalie said.

"That's what Godmothers are supposed to do."

"How have you been?" Natalie asked.

Flo started to say something and stopped. "I was about to say, 'Fine' – like your always smiling, always cheery Whitney's salesgirl. Every morning, minutes before the doors open, our floor manager, *Mister* – absolutely never Herman – Jenkins gathers his *girls* together, reminds us to always smile no matter how idiotic the customer acts, gives us all a once over, which is a nickel this side of a leer, to make sure we're properly attired, and sends his *girls* off to sell notions, hosiery, better dresses, and what not." She put her coffee cup down with a bang.

Marcia peeked in. "Is it time for a story?"

Just a few more minutes," Natalie said.

Flo continued, "Even with my employee's discount, I'm spending a hefty chunk of my salary on dresses and stockings. Wearing the same dress twice in a week gets a scowl and a *word* from Mr. Jenkins." Flo took a gulp of coffee. "I'd like to see him stand all day behind a counter in high heels."

Natalie reached across the table and laid her hand on Flo's. "Are you alright?"

She shrugged. "One of the sales*girls* in maternity had a death in the family, and I had to fill in."

"Sometimes it takes time," Natalie said.

"Almost three years?" Flo glanced toward the living room. "We're going to see a doctor. Maybe something's wrong with me."

"Or Bob. I'm sorry," Natalie stammered. "Nothing's wrong with either of you."

"Maybe my girdle is the culprit. Stuff Jenkins in one of those every day, and we'd see how cheery he'd be."

Natalie gestured to take in Flo's flowered print shirtwaist dress. "At least you don't have to hide your good looks under coveralls, safety goggles, and a paisley bandana."

"I don't miss that," Flo said. "I'll take something between the Arsenal and Whitney's notions department." She paused. "Have you thought about going to work?"

"Every day," Natalie said. "I'd love a job like I had at the Arsenal. I was doing something that was important. It was a challenge. I did things I never realized I could do." Natalie glanced toward where Marcia was surely waiting for a chance to return to her spoiling Aunt Flo. She was bored. Marcia filled her day with demands for stories, games, and jaunts to the playground, but it didn't stretch her. But she also couldn't imagine joining the two, three, and now four-children families cramming into Sunday Mass. She hoped Flo's dreams of a houseful of kids came true, but not for her. Natalie wondered if she was cut out for motherhood at all.

Flo said, "Maybe the Soviets will start another war."

"Something not as dramatic," Natalie said. "I ran into Gene Farley at a First Communion party. He's moved from the Arsenal to the Ford radiator plant on Green Island as a line supervisor. They're expanding, and I told him he should hire some of the women who worked at the Arsenal."

"Not a chance," Flo said. "When I decided to get a job while Bob finished school, I tried Ford, Bendix Brake, and all the other factories around here. They wouldn't even let me fill out an application. Sitting at a bench and sewing collars for Arrow for peanuts was the only factory job open. I could do any job on the line at Ford – and get three times what I make as a sales *girl* at Whitney's."

"Get off the line and back in the kitchen," Natalie said. She and Flo had been around and around on this, so Natalie was only a little sorry she came back to where Flo would love to be: in the kitchen surrounded by four or five children.

Flo said, "Sometimes in my head I can still hear the hellish banging of the forges and the screaming lathes. All day at Whitney's I hear these delicate little tinkling chimes signaling the urgent need for a supervisor to handle a crisis of whether the stockings the customer has selected are indeed the ones advertised on sale in Sunday's *Knickerbocker News*." Flo gulped her coffee. "These people – including Mister Jenkins – would faint if they had to deal with a breakdown of a gun tube reamer."

Natalie felt guilty letting Flo get her frustrations off her chest because she felt the same – bored.

"I'm sorry," Flo said. "I shouldn't unload my complaints on you."

"That's what friends are for."

Flo took two sips of her coffee. "So, as a friend, how are you?"

They both knew what she was asking. Cautiously at first, but more frequently over the past two and a half years, Natalie had been sharing her concerns, now worries, about Bill. "Not much better," she said.

"Bill seemed okay when you two came for dinner."

"You're being kind. I'm afraid Bill was sliding into another funk. For two, maybe three weeks before, we were an almost normal family. He went off to work and sold a few cars. He took Marcia to the playground and helped around the apartment..." Natalie felt her throat squeeze. "Sorry."

Flo patted the back of Natalie's hand.

Natalie let out a bitter laugh. "I almost prayed. Maybe. Just maybe, he's finally digging out of the hole he's been in. Maybe this is the nice guy I married." She shrugged. "But then the signs returned. Sulky. Brooding. Touchy. And then going off over the smallest thing, or something only he can see. Did you see the story in the *TU* last week about the unexploded bomb in London that finally did explode and kill seven people?"

"I did," Flo said.

"I thought about people all over England and France and Germany trying to put their lives back together: thousands of bombs, hand grenades, and mortar shells buried under their feet waiting to go off at the slightest jiggle. Maybe I shouldn't complain."

Flo stared at her coffee cup for several seconds. "He hasn't hit you or anything?"

"No," Natalie sighed. Not yet, she thought. "The problem is that when he falls into those deep funks, he doesn't want to go to work. Even though his brother owns the dealership, I'm afraid he'll get fired or quit – like he did in the jobs before Mike took him in."

"Have you suggested that Bill see someone?"

"I broached it in what I thought was the most gentle way possible. You know, talk to someone. I didn't even say 'doctor.'" Natalie blanched at the memory of what happened before she continued. "Bill swept a plate off the table, and barged out of the room yelling that he wasn't going to see a shrink. And he'd be fine if people stopped harassing him and gave him a fair shake instead of lying to him and cheating him out of what he was due."

"Is it time for a story?" Marcia called from the doorway.

Natalie said, "Yes, honey. Aunt Flo can't wait to spoil you."

Grinning, Marcia ran to Flo. Flo took Marcia's hand and picked up the shopping bag she'd left by the door. They walked toward the living room, where Flo would read a story and then, like a magician pulling rabbits out of a hat, would discover a toy and probably one or two cute outfits in the bag.

And Natalie will let Flo play with Marcia while she wonders whether it was the mixture of love and pain she felt for Flo or the fear Natalie had for their future that had her sniffling. Maybe she was letting her life slither away pining for a past that can't be repeated, she thought. Then Natalie remembered her conversation with Gene Farley – and kicked herself for forgetting about Tony Spadaro.

30

Appliance Sales Higher: Hotpoint Steps Up Output

Natalie nervously settled into a chair across from Tony Spadaro's desk as he put down the phone.

Tony said, "You weren't very specific when you called, so why don't you fill me in on your ... whatever."

"Proposal," Natalie said. "When we talked at my cousin's party, you said you were having problems with scheduling orders from manufacturers, deciding how much to keep in inventory, where to store your appliances and matching deliveries to the stores where you most needed your appliances." She was afraid she was speaking too fast.

Tony leaned back in his chair. "Whoa. You've got a good memory."

"Not good enough," Natalie said. "I was probably wondering whether my daughter was getting into trouble when you were telling Nick about your problems managing three stores."

Tony gestured toward the phone. "That call was from the manager of my Central Ave. store. Yesterday one of the salesmen sold a top of the line Amana range and refrigerator." He made a sour face. "Except the models they wanted weren't in the back of the store or in the new warehouse like his inventory sheet read, and they won't be until the next shipment from Iowa in three weeks. So the couple took a hike. The ex-customers aren't happy, the salesman who was already figuring his commission isn't happy, the manager isn't happy, and I'm not happy."

"Good," Natalie blurted. "Sorry. I mean that's what I wanted to talk about. I can fix it."

Tony looked doubtful.

When Natalie practiced what she was going to say to Tony, at first she was too cautious, 'suggesting I might be of assistance.' Too timid. It took her several practice tries standing in front of the bathroom mirror while Marcia napped to screw up the courage to say what she did. 'I can fix it."

"That's pretty bold," Tony said.

Natalie wished she'd spent more time practicing answers, but she charged on. "That's what I did, Tony. I was running Inventory Control at the Arsenal, and by the time I left I was trouble-shooting problems like yours for the Director of Operations."

"Nick says you were a secretary."

How Natalie wished Mr. Vincent hadn't died. In her purse was the letter of commendation, but she didn't think Tony was going to be convinced by a piece of paper. "Logistics," she said.

A question formed on Tony's face.

Before he could ask the question, Natalie rushed on, "Coordinating supplies and people and processes." She ignored the baffled stare on his face because she doubted many civilians knew the term. "Making sure the necessary breech rings and firing mechanisms for howitzers are in inventory. Getting the right parts to the assembly lines on time. Reassigning lathe operators to where they're most needed." Natalie hoped that wasn't too much because Tony seemed stunned. More slowly Natalie said, "I did that at the Arsenal, Tony, and your problems are the same, different scale, different products, but they're the same."

Natalie pointed to the telephone. "The customers who didn't get their fridge and range. That's inventory control. From what you said at the party, that's not the first time that's happened, right?"

Natalie was encouraged by what she thought was a glimmer of understanding on Tony's face. "If that's happening too many times, I'll bet on some days you've seen your delivery guys standing around for hours – on your clock – and then on other days you get angry calls from customers because your managers over-booked deliveries."

"Jesus H. Christ – excuse me"

"Tony, I spent two years at the Arsenal. I heard worse every day."

"Okay, you nailed some of what's going to give me an ulcer. So how does this get fixed?"

Natalie wished he'd asked how *I* get it fixed, but she pushed on. From her purse Natalie pulled out the map of Albany County she snuck out of the Watervliet Library. "May I?" Before he answered Natalie stood and spread the map on Tony's desk. "Here are your stores," she said and pointed to the locations she'd memorized. She wished she could have marked them in red pencil, but she planned to sneak the map back into the library.

"Far apart," Tony said. "I bought a building for a warehouse. Right now, it's mostly for overload for what I don't have room for at the stores. But I haven't had a chance to get it organized."

"Good," Natalie said. She hoped she didn't sound like she was patting a child on the head. Tony may have discovered a talent for selling appliances, but she didn't think he saw the big picture. "That was number one on my list of things I propose." Natalie wanted to sound confident and hoped she wasn't presuming too much. "But you're expanding. You *are* the appliance king." And vain as well, she thought. "With three stores, you've got a lot going for you. You should get bigger discounts from your manufacturers and wholesalers for bigger orders delivered to one central warehouse instead of three smaller orders to each store." When Natalie caught a glimmer of surprise in Tony's eyes, she wondered if his ship was really going to sink. "With a central warehouse, you've got to schedule deliveries to the stores so they've got enough on the floor to show customers." Natalie paused. "The new warehouse is great, but you have to figure out how best to use it."

"Jesus H., Natalie. Have you been sneaking into my stores at night?"

"If we do it right, you can cut back on storage at each store and expand the sales floor." Natalie was afraid to see if Tony picked up on exactly what she'd said. "Tony, that's just a few of the ideas I have." She didn't want to load too much on Tony's plate and sat down.

"That's a lot to take in," Tony said.

"I could go on, but you get the idea."

"What do you propose I do?"

"At the party, you talked about hiring a business manager." Natalie was sure he didn't have one or they wouldn't be still talking. "Hire me."

"You have a kid – Mary or…"

"Marcia." Natalie also guessed Tony's response. "Tony, I'm positive I can help you fix these problems working part-time – about twelve to fifteen hours a week. We can review orders and shipments on Monday, go over inventory on Wednesday, coordinate sales, and deliveries on Friday. Morning or afternoon. No more than fifteen hours." She hoped.

"And your daughter?" Tony said as though Natalie was going to put her up for adoption.

"My mother's going to babysit her," Natalie lied.

Tony shrugged. "I don't know."

"We can give it a trial run. I'll start at whatever you're lowest paid employee is making. "But Natalie didn't think he was convinced. "Give Gene Farley a call." Natalie took out a slip of paper with Gene's phone number and pushed it across the desk. "I have got strong letters of recommendation," she said and pointed to her handbag. "But I worked with Gene. He knows what I did for him, and he knows about the other time-saving, and *money* saving, projects I worked on at the Arsenal. I will cost you a lot less than a full-time business manager – and I'll save you my salary five times over."

Tony picked up the paper with Gene's number. "Let me think about it. You hit me out of the blue."

Natalie felt him slipping away. "Tony, we can't wait too long. I can keep you from sinking – help you make more money and get more sleep." She said, "Please call me by the end of the week so I can make arrangements with my mother."

Tony stood, and Natalie reached across the desk and grasped his hand. "This will be good for me – and for you."

Thirty minutes later Natalie was walking up the sidewalk to her parents' house. Her stomach, finally unclenched after her meeting with Tony, was tightening again. She was afraid she'd lost the confidence she gained working with the managers and supervisors at the Arsenal. She hoped she didn't come on too strong with Tony, but she didn't want him dithering. But now Natalie had to deal with a more difficult case – Mom.

Natalie checked to see that Marcia was occupied and said to Mom, "I'm thinking of getting a part-time job."

"Go back to work?" she said as though Natalie had announced she was taking up street-walking.

"Only part-time, and it could be flexible." A frown formed on her mother's face. "Mom, I need to do this." Her mother gave Natalie the, *I don't know how I raised such a difficult child* look.

Mom glanced toward the dining room where Marcia had set up house under the table. "And what about Marcia? A child needs her mother at home."

"She's got you." Natalie reached across the table and put her hand over her mother's. "I need you."

"I would have thought that with the war over, and Bill back home, you'd be happy being a homemaker. You could have more children."

Natalie, Mom, and Dad had gingerly stepped around Bill. They'd pretended that sitting wordless through an entire Sunday dinner and or loudly complaining about Mike's wrong-headed running of the dealership on the next Sunday – and the dozens of other weird behaviors they pretended weren't happening would somehow, someday evaporate. 'He'll get over it. It takes longer for some men', were the only cautious remarks they allowed themselves.

"Mom, having more children isn't going to fix Bill's problems. He's not getting better." Natalie stopped herself from telling Mom it was getting worse. "He's not doing well at his job, and I'm afraid he'll quit or get fired."

"Your father and I can …"

"No, you can't," Natalie interrupted. "Not with money. I appreciate what you give me now on the QT." Natalie squeezed her hand. "What you can give me is three mornings or afternoons a week, ten or so hours." Natalie hoped to God she didn't have to play her trump card. She knew Dad and Mom were helping out Nick. Once when Natalie protested the twenty he slipped in Natalie's hand, Dad make a veiled reference to what they were sending to

Nick at Syracuse.

Another sigh. "I'll talk to your father."

"Thank you, Mom. It will mean a lot to me – and Marcia." *Bless me, father, I shamelessly manipulated my mother.* Natalie knew she'd do it, and Natalie would gladly put up with whatever sighs Mom would pull out of her repertoire and make whatever allusions to what she believed was best for families. Now Natalie had to deal with her next problem.

***

"I can provide for my family without my wife having to go to work," Bill said.

Natalie put her hand on his shoulder and gave it a loving squeeze. "I know you can, Bill. It's not really going to work." It was Thursday, and Natalie hadn't heard back from Tony. But if he called, she couldn't tell him to hold off until she cleared it with her husband. It had to work.

Natalie wasn't surprised by Bill's reaction to the idea of her going to work for Tony. She'd waited all week for the right moment to bring it up. Finally, when Bill came home with the news that he'd sold two cars that day, Natalie hoped she'd catch him on a high.

"It will only be a few hours once or twice a week. And Mom will be delighted to take care of Marcia." Natalie was glad that all she got was a sour look from Bill before he pulled a beer from the fridge.

Bill flipped the cap off the bottle with a church key and took a long swig. "I'm not crazy about you working. I was never that keen on Tony, and now he thinks his shit don't stink. Mister Appliance."

"Tell me about your sales."

Bill plopped in a chair at the kitchen table and took another long pull on his beer. "Two Commodores and I'm pretty sure I got a hot prospect with a guy coming back

249

tomorrow. Things are turning around, Natalie. You won't need a job."

Natalie kneaded his shoulders. "You're hitting your stride. This thing with Tony will just be icing on the cake." More like filling in the wide cracks in their budget, she thought. It was terrific he'd sold two cars today and maybe another tomorrow, but that made four in the past three weeks. And Natalie was behind on her tab at the grocery store.

"It felt good to stick it to that asshole Stenson. Made a big stink about the guy I sold one of the Commodores to was his customer, like they had a blood brother contract or something. He took the day off, tough shit."

"Bill, Marcia," Natalie said quietly. She felt Bill's shoulders tense under her fingers. Natalie didn't want him swinging into another rant about how Stenson and the other salesmen, the sales manager and everyone else were treating him unfairly. "Good for you," she said. "Put Stenson behind you. You're on a roll. My little thing with Tony will be just a little sideshow. Egg money, the farmers' wives say." She felt a shrug.

"I guess. Just don't bandy it around that you've gone back to work."

An hour later, Natalie took the dinner dishes to the sink. All through dinner, Bill acted as though they were the happiest family in the world, grinning and complimenting her on the dinner she'd cooked.

Bill grabbed a surprised Marcia and pulled her onto his lap. "Come here." He wrapped his arms around her and squeezed her.

Marcia squirmed and said, "Daddy, you're hurting me."

"Sorry, darling. I guess I love you too much." He

released Marcia. Her messy hand left a smudge on Bill's pant leg. "That's okay, honey," he said.

Natalie handed him a dish rag, and he wiped his pant leg. "Mommy will clean up after me. She always does," he said with a wide grin.

Two Commodores and he's Bob Hope and Groucho Marx rolled into one. Enjoy it Natalie told herself, but she felt like the weather man on WGY: 'Today's high pressure will be followed by a low pressure system coming in from the west.'

Natalie slipped her nightgown over her head. She felt Bill's eyes on her. Where's that low pressure? He kept up the joking, the hugs and kisses all evening. He even insisted on helping Natalie put Marcia to bed. She wished he'd do that every night, but tonight she was afraid of what it meant.

Natalie slid into bed, and immediately Bill rolled toward her. One arm was across her chest, and his hand was on her breast. "We have such a beautiful daughter, Natalie. We should have a son, even more daughters."

Natalie loved Marcia, but she didn't want more children, even if they could afford them. So what if Bill doesn't have a son. God, she was only twenty-five. At this rate, she could have – she didn't want to count – before her change. Natalie pictured the Zappellos trooping into Sunday Mass, three already and another on the way. The Hogans and their five children spilled out of their station wagon like a circus act, beaming in their two pews as Father Eagan fawned over them as though he'd harvested a bumper crop of pole beans. Everywhere Natalie turned at ten o'clock Mass she was surrounded by squalling and squirming children.

Bill's kneaded her breast, and Natalie counted the

days since her last period. The Pope must have more regular periods than she did if he thinks his rhythm method will work. Natalie put off Bill for as long as she could after Marcia's birth, but he was right that it wasn't natural for them not to have sex. But it was difficult to enjoy it when all she was thinking was whether she'd get pregnant.

As soon as Bill pulled out, Natalie slid out of bed. "I've got to clean up." In the bathroom, she dug the douche bag out from the back of the vanity. She didn't know if Bill realized what she was doing or not, but she wasn't going to join the circus.

***

She'd been over the moon since Tony called. They'd talk about the job. No promises. Now standing in Tony's new warehouse a week later, Natalie struggled to not smile. It was a complete mess, and she loved it.

From the way Tony described his telephone call with Gene Farley, Natalie sensed a hint of ambivalence and hoped Gene didn't come on too much about how she'd kicked his behind. Tony was sensitive. Natalie needed to calm down and hit a balance between being someone who could help him and a pushy woman who was going to straighten out the mess he'd made. But God, what a mess. Natalie wondered how he managed to open three stores with the jumble of inventory and records she'd already seen here.

With the inventory sheet Tony gave her in hand, Natalie cautiously asked, "Could you show me the thirteen Maytag washing machines?"

Tony pointed to a row of large cardboard cartons along the wall. "That's them."

Natalie didn't know whether to ask why there were only eight cartoons, but thankfully Tony beat her to it.

"Yeah. Not thirteen. We had a sale. Went well. Haven't had a chance to update the inventory records."

"How often do you do that?"

"As soon as I can." He made a face. "Not often enough."

Natalie was afraid that her standing there with the incorrect inventory might make Tony feel guilty. She chanced a playful punch on his arm. "That's because you're selling at such a fast clip. You're outrunning your paperwork."

"And you're going to set me straight?" he said.

"We'll figure out how to make sure your guys aren't selling what they don't have in inventory."

Two hours hour later, Natalie and Tony were sitting in a booth at the Westgate diner after going through the stock room and sales floors of the Latham and Central Avenue stores. There were the same issues she saw in Cohoes: inventory records not matching what was in the storerooms or on the floor, managers, under gentle prodding, reporting delivery delays, and tug-of-wars between stores dragging their heels on shipping best-selling-appliances in short supply to other stores.

Tony leaned back in the booth. "You see why I'm working on an ulcer?"

Throughout the morning, Natalie felt Tony's prickliness ease. She was on his side when the managers raised their complaints. "I think the warehouse is going to be an enormous help." She took a sip of coffee. "But, you need me to come in three times a week to handle the issues we've seen." Natalie didn't want to keep hammering on the problems she'd laid out earlier or pile on the others she'd seen on their tour. She knew she could fix them, but she was afraid it might take more than the three or four hours three times a week she'd proposed. "All I need is a tiny desk, an adding machine, and a jar of Number 2 pencils." She was relieved when Tony laughed.

"I'm seeing what Gene Farley hinted at."

"Look at it this way," Natalie said. "You'll have me to blame when I ration hard to get appliances among the stores, schedule deliveries that keep the guys you're paying delivering instead of sitting around in the store room, and not tying up your money with shipments that sit in the warehouse too long."

Tony spread his arms wide. "I surrender."

"When do I start?"

31

Husbands Give Views on Working Wives at Parley on Jobs and Futures

Three weeks later, Natalie got out of her car and breathed in the warm air. June was busting out all over, and while she loved her job, she didn't love being stuck inside all day. It was great, but the small price to pay hit her when she opened the front door of the warehouse and sniffed the air. Yards of sheetrock and paint for the front end and buckets of lye on the floors in back hadn't erased the ghostly aroma of seventy-five years of steaks, pork chops, and ground chuck seeping out of the walls of the old Freeman's meat packing plant Tony had purchased for the warehouse.

The door from the storeroom popped open, and Ralph Turner stepped in and quickly closed the door behind him. He looked surprised to see Natalie. "Good morning, Mrs. Costello," he said as though he was greeting one of his teachers.

"Good morning, Ralph," Natalie said. So far, he'd been the perfect warehouse guy: big and strong and able to do pretty much exactly as he was told.

"Ready for a good day?" Natalie said and started toward the small office they'd carved out of the front. It may still smell of stale meat, but it was her office and she didn't have to share it with Agnes or worry about a Mr. Holt. She was about to hang up her sweater when she realized something wasn't right. She turned back to Ralph. His face was flushed and there were sweat circles under his armpits. The moment his head dropped to hide the guilty look on his face, Natalie heard voices from the back.

Natalie slipped around Ralph and opened the door to the back. When she saw Walter Hawkins, the warehouse manager, and Howie Grant, the manager of the Central Ave store standing next to a row of Frigidaires, she knew her day was off to a lousy start.

Walter said, "I thought you were coming in this afternoon." He stole a sideways glance at Howie.

Caught with their hands in the cookie jar – again. "My mother had to do something, and we switched off her babysitting Marcia." Natalie was sorry she was explaining why she was here. The problem was she knew why Howie was here. Natalie hoped she'd get this settled quickly and without too much of a fight. "What's up, Howie?" He looked as though he was deciding whether to lie or argue.

"It's urgent," he said. "Walter told me you weren't coming in this morning, and I couldn't wait. Figured we could straighten out the paperwork later."

Bald-faced liar. Natalie shot a black look at Walter. Unlike Ralph, Walter didn't always do exactly what he was supposed to do. He followed instructions until the last store manager had brow-beaten, lied, or cajoled him into *just this one* end-run for extra items or quicker delivery. Natalie saw four tall cartons ready to be loaded into the Central Ave store's truck – four Frigidaires that were definitely not scheduled for delivery and not going to be straightened out later. Now what? She wasn't Walter's or Howie's boss. Her choices were very limited. Natalie stifled the urge to yell at them. Walter and Howie along with too many other men she'd worked with since she started couldn't seem to deal with women in any job other than school teacher, nurse, secretary, and shop clerk. "What's so urgent?" Natalie asked as though she might be reasonable.

Howie gestured toward the refrigerators. "I'm completely out of that model."

Don't keep lying, Natalie wanted to say. Natalie cocked her head in the direction of her office. "All out?" she asked as though the hint that she might be reasonable was quickly evaporating. Howard knew her paperwork was never wrong because she was meticulous when she was working here – and when she took it home and double and triple-checked it while Bill snored on the sofa.

"Well, almost," Howie said as if he sensed a chance to negotiate. "Had a great day yesterday. And I've got two customers I'm sure are coming back after work today for those models. I've got to have them on the floor or in the back." He spread his hands in a gesture of appeal. "They sell better when they can open and close the doors."

Natalie didn't want to go back to her office to check the figures, but she was positive she remembered them. "How great a day?"

"Sold three," he lied.

"Even if you really sold three – I'm guessing two – that leaves you with one on the floor and two in the stockroom." The wrinkled brow on Howie's face told her he was struggling to do the math.

Walter shook his head. "I don't know how she does that."

Howie shot him a nasty look.

"I do it because I keep very careful records of inventory and deliveries." Natalie stared at Howie for a few seconds. He knew that if she didn't sign off on this hijacking – now or when the paperwork supposedly got straightened out – he was going to have a problem accounting for his sales at the end of the month. And Natalie knew he'd complain to Tony that this – he won't say it but will make clear – *female* paper-pusher was slowing down sales. And they'd have a long and useless meeting which would solve nothing and leave everyone angry.

Still, Natalie couldn't let Howie get completely away with it. She grasped Howie's arm and pulled him toward the loading dock. When they were out of Walter's hearing, Natalie said, "Howie, you and I know where this is going. Here's what I propose. You take *one* of those Frigidaires, and I'll sign off on the delivery." Natalie felt him relax. She turned to face him. "But if I hear that you're telling the other managers that I can be buffaloed, or you go behind my back and complain to Tony – let me count the ways I can make your life miserable."

For a couple of seconds, Howie seemed to be figuring the pros and cons. "Three?"

"Two." Natalie gave him a mirthless smile. "And if you behave yourself, you might be first in line for the next hot items." She pursed her lips and cocked her head as though conjuring evil deeds. "And if you backslide, I'm not good at absolution."

"Okay," Howie said.

Natalie called to Walter. "Why don't you and Howie move two of these units back where they came from?"

Walter glanced toward the stockroom door.

"Give Ralph a break. He's beat."

Thirty minutes later, Natalie and Walter were on the loading dock watching Howie drive away. It was a good time for the heart-to-heart talk she needed to have because this wasn't the first end-run Walter aided and abetted.

Natalie was about to begin when Walter said, "Sorry, Natalie. It won't happen again."

She'd like to believe him, but he was too much of a nice guy and a pushover. "Walter, I'm not your boss, and you're not mine." God, how she missed the military hierarchy at the Arsenal – and the authority she wielded as Mr. Vincent's trouble-shooter. "We have to work together. I know my paperwork is accurate, and I'll vouch for it to Tony, his accountant, lawyer, and whoever wants to check the numbers." Natalie paused for a few moments to let this sink in. "If the inventory doesn't match my paperwork, I'm sure *I'm* okay."

"Cripes, Natalie. I hope you're not suggesting…"

"Of course not," she interrupted. "But you don't want to let yourself be pushed out onto the end of a limb and have somebody get the wrong idea if it all doesn't add up." She was glad Walter seemed anxious. Natalie gave him a pat on the arm. "Give me a few minutes and I'll be back to go over what we've got coming in from suppliers."

Back in her office, Natalie settled into her chair and tried to remember what she'd planned to do that morning. Getting this warehouse up and running had been more draining than she'd hoped. She felt terrible about asking Mom to babysit more than the 'ten or so hours a week' she initially asked. It's been more *'or so'* – like fifteen plus, and Natalie didn't see it getting less soon. When Natalie first saw the mess Tony was in, she was delighted. It was something she could fix. And although she was fixing inventory control, it was the Walter's and Howie's she was struggling to fix. Natalie pushed the other thought away but she couldn't. How was she going to fix Bill?

Later Natalie leaned against a Whirlpool washing machine and sniffed the shoulder of her dress, smelling the mix of dust kicked up from moving the stock, the peculiar aroma of cardboard, and sweat. She wondered if she ought to get some overalls like she had at the Arsenal. This was supposed to be an office job, but Natalie found herself digging around among the cartons trying to locate stock that had been delivered and not stacked where she wanted. Walter was too damned nice, and he let the drivers drop the deliveries inside the loading dock instead of where they should be. It wasn't exactly the mess of howitzer parts in Building SH at the Arsenal, but different brands and models of fridges, ranges, washing machines, and dryers were scattered throughout the warehouse.

Natalie hoped she was making progress with her plan for organizing where the different appliances should be located. She'd explained to Walter that if he let the teamsters drop the supplies wherever it was easiest for them, he and Ralph were the ones stuck with pushing and hauling stock around for deliveries to the stores. She wasn't ready to run to Tony to explain how much wasted time and *money* that cost.

Natalie stepped away from the rows of washing machine and clothes dryers. Farms all over Albany and Rensselaer counties were growing three bedroom ranches, so if the new owners were coming in to buy a washing machine, there was a good bet we were selling them a dryer. Now the washers and dryers that used to be scattered all over the warehouse by brand were in adjoining rows. She wanted to start on reorganizing refrigerators and ranges, but she needed to pick up Marcia at Mom's. She felt terrible that she was asking Mom to babysit more hours than Natalie had promised. But for the first time since she'd left the Arsenal she felt as though she was putting together a real life. Now if she could only get Bill to come along too.

32

Soviets Blockade Berlin: Airlift Backfires on Russians

Natalie stepped into the bedroom. Bill was sitting on the edge of the bed. "Bill…"

He gave Natalie a startled look and slammed down the cover of the metal box in his lap. "Don't sneak up on me like that."

"I'm not sneaking," Natalie said. "What's in the box?" The brown metal box came home from the service with Bill and was shoved in the back of the closet under the Ike jacket and tan trousers of his uniform. 'Souvenirs' he'd said. That was a surprise because Bill didn't talk about the war. Whenever anyone asked him about D-Day or the Battle of the Bulge he'd clam up. The one time Natalie asked him about his experience as a Prisoner of War, the angry look on his face made it clear that topic was *verboten.* Flo said that Bob was reluctant to talk about the war in Italy, only eager to tell whoever wanted to listen about how Roman ruins had inspired him to be a history teacher.

Bill had been awarded the Purple Heart, but he never showed Natalie the medal. She'd seen a picture of one in *Life,* and she wanted to see Bill's. There had to be more in the box than Bill's medal because when Natalie picked it up one day when he was out, it was heavy. She didn't want to shake it, but as she tipped it to put it back, she felt something heavy shifting inside. A shiver had gone through Natalie as she thought about what might be locked in the box. She was afraid to try the several keys Bill kept in the corner of his dresser drawer. Natalie had an unclear memory of a short story she read in high school, but did recall that it didn't turn out well for the person who pried.

"Come on, Bill," Natalie said. "Secrets aren't good for a marriage." She felt a flush on the back of her neck when she heard her words.

"Nothing. Just stuff I should have never brought home. I should have thrown it out anyway."

"I'd like to see your medal." Natalie sat down next to him, and he quickly shifted away, turning so the box was largely hidden from her view. "Please."

Bill sighed and lifted the lid of the box a few inches. His hand slid in, scrabbled around for a moment, and came out with the Purple Heart.

Natalie took it from his hand. "You're a brave man."

He snorted and took it back.

"What else is in there?"

"Junk. Discharge papers, my pay book. Crap I should throw away." He started to rise and turn toward the closet.

Natalie put her hand on his arm and held him back. "Bill, there's more in there." She paused wondering if her confession would anger him and make him unwilling to tell her. "I was cleaning the closet, and I moved the box. It's heavy. There's something heavy in there."

Bill's eyes became defensive, and he shifted away from Natalie.

She pulled him back. "I *need* to know what's in there."

Bill stared at the box for several seconds. He slowly opened it, still keeping Natalie from seeing inside. He pulled out a sheaf of papers and laid them on the bed. "My discharge papers and a letter from General Eisenhower thanking me."

"Did you keep my letters? I kept yours."

"Sorry. Lost them."

"That's okay, you had a lot going on." She paused. "What else?"

Bill pulled out a folded black and red flag. "Nazi flag. I don't know why I wanted it." He put the flag back in the box and started to close the lid.

"Bill, I have to know about the heavy thing."

"It's nothing you should worry about. I shouldn't have brought it home."

"Show me."

Bill slid around so Natalie could see into the box. There was a large black gun laying in it.

Natalie flinched as though she'd seen a cobra in there. "A gun. Bill, why did you bring home a gun?"

"It's a pistol, a forty-five – officer's weapon."

Incredulous, Natalie said, "The Army let you take it home?"

"At the embarkation ports, it was like an Arab bazaar. There were guys with stacks of forty-fives, Lugars, rifles, two bucks, twenty bucks." He let out a rueful laugh. "Hand grenades, even. I can't believe anybody'd be stupid enough to put a grenade in their kit."

Natalie bit back saying how stupid it was to bring a pistol home. "They let you bring that stuff home?"

"Some guys were selling and trading guns for peanuts on the ship coming home. Officers said they'd take it from us when we landed. We get to port, and there's thousands of GIs piled up itching to go home. There's heaps of guns, helmets, canteens some guys threw away. Other guys are picking up what they wanted. We get assembled. A Colonel gets up on a stage and sees a couple thousand GIs ready to riot. He says to get the hell out of here and everybody storms toward the gates with their train ticket and whatever they wanted to carry home."

"Why did you want that?"

"I don't know."

Natalie was afraid to ask, but finally said, "Is it loaded?

He slowly nodded.

"Bill, it's dangerous. Marcia." Crazy, scary images skivvied through her head.

"It's locked. Marcia couldn't open the box."

"Bill, please get rid of it."

He stared into the box for several seconds. "Yeah. I should get rid of it. There's guys I see at the dealership who want these souvenirs."

"Give it back to the Army. Throw it in the Hudson. I'd feel terrible if you gave it away or sold it, and someone got hurt."

Bill closed the lid, and locked the box.

Natalie wanted to see what key he was using so she could find it later and throw the gun away. "Soon, Bill. Please."

33

900 Jews Land at Haifa: Arrive From France as 2,000 More British Troops Depart

Natalie dropped the groceries on the end of her kitchen table. "I'm sorry I took so long. Another snafu at the warehouse." She felt terrible. This was the second time that week she'd been longer than she'd promised. Mom started to get up. "I'll get them," Natalie said. "Marcia probably wore you out."

"Never. I love watching her. She's a darling."

Natalie put boxes of Cheerios in the cupboard, milk in the fridge, cans of Campbell's Chicken Noodle soup on the counter. "Why is it she never fusses when you watch her?" She finished putting the groceries away. "Would you like a cup of coffee?"

"No thank you." Mom hesitated. "Well, maybe."

Natalie reached for the coffee pot and the tin of Maxwell House. That's odd, she thought. I always offer, and she always refuses, with an excuse about some chore at home that needed doing.

The percolator began bubbling, and Natalie set the timer on the stove. Mom appeared distracted and was glancing toward the living room where Marcia was singing a song to her doll. "Is there something you want to tell me? Was it something about Marcia?"

Mom turned away from the living room as though she didn't want Marcia to hear. "You like Dr. Schwartz?" Mom asked in a whisper.

Natalie poured the coffee. "He was nice." Natalie

knew she shouldn't have cancelled her annual check-up, but she'd been feeling pretty good, and they didn't need another bill. She wondered what was on Mom's mind. "So?"

"He does the other things too, not just delivering babies," Mom said.

It took Natalie me a moment to figure out what she was asking. "You mean G-Y-N?"

Mom said, "I can never get them straight. Which letters are for what thing."

Natalie recalled seeing women of a certain age in the waiting room when she went in for her pre-natal checkups. The change Natalie figured. But Mom was only fifty-two, no fifty-three. She might be starting early, not that anyone would know. "He does gynecology."

From the look on her mother's face, Natalie expected to be scolded for using bad language. "Female problems," Mom offered cautiously.

Natalie reached across the table and covered her mother's hand with hers. "Mom, a lot of women have female problems. If something's the matter, you should make an appointment. Go see him."

"I don't know," Tess said. "I shouldn't have bothered you with it." She started to get up.

Natalie wouldn't let go of her mother's hand. Her mother was stubborn and likely to ignore whatever this problem was, expecting it to go away with prayer and *zabaglione.* "Mom," Natalie said in a whisper. "What's the matter?"

Mom settled back resigned and gave Natalie the shrug that implied *the Russians have invaded New Jersey – but we'll be alright.* She finally said, "A lump."

"A lump? On your breast?"

"A little lump," Mom said as though Natalie

shouldn't be concerned. "I'm sorry I brought it up."

"Where? When did you discover it?"

After a moment, a cautious finger pointed to her left breast. "I felt it in the bath tub." She lowered her eyes.

Natalie wanted to shout, 'Good God, Mom, examining your breasts in your bath is *not* a mortal sin. Instead she asked, "How long? When did you first feel it?"

"A few months ago. Maybe six."

Six months and she hadn't said or done a thing about it. Natalie wanted to yell at her, but she knew that if she pressed too hard, Mom would pull her head in like a turtle. As gently as Natalie could manage, she said, "Has it gotten larger?"

Another shrug. "A little."

A lot Natalie guessed. "Have you talked about this with Dad?" As soon as the words left Natalie's mouth she realized the foolishness of expecting Mom to discuss her *female problem* with her husband of twenty-eight years.

"Your father is under a lot of pressure with the new shop. He doesn't need something else to worry about."

Natalie said, "It's great the business is doing so well, but he needs to know." Natalie didn't say that it would destroy him if he found out his wife didn't tell him she had breast cancer because she didn't want to bother him.

Mom finished her coffee, and pushed away from the table. "I'll say good-bye to Marcia."

Natalie knew where this is going – nowhere. "Mom, do not let this go. It will not get better by itself. It is probably nothing, but you need to have Dr. Schwartz take a look."

"I will."

"Damnit, I'm not kidding. I'm going to call you tomorrow afternoon. If you haven't made an appointment with Dr. Schwartz, I will." Mom gave Natalie the snotty teenager look.

Natalie decided to drop the A-Bomb. "Mom, this is serious. It could be nothing, but if it isn't, then you have to take care of it as soon as possible." She paused. "And if you don't make that appointment, I'll tell Dad." Now Natalie really got a *Go to your room and don't come out until you're ready to apologize.* But there was a surrendering sag in her mother's shoulders. She'll do it – she hoped.

34

Employees Held in $180,000 Theft: Officials of General Electric Subsidiary Are Accused in Swindle

"Thanks," Natalie said to Walter and Ralph. "You guys are great." It had taken all morning, but they finally got all the large appliances rearranged. Natalie was beat, and from their sweat-stained shirts she was sure they were too. Natalie did as much shoving and pushing as they'd allow, but she hoped Walter finally realized how much easier his life was going to be. And Natalie wouldn't have to waste time matching shipments to the warehouse with deliveries to the stores when Ralph lost count because he and Walter were running all over the warehouse for a GE fridge here and an Amana fridge over there. Natalie glanced at her wristwatch. She was going to be late picking up Marcia again. "Got to go," she said and started toward her office.

Natalie was halfway there when she noticed the stack of toasters was smaller than she remembered from the other day. She doubled back to where the guys were resting. "Walter, am I imagining things, or are there fewer toasters on the stack against the back wall?" She pointed to where the small appliances were stored.

"Probably," he said. "I think a dozen went out with the Latham order yesterday."

Darn. It took Natalie three weeks to get the ranges and fridges rearranged. She didn't have as good a handle on the small appliances. "Okay," she said and started toward her office. But something was still bothering her. She was late, and Marcia was going to get cranky and need a nap. She should go home. "Hey, Walter," she called. "Sorry, but do you have the paperwork on that delivery?"

"Sure," he said.

Natalie followed him to his desk at the back of the warehouse. A few minutes later, Natalie was running her finger down the list of large and small appliances delivered to the Latham store yesterday. "Do you have the list from the last delivery?"

Walter dug through a sheaf of ship orders and handed Natalie the list from the last delivery.

"One more, please," Natalie said. "The one from the week before."

Walter rifled through the papers and handed Natalie another list.

She scanned it and decided to press her luck because something was not making sense. "Walter, I know you'd like to clock me on the head, but I need one more favor, the delivery lists for the past three weeks for Central Ave."

Walter found another stack of paper and after shuffling through it, handed Natalie three sheets of paper. It didn't take Natalie three seconds to see what was scratching at the back of her brain. "Thanks, Walter. I really appreciate you putting up with me." She handed the papers back to him and headed for the door.

***

The next morning, Mom walked into the kitchen and hugged Marcia. Even at two, Marcia realized that Grandma two days in a row was different.

"I can't thank you enough, Mom. I know. I know," Natalie said. "This is important and can't wait."

Twenty minutes later, Natalie squared her shoulders and opened the front door of the Cohoes store. Slowly, she made her way along the row of clothes washers.

"Can I help you, Ma'am," a salesman said. He patted

a Whirlpool. "Top of the line, and they're on sale until Saturday."

"Thanks, I've got one," Natalie said. She scanned the sales room and stepped toward the shelves of toasters, electric percolators, clock radios, and steam irons. Natalie took as much time as she dared, keeping her face away from the glassed-in office at the back of the store.

The salesman pointed to an electric percolator. "When I got back from the service, my wife refused to use an electric. But after four years of GI bilge I couldn't get enough good coffee, and she got sick of making three and four pots a day." He pointed to a GE Hotpoint. "They're the best. Just plug it in. I hear they're working on ones with timers built in."

"Thank you," Natalie said. She glanced at her watch. "Goodness, I lost track of the time. Have to run. Thanks." She scurried toward the door.

Natalie pulled out of the parking lot as though she was driving the getaway car at a bank heist. Maybe she should have introduced herself, she thought. Maybe she should have asked Tony for a tour of the stores instead of the quick run-through before she started. He offered later but then she got so busy at the warehouse, they'd put it off. But Natalie thought she got enough of a picture.

Twenty minutes later, Natalie stepped in the door of the Latham store. Uh, oh, she thought. Frank Collins, the manager was right in front of her talking to a salesman. Frank's furrowed brow told Natalie he was wondering why she was here. "Natalie?" he said.

"Good morning, Frank," she said with a casual wave.

Frank said, "What brings you here?'

"You know, Tony and I talked about me taking a tour of the stores, but we kept putting it off. I had to visit a sick friend out this way, and I thought I'd stop by."

Frank swept his arm around to take in the salesroom. "Well, this is it."

He didn't sound as though he wanted to give Natalie a guided tour. "Thanks. You know, out there in the warehouse, I see cartons of fridges and ranges coming and going." She pointed to a Frigidaire. "It's nice to see them gleaming on the floor."

Natalie waited to see if Frank was going to show her around, but he was saying something to the salesman. "Mind if I look around?"

Frank shrugged.

Natalie made a show of slowly taking in the large appliances: opening and closing the doors of a couple of fridges and range ovens. She moved cautiously toward the area where shelves displayed toasters, percolators, and other small appliances. Natalie resisted picking up any of the small appliances and hoped she looked as though she was uninterested in them. She moved toward the back of the store and Frank's glassed-in office. Frank stared at her. She couldn't read his face. Natalie screwed up her courage and called, "Hey, Frank. I'll take a quick gander at the storeroom and get out of your hair."

Frank walked briskly to stand beside her. "Nothing but a storeroom."

Natalie realized he was struggling to not seem to be blocking the door. "I might get some good ideas about how to arrange the inventory at the warehouse." Natalie opened the door and stepped into the storeroom. It was a storeroom.

Natalie said, "Everything fine with you on how we're handling deliveries?"

"It's okay."

She chanced a pat on his arm. "Come on, Frank. I'll

bet you're getting the sales delivered to the customers much faster. Give a girl a break," Natalie meandered around cartons of large appliances, her eyes darting around. And then Natalie located what she came to see, and in a second she understood what was going on. "I better get on my way. If you have any problem, please call me. We'll get on it."

"Sure thing," Frank said flatly and led her to the front door.

***

Two days later, Natalie sat across from Tony in his office. "You should have let me know you were going to do a tour," Tony said.

"Jungle drums, right?"

Tony said, "Frank called Chet, and they both called me asking why my inventory manager was snooping around. And Chet was annoyed you didn't tell him you were in the store."

"Tony, I'm sorry. But I needed to see it for myself before coming to you."

"See what?"

"How many stores have you got?"

"What kind of question is that? Three, for crissakes. You know that I hope."

Natalie said, "I'm going way out on a limb, but if what I suspect holds up, you may have four."

"What are you talking about?"

"Here's what I know," Natalie said. She put the sheaf of papers she'd pulled from her purse on Tony's desk. "I'm sorry I didn't catch this before, but I've been working to get the large appliance storage in shape. I went back through the inventory and delivery records for the Latham, Central Ave, and Cohoes stores for past five months." She spread the papers out. "The thing is, Tony, we ship Latham fifteen, some months twenty, percent more small appliances than we ship to Central Ave and Cohoes."

"So, maybe Frank's got a good thing going with small appliances."

"I hope so. But if you check your financials, and the receipts match the deliveries we made from the warehouse, I'm wrong and very sorry. If not, someone is running a small appliance store – and it's not you." Natalie sat back in her chair waiting for Tony to see the light and congratulate her on her discovery.

Tony fixed her with a cold stare. "Frank Collins," he said in a venom-tinged voice. He speared her with a black glare that frightened her. "Frank and me. That's all there was back in forty-five." Tony jabbed his hand in the direction of the door. "We didn't know if we were going to make it. The two of us, ten, twelve, fourteen hours a day, Saturdays, Sundays. A couple of weeks, I couldn't pay him his salary. We split the day's cash receipts so we could buy groceries for a few days."

Tony stared at the ceiling as though recalling those times. He turned back to glare at Natalie. "And when we finally got this going, Frank sweat blood to get the Central Ave store up and running. Again, twelve, fourteen hours a day hiring and training salesmen, shoving and hauling the inventory like he was a coolie. Frank wouldn't let me hire more help because he said we didn't have the margins yet."

Tony stopped as though he couldn't remember what he was going to say. "And when everything was ship-shape he dives in to help set up Latham." Tony stared at the papers on the desk.

Stunned, a tight knot gripped the middle of Natalie's chest.

After what seemed minutes, Tony said, "You should

go." His voice had changed. It was as though he was dismissing a manufacturer's rep who was wasting his time.

Oh, God, he's firing me, Natalie thought. "Where?" she finally asked in a whisper.

Tony looked at her as though she was a nobody. "Out of here. The warehouse," he said but Natalie heard a trace of doubt in his voice.

She couldn't tell him it was her day off and she needed to go home so that Mom could go to her doctor's appointment. Was she being fired? The lists and figures she'd prepared were in front of him, and Natalie wondered if she should take them with her. She didn't know what to do.

"Now," he said and swiveled his chair away from Natalie to pull out a drawer in his desk.

"I, ah…" Natalie didn't know if she should apologize. She didn't know what to say. Her hands trembled, and she stood. Tony was riffing through some file folders as though she wasn't there.

Natalie left Tony's office. As she forced herself to walk, not run, to the door, she was sure his secretary and the billing clerk in the outer office were staring at her, already knowing that she was going to be fired.

35

*Bids Doctors Use Caution: Dr. Rusk Would Avoid
Creating Anxiety in Cancer Cases*

Mario puts his hand on mine. "Tessie, it's going to be alright.
The doctor said it could be a cyst, or a plugged-up lymph
node. Don't rush to the worst conclusion."

"Or it could be cancer."

"Come on, Tess, you're too tough."

"Pray for me, Mario." There's a surprised look on his
face. Mario goes to Mass with me. He makes his Easter Duty,
but Mario is not a man who prays.

"You got a million prayers stored up. God's not going
to let you get cancer."

Enough of this. God is going to give me cancer for
what I've done. I don't remember exactly when I got mixed
up or when I stopped. Maybe a year or two after it happened
I go into the confessional. The grill slides open, and I say,
"Bless me, father for I have sinned." The priest says, "Yes,
my child." I remember it like it was yesterday. Father
Cameron I could tell. He always chewed those mints, but
they never covered the smell of whiskey. I confess lying to
my husband about how much I spent on groceries, being
impatient with colicky Natalie – and then I stop. I was going
to confess what I did, but I couldn't. I didn't. "Is that all, my
child," the priest says. He waits. I can't get the words out of
my mouth. Finally, I say, "Yes." The priest gives me
absolution, and I make the Act of Contrition. I lied in
Confession. That surely must be a mortal sin. I can confess it
next time and be absolved. But Sunday, I go to Communion

with a mortal sin on my soul – a sacrilege.

***

I shouldn't have let Natalie talk me into this. What's going to happen will happen. I feel like a fool – an old fool. Me and that other woman sitting near the door the only ones not big as a house or holding a newborn. She looks like a complainer. Reminds me of Velma Owens. To hear her talk about it – and she never missed a chance, at the meat market, standing on the bus stop, coming out of Mass – her change was like the stigmata of St. Catherine of Siena. You get over it.

I told Natalie I could get here by myself. I'm not senile. I know the bus routes. Sitting next to me like I was going to skip out. She said I should have a pelvic exam and have a pap smear as long as I'm seeing this OB-GYN guy. I don't even like the sound of it – gynecology. I told her I'm cancelling the whole thing. Okay, we got that settled. Only my left breast, and I don't like that. I'll take off my blouse. I can slip off that side of my slip and undo my brassiere. That's it.

A tiny cry and I can't help turning my head toward the woman holding an infant in a pink blanket. One month. You don't have to ask or look. There is no other sound in the world like a hungry one month old. I shouldn't have come. Why waste everyone's time? Why put off what I know is going to happen?

I wouldn't let Natalie come in with me. When he finally got to it, I stared at the picture of a doe and fawn on the wall. I memorized every last detail, the trees, the stream they were drinking from, the flowers and the bushes. I couldn't look at him. What's the use? I knew what he was going to say.

I wouldn't tell Natalie what he said until we were out

in the hallway. 'Biopsy' – the second worst word in the English language. She couldn't bring herself to say the worst one. Talked around it: 'don't imagine the worst,' and 'it could be nothing,' and 'didn't the doctor say it could be benign.' That's the best word, but I know it won't be. Why are they going to make me go through this?

***

I'm freezing sitting here on the end of the examining table. How was I supposed to tie those strings at the back, and why did I have to take off all my clothes for them to get a sample from one small lump on my breast. I tried to cover myself at first, but why bother. I know what they'll say. They wouldn't change the date. If I was ever to believe in signs, this is one. Any other day, I pleaded. What did I think, I could avoid my fate?

I told Mario he didn't need to come with all the jobs backed up at the shop. That's good. I wonder how he'll manage when I'm gone. I guess Natalie and Marcia could move into our house although I don't think Mario and Bill could manage that.

I can get dressed now, the nurse says. I don't remember anything after that young doctor stuck me with the needle. I feel the bandage where the lump was.

The nurse says, "You'll feel some discomfort as the anesthesia wears off. Aspirin should help."

I start to slide off the table when she bustles out of the room. Aspirin. I should start getting used to pain. I remember visiting Lucy Amato maybe a month or two before she died: could hardly talk with the pain of the cancer in her uterus. Uterus, breast, the curse of Eve. What difference does it make? I'm getting what I deserve.

The doctor comes in the room, and I yank the thin striped robe closed as best I can.

"Sorry, Teresa," he says.

He doesn't look sorry.

"We'll have the results of the biopsy in about a week. Call the office next Thursday, and they'll set up an appointment for us to discuss the results." He gives me a fake smile. He looks at the chart in his hand. "The nurse will tell Mario he can come in to help you get dressed."

Teresa. Mario. He'd probably have a cow if I called him Herman. And I've managed to dress myself since I was three.

Mario pokes his head in the door. "You okay, Tess?"

"I'll probably be a little sore they say. I'll take an aspirin."

"You want me to help?" he says as I pick up my clothes off the table.

I start to get dressed. All of a sudden I'm crying.

Mario puts his arms around me. "You'll be alright, Tess. I know it."

"I'm crying for you. I'm going to leave you alone."

"You don't know that. We wait for the results. Even if it's not so good, they can do stuff now that wasn't around a few years ago."

I run my hand across my face and point to a box of tissues. "Give me one of those," I stop crying. "Of all days. We might as well get used to what's going to happen."

36

New Ways to Halt Cancer Are Shown

Flo slung her purse on the kitchen chair and gave Marcia a hug. Natalie had been waiting all day for Flo to stop by after work. When Natalie returned from her meeting with Tony, she tried to tell Bill about her suspicions about Frank and the small appliances. It didn't seem as though he understood or even cared. 'He might be stealing,' Natalie said. But Bill simply shrugged and flopped on the sofa where he sat until Natalie had to lever him up to join her and Marcia for dinner. She wondered how he was acting at the dealership and how he could sell cars when he didn't seem connected to reality. But then again, he wasn't selling many cars.

Flo gave Marcia a big kiss, and took a picture book from a shopping bag. "Look at this new book in the living room while I talk to your mommy."

Natalie didn't protest.

"You sounded upset," Flo said.

"I don't know where to start." Natalie blurted as she struggled to hold back the tears that had been coming and going all day.

"Start wherever you want."

"Bill, my job, my mother."

"So start with Bill," Flo said.

Natalie said, "Right now that seems to be the least of my problems. For the moment it's the same. Most days I think I'm married to a zombie, and on other days he ping-pongs around the apartment like a windup toy with a too-tight spring. He's not selling many cars, and if it wasn't for my part-time job we wouldn't make the rent."

"That's the *least* of your problems?" When Natalie nodded, Flo said, "He still won't get help?"

"No, and my other problems are a one-two punch. My job and Mom."

"What's wrong with your mother?"

"She felt a lump in her breast – *six months* ago. I had to threaten a holy war to get her to make an appointment with Dr. Schwartz."

"What did he say?"

"He gave her a referral for a biopsy, and now she's sure she's going to die."

Flo got out of her chair and put her arms on Natalie's shoulders. Natalie twisted around. "And you know what?" she said in a bitter voice. "I don't want my mother to die – but I can't stop thinking about who will take care of Marcia or how can I keep my job if Mom is sick – or she dies." Natalie burst into tears. "I am a terrible, selfish person."

"You are not." Flo gave Natalie a squeeze and sat down. "It's all mixed together. Your mom's health is important, but my mother always said, 'Don't borrow trouble.' One step at a time."

Natalie calmed down and poured them coffee. After a few sips, Flo said, "Is there a problem at your job?"

"Number three or number one or number two on my list? It depends whether I have to cajole Bill to get out the door to work in the morning or when Tony's going to fire me."

"Why would he do that?" Flo said. "You told me you were doing great organizing the warehouse."

"I was. I am – that is until I discovered that the manager of one of his stores is probably stealing. I think he's selling toasters, and clock radios, and percolators at knock-down prices to his friends and relatives. But I only had half the story: records showing unaccounted inventory. I brought it to Tony and told him he needed to match the inventory to sales receipts to prove it." Natalie shook her head. "I was so proud of myself. I expected Tony to put a gold star on my homework. Instead I got a story about how he and the manager go back to day one in the business, a prince of a fellow who works his heart out for Tony – blood brothers. He was angry at *me.* I thought Tony was going to fire me on the spot."

"He was shocked," Flo said. "I can see how he might not want to believe it. But he's got to wise up if this guy is actually stealing."

"I hope. I didn't get fired – for now – but the word has spread, and it's like working in the walk-in cooler at the meat market. Nobody wants to talk to me."

Flo said. "I'll bet he's angry because a woman had to tell him he was being taken for a ride. You pick up a magazine, and it's all about how we're supposed to forget about the jobs we did during the war and go back to the kitchen and bake cookies and make babies."

"Isn't that what you want?"

"Yes and no," Flo said. "When Bob finishes college and gets a teaching job, I'll be happy to be a housewife – and I hope a mother. But no way I'm going to let him walk all over me. I had to deal with some pretty tough characters at the Arsenal. I can handle myself – and Bob."

"You and Bob have a clear vision of your future," Natalie said. "I feel as though I'm dragging my old life along like a huge black anchor tied around my waist clanking behind me with each step I try to take. But where am I going? I keep recalling those last years at the Arsenal. I know I can't go back, but I miss the wonderful feeling when

I solved a problem with what I never knew existed in me. I had a champion in Mr. Vincent. I gained allies when I worked with managers. I overcame ones who opposed me." Even though Flo knew about her and Jack, she couldn't tell Flo that while she would never shed the shame of what she did with Jack. She had never felt more alive as a woman.

"Natalie, face it. You're not happy unless you're at war."

Natalie was glad Flo had broken through the gloom. "My Aunt Emma had this enormous Bible. It had gold on the edges of the pages, a leather cover, and pictures of Adam and Eve getting kicked out of the Garden of Eden, pairs of animals walking up a ramp to Noah's Ark. Somewhere toward the end was a picture of the Last Judgement. I was fascinated by it. On the right half devils were shoveling sinners into Hell. Below the damned were boiling in vats while other devils carved up sinners with huge cleavers."

"I remember seeing something like that. Father Eagan had a sermon on the torments of Hell for us sinners –'an eternity of incomprehensible suffering', he thundered. My father said he usually did that sermon after a three-day bender."

"Yeah, and on the other side were the saved sitting in rows of pews with smug grins on their faces." Natalie leaned towards Flo. "Heaven confused me. What happens for an eternity after you've checked below to see that Genny LaFleur is getting boiled in peroxide, said hello to this or that saint, saw whether Helen of Troy was there, and found your grandmother? I really thought about it, Flo. It could be very boring for ever and ever."

"Boring beats what I hope happens to the guy who broke up with me a week before the Junior Prom," Flo said. "Is there a point here?"

"The point is I hoped when the war was over I'd start a new life with Bill, perhaps not the same as yours and Bob's but something different and exciting. What if Bill miraculously recovers, my mother doesn't die of breast cancer, and Tony sees the light? Then what? I lie awake and try to imagine a beautiful life, even a satisfying life, but I can't peer through the fog. I'm fighting three wars, and I don't know what a victory looks like."

"Mommy, I have to go potty."

Flo and Natalie burst into laughter. Marcia's face crumpled, and she began to bawl.

***

Three days later, Tony's Caddy was parked outside the warehouse when Natalie arrived. She opened the door. Ralph and Walter, ashen-faced, were pressed against the wall as though standing in front of a firing squad.

Tony wheeled around and fixed Natalie with a glare. "In here," he said in a nasty tone. He stalked toward Natalie's office. He turned back to Ralph and Walter. "Don't touch a fucking thing," he yelled. His arm shot toward the door to the back room. "One single item of stock moves an inch back there and I'll …."

Tony sat behind Natalie's desk. She was left standing like a misbehaving student in front of the principal. A hot flush crept up her back, but she was afraid to take off her jacket.

"When did you figure there was a discrepancy in the small appliances?"

It was an accusation rather than a question. Natalie got herself under control and thought of telling him she quit. He had no right to talk to her in that tone of voice. "About a week or ten days before I came to you about it."

"Why not sooner?" Tony snapped.

Natalie said, "Because," she said as evenly as she could, "In addition to getting the mess in the warehouse straightened out, I needed to check and recheck the records."

Tony looked as though Natalie was a student sassing the principal.

"So you didn't know anything about the missing toasters and clock radios and the other shit that walked before?"

Natalie told herself to count to ten, but she only got to five. "I don't know where this third degree is coming from but I don't like it." She pointed in the direction of the back room. "I'm saving you money by taking that rat's nest you called a warehouse and turning it into an efficient operation. I haven't, but I can tell you how much money I'm saving *you* by not having Ralph and Walter running around half the day trying to locate stock. *I* figured out something wasn't right with the small appliances. *I* went, on my own time, to see what was in the stores – hoping I was wrong and there was a reasonable explanation for the discrepancy between what's delivered and what's actually there. I brought it to you, and you all but kicked me out of your office. If you're going to fire, me, do it because otherwise I'm quitting." Natalie turned toward the door, anger wafting off her like dark mist.

"Wait," Tony said. "I'm sorry."

He didn't sound sorry, but Natalie stopped.

"Sit down." Tony stood and motioned for Natalie to sit behind her desk. He perched on the edge of her desk. "You were right."

"About the small appliances?"

"Shit. Small appliances and a lot more. Frank was running a small appliance outlet out the back door. I hired a private investigator. He and his partner got great discounts on toasters, clock radios, everything on the shelves."

"I'm sorry."

Tony asked, "Why?"

"Frank was your friend. You told me how he worked so closely with you at the start."

Tony glared at her. "Friend. My lawyer brought in an outside accountant. He audits the books and sees the small appliance scam." Tony shook his head. "And then he asks me why so many of my large appliances are discounted for scratches and dents. My friend Frank and my business manager are in cahoots on a scratch and dent scam."

"I don't understand."

Tony stared at Natalie as though she was thick. "The customer pays the list price. Frank books it as a discounted scratch and dent and pockets the difference. My trusted business manager sniffs it out. Does he tell me? No, he decides to go in on it and take a cut." Tony swept the in-basket, pencil holder and everything else on the top of Natalie's desk into a pile on the floor. "*Jesus*, is everyone stealing from me?"

"I'm not," she snapped. She wished she could vouch for Ralph and Walter, but how could she tell.

Tony kicked the wastepaper basket. "Frank says I should have made him a partner. All this time, he's holding this grudge, getting back at me because I didn't make him a partner. The son-of-a-bitch told me he was owed."

Natalie thought Tony was trying hard not to cry.

"What happens now?" Natalie said.

"I fired the bastards. I wanted to call the cops, but my lawyer says it would take a year to calculate what they stole. He says it's not clear whether I could make a charge of embezzlement or whatever stick." Tony stared at the wall for several seconds as if he was trying to remember something. He knocked the calendar off the hook, and it fluttered to the floor.

"Did you come out here to wreck my office?"

"I don't know what I'm doing. I went over to Central Ave and screamed at everybody there. I told them I'd have them making license plates if so much as a clock radio was unaccounted for." He looked around as though reminding himself where he was. He pointed in the direction of the back room. "Two hundred, three hundred thousand in inventory back there. How the hell do I know what's what?"

"I know what's what here," Natalie said firmly. "I'm not stealing, and I'm sure that neither are Ralph and Walter."

"Who doesn't have their damn hands in my pockets?" Tony wheeled around and crashed out of Natalie's office.

Cautiously Natalie followed a couple of steps behind. Ralph and Walter were still pinned to the wall.

Tony pointed his finger at them. "You fucking steal from me, and I'll break your arms before I call the cops." He slammed open the front door and stormed out.

***

A week later, Flo sat at Natalie's kitchen table. "It must be awful," Flo said.

Natalie took a sip of coffee. "Chaos. An outside accountant brought in a business manager, but I think he's only there until Tony finds a permanent replacement. The assistant manager at the Latham store is filling in as manager. Tony went crazy. He didn't outright accuse anyone of stealing, but everyone is under suspicion. The manager at Central Ave refused to work under those conditions and quit."

"What about you?" Flo said.

"I don't know. At the warehouse everything is

moving at half-speed. Walter won't let anything go out unless he triple checks the ship orders. The drivers act as though they're driving Brinks trucks. The guys at the stores count and recount everything that's off-loaded before they sign off on a delivery."

"Serves him right."

Natalie said, "What galls me is in some perverse way Tony blames me. If I hadn't discovered the scam, his life would have continued in ignorant bliss. Crazy I know, but it's there."

"What are you going to do?"

"For the time being, keep going to work. We need the money. I'll do my job, but no more. I see a dozen things that could be done better, but he gets exactly the job and the hours he pays me for." Natalie paused. "I hate it."

37

Need for Local Aid to Veterans Seen: Warning that Agencies Must Not Bungle Made at Parley

Bill leaned over Natalie's shoulder and kissed the back of her neck. "Good morning," he said and cocked his head toward the coffee mug in front of her. "Would you like a refill?"

"Thank you." Bill was clean-shaven and wearing the pair of weekend trousers and the plaid shirt Natalie gave him for his birthday.

Bill set the mug in front of Natalie and poured just the right amount of cream. Sitting across the table from Natalie he asked, "Done with the sports page?"

Natalie pushed the section from the Sunday *Knickerbocker News* across the table. Their little joke. She never read the sports, and Bill called the obituaries his grandmother's sports page. Natalie hadn't taken her to a wake in a month, and she was sure right now she was prospecting through her copy of the paper for an excuse to meet her friends at Parker Brothers. Thankfully, Marcia was sitting quietly, enthralled with the picture book with fuzzy animals Flo brought her the other day.

Pushing the sports to the side, Bill reached for another section. "I can't stand it. How could they lose to the Washington Senators?"

Natalie gave him a playful shrug and went back to the local news. She'd save the want ads for later. If Tony continued to treat her like a leper because she discovered his blood brother was stealing from him, she'd find another job. And if Bill continued to bring home a decent paycheck like he'd done for the last three weeks, maybe she wouldn't have to jump at the first job offered.

"That was fun yesterday," Bill said. "Want to go to the park again after lunch?"

"We have to get out and enjoy this great September weather while it lasts," Natalie said. "Where else can we go?"

"Mommy. Look at this one," Marcia said. Her book was open to a page with a smiling horse with black and white fuzz glued to its body.

Natalie rubbed her finger over the fuzz. "I've got it," she said. "How about a Sunday afternoon ride? Flo said there's a farm out in Schodack that's got baby lambs and calves. It's like a little zoo," she said.

"Yay," Marcia shouted. "Let's go see baby lambs and calves on a farm."

"The whole country's on the road every Sunday afternoon," Bill said.

"They're still getting over rationing." Natalie didn't say that means they'll keep buying cars because she didn't want to jinx the roll Bill's been on at the dealership.

After lunch, they managed to get Marcia and her paraphernalia into the car and on their way to rural Rensselaer County.

"Wow," Bill said. "Will you look at all the new houses out here?"

Natalie patted Bill's arm. "Soon, Bill. Soon."

"I want to see baby lambs," Marcia shouted from the back seat. "And maybe baby cows."

"Take the left onto sixty-six," Natalie said. "I called Flo for the directions." Natalie didn't understand why Flo kept doing this to herself, taking Sunday afternoon rides to farms full of children. Natalie had seen her at playgrounds sitting on a bench watching the children play as though she was waiting for her son or daughter to climb down from the monkey bars and walk home with her hand-in-hand. A few miles down the road, a line of cars was parked on the shoulder. Flo said that Wyland's Farm had become a family destination. Flo said the Wyland's loved seeing children handing out oats and hay to feed the lambs and other animals through the fence.

Natalie pointed to the last car in the line. "There's a spot behind that Hudson."

They clambered out of the car and walked toward the farm. As they approached the large fenced area where families were petting and feeding the animals, Natalie realized that Bill had fallen back. "Come on, Bill. I need you to help keep track of Marcia." He seemed hesitant, as though he was struggling to remember something.

They found a spot along the fence. There were a couple of goats, a donkey, a gaggle of turkeys, and chickens inside the large open area. A pony poked his head out of a small stable. Toward the back, two lambs nuzzled under a ewe. A donkey brayed and pooped. The boys cheered, and the girls made faces.

A man approached. "Get ready children. When the lambs see Mrs. Wyland come out with her burlap bags, they'll come running."

The door to the farm house opened. Bill seemed rooted to the ground, his mouth hung open and his head swiveled side to side from the barn, the sheds, and the farmhouse. His face screwed into a frightening mask, and mewing sounds rose from the back of his throat.

The woman at the farm house door glanced back into

the house and shook her head. "Oops. Forgot one," she said. She let the door go, and it made a sharp bang as she stepped back inside.

A guttural gasp shot from of Bill's mouth. People turned toward him. Bill stepped backwards. His hands were lifting over his head. The woman reappeared with a two burlap bags in her hands. She nudged the door open with her toe, stepped out onto the stoop, and let the door behind her slam with another loud bang.

Bill screamed and dropped to the ground. He crawled on his hands and knees toward the fence. He rolled under it and scrabbled toward the car. People gawped at him then turned back toward the animals when Mrs. Wyland arrived at the corral and the lambs gamboled toward her.

"Mommy, why is Daddy running away?"

Natalie yanked Marcia's hand. "Come with me."

"Mommy, I want to see the lambs."

"Do as I say." Natalie pulled Marcia toward where Bill was standing by the side of the road, twenty feet from their car. They approached, and Bill turned. A dark splotch spread across the crotch of his trousers.

"Go back," he croaked. "Please, go back."

'Bill, can I...?"

"*Please,* Natalie. Go away."

Natalie hesitated but finally guided Marcia back toward the farm. Marcia had a shocked look on her face. "What's wrong with Daddy?"

"Daddy's not feeling well. But he'll be okay. Let's go back and watch the lady feed the lambs."

By the time they got back to the corral, all the oats have been handed out, and the lambs were trotting back to their mother. Some of the children were petting the goat and the pony through the wide wire fencing. A woman took the hand of her son and tugged him away from Natalie and Marcia.

"Let's pet the goat," Natalie said.

"We missed the lambs," Marcia whined.

Natalie finally got Marcia interested in petting the goat and watching the chickens. She nudged Marcia toward a pen holding two peacocks. "Now let's see what that bird does."

On cue, the peacock spread his tail. Marcia said, "Wow." The peacock let out a loud screech, and Marcia screamed.

"Let's go home," Marcia said. "This place stinks."

Natalie had no idea about what shape Bill was in, but she didn't know what else to do but walk to their car.

Bill stood next to the door.

"Are you alright?"

"Just get in."

Natalie arranged Marcia in the back seat and came around to the side of the car. She caught Bill's eye, then decided to concentrate on getting herself settled into her seat. A couple of rags Bill kept in the trunk for when he changed a tire were laid on the driver's seat. Bill quickly got in. A rank odor made Natalie's eyes sting. Bill rolled down the window on his side. Natalie rolled down hers.

"It smells," Marcia said.

"It's the farm animals," Natalie said.

They drove too fast back to the apartment. Almost before the car came to a stop, Bill dashed out of the car. Natalie took her time getting Marcia out of the back seat. "Let's go to the park for a little while."

An hour later, they entered the apartment. Natalie was about to take Marcia into the bathroom, but decided to check first. Bill's underpants and trousers were soaking in the tub. Natalie pulled the shower curtain closed before she let Marcia in to pee.

Natalie got Marcia settled with books and games and cautiously went into the bedroom. Bill was sitting on the edge of the bed. His head was in his hands. Natalie sat next to him and put her arm around his shoulder. "It's alright, Bill. It's alright."

"It's not alright." He stared at the palms of his hands as if something was written there. "I can't. Three years and I can't do it."

"What Bill? What can't you do?"

"I'm useless. It's getting worse. What am I going to do, shit my pants every time a car backfires? I can't go on like this."

How many times had Natalie heard someone say 'I can't go on like this?' A line tossed off about some trivial persistent problem. But she heard something more ominous in Bill's statement. She was afraid. "What if you talked to someone about it?"

He let out a snort. "Go to the VA and tell a shrink Mom liked Mike better than me?"

Natalie patted Bill's back. "It's more than that. You went through a lot."

"Ten million men went through a lot. They didn't come back a useless mess like me."

"Bill, there's got to be thousands of men like you."

"Yeah, and they're in the VA funny farm out in the Finger Lakes."

"Think about it, Bill. Talk to Doc Evans. Ask him if he knows someone you can talk to about this." Natalie felt a shrug. He has to. When he said, 'I can't go on,' an ice pick pierced her heart.

38

Radio Phosphorus Used in Brain Tumor: New Type of
Geiger Counter Inserted in Brain

Mario was holding Tess's hand so tight it hurt, but she
didn't want him to let go of her.

The nurse showed them in to Dr. Schwartz' office. He
was sitting behind a desk wearing a long white coat over his
shirt and tie. A stethoscope looped around his neck.

The doctor pointed toward the two chairs in front of
the desk. He picked up a folder. "Now, Mrs. Flaherty, let's
see what we have."

"Pisano," Mario said. "She's Mrs. Pisano."

Dr. Schwartz looked at Tess as though he'd never
seen her before. She supposed he only saw her left breast,
but you would think.

"Of course. Sorry," Dr. Schwartz said. He looked at
the folder in his hand as though he couldn't imagine how it
got there. He shuffled through three or four folders stacked
on the desk.

Tess wondered how Mrs. Flaherty made out. Maybe
she should want the results of her biopsy. There wasn't
anything in the world that makes time stand still than
waiting for the results of a biopsy.

"Yes, of course. Here we are," Dr. Schwartz said. He
opened the folder and studied the contents for several
seconds.

Tess knew what was in there. For every one of those
thousands of minutes from when she first felt the lump to
now, she'd known she would have to pay for her sin. Dr.

Schwartz cleared his throat and said, "You have breast cancer, Mrs. Pisano. I'm sorry, but there is nothing we can do."

"I know," Tess said. "I'm going to die of breast cancer."

"Tess," Mario said loudly. "Are you crazy? He said it was benign. The lump wasn't cancer."

Dr. Schwartz had a startled look on his face. He shot a look at the other folders on his desk as though Tess and Mrs. Flaherty and who else was in those folders got mixed up. He looked at Tess's folder again. "No, your husband's right. I said the biopsy was negative as to a carcinoma – cancer. You don't have cancer. It was probably a blocked lymph duct." He put the folder down. It seemed like he wanted to get them out of the office and bring in Mrs. Flaherty.

They stood. "Thank you," Mario said to the doctor. Tess didn't say anything. Mario gave her a look as though she was being rude to the doctor. Tess's mind was fuddled. She walked out of the office. She couldn't look at the couple waiting to go in. It wasn't fair. She didn't commit the sin. I did. I should pay, not her.

Mario walked Tess out of the doctor's office like she was an invalid. Tess felt a little pull where they took out the lump, but she was fine. Still, it was nice having Mario hold on to her. He's a good man and a wonderful husband, but the moment she finally heard what the doctor really had to say, she knew what she had to do – what they had to do.

Mario opened the door for Tess, got in the car, and started to put the key in the ignition. Tess put her hand on his wrist. "Mario. Wait. We need to talk."

"Here? Now?"

Tess wondered if he suspected what she was going to say. She couldn't wait another minute. She didn't want to go home and let the memory of what happened then and today fade away. "Mario, I have to see her. We have to see her. If you don't want to do it, I'll do it myself."

"Tess, why don't we talk about this at home? You're upset. The lump, the biopsy—you've been under a lot of stress."

"That's true, but all this has shown me what I have to do. I'm confused about whether God sends signs, but I'm fifty-eight years old. Maybe it wasn't cancer this time, but what happened weighs on me more. I can't go to my grave without facing it."

Mario let out a long sigh. "Okay. Let's go home."

"You're not just saying that to put me off are you? You agree?"

Mario said, "If that's what you – we – have to do, I'll be with you. It was *us*, Tess, not just you."

39

Mental Hospital Crowding Eased: Report Stresses Effort at Curative Over Custodial Car

Mario pulled off the highway and onto a wide circular drive. "That must be the headquarters," he said, pointing to a four-story building at the middle of the circle.

"It looks like a mansion," Tess said. I'm confused, she thought. Maybe this is not a bad place after all. Three men were trimming a hedge. One, holding a gardening shears, had a large misshapen head. Another man Tess couldn't see well was kneeling and picking up the clippings. The third man was leaning against a post and smoking a cigarette. He didn't look like the other two. She supposed he was watching them.

Tess had been gripping her knees more and more tightly as they got closer, and her hands were sore. She was sure she wanted to do this. She talked it over with Mario for so many evenings after dinner and made him take time away from the shop to write to this place and make the arrangements for their visit. She even went to the library and read about movie stars and that famous writer whose children were in places like this.

Mario said he wanted to do it, but now Tess wondered if it was the right thing to do. She wanted it and couldn't see how she could do it without Mario, even though he kept reminding her that it was both of them, not just her. Mario found a vacant spot where the sign said, 'Visitors.' He turned off the engine, and they sat. Mario reached across the seat and put his hand on Tess's wrist.

"We're doing the right thing, Tess."

"Why did it take us twenty-seven years to do the right thing?" Tess said.

Twenty-seven years, and it was still like it was yesterday. Fifteen hours of labor. The nurses telling her to push. One making cracks to joke her through the pain. Doctor Petosa muttering. Tess burning a hole in the ceiling with her eyes. 'Okay, here she comes, ready or not' the funny one said. Tess felt the baby slide out. She turned her head, but she couldn't see much because of the sheet drawn up. There was silence. Then Tess heard them whispering. One of the nurses came around to wipe her forehead, and Tess would never forget the look on her face. 'Everything's going to be alright,' she said, but Tess could tell it wasn't. Tess sensed hurried movement on the other side of the room. She knew something was wrong. She hadn't heard a cry.

"I want to see my baby," Tess said to the nurse. "What's wrong with my baby?"

The nurse wiped Tess's forehead again and shot a worried look toward the other side of the room.

Tess heard a sound, but it wasn't a newborn's cry. It was like a strangled gurgle – another sound she would never forget.

Dr. Petosa poked his head around the sheet. The look on his face froze Tess's heart. "Mrs. Pisano, there's a bit of a problem. We're taking your baby to the intensive care ward."

"What's wrong?"

"You had a difficult birth," the doctor said. "We'll do everything we can."

"Is my baby going to die?"

He hesitated a moment too long before answering.

"We'll do everything we can." His head disappeared.

"Wait," Tess called out. "My baby. A boy or a girl?"

A nurse poked her head in where the doctor was. "A daughter," she said. Her voice was flat, but Tess heard a hint of sadness in it.

For three days Tess kept asking to see her daughter. Finally, Dr. Petosa came to her room. Mario was standing next to him. From the looks on their faces, Tess knew something was terribly wrong. "Did she die?"

"No," Doctor Petosa said, but he sounded disappointed. "But I'm afraid your daughter suffered damage to her brain because of a lack of oxygen during her birth."

Tess heard his words, but she didn't want to listen. "What does that mean?"

Doctor Petosa said, "Your daughter is mentally retarded."

"Can't you do something for her?"

Doctor Petosa said, "I wish I could say, 'yes' but I'm afraid not. We've done a number of tests, and the results are definitive. They won't change."

"What's going to happen?"

The doctor looked at Mario, but Mario simply nodded his head as though it was useless to ask him for an answer. "Your daughter might survive this initial trauma but she will need special care."

Tess asked, "Can't we take care of her at home?"

"I'm afraid not," the doctor said. "Fortunately, there is an opening at Syracuse State School. I went to med school with the director. He's agreed to admit your daughter to a special program."

"No," Tess said, and Doctor Petosa gave her an annoyed look.

"Mrs. Pisano. Under the circumstances, you and your husband are fortunate I have this connection. The state schools usually don't admit infants. It will be best for you, your husband, and your daughter."

The doctor left, and Mario and Tess cried. Tess was in the hospital for a week. After four days, they let Tess see her daughter. All this time, she called her, 'my daughter.' It was as though naming her would somehow put a curse on her. She was in a crib in a special room, tubes stuck into her. She was mostly purple. "Margaret," Tess whispered.

A week later, Mario and Tess were crowded in an office at the hospital. There was Doctor Petosa and two other men, all of them wearing white coats over their shirts and ties.

Doctor Petosa said, "This is Doctor Moran. He is the Director of the Neo-Natal Unit here at the hospital." He waved his hand toward the man sitting next to him. "This is Doctor Cummings. He is the Deputy Director of the Syracuse State School." The man said, "I'm afraid my med school lab partner wasn't able to be here today. Still running behind schedule."

The man from Syracuse chuckled, and Tess wondered what was the joke.

"Well then," Doctor Petosa said. "Doctor Cummings, please explain what is planned for the Pisano's daughter."

"Margaret," Tess whispered.

Doctor Cummings shot Tess a scolding look. "This may seem harsh, Mrs. Pisano, but our experience tells us that the best course is for you – and your husband – to take leave of your daughter."

He must have seen the dismay on Tess's face.

"There is nothing you can do. At the state school we may be able to address some or perhaps most of your daughter's immediate physical complications." He paused. "But we will not be able to reverse the mental damage. She – and you – will be better served by a complete separation."

"For how long?" Tess asked.

Dr. Cummings said, "Mrs. Pisano, I have a dear cousin who chose to join a Carmelite convent – an enclosed life they call it, one of prayer and contemplation away from the world. Perhaps it will help you and your husband to adjust by thinking of your daughter as entering an enclosed life. And as with the nuns, it is much better for all concerned to make the break complete and irrevocable." He glanced at his wristwatch and then at the other two doctors.

"Can I see my daughter – Margaret – before she goes to Syracuse?"

"I think it is best if you don't," Doctor Petosa said. He stood, and the other two doctors also got up from their chairs. "Doctor Cummings is a very busy man. We should be very thankful he has agreed to come to Albany and thankful that the director of the state school still remembers how many of his lab reports I helped him complete."

The three men chuckled again. Tess wanted to slap their faces.

Tess never saw her daughter. She let them take her away. She never held her. She never said goodbye.

Tess squeezed Mario's hand. She didn't know what was going to happen, but they'd come this far. "Let's go in."

Inside the Administration Building, the woman at the front desk checked them off in a book she had open. She picked up the telephone on her desk, and in a few moments a man appeared. He seemed to be about forty or fifty years old. He was wearing a gray shirt buttoned to his throat and gray work pants.

"Arthur," the woman behind the desk said. "Please

take Mr. and Mrs. Pisano to Dr. Hanoush's office."

"Yes, Miss Brody," he said in a careful, dull tone.

Tess and Mario followed Arthur down one hallway and another. The building looked like a mansion from the outside, but the inside was cut up into beaverboard cubicles. Wooden and metal desks and mismatched chairs were jammed together along the walls. Two women were washing windows. They appeared to be in their twenties, about the same age as Margaret.

Inside the Deputy Director' office, Mario and Tess were seated in front of a gray metal desk. Ever since they walked into the building, Tess's heart had been fluttering. Doctor Hanoush told them he'd reviewed what Mario discovered when he began making inquiries about visiting Margaret. She had been in a special children's program at Syracuse until she was eighteen years old. Then she was transferred to Rome State School.

Consulting the folder in his hand, Dr. Hanoush said, "It appears that your daughter has adjusted well here at Rome. I see that she has had no unusual medical problems aside from an appendectomy in – let's see – thirty-five." He looked up from the chart and paused.

Tess squeezed her hands into fists when she saw the look on the doctor's face.

The doctor said, "The appendectomy was routine. Apparently, the surgeon felt that as long as she was under anesthesia, and given her overall situation, he performed a hysterectomy. It isn't something we would do as a matter of course, but he may have observed an abnormality. And, well, there you have it."

Dr. Hanoush gave Tess and Mario a few more details about Margaret's life. He said she Margaret was 'trainable' but not quite 'educable.' She was capable of largely caring for herself and able to participate in many of the activities of the institution. When he was done, he summoned a staff member. "Miss Harris will accompany you," Dr. Hanoush said. "In situations like yours, where the child hasn't had contact with the parents, we find it best to go slow."

Miss Harris, a tiny scrap of a woman, led Tess and Mario across a wide lawn to another building. "It's one of our staff dining rooms," she said. "Margaret is a great help in the kitchen."

Tess didn't like her. Her voice was too bright, like a real estate agent taking them on a tour of a model home out in Delmar.

They entered the front door of the building. Miss Harris said, "We told Margaret she would have visitors, but I'm not sure she's prepared for too much emotion."

Tess wasn't prepared either, no matter how many times she tried to imagine seeing Margaret.

Miss Harris directed Mario and Tess to stand at the end of the empty dining room while she went into a door at the back. Tess had to tell herself to breath normally. After a few moments, Miss Harris emerged holding the hand of a young woman wearing plain cotton flowered dress. For a moment Tess was afraid to look at Margaret. When she did, she saw a pleasant looking twenty-seven year old woman. When Tess was planning to visit Margaret, she hated the words in the articles she'd read at the library: idiot, imbecile, moron. Not from cruel people or kids who didn't know any better, but doctors who wrote the articles. Margaret had an uncertain smile on her face.

Tess was in a swirl, afraid she'd frighten her.

"Margaret," Miss Harris said. "These are the visitors I told you about."

Tess wondered if Margaret had any idea of who they

were.

"Hello," Margaret said politely as a child who had been taught proper manners.

What do I say? What do I do? Tess wondered. She looked to Miss Harris.

Miss Harris gestured toward a small table where there were four chairs. "Why don't we sit for a moment? Would you care for some lemonade?"

Tess and Mario nodded, and Miss Harris went through the door from which Margaret emerged. Tess was afraid of being left alone with Margaret. Across the table, Margaret was staring at her hands in her lap.

"Do you like it here?" Tess asked.

Margaret glanced toward where Miss Harris had gone. After a few moments, she said, "Yes."

Tess asked. "What do you do here in the dining room?"

Margaret seemed to be searching for the answer. "Open the tins. Peel the potatoes. Put the food in the pans."

"Do you like working in the kitchen?" Mario asked.

Margaret looked toward where Miss Harris had gone. "Sometimes I help putting the dirty dishes in the big dish washer."

Tess was relieved when Miss Harris returned with four glasses of lemonade on a tray.

"Do you have any special friends?" Tess asked Margaret. Again she seemed confused.

"Why don't you tell your... Mrs. and Mrs. Pisano about Alice?" Miss Harris said to Margaret.

Tess thought she saw a glimmer of a smile on Margaret's face. "Alice is my best friend. We eat together every day."

"Margaret and Alice are quite the pair," Miss Harris

said.

For several minutes, Tess and Mario asked Margaret simple questions about what she did every day. Some questions seemed to confuse her. To others she provided short responses and often looked to Miss Harris for the answer.

Tess and Mario seemed to have exhausted questions for Margaret, and Miss Harris said, "Perhaps that's enough for now." She glanced at her watch. "Let's walk Margaret to her program."

Tess and Mario followed Miss Harris and Margaret across wide lawns toward a large building. Along the way Tess tried to form a sense of Margaret's life here. Inside the building, Miss Harris prompted Margaret to say 'goodbye.'

Margaret extended her hand as though repeating an exercise she'd practiced. "Good bye," she said.

Instead of grasping her hand, Tess stepped forward and wrapped her arms around Margaret. "Good bye, Margaret," she said through the hard lump in the back of her throat.

Margaret looked at Miss Harris when Tess released her. Miss Harris and Margaret walked toward the row of long tables where dozens of men and women were working with objects Tess couldn't identify laid out in front of them. Tess followed Margaret's walk until she sat at a vacant chair next to another woman about her age. Alice?

"I don't know if I was supposed to do that," Tess said to Miss Harris.

"I realize it's difficult. I'll walk you back to the Admin building."

"Can we see where she lives?" Mario asked. An uncertain look flitted across Miss Harris's face. "Where she sleeps," he added.

"It's not on the way to your car."

"We have time."

Miss Harris pointed toward some long buildings about one hundred yards to their left. "It's way over there," she said as though the building was miles away.

"That's okay."

Miss Harris let out a sigh, and they headed toward the building. "You have to keep in mind that the state is working as best it can to relieve over-crowding."

They arrived at the building. Miss Harris asked Tess and Mario to wait outside and entered. A few minutes later, she came out. "I'm not sure this is the best time to visit. Perhaps when – if – you visit again."

"We want to see where our daughter lives," Mario said.

Miss Harris and Tess turned to him. He had a determined look on his face, and the forceful way he'd spoken seemed to overcome Miss Harris' reluctance.

"Alright," she said. "It's not ideal, but we are working on it."

They stepped inside the building. Along each long wall twenty or thirty beds were lined closely together. A locker was at the foot of each bed and a tall cabinet between each bed.

"Which one is Margaret's?" Tess asked.

Miss Harris said, "I don't know." Another sigh as she glanced toward a woman at the far end of the building. "Do you want me to ask?"

"Yes," Mario said firmly.

Miss Harris returned and let Tess and Mario to one of the iron beds. They stood at the foot of the bed. It was barely more than a cot. It appeared clean, but there was no more than two feet between Margaret's bed and the ones on either side. Tess stared at the bed trying to imagine Margaret getting ready for bed, putting on a nightgown and sleeping in a room with forty or fifty other women. Tess could press Miss Harris to show them the bathroom, but they'd seen enough. Tess turned to follow Miss Harris, but Mario remained staring at the rows of cots.

"How many people live here?" Mario said.

"In this dormitory?" Miss Harris asked. "I'm not exactly sure."

"How many in this whole place?" Mario asked.

Miss Harris hesitated. "A little over five thousand. But…"

"You're working on it." Mario said. He turned and walked out of the building. Miss Harris and Tess followed.

Tess and Mario walked back to the Administration building. Miss Harris told them again about the plans to relieve over-crowding, plans for expansion of living quarters and plans for new state schools.

Fifteen minutes later, Mario and Tess stood next to the car staring back at the buildings.

"She seems okay," Mario said. "Clean and content I guess. We can come back often and make sure she's okay. I don't know what else we can do."

Tess took another long look at the several buildings she could see from the parking lot and recalled the others they saw from the entrance. Tess turned to Mario and took his hand in hers. "We can give her a better life."

40

DiMaggio Smashes 3 Homers as Yankees Beat Browns Twice

I lean against the fender of the Commodore. "One thousand, three hundred," I tell him.

The guy says, "Okay, that's the civilians' price. Now give me the veterans' price."

"That's the price."

The guy puts his hand on my shoulder like we're best buddies. "Come on. Don't bullshit me," he says. "I know there's a lot of slack in your price. Guys who fought the Nazis made it possible for you to even be here, so let's have the real price."

I shake the guy's hand off my shoulder. He scowls at me. "That's it," I say. I feel a headache coming on. There's a black cloud at the edge of my eye. I start to step away.

"Hey, I'm talking to you."

Dave walks over. "What's the matter?"

The guy shoots his hand toward me. "This jerk won't give me a break on the price. I'm a veteran, and I got to take shit from him. Probably was a conchie."

Dave says, "Take it easy, friend. Bill was in the service. Fought in Normandy. Spent time in a POW camp."

The guy makes a sour face and shakes his head. "I should have figured. Dropped your rifle and quit, huh? *Hande hoch.* Hands up," he mocks. "Finished out the war on Red Cross handouts while we kept on fighting."

I don't remember hitting him. He's flat on his back, and I'm straddling him punching his face. Blood from his nose and busted lip is splattering on my shirt. Dave's grabbing me, trying to pull me off. I keep pounding the son-of-a-bitch.

"Bill, stop for crissakes!" Dave's screaming.

More hands pulling on my arms and shoulders. They pull me up, and I give the guy a kick in the side.

"Take it easy," Dave says.

I punch Dave. I'm swinging at everyone that's close.

Mike comes running out of his office. "Jesus, Bill. *Stop.*" Dave and Mike are pinning my arms, pushing and dragging me across the showroom floor into the small office at the end. They slam me down into a chair.

"Keep him here," Mike says to Dave. "I got to see what the hell he's done."

I sit with Dave's hand firmly on my shoulder. I'm not going to get up. I'm trying to piece together what I did. His face. There was something about his face. I can't see it at first, then I get a blurry picture of the kraut with the machine gun. Same eyes. The shape of his head. Fucking kraut with the machine gun. *Hande hoch.*

Ten minutes later, Mike comes in the office. "You've really done it this time."

"He shouldn't have said what he said."

"So he's an asshole. Once a week, some vet comes in expecting a free car because he got trench foot on Iwo Jima. We put a hand on his shoulder, tell him we understand how tough it was, nod toward my office like you're going to tell him a secret, and then whisper the vet's price in his ear – which is the same goddam price we give everybody. We don't beat the shit out of them."

"I'm sorry."

Mike cocks his head at Dave, and Dave leaves. "You got to go, Bill."

"Go where?"

"Right now, go home. You got to get out of here."

"Why?"

"I tried to apologize. Told him you were under a lot of pressure. The thing is he went out the door yelling he was going to the police and get a lawyer and sue."

"I'll pay for his broken nose."

"Bill, get out of here. Now."

***

Natalie put her key in the lock, but the back door to the apartment opened. She was sure she locked it when she and Marcia left for the playground. Perhaps she forgot while getting all of Marcia's stuff packed.

Inside the kitchen, something was wrong. A chair was tipped over. There was broken glass on the floor. Natalie pushed Marcia behind her. A burglar? She was about to rush back down the stairs and out the door when she heard a shout and crash in the bedroom. Sweet Jesus. It was Bill. It was a little before noon, and Bill should be at the dealership.

Natalie heard another crash. There was broken glass on the kitchen floor. A coffee cup? A water glass? She grabbed Marcia's hand and shoved her along in front of her to the living room. The door to the bedroom was closed, but she heard Bill swearing though the door. "Stay here," Natalie said to Marcia. "Don't move." She realized she'd frightened her, but she needed her to stay out of the way.

Natalie rapped on the bedroom door. "Bill." She jumped back when she heard another crash. She pushed open the door. Bill was standing in front of her dresser. There was nothing on the dresser top. Natalie's perfume bottles, the framed photograph of their wedding – everything had been swept into a pile in the corner. A pillow from their bed was under the window where the Venetian blinds had been knocked off their brackets and dangled at a crazy angle. Whatever was on Bill's dresser was on the floor.

Bill faced Natalie. His face was a pulsing red mask. His breath was coming in gulps. The furious glare on his face backed Natalie into the door. He took a step toward Natalie. She held up her hand. "Bill. Stop. What's going on?"

"Fucking asshole," he shouted. His left hand was a tight fist. He jabbed his right hand at Natalie. "That's it, I said. I don't have to take this shit anymore."

"What? Where? At the dealership?"

"Did he think it was a vacation?"

Natalie didn't know what he was talking about. And he was shouting at someone or something over her shoulder. "I don't understand." She reached for Bill, but he slapped her hand away.

"POW he says, like he won the war single-handed, and I'm sitting on a beach with a cold beer."

Natalie was finally able to grasp Bill's forearm. "Who?"

He wrest it free, and hit Natalie across the face. "That'll teach you. You son-of-a-bitch."

Natalie stumbled back, hit the edge of the bed and slumped to the floor. Bill took a step toward her and pulled his fist back as if to hit her again. "Bill, stop," she screamed.

"Mommy."

Bill and Natalie turned toward the door.

"*Mommy*," Marcia cried again.

Natalie scrabbled to her feet, hunching away from Bill in case he was going to hit her again. She opened the door a crack. Marcia stood rigid with fear. "Go back to the living room. Everything is alright." Marcia gawped at Natalie's face. Natalie touched her fingers to her cheek. There was blood on them. "I slipped and fell. I'll be alright."

Cautiously, Natalie turned. Bill stared at her as

though he'd never seen her before. His head swiveled around as though he'd just discovered the wreckage of the bedroom. He gaped at his balled fist and back to Natalie's bleeding face. "Oh my God, what have I done?" he cried and fell back on the bed in a faint.

Oh, God. A stroke? Bill eyes rolled back in his head. He muttered nonsense words.

Natalie knelt on the bed next to him. "Bill. Bill. Are you alright?" He wasn't alright. Should she call the police and get an ambulance? Bill raised his left hand, and Natalie flinched. He wiped his hand across his forehead. "Whaa?" It was as though he'd awakened from a nightmare. He bolted upright and they knocked heads.

"Oww."

"I'm sorry," Bill said and rubbed his forehead.

It was as though he didn't remember hitting Natalie moments ago.

Slowly Bill surveyed the room. At first there was a questioning look on his face and then flickers of recognition until his mouth dropped open. "Oh, God. What did I do?" He slumped foreword, buried his face in his hands, and cried.

Carefully, Natalie put her arm around his shoulder, but that seemed to bring more sobs. After a few minutes, the sobs lessened, but his face remained buried in his hands. When Natalie thought he was somewhat under control, she said, "Stay here. Stay calm. I've got to see what's happening with Marcia."

Natalie opened the bedroom door. Marcia was terrified. "It's alright. Everything is alright," she said and hugged Marcia to her. "Daddy... had a spell." Marcia stared at Natalie's face. "And I slipped and hit my head on the dresser. I'm alright. Daddy's alright. Mommy's alright."

Everything was alright – except it wasn't.

"I'll bet you're hungry. Let's have lunch." She opened the bedroom door a crack. Bill was still sitting on the edge of the bed. "Bill, I'm going to get Marcia's lunch. Can I get you anything?" He shook his head. "I'll be back in a few minutes."

Natalie took Marcia into the bathroom and was shocked to see the cut under her eye and the smear of blood on her cheek. A red bruise was starting to turn blue on the other cheek. No wonder Marcia was frightened. Natalie quickly washed the bloody smear and pressed a cold cloth against her cheek while Marcia gave her fearful glances from her potty chair.

Back in the kitchen, Natalie was a hyper Betty Crocker handing around peanut butter and jelly sandwiches and passing out chocolate chip cookies usually saved for snack. Marcia eyed her suspiciously.

Thirty minutes later, Natalie got Marcia down for a nap and checked on Bill. He was still in the same position on the bed. Natalie sat on the bed beside him. Afraid she'd provoke another rage she cautiously asked, "How about some lunch?" He shook his head. They sat silently, until Natalie finally asked, "What happened?"

"I hit you."

"I'm okay." Natalie waited a few moments. "Why? What made you to do this?" She waved her hand at the mess strewn around the room.

"I blacked out – again."

"Again?" Had this happened before and he hadn't told her?

"Natalie, I've really messed up."

Natalie put her hand on his arm. "Bill, please tell me what happened."

"A customer came into the dealership and made a big deal about being a vet. I gave him the price, and the guy went off on me. He said the guys who saw action like him should get a better deal. He accused me of being a conchie."

"Jerk," Natalie said.

"Dave stepped in and told the guy that I was in the infantry, Normandy. I could have handled it. Then Dave says I was also a former POW. The guy accuses me of dropping my weapon and surrendering instead of fighting. That's when I punched him."

Natalie tried to picture Bill swinging at this customer, hoping it was more of a push. "Just a punch?"

"More than once. Several times. I knocked him down. I couldn't stop hitting him."

Natalie gave Bill a sympathetic squeeze, but she was scared. This was new. This was different. And what if it happens again?

"Dave and a couple of the other guys pulled me off. The guy's face was pretty bad. He took off. Said he was going to press charges. Said he was going to sue."

Natalie pointed to the broken bottles and picture frames. "What happened here?"

Ignoring her question, Bill said, "Mike told me to get out. Go home. I still couldn't stop even when I got home." Bill put his fingers on Natalie's cheek.

Natalie tried not to flinch, but she couldn't. "It's nothing."

"I hit you. I can't believe I did this to you."

"Nothing that can't be replaced or fixed," Natalie said. But she couldn't help thinking about the other episodes, the wild mood swings, the constant complaints about being treated unfairly and his inability to be successful, even adequate, in his jobs. It's gotten worse, not better. And what happened today was dangerous. She feared Bill couldn't be fixed.

***

Natalie heard Bill's tread on the staircase, and her heart sank. She didn't have to glance at the clock over the stove to know that it was not yet noon. It had been two days since Bill attacked the man at the dealership: two days of phone calls with his brother, two days of refusing to tell Natalie what was going on, and two days of him sitting on the edge of the bed staring at the wall. Although Bill offered only vague allusions to what his brother said in the last call, Natalie was sure it was an ultimatum that finally got him to grudgingly get dressed and go in this morning.

The door opened. Natalie was afraid to look at him. Marcia turned toward Bill and applesauce dribbled down her chin. Natalie spent the entire morning rehearsing what she'd say to Bill if the news was good – or bad. Now that he was here after no more than a couple of hours at the dealership, she knew it was bad, and she didn't know what to say.

Bill stood in the doorway as though afraid to come into the apartment. His jacket was draped over his arm, and his shirt was soaked in sweat. "How did it go?"

"I'm done."

At the same time Natalie wondered what she'd say, she thought about what they'd do if he lost his job. She didn't have any answers to that either. Marcia stopped eating her lunch. Even a two-year-old felt the tension in the room. Natalie wanted to hear what happened away from Marcia. "Finish your lunch," she said. "Why don't you tell me about it in there?" Natalie pointed toward the dining room.

Slowly Bill walked by Natalie, and she smelled the

stench from his sweaty shirt. "You're hot."

"I had to take the bus home."

Natalie realized they'd fired him, and he had to hand in the keys to his salesman's car.

Natalie stood in the dining room hoping she and Bill could talk, but Bill went into their bedroom and angrily stripped off his shirt. She decided she might as well get it out in the open. "Mike fired you?"

"Who was the jerk who said blood was thicker than water?" Bill tossed the shirt into the corner of the room.

Mike had put up with a lot, but Natalie didn't think he'd go so far as to fire Bill. Then again, Bill had never beat up a customer before. "Are you alright?" Natalie said even though she realized how ridiculous her question was.

Bill seemed to recognize it, and plopped down on the bed with a shake of his head. "Did he think I'd eat the shit he offered?"

"What do you mean?"

"Parts. *Assistant* manager of parts. Our father started the damn dealership. I'm the son of the owner," Bill shouted at someone – not Natalie – on the other side of the room.

Natalie felt her anger rising when she realized that Bill wasn't fired. He must have quit. But this was not the time to remind Bill that after his father died, he demanded Mike buy out his share of the business so he could invest their savings in the can't-fail soda dispenser franchise his old Army buddy was pitching. And three other failed jobs after that. They'd been damn lucky blood was thicker and Mike took him in as a salesman. "He offered you another job?"

Bill looked at Natalie as though she might be a sympathetic judge. "A gray shirt with a little oval badge with 'Bill' over the pocket from Capital Uniforms." He gave Natalie a pleading look. "A couple of bucks an hour. Can you believe it?"

"You didn't take Mike's offer?"

"Offer?" Bill spit. "He was rubbing my nose in it, hoping I'd quit. Whining about what he paid out to the asshole I punched. Made it sound like he was doing me a big favor."

Natalie did the math. His monthly draw barely made their weekly grocery budget. Then she remembered that Bill would lose the car from the dealership, and then she figured the bus fare back and forth. Her brain was spinning with *and then whats.* Stop. She put her hand on Bill's shoulder, and he slumped under her touch. "I can see why you're upset," she said quietly. "Take it easy this afternoon. Think things over."

"There's nothing to think over." Bill flopped back on the bed. Blank eyes stared at the ceiling. "I'm done."

41

*Dr. Yepsen Tells States at Parley to Fight Mental
Deficiency and End 'Appalling' Neglect*

Mom started to clear the dessert plates. Across the table,
Nick looked as unsettled as Natalie felt. When Nick said
Mom and Dad asked him to come home for the weekend,
Natalie was sure something serious had happened. Her
mother and father had moved so cautiously around their
own house, it was as though Governor Dewey had been
invited to dinner.

When they learned that the lump on Mom's breast
was a cyst, Natalie hoped her spirits would pick up. But then
there were those unexplained days out of town. They'd
never taken a vacation. As far as Natalie knew they didn't
have relatives that lived outside a two mile radius of
Watervliet. If there was something more than the cyst, Mom
would go to Albany Med, not out of town. When Natalie
mentioned it, Mom said, 'Something we had to do,' in her
that's all I'm going to say about it tone.

Mom returned from the kitchen, and Natalie
blanched when she caught the deep seriousness of the look
that passed between Mom and Dad. Something wrong with
Dad?

"Your father and I have something to tell you," Mom
said. She looked at Dad.

Dad reached across the table and took Mom's hand in
his. "You can tell them," he said in a grave tone.

Oh, Jesus. It's going to be awful.

Mom looked at Natalie and then Nick. "You two have

a sister."

Natalie thought she'd heard her words correctly, but they didn't make sense.

Nick said, "I have a sister?"

A tear trickled down Mom's cheek. "I let them take my baby away."

"Tess," Dad said. "You didn't let them. We did what we thought we had to do."

Natalie's head ping-ponged between Mom and Dad. What were they talking about? Natalie gawped at Mom. Did she have a baby out of wedlock and put it up for adoption? She didn't understand.

"Two years before you were born, I had another baby."

Natalie's mind raced to do the math. She glanced toward the living room where Marcia was playing with a doll.

"Margaret," Mom said.

"She was damaged," Dad said. "She had the mental retardation. We couldn't take care of her. They took her away."

Mom sniffled. "We could…"

"There was no way we could have," Dad said. "That's what happened then, even now. Sometimes the doctors think the baby won't live."

"But she didn't die?" Natalie asked.

"No," Mom said. "They took her to a special program at Syracuse."

Natalie said, "You've been going to Syracuse? These out of town trips?"

"She's in Rome now," Dad said. "I guess they did all they could for her at Syracuse and then she went to live at Rome at the state school there."

"She goes to school in Rome?" Bill said.

Natalie gave him a look as though she forgot he was there.

"It's not really a school," Dad said. "It's a…" He turned to Mom.

"It's an institution," Mom said with bitterness in her voice.

"And you've been visiting her in Rome?" Natalie thought she sounded like – well – she didn't know but it was as though her parents were telling her she was adopted or Dad had another wife in the old country.

Dad squeezed Mom's hand. "The doctors said it was best if we didn't see her. That's what they did. They told us at Rome that a lot of the people there don't know their parents."

"We should have never listened to them. I shouldn't have let them take my baby, and I should have gone to see her," Mom said. "That's why I got the cancer."

"Tess, it wasn't your fault, and you didn't get the cancer," Dad said.

"I should have for what I let them do."

"Tess, we decided that it's water over the dam. We can't go back and change what happened twenty-seven years ago. It seemed like we didn't have a choice. We didn't know any better."

Mom slid her hand out from under Dad's and smacked the table top. "But now we do. Now we can make it right."

"Those times we were out of town," Dad said. "We have been visiting her…"

"Margaret," Mom said.

"We've been visiting Margaret," Dad continued. "Getting her used to us."

Nick said, "Is she...?"

Dad said, "She – Margaret. She works in the kitchen. She talks to us pretty good. She's getting used to us."

Natalie tried to recall mentally retarded people she'd seen. "Like Joey Casatto?" she asked as she called up an image of the short teen-aged boy with flat features who closely followed his mother at the grocery store.

"No," Dad said. "What Joey's got came from a bad gene. What Margaret got was from not enough oxygen when she was born."

Tess said, "I talked to Anita Casatto. They wanted to put him away too, but she wouldn't let them."

"Tess," Dad said. "It's different now. What happened twenty-seven years ago is over. Now is now."

Mom said, "And now we're planning to bring Margaret home."

"Here?" Bill said. He shot a look toward the living room.

Dad said, "We're going slow. We visit. We talk. Last time we took Margaret out for a ride and had lunch at a diner outside Rome."

"Does she realize you're her parents?" Natalie asked.

Dad said, "We've talked about that. We tried to explain it to her. For most of the people there, they don't have parents – or ones that visit – so they have a hard time understanding."

"What's going to happen?" Natalie asked.

Mom said, "We're going to keep visiting, maybe once every week or so to get Margaret more comfortable with me and Mario." She paused as if she was gathering her courage. "And then we're going to bring her home to visit and see how that goes." She paused. "And if it does, we'll bring her home for good."

"To live?" Bill said.

"She's our daughter. This is her home," Mom said.

"When?" Natalie asked. Her mind raced as she tried to imagine what that would mean. Natalie couldn't conjure a picture of how her mother's and father's lives would change and what it would mean for her. Her sister? Natalie couldn't make sense of that. Mom and Dad were in their fifties. What happens when....? Natalie tried to shut her brain down. She was going too fast.

"When she's ready," Mom said.

Marcia started to fuss. Natalie had dozens of questions, but she had to get out of the house and away from this news that was turning her head inside out. She didn't know what to say to Mom and Dad. Congratulations? I hope this works out? It sounded so trivial for this earth-shaking event for them, for her. "We better go," Natalie said. An anxious look crossed Mom's face. Natalie gave her a hug and a kiss. "I'm glad for you and Dad." She gave Dad a kiss. "We'll talk."

"Mom," Nick said. "Margaret's birthday. The day you stay in your room all day?"

Mom surrendered a shrug.

"And the ... jokes," Nick muttered. "I'm sorry."

"You didn't know."

"Maybe you can come with us the next time we visit," Dad said.

"Yeah, sure," Nick said.

Natalie had to get out of the house. She needed to think.

42

Anti-Clotting Aids Cut Heart Deaths: Experts Assert Use Will Cut Fatalities

I don't have time for this, but I'd better sit down. The aspirins aren't working. The dull pain's now creeping up and down my arm, and I got a knot in the middle of my chest.

"Mr. P., you all right?"

"Just a little winded," I say, but Jimmie's giving me a queer stare.

"You want I should call somebody?"

"No, Jimmie. I took on too much this morning." I try to laugh, but when I do I get a stab in my chest. "Don't get old, Jimmie."

"You're not old, Mr. P. Let me get you a glass of water."

Where's Jimmie and the water? I reach up to take off what's stuck on my face, but a hand grabs mine. Who's looking down at me? I try to sit up, but there's a strap across my chest. I'm in a truck. We're moving.

"Take it easy, Mr. Pisano."

"Mike?"

"Yeah, it's me, Mike Ryan from Engine 1."

"What the...?"

"We're on our way to Memorial. They're closest."

"Tess..."

***

"Mr. Pisano. How do you feel?"

I keep staring up at people. Who's this? "I don't know," is all I can manage with something stuck in my nose.

"I'm Dr. First. You're in the Intensive Cardiac Care Unit at Memorial Hospital."

"Tess. My wife?"

"Mrs. Pisano was in to see you a little while ago."

"I had a spell."

The doctor laughs. What's so funny? I don't feel so good.

"I'm afraid it's a bit more complicated than that," the doctor says. "All the bloods aren't back, but it looks as though you had an MI, a myocardial infarction."

"What's that?"

"In general, a heart attack, but we need to nail down exactly what kind."

"When can I…?" I can't finish what I want to say.

"You need to take it easy. We think you're out of the woods, but we don't need a repeat."

***

"Mario."

"Tess?"

She's sniffling, and she kisses me on the forehead. "You okay?" I say.

"If it wouldn't give you another heart attack, I'd hit you," Tess says. "I'm okay. It's you that's got to get better."

"The doctor told me. I had an M something."

Tess says, "He told me and Natalie. He says that now that it's more than forty-eight hours, he was…carefully optimistic."

"Two days?"

"Mario, you've been here almost three days."

"Holy smokes. The shop. What's…?"

"*Enough.* I'm too young to be a widow. You do

nothing but rest. Jimmie's there. Natalie's been going in calling the customers, getting things organized." She puts her hand on mine. "Jimmie saved your life. You kept telling him you were going to be alright, but he called the fire department right away." She kisses me on the forehead again. *"Testa dura."*

43

Russia Vetoes Plan for Bomb Control with 26th Negating Action in U.N.

Sitting across the kitchen table from Natalie, Nick looked like death warmed over. "You think he's going to make it?" he asked.

"The doctors are, as Mom says, 'carefully optimistic." Natalie took a long look at Nick. "What's bothering you?"

"I'm worried about Dad."

"We all are, but I think he's going to be alright – eventually. Is it just Dad that you're worried about?"

Nick sighed. "I'm afraid I'm going to flunk out."

"How do you flunk out of sociology?"

"By not going to class," Nick said. "I hate it."

"So change your major."

"I don't know if I want any major. Remember, I went in right after I graduated in June and got discharged in January. That only gave me a total of twenty months on the GI Bill. The government's only paying me for another six months."

"I'll bet Dad said he'd help you with the tuition and expenses until you graduated."

"Yeah," Nick said. "He was sending me fifty bucks a month. I feel terrible, Sis. I know it's been hard for you and Bill."

Natalie put her hand over Nick's. "Don't. Dad was slipping me at least that much on the side. Along with paying off the new equipment, it's a wonder he didn't have a heart attack sooner."

"What do we do?"

"Come back to Watervliet and work with me in the print shop – at least until Dad gets back on his feet."

"I don't know anything about printing."

"Neither do I, but I went in right after Dad's attack, thinking I'd clean up and tell his customers everything would be on hold until Dad got back."

"Jeez," Nick said. "Mom says he's got at least a few months of recuperation. And then he's supposed to take it easy."

"Once I knew that Dad would survive, I wondered if the business would."

Nick said, "We don't know how to run a print shop. What can we do?"

"For starters, ask Jimmie."

"Jimmie?"

"Right, Natalie said. "I was about to call Dad's customers to cancel the jobs he had in the pipeline, when Jimmie chimed in and showed me what to do to finish the job Dad was doing when he had the attack. Remember Jimmie followed his father around for years and then Dad. Turns out, he was always watching."

"You mean Jimmie can do the jobs? He's kind of…"

Natalie said, "Jimmie does okay inside a narrow, well-defined world. I asked him about the job Dad was working on. Jimmie said, 'Now, Mr. P. fills the ink reservoir. Then Mr. P. gets the Number 7 paper and loads it there. And then, Mr. P… Damned if I didn't finish the job with Jimmie telling me what to do every step of the way."

"Wow."

"And then I take the next order off the stack, and it's 'Mr. P. does this' and 'Then Mr. P does that.' I asked Jimmie if he could do the jobs. No way. Absolutely not. Can't do it.

But show him the order, and he's a walking owner's manual. It was like following a recipe."

"And you want me to go in and follow Jimmie's instructions?"

"Once Dad is out of the hospital, I can handle the customers, the orders, and probably pick up the business stuff. You can be Jimmie's printer's devil." Natalie reached across the table and grasped Nick's hand. "We can do it, Nick. We have to do it."

44

Msgr. Sheen Delivers Sermon at St. Patrick's on 'The Perils of an Easy Conscience'

This can't go on, Natalie thought. It's been weeks since Bill refused to go back to work. Almost every night Bill bolted awake screaming and shouting at unseen people on the other side of the bedroom or collapsing into crying jags and spouting nonsense phrases. By morning, Natalie was exhausted and he'd dropped into a near coma.

Natalie had to get Marcia ready to take to Mom's house. She'd cut down her hours at the warehouse, but that and what she had to do at the shop took up the entire day.

Thank goodness Mom had Marcia most of the time. Bill was finally out of bed, but he walked around the house like a zombie, unwashed, unshaven, and usually only wearing the pants Natalie insisted he put on. Marcia looked at Bill and then at Natalie as though Natalie had an answer to the unspoken questions on her face. *Who is this man who looks like my father? Why does he act so strangely? Why doesn't he seem to recognize me?*

Bill refused to see their doctor, but Natalie called him anyway and described Bill's behavior. He suggested Bill contact the Veterans' Administration. When Natalie gently hinted that Bill follow up with the VA, he wouldn't speak to her for days.

Last night was the last straw. Bill woke screaming, 'Watch out,' 'Sarge. Where's Sarge?' and something that sounded like German, *'Aufstehen.'* Then he jumped up and dove under the bed. But Natalie had thought several other episodes were the last straw. Reluctantly she asked Mom to give Marcia her supper. She needed to confront Bill without having Marcia home.

"Bill, you have to get up," Natalie said. He rolled over. She wouldn't let him ignore her. Natalie yanked his shoulder and pulled him over. "Get up!"

Bill slowly dragged himself to the edge of the bed where he leaned forward with his head in his hands. "I'm tired."

"Up," Natalie said.

Slowly he rose. Natalie yanked down his shorts and pulled his undershirt over his head. She pushed him toward the door. She braced for resistance, but he let her nudge him along to the bathroom. Natalie filled the tub and urged him into it. When he lay back as docile as a child, she bathed him. Natalie stood him next to the tub and dried him. "Shave," she said. He found his shaving gear and carefully shaved the three or four days of stubble from his face. "Stay here," Natalie said and rushed back to the bedroom for clothes.

Natalie got Bill dressed. It had been a couple of weeks since he'd been fully dressed. She guided him to the kitchen and sat him at the table while she made a pot of coffee.

Natalie and Bill sipped their coffee. She poured Bill another cup. He drank it and gave Natalie a suspicious look. "What do you want?" he asked.

"You." Natalie put her hand on his wrist. "I want you, Bill."

"Thank you for the bath. It felt good."

"In sickness and in health," Natalie said. "Bill, you're sick. You need help."

Bill's face hardened. "I'm not going to the VA."

Natalie was afraid he was going to dash back to the bedroom. "Let's not talk about the VA," she said. Not yet, she thought. "For now, I want you to get up every day. Wash, shave, and get dressed."

Bill said, "I can't sleep."

They sat silently for a few minutes. "The nightmares, the shouting, and the other things," Natalie said. "You've got to stop re-living the war."

Bill looked at the hands in his lap. "I wish I could. But I can't let it go."

"I'm not saying you have to go to the VA, but maybe if you talked to someone about what happened it might help make the memories go away, or fade."

"You think I'm crazy and need a shrink."

"You're not crazy, Bill. But you're not getting any better, and you and I and Marcia, but mostly you, can't go on living like this."

"All right," Bill said. "You want to hear about what happened? I'll talk to you."

Natalie was startled. They were the most normal words he'd spoken in a normal tone of voice in weeks. "I'll listen. Of course."

Bill stared at Natalie. "I cheated on you. Is that what you want to hear? When I was in France after the invasion I slept with a whore I picked up in a bar." He slapped the table. "*There*. I don't feel any better. Do you?"

He was away for more than three years – in combat, in a POW camp. Was having sex with a prostitute all that was making him crazy? Natalie couldn't expect that he'd led a celibate life for three years. It was always off limits. But as he looked at Natalie as though expecting a shock on her face, she knew all that was there was her stinging blush. Natalie looked into Bill's eyes for several seconds. "Bill, I cheated on you. I betrayed my vow to you. More than once."

"I heard the rumors," he said softly.

Natalie started to cry. She put her hand on his arm. She expected him to brush it away, but he left it. She wasn't surprised. She was sure there was no shortage of folks who couldn't wait to pass their suspicions about her and Jack. "They weren't rumors. I'm so sorry, Bill. I should have been faithful to you. I wasn't."

Bill and Natalie embraced and sobbed in each other's arms. Bill gently pulled back and held Natalie at arm's length. With a wry smile, he said, "We're even. We don't need to talk about it again."

They weren't even, Natalie thought. A one-night stand – maybe more – with a prostitute thousands of miles from home in the middle of a war was nothing compared to what she did with Jack Mahoney. She couldn't imagine how she'd ever make it up to him. What could make it even? "Thank you," Natalie said and kissed him. She was afraid to push too hard too soon, but she said, "Can you talk about the other things?"

Bill said, "I want them to stop. I can't make them stop."

"What needs to stop?"

"I can't describe them. I think the memories have gone away. I try to think about the better times, my buddies, seeing different things, but then they come back." Bill put his head in his hands. "I can't make them stop."

"We need a plan, Bill."

He said, "It's been almost three years. I don't know what to do."

After a few moments Natalie said, "I don't either. But for starters, here is what I want you to do. Every day I want you to get out of bed in the morning. I don't care whether you slept the night before or not. Get up and get dressed. Okay?"

"I guess."

"Don't guess, Bill. I have no idea what will work, but all we can do is take one step at a time. Get up. Get dressed. Eat breakfast."

"That's three steps."

Natalie said, "Good grief. I wondered if you'd left your sense of humor in France."

Bill let out a long sigh. "Okay. I'll try."

45

Natalie set Jimmie to packing the new menus for the Old Daley Inn and had Nick set up the press for a new batch of tickets for the Palace. She needed to stop at Jack's Oyster House with the quote for their menus. Natalie wanted to wrap up as many restaurants as possible before the competition started matching their prices.

Natalie thought she should swing by her parents' house. She was sure Marcia was getting a cold. Mom had too much on her plate already with babysitting and trying to keep Dad occupied. Natalie only let him into the shop for an hour – and only after he'd sworn he'd taken his nap. Still it was a challenging hour of, 'Did you remember to order a replacement die cutting jacket' and 'Do you think it's a good idea to order that many rollers?' and a dozen other poorly-disguised worries in his questions. Growing up poor and struggling through the Depression made him too cautious. When Natalie finally got a handle on how he'd been ordering supplies, she realized he was spending way too much in shipping for small orders of ink and paper. Dad joked that she was going to give him another heart attack when she began her first bulk orders. But every time she and Dad were together, she really did worry he might have another heart attack. What if never fully recovered, and she and Nick and Jimmie would struggle to keep the business afloat – or limp on until it folded?

Natalie remembered Mr. Vincent calling her 'a Whirling Dervish' as she dashed from one to the next of his assignments and the ones she'd proposed. She made sure they took up virtually every minute of each day grappling with what needed to be done to complete the project and what might be the next project. Most importantly, they crowded out the shameful memories of her and Jack that haunted her idle moments.

Now she was again a Whirling Dervish. She still squeezed in as many hours as she could at Tony's warehouse. They needed the money, but since the appliance scam blow-up, her heart had hardened toward Tony. He still got more than what he paid her, but she'd forced herself to ignore ways she could improve what they were doing.

The shameful thoughts that haunted her now were about what lie ahead. When she picked up Marcia the other day, her parents looked old. Even slowed by his heart attack, Dad didn't want to hear a word about retiring.

She felt guilty asking Mom to take on more baby-sitting, but after all, with what Natalie was doing at the shop along with her job at Tony's warehouse, she had more than a full-time job. Last week when Natalie wanted to take up Flo's offer for the two of them to spend a Sunday having lunch and peeping leaves in Columbia County, Mom announced that she and Dad were making a trip to Rome. When she got off the phone, she'd burst into tears.

Damn it. She deserved an afternoon off with a friend. Natalie and her mother didn't have what she imaged was an ideal mother-daughter relationship. But she had been the only daughter no matter how fraught their lives had been. Now Margaret had dropped into their lives. Natalie felt a sting of being nudged to the sidelines as Mom and Dad took trips to Rome and now planned to bring Margaret home for a trial weekend to ease her into living permanently with them. She had to admit her anger and jealous tears masked the greater fear that stalked her in those early morning moments before she was fully awake. Instead of the half-formed memory of Joey Cassatto trailing his mother around the grocery store, it was Margaret following Natalie. Enough. She was driving herself crazy.

An hour later, Natalie pulled away from the curb on State Street and felt good hoping the surprised look on Arnold's face meant her quote would add Jack's as a customer. She turned on Broadway and wondered whether she should go home before she checked on Mom and Marcia. Natalie had never been more worried about Bill. After their confessional heart-to-heart, things got better – for a week. But then Bill slid back into what seemed to be an even deeper depression. The nightmares continued. He wouldn't get dressed, and he never ate meals with her and Marcia. He was like a feral cat barely keeping alive scrounging bits of cold left-overs from the fridge. Natalie felt as though she'd failed him. She decided she'd better go home.

She paused at the door to the apartment. Finding Bill at the kitchen table in his underwear would be an improvement. When Natalie did come home to check on him, he was usually asleep or sitting on the edge of the bed staring at the wall. 'Nervous breakdown,' Doctor Evans said when Natalie described Bill's condition. If this went on any longer, she was going to have a nervous breakdown. Natalie pushed open the door. She was startled. Bill was sitting at the kitchen table. But instead of an unwashed, unshaven lump plopped down in his underwear, Bill was completely dressed. He had on a jacket, clean white shirt, and even a tie. As if she discovered a strange man in their house, Natalie called out, *"Bill."* She was sorry it came out as though she was shocked, but it took her a few seconds to take in this complete overhaul.

Bill beamed a broad smile. "Hi, Natalie."

Natalie told herself to calm down and act as though Bill looked like a normal person every day. She kissed the top of his head and slid into a chair across the table. "How are you doing?" Natalie forced herself to act naturally, afraid calling attention to this radical change would prompt him to retreat to the bedroom.

"Good," Bill said as though he'd finished a positive inventory of himself. "Very good."

Natalie waited to hear Bill explain why he'd dressed as though going off to work. When he didn't answer, Natalie asked, "Can I make a pot of coffee?"

"No thanks. I made one earlier."

The coffee pot, basket and a rinsed out cup were on the counter next to the sink. For weeks, he'd been barely capable of pouring himself a glass of water. Natalie told herself to go slowly. As casually as she could, she asked, "Going somewhere – or just feeling like getting dressed?"

Bill looked at Natalie for several seconds. "I've been thinking."

Natalie waited for him to explain. Finally she asked, "About what?"

"About us."

Natalie was taken aback by the broad grin covering his face. He was looking at her with affection – love – something she hadn't felt from him for … she wasn't sure what to do or say. Natalie put her hand on his. "I'm glad."

Bill went back to staring the table. After a few moments, he said, "I know it's been difficult for you. I've been difficult."

"We'll work it out," Natalie said. She chanced a sweep of her hand at his clothes. "You look good. I'm glad to see you up and dressed." She didn't know how far to take this, but she said, "A step in the right direction."

"All that time in there," he frowned and tilted his head toward the bedroom. "Sitting, staring at the wall."

"But now you're up."

"Thinking," he said as though he hadn't heard her. "Thinking about the good times," he said. "Remember our first date at the roller rink? I wanted to impress you with how well I could skate."

"And you fell and broke your wrist."

"Showing off. I was sure you'd never go out with me again."

"You were too handsome to dump after one date. And brave," Natalie said. "I guessed you liked me a lot because I could tell how much it hurt and you wouldn't take me home and go to the Emergency Room."

"I was so happy you agreed to go out with me, I didn't want the night to end."

They stared at the top of the table, smiling.

Bill asked, "Do you remember the first movie we saw together?"

Natalie wished she could, but she finally shook her head.

"*The Maltese Falcon.*"

"Humphrey Bogart. You have a great memory."

"I remember because I worried for a week about whether you'd like it, or hate it – and me."

"You were such a handsome guy – still are. I was worried I didn't measure up to Sam Spade's *femme fatale*. Can't remember her name."

Bill said, "How about the time we went dancing? I asked around, and your girlfriends said you liked to go dancing."

"I did," she said. Natalie wondered where this trip down memory lane was heading.

"I was so afraid I'd stomp all over you, I asked my cousin Paul to give me some pointers. Heard he knew how to dance. I was so embarrassed when he grabbed me like a girl and showed me some basic steps. I gave him five dollars to keep his mouth shut about it."

"Didn't he go off to New York?"

"Another story." Bill leaned eagerly toward Natalie. "The dancing, roller skating, that diner in South Troy we'd go to after the dances. Those were great." He pursed his lips. "But you know, Natalie, all those great places and good times don't come close to the one place and one time. The best." Bill looked at Natalie as though waiting for an answer.

"You tell me, Bill. You're the champion Quiz Kid."

"Tomhannock Reservoir. "

Natalie couldn't help herself from laughing although she wasn't sure Bill would think it was funny. "Of all the places we went, you pick a lover's lane out in rural Rensselaer County."

"March third, nineteen forty-two."

Natalie tried to cast her mind back six years. Of course.

But before she could say it, Bill said, "The place and date you agreed to marry me. The happiest day of my life."

Natalie squeezed his hand. "You're right. Then and all those other happy times." She decided to dip her toe in troubled waters. "And now," she said gesturing again to his jacket, his white shirt, and the blue tie she gave him as a Christmas present. "Now we can go on to more happy times."

Bill didn't seem to have heard her. "You know, Natalie. All those times when I was overseas…" His voice caught. "In France, seeing what I saw." He scrubbed his face as though trying to erase memories. "All the things I did and what happened to me. When it was the worst, it was the one thing I'd think about to push the bad stuff away."

"I'm glad, Bill." Natalie made her voice bright. "Let's put the bad stuff behind us." Again, she gestured to his jacket. "Up and at' em." She then asked the question he didn't answer earlier. "Were you planning on going somewhere?"

Bill seemed to ponder the question. "Just thought it was time to move on. Get dressed and face the day."

"I'm going back to the shop. Would you like to come along? What do they say, all dressed up and..." Natalie stopped. It sounded cruel.

Bill said, "I was thinking I'd go out."

Natalie couldn't imagine where he'd go. He certainly couldn't go to the dealership. The park, the library, dressed in a jacket and tie? She glanced at the clock on the stove. She needed to get back to the shop. "I could take you to wherever you want to go."

Bill looked at Natalie for several seconds. It made her uncomfortable. "You know what, Natalie. How about I drive you back to the shop? Nick can drive you home when you close up."

Why shouldn't he have the car to drive around? He hadn't been out of the apartment for weeks. Yet she wasn't comfortable and didn't know exactly why. "You sure?"

"Yes," Bill said. "I need to get out."

"Okay. Why don't you pick me up at five? Nick might need to go somewhere, or he might be out delivering orders."

"Good," Bill said.

All afternoon Natalie hadn't been able to concentrate. She knew she should be delighted Bill was looking and acting like a normal person, but the sudden change from the zombie he'd become made her wonder what happened. Did a switch get thrown in his brain shutting off his nervous breakdown, battle fatigue or the other explanations they'd heard for his bizarre behavior? And Natalie couldn't stop replaying what he'd said and did when he dropped her off in front of the shop. Natalie asked him again if he wanted to come in and say 'hi' to Nick and Jimmie and take a look around the shop. 'No,' he'd said. And then he took Natalie's shoulder and pulled her toward him. He kissed her and said, 'Good bye, Natalie.'

All afternoon Natalie kept replaying, 'Good bye, Natalie.' She was driving herself crazy repeating and repeating it, trying to make it sound like a normal good bye, hoping he was out driving around town, maybe even stopping in at the dealership to show off the new Bill.

It was four o'clock, and Natalie hoped every car she heard on the street was Bill coming to pick her up. She grabbed Nick. "Take me home."

Nick looked at the clock. "Now?"

"Right now." Natalie tried to keep the urgency out of her voice, but Nick gave her a questioning look.

"Jimmie," she shouted. "Wrap that up. We're closing."

Jimmie seemed unsure about what Natalie said. "I'm almost done with…"

"Right now."

"Okay, Mrs. C." Jimmie said as though he was being scolded for making a mistake.

Natalie hustled Jimmie and Nick out the door. It took her a couple of tries before she could fit the key to the shop in the lock.

"You alright?" Nick asked.

"Let's go."

The ten minute drive from the shop to the apartment seemed to take an hour. And in every minute of that hour, the thought that Natalie had shoved to the back of her brain all afternoon kept forcing itself out.

Nick pulled in front of the apartment, and Natalie bolted out of the car. She took the stairs two at a time and flung open the back door. Bill was not in the kitchen. She called out, "Bill," but didn't expect an answer. Inside the bedroom, Natalie stumbled around the end of the bed and opened the door to the closet. It was still there. But she was afraid of what she had to do next. Natalie reached into the back of the closet. A moment after she'd grasped the brown metal box she had the answer to the terrible thought that lurked in the back of her mind all afternoon. She shouldn't have waited. Natalie picked up the box. She knew it was too light, but she shook it. Nothing rattled or thumped inside. "Oh, Bill," she cried. "I'm sorry." She shouldn't have left him alone and let him take the car. She should have come home earlier.

Natalie dashed out of the bedroom. Nick was standing in the kitchen.

"What's wrong?"

"We've got to find Bill." Natalie thought she should call Mom and tell her she'd be late picking up Marcia, but she didn't have time and couldn't explain why.

Nick asked, "What? Where?"

The moment she picked up the box, she also realized where Bill was going. "Tomhannock Reservoir." Natalie pushed Nick toward the stairs. "Let's go." March nineteen forty-two. It was dark, and she couldn't remember how they got there. The reservoir must be two or three miles long.

Once they were inside the car, Nick's said, "Tomhannock Reservoir? Which end? Melrose or Raymertown?"

Thank goodness most young men around here knew about the area's lover's lane. Unfortunately, Reservoir Road ran along the entire length. Nick started the engine. "Wait." Good God, it was six years ago. Natalie buried her head in her hands and tried to remember where Bill and she were before they drove out there. Yes! The South End Tavern. They crossed the bridge at the south end. "Take seven."

Apparently sensing Natalie's urgency, Nick did a quick U-turn and headed toward Route 7 at a rapid clip. "What's going on?"

Natalie was afraid to admit it to herself and afraid that telling Nick would somehow make it happen. Finally, she said, "I'm afraid Bill might hurt himself."

Nick shot her a quizzical look. "Like?"

"He has a gun. A pistol he brought back from overseas."

"Do you think…?"

"I don't know, but we have to find him."

Nick sped through Raymertown. Natalie didn't know whether she wanted them to be picked up by a State Trooper or not. They crossed the bridge and turned left onto Reservoir Road. It didn't look familiar. Six years ago. It was night, and she wasn't driving. They slowed as they passed dirt cut-offs down to the water, trying to see if their car was parked on one of them. "Oh, Bill, please," Natalie cried as they bounced over ruts and loose gravel.

"There! There!" Their car was pulled off into the weeds on the left side of the road. A foot path led to the water. Nick pulled over and they jumped out of the car. "Please, God,

don't do it," Natalie whispered over and over as she and Nick started down the wide dirt path.

Thirty feet from the water, Bill was sitting on a log. Thank God, he was alive. Natalie took two quick steps toward Bill, but Nick grabbed her shoulder.

"Careful. Don't startle him."

Natalie's heart was pounding in her ears. She tried to take careful steps on rubbery legs. Nick was beside her. Carefully, they circled to Bill's right until they were about fifteen feet to his side. They stopped. Bill was staring at the water, and after a few moments he slowly turned toward them. Tears streamed down his cheeks.

Natalie slowly walked toward him. Bill held the pistol in his lap. "Bill," she said gently, "Why don't you put that down – on the ground?"

Bill had a pleading look on his face when he turned to her. "I couldn't find it, Natalie."

She took another cautious step toward him. "What couldn't you find, Bill?"

"I drove up and down the road, but I couldn't find it." His head slowly shook, and his face had a look of deep disappointment. "Where I asked you to marry me. I couldn't find it."

Natalie took two more careful steps toward Bill and gently placed her hand on his shoulder. "It's alright, Bill. The important thing is you asked me, not the exact spot."

"I'm sorry."

Natalie rubbed Bill's shoulder, and he leaned his head on her arm. "There's nothing to be sorry about." He still had the pistol in his hand. Natalie didn't know if she should say anything about it. Nick took a step toward them, but Natalie shook her head. "Bill, why don't you put the gun on the ground?"

Natalie's gut clenched as Bill lifted the pistol, holding it in front of him.

"Bill, please put the gun down."

Turning his face to Natalie with tears still tracking on his cheeks, he said, "I couldn't. I'm a coward."

"You're not a coward, Bill." With her right hand Natalie slowly reached out and gently took hold of Bill's wrist. She lowered his hand and the pistol to his lap. "You're not a coward. And there is no reason for you to harm yourself."

Bill let the pistol drop to the ground. He twisted toward Natalie and buried his face in her torso. "I'm so sorry," he said over and over, sobbing.

Natalie pressed Bill into her and rubbed the back of his head. After a few minutes, she urged him up. "Let's go home, Bill."

46

Natalie pulled open the drawer next to the refrigerator and wondered where Mom put the potato masher. It wasn't like her to make changes, but over the past couple of months it seemed as though she'd faced the larger changes ahead by re-arranging small things: kitchen utensils in different drawers, her Sunday best cups and saucers on the first instead of the second shelf of the hutch and the blue upholstered chair in the living room now on the left of the sofa rather than on the right where it had sat since Henry Hudson sailed the Half Moon up the river.

Nick poked his head in the kitchen. "Natalie, can I help with anything?"

"Thanks Nick. Just keeping an eye on Marcia has been an enormous help. I lived here for more than twenty years, but cooking in Mom's kitchen has me even more nervous."

"It's going to be fine."

"Yes, but today is different. This is it."

Nick said, "I pulled Marcia's trike around behind the house. Okay?"

"Thanks, I don't want her messing her good dress or scraping her knees – at least until later."

Nick said, "If they did manage to leave after lunch, they should be here any minute. If they build that Thruway, I'll bet they could make it in two hours instead of the four it takes now. And maybe four hours to…" Nick gave Natalie an apologetic look and said, "Sorry, Sis."

"Don't be sorry," Natalie said.

"It was the right thing to do."

"Actually, I don't mind staying over. I found a nice motor court on Route 5 with five or six of those little cabins. It was like staying in a doll house. And when I visit Bill, sometimes we take walks in Sonnenberg Gardens."

Nick asked, "Are they part of the VA hospital?"

"I'm not sure," she said. "One of the administrators told me that when the VA bought the Thompson farm, the mansion and gardens were included. The mansion is a bit run-down, but the rose gardens are still beautiful. Some of the patients and staff are trying to maintain the walled gardens and plantings."

"I can't see Bill tending rose bushes," Nick said. "Sorry."

Natalie took her hand out of Nick's grasp and gave him a playful punch on the arm. "Quit apologizing. It's where he has to be. We don't know for how long, but he's safer there. At least he might understand he's not the only veteran still suffering the after-shocks of the war."

"Let's hope so," Nick said.

"The last time I visited, we took a drive to the lake. It's only a mile away, and there's a big amusement park right on the shore – Rose Land. And Canandaigua is a lovely town. Maybe I'll take Marcia. She'd love to stay in one of those doll house cabins." As soon as the words were out of her mouth, Natalie realized she'd said aloud what none of them had fully admitted. Her voice caught. "It will take a while before Bill's war is over."

Nick put his arms around Natalie. "I hope your war ends too."

"I'll put the roast in now," Natalie said. "When they arrive, we should ease into dinner. I made some celery sticks

348

with cream cheese. It seemed to work well the last time."

"Do you think she'll realize it won't be like the last time?" Nick asked.

"They've been taking it one step at a time," Natalie said. "They've spent more time each visit. When she stayed here for the weekend, she seemed fine, but a little confused."

Twenty minutes later, Dad's car pulled into the driveway, and Natalie felt her heart knocking. She went to the living room window. Nick stood next to her, and Marcia clung to Natalie's legs.

Dad got out and opened the back door. Mom and Margaret stepped out and stood in the driveway. Dad opened the trunk of the car and pulled out a suitcase. Natalie fought back tears as she realized that everything of her sister's was contained in one small suitcase.

Mom had Margaret's hand as they mounted the front steps. Natalie opened the door, and they entered. Mom and Dad, Margaret, Natalie and Marcia and Nick were crowded in the small foyer. For a moment, they stood silently. Natalie wrapped her arms around Margaret. "Welcome home, Margaret."

Natalie pushed back to hold Margaret at arm's length. A question formed on Margaret's face. She looked at Mom. Tears were running down Mom's cheeks. Dad was crying. Mom and Dad put their arms around her. "You're home," Dad said. "This is your home – for good."

Marcia hovered behind Natalie, and Natalie kneeled next to her. "Remember when your Aunt Margaret visited before?" she said. "Margaret is my sister and Uncle Nick's sister too."

Natalie gestured toward Mom and Dad. "Margaret is Grandma and Grandpa's girl. Grandma is her mom."

Margaret smiled at her mother. "Mom."

.

ACKNOWLEGEMENTS

Several people made important contributions to the completion of Natalie's Wars. Tina Lincer and Wayne Lindeman read early drafts and made suggestions for the overall direction of the novel. Dawn Lajeunesse , Darrell Laurant , Gay Malin, and again Tina Lincer made a number of comments and suggestions on later drafts. Throughout the long process, Donna Castellani provided constant encouragement and painstaking editing.

Natalie's Wars draws on the rich fiction and non-fiction literature on the roles of women during and after WW II and PTSD in veterans. Other crucial sources of material for the novel were interviews, letters, diaries and oral histories of men and women who worked in defense plants, served in combat, and had other wartime and post-war experiences.

Additional background on key aspects of Natalie's Wars included a history of the Watervliet Arsenal: *Watervliet Arsenal: A History of America's Oldest Arsenal,8th edition*. 2013. Watervliet Arsenal. Watervliet, NY. John Snyder, Watervliet Arsenal Public Affairs Officer generously contributed supplemental information and answers to several questions. Bob Pfeil at the Watervliet Arsenal and Tom Ragosta at the Watervliet Historical Society and Museum provided other source material for the novel. I hope they will forgive me for the extensive liberties I took in fictionalizing the work of the men and women at the Arsenal during World War II.